The Forgiven

Keepers of the Promise, Book One

"A tender novel of second chances, endearing characters, and a can't-put-it-down story."

—Suzanne Woods Fisher, author of *The Revealing*

"Tender, touching, and full of gentle wisdom as [Perry] explores the flaws and struggles of her Amish characters. There is so much to enjoy here that it's hard to know where to begin, but I especially liked the weaving of past with the present as Grandmother Lapp passes her legacy of memories to three special granddaughters. I can hardly wait to see what happens with Barbie and Judith! This is going to be a terrific new series, and I'm confident readers of Amish fiction will love it, beginning with *The Forgiven*."

—Linda Goodnight, *New York Times* bestselling author of the Buchanons series

"A gently drawn portrait of two lives renewed by the power of love. In this story of second chances, readers will come to care deeply about Rebecca and Matthew, as I did, and will look forward to the next book in this series."

—Robin Lee Hatcher, bestselling author of *A Promise Kept* and *Love Without End*

"With exquisite grace and unflinching honesty, Marta Perry once again takes us into the Amish world . . . The slow, sweet realization of Rebecca and Matthew's growing love takes us on a journey of healing and victory over difficult circumstances. This story touched my heart and held me captive until the last page. *The Forgiven* is a wonderful read that will bring a perfect peace to your heart while you escape into a place that brings hope to all of us."

—Lenora Worth, *New York Times* bestselling author of *Bayou Sweetheart*

continued . . .

"Five stars! Marta Perry's tender family saga of love and faith will touch your heart." —Emma Miller, author of *Plain Murder*

"A born storyteller, Marta Perry skillfully weaves the past and present in a heart-stirring tale of love and forgiveness."
—Susan Meissner, author of *A Fall of Marigolds*

PRAISE FOR THE PLEASANT VALLEY NOVELS

Susanna's Dream

"[Perry] has the ability to make the reader feel what the characters are feeling and thinking. That is truly a gift."
—*I'm Hooked on Books*

Lydia's Hope

"I'm a big fan of Ms. Perry's writing style, and it was no surprise that I fell in love with this newest addition to her collection. I'm so glad that I stumbled upon this book . . . This is one you shouldn't pass up!" —*Night Owl Reviews* (4½ stars)

Naomi's Christmas

"[Perry] never disappoints." —*The Mary Reader*

Hannah's Joy

"An enjoyable Mennonite romance starring two fascinating individuals . . . Fans will enjoy this warm tale of love and belonging."
—*Genre Go Round Reviews*

Katie's Way

"A great story of friendship, second chances, and faith . . . Wonderful."
                                    —*Reviews from the Heart*

Sarah's Gift

"Perry's fourth Pleasant Valley book places her well-rounded characters in a sweet, entertaining romance."   —*RT Book Reviews*

Anna's Return

"Those who enjoyed the first two series titles will eagerly await this third entry, which does not disappoint. It will also appeal to fans of Amy Clipston and Shelley Shepard Gray."   —*Library Journal*

Rachel's Garden

"A large part of the pleasure of this book is in watching Rachel be Amish, as she sells snapdragons and pansies to both Amish and 'English' at an outdoor market, taking in snatches of Pennsylvania Dutch."   —*The Philadelphia Inquirer*

Leah's Choice

"What a joy it is to read Marta Perry's novels! *Leah's Choice* has everything a reader could want—strong, well-defined characters; beautiful, realistic settings; and a thought-provoking plot."
                    —Shelley Shepard Gray, *New York Times* bestselling author of
                                                                Snowfall

THE FORGIVEN

Keepers of the Promise
BOOK ONE

MARTA PERRY

BERKLEY BOOKS, NEW YORK

THE BERKLEY PUBLISHING GROUP
Published by the Penguin Group
Penguin Group (USA) LLC
375 Hudson Street, New York, New York 10014

USA • Canada • UK • Ireland • Australia • New Zealand • India • South Africa • China

penguin.com

A Penguin Random House Company

This book is an original publication of The Berkley Publishing Group.

Library of Congress Cataloging-in-Publication Data

Perry, Marta.
The forgiven / Marta Perry. — Berkley trade paperback edition.
pages cm. — (Keepers of the promise ; book one)
ISBN 978-0-425-27141-4 (trade)
1. Single women—Fiction. 2. Amish—Fiction. 3. Cousins—Fiction.
4. Family life—Fiction. I. Title.
PS3616.E7933F68 2014
813'.6—dc23
2014016701

PUBLISHING HISTORY
Berkley trade paperback edition / October 2014

PRINTED IN THE UNITED STATES OF AMERICA

10 9 8 7 6 5 4 3 2 1

Cover art by Shane Rebenshield.
Cover design by Sarah Oberrender.

This story is dedicated to my granddaughter Georgia Lynn.
And, as always, to Brian.

LIST OF CHARACTERS

Rebecca Lapp Fisher, widow of Paul Fisher; mother of Katie, 7, and Joshua, 5

Simon Lapp, Rebecca's brother

Elizabeth Lapp, Rebecca's grandmother

Barbara "Barbie" Lapp, Rebecca's cousin

Judith Wagler, Rebecca's cousin

Matthew Byler, a furniture maker

Silas Byler, Matthew's uncle; husband of Lovina

Isaiah Byler, son of Silas and Lovina; Matthew's cousin; Sadie's brother

Sadie Byler, daughter of Silas and Lovina; Matthew's cousin; Isaiah's sister

Anna Esch, Lapp family ancestor; lived through World War II

Jacob Miller, Anna Esch's beau

Seth Esch, Anna's brother

Glossary of Pennsylvania Dutch Words and Phrases

ach. oh; used as an exclamation

agasinish. stubborn; self-willed

ain't so. A phrase commonly used at the end of a sentence to invite agreement.

alter. old man

anymore. Used as a substitute for "nowadays."

Ausbund. Amish hymnal. Used in the worship services, it contains traditional hymns, words only, to be sung without accompaniment. Many of the hymns date from the sixteenth century.

befuddled. mixed up

blabbermaul. talkative one

blaid. bashful

boppli. baby

bruder. brother

bu. boy

buwe. boys

daadi. daddy

Da Herr sei mit du. The Lord be with you.

denke. thanks (or *danki*)

Englischer. one who is not Plain

ferhoodled. upset; distracted

ferleicht. perhaps

frau. wife

fress. eat

gross. big

grossdaadi. grandfather

grossdaadi haus. An addition to the farmhouse, built for the grandparents to live in once they've "retired" from actively running the farm.

grossmutter. grandmother

gut. good

hatt. hard; difficult

haus. house

hinnersich. backward

ich. I

ja. yes

kapp. Prayer covering, worn in obedience to the Biblical injunction that women should pray with their heads covered. Kapps are made of Swiss organdy and are white. (In some Amish communities, unmarried girls thirteen and older wear black kapps during worship service.)

kinder. kids (or *kinner*)

komm. come

komm schnell. come quick

Leit. the people; the Amish

lippy. sassy

maidal. old maid; spinster

mamm. mother

middaagesse. lunch

mind. remember

onkel. uncle

Ordnung. The agreed-upon rules by which the Amish community lives. When new practices become an issue, they are discussed at length among the leadership. The decision for or against innovation is generally made on the basis of maintaining the home and family as separate from the world. For instance, a telephone might be necessary in a shop in order to conduct business but would be banned from the home because it would intrude on family time.

Pennsylvania Dutch. The language is actually German in origin and is primarily a spoken language. Most Amish write in English, which results in many variations in spelling when the dialect is put into writing! The language probably originated in the south of Germany but is common also among the Swiss Mennonite and French Huguenot immigrants to Pennsylvania. The language was brought to America prior to the Revolution and is still in use today. High German is used for Scripture and church documents, while English is the language of commerce.

rumspringa. Running-around time. The late teen years when Amish youth taste some aspects of the outside world before deciding to be baptized into the church.

schnickelfritz. mischievous child

ser gut. very good (or *sehr gut*)
tastes like more. delicious
Was ist letz? What's the matter?
Wie bist du heit. How are you; said in greeting
wilkom. welcome
Wo bist du? Where are you?

PROLOGUE

*E*lizabeth Lapp made her way slowly and carefully up the steep attic stairs. It was nonsense, this insistence on the part of her children and grandchildren that she change the habits of a lifetime. Seventy-six wasn't old, even if that young doctor acted as if she were teetering on the brink of the grave.

Pausing, she gripped the railing, grateful for its support as she caught her breath. Ach, maybe she *was* getting on in years, but that didn't mean she had nothing to contribute. There was an important legacy to be passed on, and she'd promised herself she wouldn't delay any longer.

Her three granddaughters would be arriving at the old farmhouse soon. Before they appeared, she needed to take one more look at the treasures collected in the attic.

Cautiously, conserving her strength, she made her way to the top and paused again, feeling a flash of annoyance at how shallow her breathing was. The straight chair she'd used on her last trip to the attic stood where she'd left it. Using her cane as a hook, she drew it toward her and sat.

Sunlight streamed through the window and played across the dozens of objects jammed into the space. Amazing, how quickly the attic of the old farmhouse had filled up. Her quest had begun with one small dower chest belonging to a great-aunt. She'd rescued it from being sent to auction at the annual spring mud sale, and it had lit a spark in her heart.

She'd known then what had to be done. Family memories, the whole history of one Amish family in America, were bound up in the items she'd collected in her attic. That history couldn't be allowed to die. Someone must see that it lived on.

Advancing years had caught up with her, and before the farmhouse was sold to a distant cousin, before she moved into her son's house, the memories must be passed on. That was why her granddaughters were coming today.

Getting to her feet, she made her way across the rough-hewn floorboards, touching a spinning wheel here, a hand-carved rocking horse there. Each of these things must find a new home. It was too much to expect that any one person would take all of them.

She'd hammered out her plan during the long, sleepless nights after the loss of her beloved William. The gifts must be made to the right person. Each object had a story to tell, and each story could influence the person who received it. She breathed a silent prayer, knowing she must rely on God to show her the way.

It all began with the girls. She smiled. None of the three would appreciate being called a girl; each considered herself a woman grown. And so they were, but that didn't mean they didn't have something to learn from the past.

Rebecca. Judith. Barbara. She pictured each one in her mind's eye. Rebecca, so lost since the death of her young husband more than a year ago. Judith. She frowned a little. Something was wrong there, but self-contained, quiet Judith would not talk about it, making it more difficult to know what to do. And Barbara. Barbie always brought a smile to her grossmammi's lips, with her pert, lively manner and her almost automatic rebellion against the restrictions of Amish life. Those three were the only ones of the right age to take on the task.

Elizabeth stood, resting her hand on a dower chest, and faced the truth. This was, most likely, the final challenge of her life. To find the object that would speak to each one of her granddaughters and, through that, to entrust to their generation the promise of their family story.

CHAPTER ONE

*R*ebecca Fisher hadn't summoned her family to meals with the bell on the back porch since Paul died. Today wasn't the day to start, she decided. Instead she stood at the railing and called.

"Katie! Joshua! Come to supper."

She stayed on the porch until she saw her two kinder running toward the farmhouse. Katie came from the big barn, where she'd been "helping" Rebecca's father and brother with the evening chores. Katie adored her grossdaadi and Onkel Simon, and Rebecca was grateful every day that Katie had them to turn to now that her own daadi was gone.

Joshua had clearly been up in the old apple tree by the stream, which was his favorite perch. Paul had talked about building a tree house there for Joshua's sixth birthday. That birthday would come soon, but Paul wasn't here to see it. Rebecca's throat tightened, and she forced the thought away.

"Mammi, Mammi." Joshua flung himself at her, grabbing her apron with grubby hands. "Guess who I saw?"

"I don't know, Josh. Who?" She hugged him with one arm and gathered Katie against her with the other. Katie let herself be embraced for a moment and then wiggled free.

"I helped put the horses in," she reported. "Onkel Simon said I'm a gut helper."

"Mammi, I'm talking." Joshua glared at his sister. "Guess who I saw?"

"Hush, now." Rebecca hated it when they quarreled, even though she remembered only too well how she and her brothers and sisters had plagued one another. She shooed them into the kitchen. "Katie, I'm wonderful glad you're helping. Joshua, who did you see?"

It had probably been an owl or a chipmunk—at five, Joshua considered every creature he encountered to be as real as a person.

"Daadi!" Joshua grinned, unaware of the hole that had just opened up in his mother's stomach.

"Joshua—" She struggled to find the words.

"That's stupid," Katie declared from the superiority of her seven years. Her heart-shaped face, usually so lively and happy, tightened with anger, and her blue eyes sparkled with what might have been the tears she wouldn't shed. "Daadi's in heaven. He can't come back, so you can't see him, so don't be stupid."

"Katie, don't call your brother stupid." Rebecca managed the easier part of the correction first. She knelt in front of her son, feeling the worn linoleum under her knees as she prayed for the right words. "Joshua, you must understand that Daadi loves you always, but he can't come back."

"But I saw him, Mammi. I saw him right there in the new stable and—"

"No, Josh." She had to stop this notion now, no matter how it pained both of them. "I don't know what you saw, but it wasn't Daadi."

His small face clouded, his mouth drooping. "Are you sure?"

"I'm sure." Her heart hurt as she spoke the words, but they had to be said. Paul was gone forever, and they must continue without him.

"Go and see, Mammi." Josh pressed small hands on her cheeks, holding her face to ensure she paid attention. "Please go look in the stable."

Obviously, it was the only thing that would satisfy him. "All right. I'll go and look. While I do that, you two wash up for supper."

Josh nodded solemnly. Rebecca rose, giving her daughter a warning look.

"No more talking about this until I come back. You understand?"

Katie looked as if she'd like to argue, but she nodded as well.

Pausing to see them headed for the sink without further squabbling, Rebecca slipped out the back door.

A quick glance told her there was no further activity at the main barn now. Probably her daad and brother had finished and headed home for their own supper.

It wasn't far across the field to the farmhouse where she'd grown up. That field would be planted with corn before too long. Daad had mentioned it only yesterday, and she'd thought how strange it seemed that Paul wasn't here to make the decision.

Turning in the opposite direction, Rebecca skirted the vegetable garden. Her early onions were already up. In a few weeks the danger of frost would be over, and she could finish the planting.

Beyond the garden stood the posts from which the farm-stay welcome sign should hang. If she was going to open to visitors this summer, she'd have to put it up soon. If. She had to fight back panic at the thought of dealing with guests without Paul's support.

The farm-stay had been Paul's dream. He'd enjoyed every minute of their first season—chatting with the guests, showing them how to milk the cows or enlisting their help in cutting hay. It had seemed strange to Rebecca that Englischers would actually pay for the privilege of working on the farm, but it had been so.

She'd been content to stay in the background, cooking big breakfasts, keeping the bedrooms clean, doing all the things she'd be doing anyway if the strangers hadn't been staying with them.

Last summer she'd been too devastated by his death to think of opening, but now . . . Well, now what was she to do? Would Paul expect her to go on with having guests? She didn't know, because she'd never imagined life without him.

The stable loomed ahead of her, still seeming raw and new even though it had been up for more than a year. They'd gone ahead with the building even after Paul's diagnosis, as a sign that they had faith he would be well again.

But he hadn't been. He'd grown weaker and weaker, and eventually she had learned to hate the sight of the stable that had been intended for the purebred draft horses Paul had wanted to breed. She never went near the structure if she could help it.

Now she had to steel herself to swing open one side of the extra-large double doors. She stepped inside, taking a cautious look around. Dust motes danced in a shaft of sunlight, but otherwise it was silent and empty. The interior seemed to echo of broken dreams.

Sucking in a breath, Rebecca forced herself to walk all the way to the back wall, her footsteps hollow on the solid wooden floorboards. No one was here. Joshua's longing for his daadi had led him to imagine what he hoped for.

A board creaked behind her and Rebecca whirled, heart leaping into her throat.

A man stood in the doorway, silhouetted against the light so that she couldn't make out his face. But Amish, judging by his clothes and straw hat, so not a stranger. The man took a step forward, and she could see him.

For a long moment they simply stared at each other. Her brain seemed to be moving sluggishly, taking note of him. Tall, broad-shouldered, with golden-brown hair and eyes. He didn't have a beard, so she could see the cleft in his chin, and the sight stirred vague memories. She knew him, and yet she didn't. It wasn't—

"Matt? Matthew Byler?"

A flicker of a smile crossed his face. "Got it right. And you're little Becky Lapp, ain't so?"

"Rebecca Fisher," she corrected quickly. So Matt Byler had returned home to Brook Hill at last. Nothing had been seen of him among the central Pennsylvania Amish since his family migrated out west when he was a teenager.

Matt came a step closer, making her aware of the height and breadth of him. He'd grown quite a lot from the gangling boy he'd been when he left. "You married Paul Fisher, then. You two were holding hands when you were eight or nine, the way I remember it."

"And you were . . ." She let that trail off. Matt had been a couple of years older than they were, and he'd been the kind of boy Amish parents held up as a bad example—always in trouble, always pushing the boundaries of what it meant to be Amish.

Now Matt's smile lit his eyes, and a vagrant shaft of sunlight made them look almost gold. "You remember me. The trouble-maker."

"I . . . I wasn't thinking that," she said. But of course she had been. It was the first thing anyone thought in connection with Matt Byler. "Are you here for a visit?"

Matt didn't have a beard, so obviously he hadn't married. That was more than unusual for an Amish male of thirty.

Surely his unmarried state wasn't for lack of chances. A prudent set of parents might look warily at Matt as a prospective son-in-law, but the girls had always been charmed by his teasing smile.

"My uncle needs some help with the carpentry business, and he asked me to give him a hand."

Everyone knew that Silas Byler had been struggling to keep his business going since his eldest son had so unexpectedly left the community. How strange life was that Isaiah, who'd never caused his parents a moment's worry, should be the one to leave the Amish while bad boy Matthew returned to take his place.

"I'm sorry about Isaiah. It was a heavy blow to your aunt and uncle, ain't so?"

Matt nodded with a wry twist to his mouth. "Funny, isn't it? Everyone was so sure I was the one headed over the fence."

It was an echo of what she'd been thinking. "You did a pretty good job of making folks think so, the way I remember it," she said.

"Ouch." Matt's teasing grin appeared. "You've developed a sharp tongue, I see."

"I've just grown up. I have two kinder of my own now." Rebecca hesitated, but she couldn't help but resent what he'd made Josh imagine, however inadvertently. "My little boy, Joshua, must have seen you here at the stable. He thought it was his daadi."

Matt's face sobered in an instant. "I'm sorry, Rebecca. Truly sorry. My uncle told me about Paul. You have my sympathy."

"Denke." Too abrupt, but she couldn't seem to help it. "Was there something you wanted here, Matt?"

He looked a little taken aback by the blunt question, but answered readily enough. "I'm looking for a building I can use for my furniture business. Onkel Silas told me about the stable and how Paul was going to . . ." He let that trail off. "Anyway, he said you weren't using the stable and might be willing to lease it to me."

Everything in Rebecca recoiled at the thought of putting another person's business in Paul's stable. "No." Her tone was sharper than she intended. "I'm sorry. It's not available."

Matt's eyebrows lifted. "It's standing empty. I can pay you five hundred a month for the space."

"It's not available," she said again, annoyed at him for putting her in this position and unable to keep from thinking about what she could do with an extra five hundred dollars a month.

Matt studied her face, his eyes intent and questioning. "You don't like the idea of turning Paul's stable over to someone else. I can understand that. But you have two little ones to raise. Can you afford to have it sitting empty when it could be earning money for Paul's kinder?"

The fact that Matt was probably right didn't make Rebecca feel any more kindly toward him. "I don't think that's your concern."

"Maybe not. But it is yours, Rebecca." He held her gaze for a moment longer, and she felt as if he was looking right into all her grief and uncertainty. Then he took a step back. "I wouldn't do any harm to the place, Rebecca. Think about it."

Matt turned and walked away. He was silhouetted in the doorway for a moment, and then he was gone, leaving Rebecca unsettled and upset.

Matthew's somber mood stayed with him as he headed back to his uncle's place. The road was obviously familiar to the buggy horse, probably more so than to him. It had been thirteen years since he'd left Brook Hill.

Not all that much had changed, from what he could see—things didn't, not in this quiet part of central Pennsylvania. The Amish of Lancaster County referred to this area as the valleys, and small groups had begun moving here as early as the sixties, propelled by the increasing cost of farmland back in the Lancaster community.

Matt hadn't expected it to be easy, coming back to the place where he was born, but he hadn't expected a challenge from so unlikely a source as little Becky Lapp. Rebecca Fisher, he corrected himself, clucking to the mare when her pace slowed.

It was hardly surprising that Becky had married Paul Fisher, was it? Matt found he was smiling to himself, remembering a small girl racing after a slightly taller boy, her apron fluttering.

Rebecca wasn't a child any longer. Her hair, once the color of corn silk, had become a light brown, but her sea-green eyes still surveyed a person with quiet gravity. Her oval face contained more than a hint of the loss she'd experienced. Her eyes were shadowed with remembered grief, and she'd held her shoulders stiffly, as if reminding herself to face up to whatever might be coming next.

He frowned. Why hadn't she accepted his offer? It would make things so simple, and Onkel Silas seemed convinced Rebecca needed the money.

Had she refused because she couldn't bear to see another use made of the stable than had been intended for Paul's dreams? Or was it because the offer had come from Matthew Byler, the troublemaker, the unreliable person who shouldn't be trusted?

Self-pity wasn't very admirable, he told himself with a flash of wry humor. No matter how enjoyable it might be.

The fact that Rebecca had turned him down might mean nothing more than that his timing was bad. He'd give her a day or two to think it over before he started scouting around for another place. Luckily he'd managed to squirrel away a nice little nest egg while he'd been living in the Englisch world, no matter how many other mistakes he'd made. His stomach tightened at the memory of the worst of them, and he forced himself to shake off the unpleasant thought.

The valley narrowed as he headed northeast, the parallel ridges rising more abruptly from the creek bed. Onkel Silas's place backed up to the woods, with enough space for a bit of pasture for buggy horses and a couple of dairy cows, a large garden, and the carpentry shop that was his livelihood. The mare turned into the lane without prompting, her pace quickening as she sensed the barn ahead.

Matt pulled her up and slid down from the buggy seat. As he began to unhitch the mare, his cousin Sadie stepped from the shadow of the barn into the sunlight, blue eyes narrowing in her now-familiar expression of dislike.

"About time you were getting back here, Matthew. Where have you been?"

Matt continued to move steadily, sliding the harness from the horse's back. It occurred to him, not for the first time, that maybe his cousin's sharp tongue had something to do with the fact that at nineteen, she still didn't have a come-calling friend.

"Well? I thought you were here to help Daad, not to give extra work to everyone."

Matt forced himself to count to ten before answering. "Had to help with the milking, did you, Sadie?" He kept his voice light. Doing the milking was hardly a big deal—Onkel Silas kept only two milk cows, not having the land or time for more.

"That's not what upsets me," she snapped. "Daad is depending on you."

His cousin couldn't know how that stung. He looked at her evenly. "Onkel Silas suggested I run over to Rebecca Fisher's place to see about renting her stable for my furniture workshop."

He led the mare past Sadie into the barn, forcing her to take a step back. It was too much to hope his cousin would let go of her grievance, but he'd settle for ending this conversation.

"You shouldn't be thinking about that furniture-making of yours. Since Isaiah left . . ." Her voice trembled suddenly, and she let the words trail off.

That betraying emotion wrenched Matt's heart. "I'm sorry." He took a breath, trying to come up with something that might make a difference to Sadie. "Onkel Silas asked me to fill in until Isaiah comes home. That's all."

A good thing. He didn't want anyone asking for a commitment he might not keep. That kind of promise went too close to the bone for him.

"If he comes back." She voiced what everyone feared. "And helping out is the least you can do after nearly killing Isaiah."

For a moment all Matt could do was stare at his cousin. So. That was what she was thinking—maybe what they were all thinking. He would never be free of that old mistake.

"Sadie, you forget yourself." Onkel Silas stood in the barn doorway. His face was shadowed by his straw hat, but no one could miss the disapproval in his voice. "You are unkind, and I am ashamed of you."

"I'm sorry, Daadi." Sadie's lips trembled, and she looked younger than her years.

"It's Matthew you must tell, not me. What happened to Isaiah all those years ago has been forgiven."

"Isaiah?" The female voice startled Matt. His aunt Lovina seldom came to the barn, and she sounded . . .

He couldn't finish the thought, because she was rushing toward him, her face alive with joy. "Isaiah. You're home."

He took her hands in his, holding them firmly when she tried to embrace him. "No, Aunt Lovina. It's Matthew. You remember me, don't you?"

The joy faded from her face, replaced by the lost look that seemed to be there too often these days.

His throat tightened. He hadn't been prepared for the changes in his uncle's wife when he'd returned, and it still had the capacity to pain him. He managed to find his voice. "Komm. I'll walk to the house with you."

"I'll do it." Sadie pushed past him to put her arm around her mother's waist. "We'll get supper on the table, ain't so?" Her voice gentled when she spoke to her mother. "The pot roast is about done."

Aunt Lovina nodded, moving obediently with Sadie, as if she were the child and Sadie the mother.

Matt watched them go, careful not to look at his uncle's face. Poor Onkel Silas. Surely nobody who knew her had expected a woman like Lovina, still healthy and energetic, to have her memory slipping away day by day.

Isaiah should be here. Matt felt a moment's intense irritation at his missing cousin, despite the fact that Isaiah was only repeating the pattern that he himself had started.

Matt didn't suppose Onkel Silas blamed him for Isaiah's defection, but judging by the look Sadie had given him as she walked away, she probably did.

And for all he knew, maybe that blame was justified.

"*If* you ask me, we should just get rid of everything." Rebecca's young cousin Barbie glanced around the crowded attic of Grossmammi Lapp's old farmhouse.

"Barbie Lapp, don't you say such a thing."

Realizing how sharp her tone was, Rebecca took a deep breath and sought for calm. She'd been ridiculously tense since her encounter with Matt Byler the previous day, and she certainly shouldn't take it out on other people. "We three promised Grossmammi we'd sort out the attic as she wants, and we will, ain't so?"

She looked for confirmation at her other cousin, Judith Wagler. Judith was thirty now, married and responsible. Barbie, on the other hand, showed no signs of wanting to settle down, even though she was in her early twenties already.

Too busy having a good time? Or was she flirting with the idea of jumping the fence? Rebecca would hate to think so.

"I'm sure Barbie didn't mean it," Judith said, with the air of one used to being the peacemaker. "We all love Grossmammi. Of course we'll do as she wishes."

Barbie's bright blue eyes flashed, and she planted her hands on her hips as if prepared to quarrel. Then, meeting Judith's warning glance, she shrugged. "Ja, all right. But I still don't understand why Grossmammi would think I'd be interested in our old family stories."

Since Rebecca didn't understand it, either, she decided not to comment. She couldn't help nursing a small feeling of disappointment. She was the one who'd always been fascinated by Grossmammi's stories of the generations of Amish women who'd gone before them. She was the one who'd cherished the family treasures stored in Grossmammi's attic. She was surely the logical one to become the keeper of their family's story, now that Grossmammi was selling the family homestead and moving in with Rebecca's parents.

Judith, as if guessing her thoughts, clasped Rebecca's hand briefly, brown eyes soft with sympathy. "Grossmammi knows how much you have to deal with now that your Paul is gone. Barbie and I are here to help. Just tell us what to do."

Rebecca blinked back a quick surge of tears. It had been close to eighteen months since Paul's death. She'd managed to reply calmly enough to Matt's sympathy, so why did she now struggle with tears at the mention of Paul's name? But even tears were easier than the panic she sometimes felt at the idea of going on without him.

Rebecca swallowed the lump in her throat and forced herself to concentrate. It was a good thing that she had this chore to occupy her today. If Matt returned to renew his offer, she wouldn't be there to face him.

"I've been thinking about how to go about it. Maybe we should just sort things out first," she said. "Papers in one area, furniture in another, quilts and such-like elsewhere."

Barbie, apparently regaining her normal good humor, nodded. "Okay. I'll move the furniture."

Barbie headed for a rickety spinning wheel that leaned against the eight-paned window. The spring sunshine slanting through the glass glistened on a silvery cobweb on the wheel, as if in mute memory of the yarn that had once been spun on it. The cobweb itself was a testament to how much Grossmammi had been failing in recent months. She'd always kept the attic as spotless as if church were going to be held there.

Rebecca turned her attention to a row of chests and boxes. She and Judith knelt beside the largest one, lifting the heavy lid together. Under cover of its creak, Judith spoke.

"How are you really, Rebecca? And the kinder?"

"The little ones are fine." It was easier to talk about her children than herself. "Katie understands better, I think. She still misses her daadi."

No point in saying that seven-year-old Katie's attempts to hide her longing left Rebecca feeling helpless.

"As for Joshua . . ." She hesitated. "He's a dreamer, like Paul was. I'm never sure what he's thinking." Had he believed her yesterday, when she'd told him the man he'd seen was Matt? She still wasn't sure.

Shaking her head, Rebecca lifted out a quilt, carefully wrapped in paper to preserve it, while Judith pulled out a bundle of letters tied with a length of yarn.

They worked in silence side by side for a few minutes. Rebecca knew she should ask about Judith's family, but she was afraid her voice might betray her. Judith's family was still complete—she had someone to support and comfort her, someone to share the burdens and the joys of raising the kinder, someone to love forever.

Not that Rebecca would ever stop loving Paul. But . . .

"I heard from your mamm that you're trying to decide whether to open the farm to visitors for the summer." Judith's tone was neutral, but her expression was wary, leading Rebecca to suspect that her mother had aired all her worries about Rebecca to Judith.

"Thinking, that's all." She paused, smoothing her hand over a log cabin quilt. "I wish I knew what was best to do. The farm-stay was Paul's dream, and he was so excited about it."

Paul had had so many dreams—the farm-stay, filling their large farmhouse with kinder, expanding beyond the simple truck farming they did to a dairy operation, raising the pure-bred draft horses he loved. It was hard to make a living farming without some sideline, and Paul had had such enthusiasm.

Rebecca might not be able to raise the horses or give him more children, but she could honor Paul by opening the farm-stay for the summer, if she had the courage. It was too bad that the very thought of entertaining strangers left her feeling dizzy.

"Surely Paul would not have expected you to carry on without him." Judith's tone was gentle. "He was good at greeting Englischers and making them feel at home. It was his gift."

"And it's not mine. Is that what you mean?" The edge was back in Rebecca's voice, and she was ashamed of it. She shook her head quickly, before Judith could respond. "Ach, you're right. I would rather just cook the breakfasts and change the beds."

"There's nothing wrong with that," Judith pointed out. "It was important to the visitors, ain't so?"

"Ja, but I have the kinder to support by myself, and I'm not sure about doing it." Her unconscious echo of what Matt had said to her brought his face back to her thoughts, and she brushed him away like she would shoo a fly.

"Your mamm and daad would love to have you move back in with them," Judith pointed out.

Pressing her lips together, Rebecca shook her head. Much as she loved her parents and appreciated their support, she would not move away from the home she and Paul had shared.

"I can handle things myself." Rebecca suspected she sounded like little Katie in one of her stubborn moods. She drew a small dower chest toward her, trying to focus on it. It was time to change the subject.

A screech sounded as Barbie moved a chest of drawers, drawing their attention to her. "Do you know what these yellow stickers mean on some of the furniture?" she asked.

Judith smiled, probably at the streak of dust adorning their young cousin's cheek. "Grossmammi mentioned that we might sell some pieces—the ones she has marked. We could . . ."

"Sell?" Rebecca's stomach seemed to turn over. "Why would she want to sell anything?" She put her hand protectively on the trunk in front of her. "These are family pieces."

Barbie made a face. "But who would want them? If I ever settle down in a home of my own, I'll want all new things."

"It's only the items no one in the family has a use for," Judith said, her voice soothing.

Rebecca's heart rebelled. "How can Grossmammi think of selling pieces of our family history?" Grossmammi, who always talked to her of the value of learning from those who'd gone before the current generation?

"I'm sure she'd let you have anything you want . . ." Judith began, but she let the words die out when Rebecca shook her head.

Her world was changing, and she couldn't stop it. Somehow she had to adjust, or—or what?

Rebecca closed the lid of the dower box. The attic seemed to lose its air. She couldn't stay here and dismantle her family's roots. Not when the ground was so shaky under her feet already.

Snatching up the box, Rebecca scrambled to her feet. "I . . . I'll take this home to sort."

She spun toward the attic stairs, aware of her cousins' faces, eyes wide, staring at her. Grasping the railing, she stumbled down the steps, wishing she could run away from her fears as easily.

CHAPTER TWO

*B*y the time Rebecca stopped at her parents' house to pick up the kinder, she'd managed to collect her ragged emotions. These periods of feeling overwhelmed surely would end soon, wouldn't they?

Or was this a lack of faith on her part? As always when she felt distressed, Rebecca let her gaze rest on the ridge above the farm. The pines and hemlocks formed dark green shadows, seeming even denser as the sun began to slip behind the ridge, painting the clouds in shades of blue and purple.

I will lift up mine eyes unto the hills; from whence cometh my help? The psalmist answers quickly. *My help cometh from the Lord, who made Heaven and earth.*

She had always found comfort in that knowledge. She had to believe that God had not forsaken her, even though sometimes she felt so desperately alone.

Rebecca drew the buggy horse up at the hitching rail by the back porch. Katie and Josh were playing ball in the backyard with two of her brothers, twenty-one-year-old Simon and her next brother, sixteen-year-old Johnny.

"Mammi, Mammi, I hit the ball!" Josh came running, forsaking the game in his eagerness to tell her.

Even as Rebecca was hugging him, she saw Katie smack the softball Simon had lobbed to her. It sailed over Johnny's head.

"That's great." Rebecca suppressed a twinge of guilt that it hadn't occurred to her to play ball with the kinder. "Your onkels must be gut teachers."

Simon grinned. "You taught me, Beck. Don't you remember?"

"A looong time ago," she said, smiling back at him. Simon would always be her little brother, no matter how tall he got. She turned back to her son. "Where's Grossmammi?"

"She didn't want to play ball," Josh announced, his tone suggesting surprise that anyone wouldn't want to do so. "We made cookies together, and she's cleaning up."

Rebecca ruffled his silky hair. "You go back to your game then, and I'll help her."

Joshua ran to the others, and she stood smiling for a moment as Johnny grabbed him and tickled him. They were fortunate to live right next door to her family, so that her little ones didn't suffer from a lack of male influence in their lives. And when her grossmammi moved in with Rebecca's folks, there'd be yet another generation close at hand.

The scent of snickerdoodles reached Rebecca even before she stepped into the kitchen, and her mamm turned from the sink, wiping her hands on a tea towel.

"Back already? I was sure you'd get caught up in all the treasures in your grossmammi's attic."

"There's plenty to be done, that's certain-sure." Rebecca

felt obscurely guilty for having come away early. "Gross-mammi was fretting over not being allowed to go up to the attic and supervise."

The doctor had forbidden much stair climbing, saying once a day was plenty for the time being, but getting someone as strong-willed as Elizabeth Lapp to listen was another story.

"Ach, I wish she'd chust move in here and let the rest of us worry about clearing the house out." Mamm's round, cheerful face clouded. "The room is ready for her, and it would be no trouble at all."

The welcome was genuine. So far as Rebecca knew, Mamm had always gotten along well with her mother-in-law. Still, though Mamm had a strong-willed streak of her own, it was nothing compared to Elizabeth's. It would be interesting to see how the two of them fared, living in the same house.

"We may as well let her do it her way." Rebecca tried to soothe her mother's ruffled feelings. "She will anyway."

"And what is to stop your grossmammi from going up those attic steps after you girls are gone?" Mamm demanded. "It would be just like her."

"She won't have a chance," Rebecca said. "We took the only key, and Judith will make sure the attic door is locked when she and Barbie leave." She followed the smell of cinnamon to the cooling racks and broke off a piece of cookie, aware of her mother's questioning look.

"You came away early, did you?"

Rebecca tried not to meet her eyes. "Just a little before the other two. I brought a chest of letters and books home with me to sort out. I can work on it this evening after the little ones are in bed."

"If you were worrying about getting home to the kinder, you know it's a joy for us to have them here," her mother said. "In fact, your daad and I would like nothing better than to have the three of you move in. You know that, don't you?"

"I know." Rebecca gave her mother a quick hug. "But we're fine where we are. As close as we are, it's almost like living together. Besides, once Grossmammi moves in, you'll have a houseful."

"There can't be too many people in the house for me," her mother declared. "I love having plenty of people to cook for and look after. Besides, as serious as Simon seems to be getting over Mary Ann King, it might not be too much longer before he's wanting to set up on his own."

"Really? Simon married?" Rebecca couldn't help the note of surprise in her voice. Not that there was anything wrong with Mary Ann, she supposed, barring a little immaturity. Still, she probably wouldn't think anyone was quite good enough for her little brother.

Mamm nodded, frowning slightly. "He seems taken with her, and she is a pretty girl. A bit silly, I've always thought, but if it doesn't bother him I have nothing to say about it."

Rebecca couldn't help laughing at that comment. "Mamm, you know perfectly well you'll tell him what you think. And her, too, most likely."

Mamm's cheeks, already rosy from the heat of the oven, got a bit redder. "Ach, I do try not to say everything that comes into my head."

"I know, Mamm. I know." Rebecca gave her another quick hug. "I'd better round up the young ones and get on home. Is tomorrow afternoon all right for you to watch them again?"

"For sure. The sooner you girls get that job done, the better. Josh and I will walk down and meet Katie after school." Mamm scurried to the counter and grasped a basket, thrusting it at Rebecca. "Chicken potpie and the children's cookies," she said by way of explanation. "You can chust heat up the potpie for your supper. You'll be tired after working in that crowded attic all afternoon."

"Denke, Mamm." She wouldn't argue, late as it was getting. "I'll see if I can't get through that chest after I put Katie and Josh to bed. That's the kind of thing that's going to take the most time in sorting."

"I suppose." Her mother sounded doubtful, and Rebecca suspected that she, like Barbie, would have made a clean sweep if it were up to her.

Fortunately it wasn't. Grossmammi had chosen Rebecca for this job, and she was determined to do it right. With a wave and smile for her mother, Rebecca headed out the back door. Katie and Joshua were reluctant to leave their game, but they must have been tired after all their activities at their grandparents' house, because they scrambled into the buggy rather than racing across the field for home.

Once she'd unharnessed the buggy horse and stabled her, there was the usual flurry of evening chores to do and supper to get on the table. Rebecca was glad of the potpie to make that part of the day easier.

Sitting around the table, just the three of them, could seem a little lonely without Paul's presence, and she made an effort to keep both the kinder talking. Supper had always been a time to catch up on what each one had done that day, and she couldn't let that custom die out.

For once neither of the kinder made any of their usual spirited efforts to avoid bedtime. Once she'd read their stories and listened to their prayers, Rebecca slipped away, leaving their bedroom door ajar so she'd hear any cry in the night.

She paused for a moment on the top landing, taking a mental inventory of the other bedrooms. If she intended to open for the summer, she ought to be getting them ready. If . . .

Pushing the thought away to be dealt with later, she went downstairs.

She'd found this the hardest part of the day since Paul was gone, and it didn't seem to be getting any easier. The house was too quiet with the children in bed and asleep. At moments like this her parents' offer seemed very tempting. At least there she'd have company.

No. This was their home, and they would stay in it. It would feel like a betrayal of Paul to move. Her thoughts flitted to that surprising offer from Matt Byler. Accepting it would help matters financially for sure, but still, she doubted the wisdom of it. Doubted him, more likely.

Switching on the gaslight in the living room, Rebecca glanced at the small dower chest, still on the table where she'd put it earlier. She should get busy sorting the contents. That would fill the time until she was tired enough to sleep, wouldn't it?

Once, this had been her favorite time of the day instead of the most difficult. She would sit in her chair with a basket of hand sewing next to her, while Paul occupied the corner of the sofa closest to the lamp, reading the newspaper. Sometimes he'd read out an interesting article to her.

There had been nothing exciting or special about those

evenings. They hadn't even needed to talk, and she'd been happy—the house quiet, the kinder asleep upstairs, and the man she loved close enough that she could put out her hand and touch him. That had been true happiness.

Shaking her head as if that would chase away the thoughts, Rebecca pulled the small chest toward her and lifted the lid. Work was the only cure for what ailed her.

The dower chest was packed to the brim with old letters, newspaper clippings, and several small books, their covers faded, which seemed to be diaries. Rebecca sorted through a few clippings, most of which were recipes. These could be safely thrown away, she thought.

She picked up the top diary, looking inside the front cover for a name. *Anna Esch.* Rebecca frowned. Esch. This didn't belong to someone in the direct family line, it seemed. Possibly the diary wouldn't be worth saving, but she'd have to read a bit of it before she'd feel all right disposing of it.

Flipping it open at random, she began to skim, half expecting a routine telling of the day's activities or an account of the weather. But there was nothing routine about the words the unknown Anna had penned. They caught Rebecca's imagination, pulling her in, and she turned to the beginning, settled back in the rocking chair, and began to read.

People say that we will soon be at war. . . .

Lancaster County, November 1941

Anna Esch put down her pencil and stared at the sentence she'd just written.

In all her eighteen years, she'd never seen words so frightening. *War.* The Amish, raised from birth on stories of their ancestors who'd been martyred for their adherence to Jesus' teachings, clung ever more tightly to their belief in nonviolence. Surely a war in far-off Europe, terrible as it was, couldn't touch them here in peaceful Lancaster County, Pennsylvania.

Anna moved to the window, peering out. She couldn't see anyone in the November dark, but she raised the window a couple of inches, letting in the chill air. Late as it was, Jacob must not be coming tonight.

Even as she thought it, the clear warble of a bobwhite floated through the night air. Anna's heart leaped. She waved, sliding the window down, knowing that Jacob, her come-calling friend, could see her standing there in the light cast by the kerosene lamp.

Grabbing the heavy black sweater that lay over the back of her chair, Anna pulled it on, buttoning it over her gray dress. She eased the bedroom door open and peeked out to make sure no one was in the hall. Seth, her year-younger brother, wouldn't give her away, but the younger ones might call out if they spotted her, making Mammi and Daadi aware she was moving around.

But all was quiet. She slipped down the back stairs to the kitchen, dark now. The only light on the first floor of the old farmhouse came from the living room. She could hear her daad's deep voice reading an article from the Amish newspaper to Mammi, who was no doubt sitting in her rocking chair with the mending in her lap. Their big family meant plenty of rips and tears to fix.

Anna skirted the long wooden table, knowing its position

even without seeing it. She opened the back door and crept out into the night.

This secrecy wasn't really necessary, of course. Her parents liked Jacob, thoroughly approving of him for their eldest daughter. Some evenings Jacob came to the door and was welcomed in. The two of them would sit in the kitchen, always aware of Daadi in the next room, always ready for Mammi to bustle in at any moment with offers of cake, pie, or cookies, as if Jacob needed to be fattened up.

That was the way things usually worked, when a girl had a come-calling friend. But sometimes, a courting couple just needed to have a little time alone together. So Jacob would wait under the willow tree, sounding the birdcall until she could hurry silently out and join him for some stolen moments of privacy.

She sidled around the corner of the house, keeping in the shadows, and went toward the willow tree, and then Jacob's hands were clasping hers. He led her to the bench screened by the trailing fronds of the weeping willow.

"Your hands are cold," she said softly, clasping them in both of hers to warm them. "Did I keep you waiting long?"

"Not long." Jacob chuckled, his voice deep and filled with warmth when he spoke to her. "I could see you writing at the table in your room, and you didn't look up for so long that I thought you'd forgotten about me."

"Ach, it's you who was late," she teased. "I thought you weren't coming."

"And I thought I'd never get away. Daad had me helping him mend the chair Abe broke, and he kept talking and talking and talking. You know how he is."

She nodded. Everyone in their small community knew how fond Jacob's father was of telling a gut story. She looked up at Jacob's face, unable to make out much in the dark, but knowing his dear features so well it didn't matter. She could see in her mind his clear blue eyes, his ruddy complexion, his straight nose and firm mouth. And the way his eyes crinkled just for her when he smiled.

"How did you finally get out?" she prompted, knowing he was fond of telling a story, just like his daad.

"Mamm got after him. She told him I had better things to do than listen to him." He shook his head slightly, and she sensed the movement. "She always seems to know when I'm coming to see you. I have no idea how."

"Mothers seem to know things," she offered. "I wonder if I will, when I'm . . ." She let that trail off, not sure she should mention the kinder she hoped one day she and Jacob would have.

"I'm sure you will." He clasped her hands a little tighter, and his voice was deep with meaning. He hesitated, and she felt as if the night had gone quiet, listening for what he might say next.

But he must have drawn back from whatever the emotion was, as if the time wasn't right. "What were you writing about with such a serious look on your face?"

She shivered a little. "Daad came home from the mill today, saying that all the talk was of war. Saying that we'll be in it before long. Jacob, that can't be true, can it? Surely the country will not go to war."

"If President Roosevelt has his way, we will." Jacob's tone was somber. "He's saying this Hitler must be stopped, and America is the only one strong enough to do it."

"All this talk of killing . . ." She shivered again. "I think Daad is worried about what might happen to us. But how can a war affect the Amish? We believe in peace. We live separate from the world, just as the Bible teaches us to do."

"We might not be able to avoid being caught up in it." Jacob let go of her hands, and she felt cold. "I've seen the effects of the war talk myself already. Some of my Englisch friends are avoiding me now because I'm Amish."

"Ach, you're imagining it." Anna tried to say the words convincingly, longing to persuade herself as well as Jacob.

"I wish I was. The last time I went to town, a bunch of boys in the grocery store started yelling at me, saying I was talking German." He shook his head again, the movement somehow sorrowful. "Anna, I just don't know what the future holds for us anymore."

The future. She seized upon the words. The future was her and Jacob getting married next November. She and Mamm were already filling her dower chest, putting in the quilts and linens that every Amish bride would expect to have.

She and Jacob would get married. Jacob's father would help them buy a farm. They'd have a family and bring them up in the faith. That was the way things were meant to be for them.

She wouldn't give that up. She couldn't. But fear seemed to slide along her skin, chilling her worse than the cold air of the November night. What if Jacob was right?

Rebecca let the diary drop into her lap, yawning. She'd love to continue reading, but morning came early. Her brothers insisted on milking the two cows she kept, just as they did

Daadi's, so she cooked breakfast for whichever of the boys came over. Usually the kinder were up by then, and it wouldn't do for her to be heavy-eyed at the breakfast table. Still, she suspected she'd be turning over and over in her dreams the story of this long-ago Anna.

By the time Rebecca went to her grossmammi's house the next afternoon, she was determined not to give in to her emotions again in front of her cousins. She would not be so foolish a second time.

Maybe Barbie and Judith feared they had set her off the previous day, because they were careful to avoid any mention of how life was constantly changing or of anything that might remind her of her loss. The three of them worked throughout the afternoon with a semblance of harmony.

Except, of course, when Barbie suggested that old letters and diaries were better off burned. Judith rolled her eyes.

"Barbie, we've been through this already." Judith was unusually firm for someone who typically was the peacemaker between quarreling factions. "Even if we don't take the time to go through them now, no written records must be destroyed without serious thought."

"I know, I know." Instead of flaring up, Barbie's eyes twinkled. "I just wanted to spark things up a little."

"If you keep doing that, one day you'll set a fire you can't easily put out," Rebecca said. "Just remember that this is your family's history, too. One day you may want to tell your children about it."

Barbie made a face that suggested she didn't plan to do any such thing. Maybe she wanted a new history to go along with the new furniture she claimed she'd have if and when she set up housekeeping.

Rebecca exchanged glances with Judith, suspecting they were both thinking the same thing. One day Barbie would fall in love, and then all her preconceptions of the life she wanted could well fly out the window.

Determined that she'd not leave any too early today, Rebecca lingered after Judith and Barbie left. Barbie was still arguing mildly, as if for the sake of argument, when they walked to Judith's buggy. Judith, as far as Rebecca could tell, was keeping her peace and probably only half listening. Rebecca smiled. Perhaps that was the best way of dealing with their young cousin.

Rebecca went back to the living room where Grossmammi sat in her favorite rocker, her sewing basket by her side.

"What are you working on?" Rebecca drew a stool next to her grandmother and sat down. "Another quilt?"

Grossmammi nodded, smoothing the quilt patch out in her lap. "It's a variation on an autumn leaf design that Ann Stoltzfus showed me. Look how the leaves seem to curl."

Rebecca touched the intricate design. "It's going to be so pretty."

Her own sewing was almost entirely taken up with clothes for herself and the kinder, to say nothing of the constant stack of mending produced by two active little ones. She admired her grandmother's skill. Grossmammi had an artist's eye. The leaves, worked in shades ranging from yellow to gold to orange to red, were remarkably lifelike.

"I love the colors," she said. "It reminds me of the ridge on a sunny fall day."

Grossmammi nodded, her faded blue eyes seeming to look off in the distance. "That's what I see, too—the blaze of beauty before the cold of winter. I think that's what it must be like to enter heaven."

The Amish seldom speculated about such things, content to live their lives in obedience to God's laws without wondering overmuch on what came after. Rebecca studied her grandmother's serene face, wondering what had led her thoughts in that direction.

Before Rebecca could form a question, Grossmammi's forehead puckered slightly.

"How is the sorting coming? Did you find the little chest of drawers with the blue paint? I want that put away for your brother Simon when he marries."

"I haven't forgotten, Grossmammi." She patted the blue-veined hand, idle for the moment atop the quilt patch. "We'll make sure everything goes where it should." Even if she and Judith had to hogtie Barbie to do so.

Grossmammi shook her head, the frown deepening. "I still think I ought to do more of it myself. I can at least tell you what to do, even if I can't do any of the bending and lifting. Where is the key?"

"Judith has it," Rebecca said, grateful that they'd thought of that precaution. "And anyway, you know what the doctor said about climbing stairs."

"Ach, he's overcareful, that's what he is. I feel fine."

"We want to keep you that way," Rebecca said. "So that means no climbing up the attic stairs."

Grossmammi's eyes flashed with a bit of their old fire. "I was climbing those steps before you were born. Besides, I know just how to do it. I could go up a few steps and then stop to rest. Then a few more. There's no harm in that, ain't so?"

Rebecca was slightly appalled that her grandmother was actually giving the project some serious thought. She certain-sure wasn't going to be drawn into agreeing. "And what if you tripped on those narrow steps? Just think how we'd feel if we came and found you lying at the bottom."

"I wouldn't be lying there at all. I'm stronger than anyone thinks. Just because I have a little trouble catching my breath sometimes, that doesn't mean I'm ready for the scrap heap."

Grossmammi's strong will was legendary, and she seemed intent on proving it now.

"No one's suggesting that you are. What use is it to pay the doctor for his advice and then not take it? Anyway, I don't have the key, so there's an end to it." Thank goodness Judith had the key safe in her hand. For all her gentle manner, Judith could be firm when she had to be. Maybe that came of being the mother of a houseful of boys.

"When Judith comes tomorrow—" Grossmammi began.

"Ach, that reminds me of something I wanted to talk to you about." A diversion was clearly in order. "I took home a little wooden dower chest so I could sort the contents. When I was looking through it last night, I found a diary that I wanted to ask you about."

"A diary?" Grossmammi took the bait, her face lit with curiosity. "Whose was it, do you know?"

"The name in it is Anna." Rebecca paused, trying to collect what little she knew about the writer. "She seemed to be writing about things that were happening just before the Second World War."

"Anna Esch, that would be. Ach, that is what I would have picked for you, and you found it on your own."

"Picked for me?" Rebecca repeated the words. "What do you mean?"

Grossmammi's gaze slid away from hers. "Nothing, nothing. I'd like to be sure each of you has something especially meaningful. I was entrusted with some of Anna's papers and such when she passed on. She must have been . . ." Grossmammi paused, seeming to search the endless files of information stored in her mind. "Maybe about eighteen or so when the war started."

Rebecca nodded. "I thought so. Her writing sounds as if she was fairly young and hopeful. She was writing about her come-calling friend." She hesitated. "She seemed a little naïve, maybe, dreaming that marriage meant being happy forever."

"That's how girls are at eighteen." Grossmammi's tone held a touch of gentle laughter. At Rebecca? Maybe so. She had to admit she'd probably been equally foolish at that age.

"Girls married a little younger then than they do now," Grossmammi said. "The war years turned everything upside down, that was certain-sure. Not that I remember much about it myself, but even a child hears folks talking."

"Anna said that the war had turned the Englisch against the Leit." Rebecca used the familiar word by which the Amish referred to themselves. "It's hard to imagine our Englisch neighbors acting that way."

Her grandmother shook her head. "Maybe. Maybe not. There's no telling how folks will react in times of trouble. We haven't always been on such gut terms with our Englisch neighbors as we are now. And even today, some folks don't understand why we live the way we do. They think we're backward."

"Separate," Rebecca said. That was at the heart of the matter, she supposed. The Amish took seriously the words that they were to live by God's standards, not the world's. *Be not conformed to the standards of the world . . .*

Her grandmother nodded. "You'll read more of Anna's diaries, I hope. She lived through a time of tumult and change. Maybe she has something to teach you."

"I guess I will," Rebecca said. Did Grossmammi have something specific in mind, or was she just intent on seeing that the stories were kept alive?

"Change isn't easy." Grossmammi said the words, her old voice as soft as a sigh. Her gaze drifted across the contents of the familiar room—the faded sofa, the rocker where Grossdaadi used to sit every evening, the mending basket that had probably once been as overflowing as Rebecca's was. "It always means giving up something."

Rebecca's heart clenched at the sorrow in her grandmother's voice. Maybe, in their concern for Grossmammi's safety, they hadn't given enough consideration to her feelings about losing the home where she'd spent most of her life.

Rebecca searched for the right words. "I know change is difficult. Maybe all we can do is try to look at the good things about it. You know how much Mammi and Daadi want to have you living with them, and the boys are looking forward to it, as well. And maybe I'm selfish, but I'm glad Katie and Josh will be able to spend more time with you. We'll love having you right next door."

"You're a gut child, Rebecca." Grossmammi's soft, wrinkled

hand patted hers. "We will make a bargain, the two of us. I will try to look ahead if you will, too."

The words startled Rebecca, bringing her gaze to her grandmother's face. "Me?"

"You," Grossmammi said firmly. "You were trying to reassure me. But what you said goes for you, too, ain't so?"

Heat rushed to Rebecca's cheeks. "I . . . I'm doing fine. Really."

"Then there's no harm in agreeing to welcome change." Grossmammi's wise old eyes held a challenge.

"No, no harm." What else could she say? And how did her grandmother manage to look into her heart so easily? "I'll try, if you will."

What that would mean for her, Rebecca couldn't imagine, but if it put Grossmammi in a better frame of mind about the future, perhaps it was worth it.

CHAPTER THREE

Matt glanced at his uncle's face as they loaded tools into the back of the buggy. He'd been a bit surprised when Onkel Silas had suggested knocking off early. The job they were doing, installing new kitchen cabinets in a home on the edge of the village, might be taxing on an older man, but Onkel Silas was as whipcord wiry as he'd ever been. Maybe his lack of energy was more a matter of losing heart now that Isaiah wasn't working next to him.

Matt shoved away a familiar sense of guilt. It wasn't his doing that Isaiah had kicked over the traces and bolted for the outside world. He hadn't so much as seen his younger cousin in years.

Onkel Silas climbed into the buggy seat, and Matt swung up next to him and took the lines. Raising a hand in good-bye to Emma King, their client, who was watching from the window, he clucked to the mare and they moved off.

"Emma seems satisfied with how the cabinets are coming," he ventured when his uncle didn't speak.

"She'll want to get back into her kitchen with all those kinder to feed." Onkel Silas sent a sideways glance at Matt. "She was your year in school, ain't so?"

Why aren't you married with a family of your own? Was that the question his uncle really wanted to ask? Matt wasn't sure.

"Ja, she was. She's changed a bit since then. I wouldn't have thought she and Joe King would make a match of it."

Onkel Silas chuckled, seeming to relax against the seat. "She led him a fine chase, as I remember. Everyone from your class is married now, ain't so?"

That, Matt thought, was as close as his uncle would come to asking him directly why a thirty-year-old Amish man wasn't married.

"Everyone but me," he said with a cheerfulness he didn't feel. "I haven't found anyone willing to take a chance on me yet."

Onkel Silas managed another chuckle at the comment, but he didn't push. A good thing, since Matt had no intention of telling him or anyone else why he wasn't married.

"We ought to be able to finish that section of cabinets tomorrow." Matt changed the subject firmly.

"Most likely."

They rode along in silence then. If his uncle didn't feel like talking, Matt was just as glad to stay silent. Conversations with his uncle seemed laid with traps for the unwary these days.

Onkel Silas glanced ahead as the mare picked up her pace, sensing the lane to the barn. "Just drop me at the mailbox. That'll give you time to run over to Rebecca's and see if she's made a decision. You'll want to get your shop set up soon as you can."

"I can take you up to the house—" Matt began.

His uncle cut him off with an annoyed look. "I'm not so old I can't walk up my own lane. Get on over to Rebecca's before she's busy with supper."

Matt nodded, not venturing to argue. This slight testiness on his uncle's part was new. Onkel Silas had always been the most even-tempered of men. Still, given all he had to deal with now, it wasn't surprising.

His uncle climbed down, and Matt headed on down the road, conquering a faint reluctance on the part of the mare, who obviously considered that she should be heading for the barn and her feed bucket. He glanced back once, to see Onkel Silas square his shoulders and start walking toward the house.

Matt's throat tightened. It had to be small compensation to Onkel Silas to have his nephew rather than his much-loved son working beside him. Isaiah should come home, the sooner the better.

As for Sadie's implication that Isaiah had been emulating Matt when he'd jumped the fence—well, that had to be a figment of her imagination. Matt hadn't been around, and Isaiah no doubt had plenty of examples of fence-jumping closer to home. Every rumspringa group seemed to have one or two kids who decided to take a bite of the apple. Most of them came home eventually, ready to take up their proper roles.

Still, Isaiah was needed here now, not later, with his daad aging, a business to run, and his mamm in the condition she was. Had Onkel Silas made any effort to find the boy? If so, he'd certain-sure never talked about it.

Sooner or later Isaiah would come to his senses. That made it all the more important that Matt get his shop set up as quickly as possible. He could only hope that Rebecca, too, had come to see the sense of his proposal. If not, he'd have to look elsewhere, and he found himself oddly reluctant to do so.

Renting the unused stable wasn't just the best solution for him, being well suited to his needs and only a few miles from his uncle's property. It surely was the best solution for Rebecca, as well. She couldn't be finding it easy, even with her family's help, raising two children on her own.

A small farm like Rebecca's was common among the Amish, and most families eked out their income with an assortment of other efforts, like a fruit stand or a quilt shop or a part-time job. That allowed the family to work together most of the time, something that was prized among the Amish, even if it was possible for the father to earn more by working at a full-time job away from home.

Matt felt wry amusement at the idea. His time in the Englisch world had convinced him the Amish ideal ran exactly counter to the modern American dream.

A few minutes later he was turning in the lane at Rebecca's. In just the last couple of days, the ridge above the house had put on its spring coat of pale green leaves, their lightness a contrast to the deep green-black of the pines and hemlocks. On the lower stretches he could see the patches of pinkish white that marked the mountain laurel coming into bloom.

Insensibly, his heart lifted at the sight. Spring was a time for new beginnings. Why shouldn't it be a new beginning for him?

Mindful of what Rebecca had said about her son seeing him

at the stable and thinking he was his father, Matt drove up to the house and stopped at the hitching rail by the back door. Country people always came to the back of a house, not the front. He'd never found that strange until he'd lived a bit in the city.

Sliding down, he gave the mare a pat as he fastened the line to the rail. Even as he turned toward the house, the back door opened and a small figure shot out.

The boy skidded to a halt as he realized the visitor was a stranger. This must be Joshua. Had Rebecca mentioned the boy's age? He didn't remember, but Joshua looked about five or six. Round blue eyes stared warily at Matt from beneath the brim of a straw hat. Joshua wore the typical blue shirt, black pants and suspenders of most Amish boys, and under the hat his hair was as pale and soft as corn silk.

"You must be Joshua." Matt squatted, bringing his face to the child's level. "My name is Matthew."

Joshua's only response was a slight nod, and he took a small step back, as if not comfortable so close to a stranger.

It was probably better not to push the boy for conversation he so clearly didn't want. "Is your mammi here?"

That got a more decided nod. Joshua turned, maybe intending to go after his mother. But the door opened just then and Rebecca emerged onto the porch. Joshua indicated him with a wave of his hand.

Matt rose to his feet, feeling a little foolish given the boy's lack of response. "Rebecca." He nodded to her, trying to gauge her expression. "I was just getting acquainted with Joshua."

The boy, as if released by the sound of his name, darted off across the yard. At first Matt thought he was headed for the stable, but instead he veered toward the apple tree behind it and swarmed up, his small figure vanishing into the cloud of blossoms.

"I didn't mean to scare him." Matt turned back to Rebecca in time to see her staring after her son. The look of maternal love on her face was so powerful it unsettled him. There was a fierceness about it that didn't match his image of a shy, serene Rebecca.

The disturbing expression faded as she faced him, her green eyes intent. "Josh is shy with strangers. Just don't pay much attention to him, and he'll warm up."

That sounded like an assumption the boy would be seeing something of him. He wasn't sure whether to take that as a hopeful sign or not. Maybe he'd better just get to the reason he was here.

"I hoped maybe you'd had a chance to come to a decision about renting the stable to me. If it's a question of the money—"

"No, no." She shook her head, a flush coming to her cheeks at the idea that she might be bargaining with him for more. "I just . . ." She let that trail off, and Matt could feel the struggle going on inside her.

Before he could speak, her face seemed to firm, and she met his gaze. "Tell me something first. Why? Why here? Why come back to Brook Hill at all? I know you said your uncle needs you, but there must be more to your decision than that."

Matt wanted to turn away from the insistence in her gaze, but he couldn't. "That would make it a long story," he said, hoping to deter her.

"I have time." Rebecca gestured toward the swing on the back porch. "Komm. Sit down."

He hesitated for a second, and then nodded. As he mounted the steps beside her, his shoulder brushed the bell that swung from the porch roof, and it gave off a faint reverberation, humming musically. Rebecca grasped the rope instantly, stilling the bell, an expression on her face he couldn't interpret.

"Sorry," he said. "I guess you don't want to call the kinder for supper yet."

Rebecca's lips were pressed together, her expression shuttered. She didn't answer, and he had a sense of strong emotion moving behind the facade. Clearly there was more here than just a bell, common as they were on farm porches. Just as clearly, she wasn't going to confide in him. Not that he wanted her to.

Matt sat at one end of the swing, hearing the chain creak. Rebecca settled herself at the other, carefully leaving a space between them wide enough for another person to occupy. She clasped her hands on her lap, pressing them against the dark green apron that matched her dress and her eyes.

She didn't speak, so she must be waiting for him to start the conversation. The trouble was that he didn't intend to tell Rebecca or anyone else his full reasons for returning to a place he'd long ago told himself he'd seen the last of.

"You already know about Onkel Silas. Isn't it natural I'd want to help out until Isaiah comes back?"

She gave a slight inclination of the head. "I suppose so. But what if he doesn't return? Will you go into partnership with your uncle?"

"Isaiah will be back." Every day he felt that more strongly. If for no other reason, Isaiah would return for his mamm's sake.

"What makes you think so? Have you heard from him?"

Rebecca's face was troubled, as if she'd seen too much of things not turning out the way they were expected to.

Matt realized he wanted to give her an honest answer, not a pat reassurance. "No, I haven't, but I think I know what kind of man Isaiah is, even though I haven't seen him in a long time." He picked his words carefully, trying to articulate to her something he hadn't bothered to spell out for himself. "Isaiah has a good heart. He's responsible. He won't be able to ignore the call of the way he was brought up."

"You sound so sure." Rebecca's green eyes seemed dark with questions.

"I am." Or at least, he was trying to make himself believe it. "After all, I did."

Rebecca's eyebrows lifted. "You? You mean you did leave the Amish?" Her hand moved in a slight gesture toward his clothing. "I thought people had all been wrong about you when they said you'd certain-sure turn Englisch."

"No, they had it right all along." Clearly she wasn't going to be satisfied unless he explained a bit more. "I think my folks thought moving out west and meeting the challenge of a new place would be enough to settle me down. Maybe it did, for a time, but eventually . . . well, I guess I was just born wanting to see what lay over the next ridge." He glanced toward the ever-present ridge that guarded Brook Hill.

"How did you get along out there among the Englisch?" She made it sound far away, even dangerous.

He shrugged, aware of how close she was. Near enough that if he moved his hand, he'd bridge the gap between them. "It wasn't as bad for me as it is for some fence-jumpers. I'd been apprenticed to a furniture maker, so I had a trade I could turn to. I did okay."

"But you still came back to the faith eventually." There was a question in the words, and it was one Matt had no intention of answering.

"I realized I didn't really fit in anywhere else. At heart, I will always be Amish." He let a little impatience creep into his voice, afraid if she asked more he might reveal too much. Rebecca was just too easy to talk to, with her sweet face and innocent eyes. "Why is my life story important to whether or not you rent the building to me?"

She nodded, as if to accept the implied rebuke. "I just want to be sure you wouldn't turn the stable into a workshop and then up and leave."

"I wouldn't."

Again he sensed the struggle in her, and he knew he had to say something more to reassure her.

"Look, Rebecca, I'm ready to make a permanent change in my life, and coming back to where I started is my choice. I can't prove my commitment to you. I'm afraid you'll just have to accept it. Or not."

Rebecca's expression seemed to grow still, and he had the fanciful feeling that his words had struck an echo in her. After what seemed a long moment, she nodded. "All right." She gave a small nod. "We have a deal. You can start moving in as soon as you want to."

He turned toward her, his hand braced against the back of the swing so that it nearly touched her shoulder. "Denke, Rebecca. You won't regret it."

He'd like to say he promised, but experience had taught him that making promises was a dangerous thing to do.

Rebecca stood by the lane watching until Matt's buggy disappeared behind the trees along the road. Was she doing the right thing? She could only pray she wouldn't regret this decision.

She'd been on the verge of saying no. And then Matt had said something about changing his life, making a fresh start. She'd been irresistibly reminded of the promise she'd made to Grossmammi about reacting positively to life's changes, and she'd been caught.

Well, having Matt working in the stable that she still thought of as Paul's would certainly be one of those changes, and she'd just have to do her best to welcome it.

Thoughts of supper stirred in her mind, and she went up the three steps to the porch, unable to prevent herself from looking at the bell as she passed it. Her stomach had lurched when Matt had brushed against it, and at just the thought, she felt the sensation again.

She reached up, her fingertips touching the cool metal. She and Paul had been moving the last few things into the farmhouse when she'd come outside and found him attaching the bell to the roof of the porch.

"Whatever are you doing?" She'd looked up at him, laughing a little at the sight of him teetering on a chair to fasten the bracket.

"I'm putting the final touch to our new home." He stepped down lightly. "Every farmhouse has to have a bell. How else will you call me for supper when I'm out in the fields, or let me know if you need me? When I was little, no matter where I was on the farm, I could hear the bell calling me home."

He swept her up in his arms with a quick movement, his face alight with joy and love. "Now this is our home, ain't so?"

"Ach, for sure it is. But you'd better put me down before someone sees." She hadn't really meant her chiding, and he knew it. She had loved feeling his strong arms around her and knowing the two of them belonged to each other.

"I won't put you down until you ring the bell for the first time." He held her so she could reach the cord.

Smiling at his excitement over something so simple, she pulled the rope, sending the bell's sweet peal singing across the valley.

Paul had pressed his cheek against hers. "Whenever I hear the bell ring, I'll know you're calling me home. For the rest of our days."

He'd never imagined that their days would be cut so short. Rebecca caressed the bell once more and then stepped resolutely away from it. She had no choice but to accept what God had sent them.

"What are you doing, Mammi?" Joshua trotted across the grass, looking at her with curiosity in his face.

"Nothing." She put a hand on his shoulder and drew him to her, sitting down on the top step. "Tell me something, Josh. Why did you run away when Matthew was here?"

Josh shrugged, his usual response when he didn't know what to say or when he didn't want to answer. Still, Josh would need to get over his shyness now that Matt would be around often.

"I know he's a stranger to you, but Matt is an old friend. He was in school with me and your daadi. There's no need for you to be shy with him."

Her thoughts flickered to the rebellious teenager Matt had been. But she had no right to judge him now by who he'd been years ago.

"Anyway, he's going to rent the stable to use for his furniture-making business, so you'll see him around a lot. You will be polite, ain't so?" She smoothed his silky hair out of his eyes.

Josh nodded solemnly. "I will, Mammi."

"What are you talking about?" Katie emerged from the house, letting the screen door bang behind her. She hopped down the steps on one foot and stood teetering a little.

"We were talking about Matthew Byler." Rebecca eyed her daughter warily, not sure how Katie would take this news. "He's the man I was talking to in the stable the other day."

"He's going to make furniture in Daadi's stable," Josh announced, preventing Rebecca from finding a gentler way of revealing a truth she suspected Katie wouldn't like.

Katie planted both feet on the ground and her fists on her hips, staring at Rebecca. "No, he's not. That's dumb."

"Don't say that word," Rebecca said automatically. "We don't have a use for the stable, so Matthew Byler wants to rent it from us. That means he'll pay us to use it for his furniture-making."

Katie stared at her for what seemed forever, her normally sunny small face setting in stubborn lines. "No. He can't. It's Daadi's stable."

Her voice trembled a little on the words, and Rebecca's heart twisted. Poor Katie. She remembered her father's dreams more than Joshua did.

"I know we built the stable for Daadi's horses. But Daadi has no need for it now that he's in heaven." The Amish weren't generally so proud as to claim they knew they were going to heaven, but about Paul she had no doubt.

Clouds gathered on Katie's face. "It doesn't matter. The stable still belongs to Daadi. Nobody else can have it."

"Katie, that is foolish." Maybe her voice was a little tart because she understood what Katie felt. "Daadi would not want the stable to sit empty when someone can use it. You know how generous Daadi was."

"No!" Katie's voice rose. "It's still not right. You can't let someone else have it."

The vehemence in her child's tone startled Rebecca. She understood the emotion that prompted it, but she could not allow Katie to speak to an adult that way.

"This is not up to you, Katie. It's a grown-up decision." She hoped that sounded final.

"I'll tell Grossdaadi," Katie flashed back. "He won't let you."

Rebecca grasped her daughter by the arms, genuinely shocked and dismayed. "Katie, that will do. This is my decision, no one else's, and I have made it." As lonely as the words sounded, they were true. "I will hear no more about it."

Katie stared at her, and Rebecca suspected she was shaken both by the decision and the fact that her mother had made it. She longed to reach out and pull Katie against her in comfort, but she couldn't allow her to get away with being disrespectful. Paul never would have, and now the burden of discipline, like so much else, was hers alone.

Katie glared at her for a moment longer. Then she whirled and ran toward the barn, perhaps to carry her complaint to her grandfather. Well, she would get no satisfaction there, Rebecca knew. Whatever her father thought of her decision, he wouldn't allow Katie to think he took sides against her mother.

Rebecca sighed, feeling as if her heart had taken a pummeling. If only she could find a way to reach Katie. She felt as if she were failing the child she loved so much.

"Is Katie mad because God took Daadi away?" Joshua, who had been a silent spectator, put the question in a small voice.

Rebecca touched his cheek lightly. In his innocence, he'd come up with the truth, she thought. "I suppose she is. But what happens to us in this world is God's will, and we must accept it."

Rebecca said the familiar words automatically, but they sounded hollow. Suddenly she knew why she couldn't seem to deal with Katie's anger. It was because she felt the same thing. The truth swept over her like a blast of wind. She was angry with God for taking Paul away when she needed him so much.

Lancaster County, November 1941

The feel of snow was in the air as Anna drove the buggy down the narrow country road toward the four-room schoolhouse attended by both Amish and Englisch children from the area.

Usually Peter and Sarah, her youngest sister and brother, walked home together at the end of the day, but Mamm had kept Sarah home with a sore throat, and she hadn't wanted six-year-old Peter walking alone.

Anna had been glad to have an errand that took her out for a bit. It had seemed to her that there was an unspoken tension in the house lately—something weighing on Mamm and Daad that was never said aloud but only hinted at through an exchange of looks, an unusual testiness in Daad's manner, a few extra worry lines on Mamm's usually serene face.

Her parents shouldn't be changing. Anna knew that was childish, but she couldn't seem to help it. Her world had always been anchored so completely by the twin rocks of family and faith. Nothing could alter that, could it?

Still, the uneasiness seemed to permeate the entire Amish community these days. She'd noticed Daad with his cousin, Amos Sitler, after worship on Sunday, and she'd been alarmed by the grave expression on Cousin Amos's face. He was one who always had a joke or a laugh when they met, but not that day. She'd drifted a little closer.

". . . will be chust as bad as it was in the last war, I'm certain-sure of it." Cousin Amos had shaken his head. "Already there have been angry looks when folks hear us speaking Deutsch. How long before it moves to worse than looks?"

"There's no call to borrow trouble," Daad said, but she'd seen how worried he looked. "God will be with us, no matter what."

"I don't doubt it, but to think of our kinder having to face that kind of trial—"

Cousin Amos had seen her watching them then, and he

turned away with a comment about the chance of snow. But what she'd heard had kept her awake that night, and she hadn't quite shaken off that sense of dread yet.

A few flakes of snow drifted onto Bell's glossy back, making brief stars before melting into the mare's warmth. Anna barely had to touch the lines to turn her into the long lane that led to the schoolhouse. Bell knew the way as well as Anna did.

Suddenly the mare's head came up, her ears pricking forward. She shook herself, setting the harness jingling, and in a moment the horse's odd apprehension touched Anna, as well. There were so many vehicles jamming the lane—surely not that many parents would come to pick up their children, no matter how cold the day. One pickup truck was stopped haphazardly across the lane, nearly blocking it.

Frowning, Anna pulled up the mare. Maybe it was best to leave the buggy here, rather than risk getting penned in with no room to turn. She slid down, speaking softly to the mare, and tied her to a convenient tree branch. As she hurried toward the building, she finally caught the scent that had alarmed the mare—the faint, acrid smell of burning.

Fear raced through her, swamping every other thought. Was the school on fire? Peter—she had to find Peter.

Pulling her skirt away from her legs, Anna broke into a run. Someone brushed past her—an Englischer, then another, hurrying toward the school.

"What's wrong?" she cried, but they didn't so much as look at her.

Fear propelled her forward. A crowd milled around the

school, and the smell of burning was stronger now. Some parents hung back, clutching their kinder to them.

"Peter!" Her cry seemed lost in the buzz of other voices.

Someone caught her arm. She swung around, breath catching, but it was Jacob—his dear face worried.

"Jacob, what is it? What's happening?"

"It's all right." He rushed the words. "You've komm for Sarah and Peter? I'll get them."

"Just Peter. Sarah is at home." She tried to pull free of his grasp. "I must find Peter. He'll be frightened."

"Go back to the buggy. I'll bring him." He was trying to urge her away from the school building, and that very fact frightened her.

"No." She pulled away from him. "I must find my little bruder."

Apparently realizing she wouldn't be dissuaded, Jacob touched her arm and pointed. "Komm. Over here. The teachers have some of the kinder by the swings."

Anna had to break into a run to keep up with Jacob's long stride, and she was too breathless to ask again what was happening. If the school was on fire—her throat tightened at the thought. She'd spent eight years in this school, Amish and Englisch children together, and it was nearly as dear and familiar to her as her own home.

Several Englisch mothers, coats pulled on over their housedresses, hustled their children away. Anna half expected to find flames scorching the schoolhouse, but the white-frame building stood as solidly as ever, though people were running in and out.

Searching desperately, Anna finally saw Mrs. Dill, the seventh and eighth grade teacher, standing near the tire swing that hung from the apple tree, a cluster of children with her. Pressed close to the teacher's side was Peter.

Anna could have wept with relief. She ran toward them, and Peter hurtled himself into her arms. He was trying hard not to cry, and he buried his face in her apron.

"It's all right now. I'm here." She held him close. "Denke," she murmured, her gaze meeting that of her former teacher.

"Take him home," Mrs. Dill directed. There was a shade of the usual command in her voice, but her face was drawn with pain or grief.

"But what has happened?" Anna looked to her for answers, as she always had. "Is there a fire in the school?"

It seemed to her that Mrs. Dill and Jacob exchanged looks, much as Mamm and Daad had been doing recently.

"No." Mrs. Dill's authoritative tone flattened on the word. "They are burning the German grammar books."

Anna could only stare, trying to understand. "Books . . ." She murmured the word.

Mrs. Dill had taught German and French to the older scholars, along with literature, history, and mathematics. Anna had always thought there was nothing Mrs. Dill didn't know, but the Englisch woman's love of language and literature had been obvious. Many of the books in the upper-level classroom were her own volumes, and she'd handled them as if they were the greatest of treasures.

A shout pulled Anna's attention to the building. A pyramid of books had been made on the grass by the flagpole, and a man she didn't recognize splashed gasoline on them from a can. The acrid odor assaulted her senses.

"But your books . . . we can't let them be destroyed. We have to stop those people."

"We can't." Jacob's voice was gentle.

She didn't want to accept that, but she could see that Mrs. Dill already had.

"Why?" Anna held out a questioning hand to her teacher. "Books can't harm anyone."

Mrs. Dill gave her an approving look. "You and I know that. But in troubled times, I fear common sense is the first thing to go."

"But surely the parents of your students will make them stop." She couldn't believe this was happening, not here.

"Some might want to, but they're afraid. They don't want to be seen as German sympathizers. It's not an easy thing, to stand up to a crowd." Mrs. Dill patted Anna's hand. "You can't do anything here. Let Jacob see you and Peter safely home now."

"We can take you home as well," Jacob said. "You don't want to see this."

Mrs. Dill's gaze softened as it rested on him, but she shook her head. "No, thank you, Jacob. I must stay."

Jacob nodded, as if he understood. He clasped Anna and Peter by the hand, and Anna was glad enough to feel his fingers around hers, communicating his strength.

They'd just started down the lane when a roar went up from the crowd. Anna glanced back over her shoulder. Mrs. Dill still stood where they had left her, her slight figure seeming as indomitable as ever.

Beyond her, the pyramid of books had blazed up in a tower of orange and red.

No, not a pyramid, not a bonfire. Mrs. Dill always insisted on precise language from her students. This was a funeral pyre.

Anna was shaken by a feeling so unaccustomed that she wasn't sure at first what it was. And then she realized. It was anger. How could God let this happen?

Chapter Four

Matt glanced around his new workshop with satisfaction a week after Rebecca had agreed to rent the space to him. He'd taken his time getting organized, methodically arranging his equipment to suit his needs and the space available in the stable.

He hadn't wanted to pull apart any of the stalls that had been built, presumably for the work horses he'd heard Paul had intended to breed. Instead, he'd worked around the existing interior, using the stalls as storage areas for the time being. The center section had plenty of space to set up his workbenches.

Now, finally, he was ready to actually get to work on some new pieces of furniture, and something that had been restless in him was stilled at the thought.

It wasn't that he didn't take pleasure in working alongside Onkel Silas in the carpentry business, because he did. Their talents blended well together. But however smoothly the work went, that job was always accompanied by a sense of obligation and an awareness that even though he'd never say it, Silas must consider him a poor substitute for the son he'd lost.

Matt ran his palm along the smooth curve of the maple rocker he was making, feeling the wood grow warm beneath his touch like a person's skin. This was where his heart was, after all. How many people had the chance to spend their lives working at a job they loved?

He turned the question over in his mind as he arranged the spindles for the rocker's back. More people among the Amish were satisfied with their work than in the general population, he'd guess. To the Amish, work was to be enjoyed as praise to God, no matter what it entailed. It was so much the better if a person could do something he really enjoyed.

The friends he'd had when he'd lived among the Englisch had seemed to see their jobs as nothing more than a means to earn money to do what they really wanted to. Still, they'd been young and restless, like him. Maybe they'd eventually find the pleasure in their work that he did when he felt a piece of furniture taking shape under his hands.

The boy was there, watching Matt as he had been for the past few evenings. Matt had spotted him peeking around the edge of a box stall a few minutes after he'd started work.

Joshua was a bit closer tonight—either feeling more daring or becoming more convinced that Matt hadn't noticed him. Matt had been careful not to let on that he saw the child, but maybe he could risk talking a bit.

"Looks as if this spindle is just a tad too long." Matt kept his voice low, as if he were talking to himself. "Pity, but I'll have to shorten it. No point in rushing through a job and ending up with less than my best."

He tackled the offending spindle, shaving a fraction of an inch off the end. "There's no hurrying in woodworking—that's what Asa used to say when he was teaching me the craft. Take it slowly and do your best. You'll get faster in time."

He fitted the spindle against the back, measuring it with an experienced eye. "Just a touch more, I think." He suited action to words and shaved off a bit more, holding the spindle so Joshua could see what he was doing.

"There's no room for temper in woodworking, either." He smiled, remembering. "I mind the time a piece I'd been working on for a good hour came apart in my hands just when I thought it was done. I was so mad I threw it across the shop."

He heard a rustle from the direction of the stall and the faint creak of a board.

"Asa just looked at me, disappointed. 'Wood will forgive a lot,' he told me, 'but not bad temper.' Far as Asa was concerned, the wood was a living thing."

"Who was Asa?" The small voice, coming after days of silence, startled him.

Careful, he told himself. Making friends with Rebecca's son was a lot like coaxing a sparrow to take a bread crumb from his hand.

"Asa Wagner was my neighbor when I lived out in Indiana. I was his apprentice. That means he taught me about woodworking so I could make furniture."

Asa had taught him more than that; he'd given his endless patience with the headstrong teenager Matt had been. It was just a pity Matt hadn't taken his lessons to heart in time to prevent some of the worst of his mistakes.

"Is that going to be a chair?" The boy's voice came from just behind Matt, and he risked a look. Joshua had crept up without a sound. His wide blue eyes were fixed on the pieces laid out on the worktable.

"A rocking chair," Matt said. "This will be the back of it."

Joshua's small finger reached out to touch a spindle, tracing the rounded curve. "It's smooth."

"I like to get every piece as finished as I can before I put it together. Otherwise it can be hard to get the sandpaper into all the curves and corners to finish them."

That had been one of Asa's pet peeves, he remembered. Every bit of a piece should be smooth as silk, even the parts that didn't easily show. That's how you could tell a piece was handcrafted, not made by a machine, he'd say, dismissing machine-made products with a shrug of his wiry shoulders.

"But how do you get it so smooth?" Joshua met Matt's eyes, his curiosity finally outweighing his shyness.

Matt reached for the box that contained his sandpaper, sorted according to grade. "You go over it with finer and finer paper each time, wiping it down completely after every rubbing. Can you feel the difference between these?" He pulled out a coarse paper and an extra-fine one.

Joshua touched each one, his small face serious. Then he nodded. "But why don't you just start with this one?" He indicated the extra-fine.

The youngster was sharp for a five-year-old, it seemed to Matt. Rebecca must have her hands full, raising two youngsters without a husband's help.

"You don't start with the fine one because the wood would be too rough at first to respond to it. You can't take shortcuts and have a piece come out its best."

Joshua grinned, his solemn face lighting up. "That's what Mammi says when Katie wants her to hurry with the baking."

"Your mammi is a wise woman," he said, wondering what Rebecca would say if she heard.

And speaking of Rebecca, someone had just stepped into the path of late-afternoon sunshine that streamed from the open door. He turned to greet her, but his smile checked when he realized it wasn't Rebecca. It took him a moment to recognize Simon, her next younger brother. He'd been little more than a child when Matt left.

"Simon—" he began, but he paused when he realized Simon was rather obviously ignoring him and staring at Joshua.

"I think your mammi wants you at the house, Josh." His face, a more masculine version of Rebecca's with its straight nose and fresh color, seemed to tighten. "You shouldn't be out here with him."

Matt found his own muscles growing taut in response. Simon made it sound as if the stable were a dangerous place now that Matt had moved in.

Leave it alone. He had no business interfering between Joshua and his uncle.

Joshua's expression clearly asked a question, but he didn't say it aloud. Instead, he gave Matt a shy smile and sprinted from the stable without a word.

"No need to scare the boy off," Matt said mildly once Joshua was gone. "He wasn't bothering me."

"It wasn't you I was thinking of." Simon took a step closer, his youthful face suddenly pugnacious. "I don't want Joshua hanging around you."

Matt squashed the tiny flare of temper. "Is that what Rebecca says?" he asked.

"That's what I say." There could be no doubt of Simon's attitude. Was his obvious opposition to Matt shared by the rest of Rebecca's family? She'd certainly given no indication of it, if that was true.

"It seems to me what Joshua does is up to his mother." Matt turned back to his worktable, hoping that would put an end to an obviously fruitless conversation. "If she doesn't want me talking to Joshua, all she has to do is say so."

He heard a hasty step behind him, and then Simon's hand gripped his shoulder as if to spin him around. Matt grasped the edge of the table. *Don't lose your temper. Whatever you do, don't lose your temper.*

He stood, rocklike, long enough to make it clear to Simon that his efforts wouldn't move him. Then he turned to face Simon with an assumption of calm he didn't feel.

"You're not looking for a fight, are you, Sim?" He deliberately used the boyhood nickname. "The church would frown on that, ain't so?"

"You should know." Simon's temper flared. "Now that Paul's gone, it's up to Rebecca's family to protect her and the kinder. I don't want you influencing my nephew or taking advantage of Rebecca's good nature. You understand?"

There was a time when Matt would have responded to those words by seizing Simon by the scruff of the neck and tossing him out the door. Those days were gone. They had to be if he expected to stay in this community.

"Is that all?" Let Simon try to figure out whether that was sarcasm or not. "Because if so, I need to get back to work."

He turned to the workbench again, reaching for the spindle.

He felt Simon behind him and imagined he sensed a certain bafflement in the air. Simon, he suspected, didn't know quite what to make of his reaction. The question was, how far did Simon want to push him?

Heavy shoes scraped on the floor. Simon's body blocked the light from the door again for a moment, and then he was gone.

Matt unclenched his fists, one finger at a time. He'd been so intent on getting Rebecca's approval for his plan that he hadn't stopped to consider how anyone else might react to his presence on her property. Maybe he should have.

And maybe he should reassess the likelihood that he was going to keep the promises he'd made when he returned to the Amish, especially here in Brook Hill. He'd thought this would be a good place to test his resolve, back where he had started. Maybe he'd underestimated the power of people here to set his rebellious temper flaring all over again.

Sometimes Rebecca thought that the more they sorted in her grandmother's attic, the more things they discovered. That was impossible, of course, but certainly the job was taking longer than they'd anticipated, and today only she and Barbie were working, since Judith's youngest was down with a fever.

Rebecca couldn't help murmuring a quick, motherly prayer that her own kinder would be spared. Spring colds seemed to go on and on, just at a time when the young ones most wanted to be outside.

Rebecca lifted a box filled with old sheets, revealing yet another dower chest beneath it. She bent, looking more closely at the front, and traced the faded paint with her fingertip.

"Barbie, komm see this."

"Another chest?" Barbie frowned, her arms filled with a quilt she'd just unearthed. "What's so special about that? The attic is full of them."

"But look at the date on this one." She knelt to get a better angle, peering at the inscription on the front. Two birds faced each other from matching apple trees, and between them she could just make out the lettering.

"Martha Esch, June 1856," she read. "Can you imagine? I wonder if it's been here in the attic that long?"

"It couldn't be." Barbie, her attention apparently caught, came and knelt beside her. "The Leit haven't been here in Brook Hill that long."

"No, of course not." Rebecca was forgetting her history. "This must have been made when the family was still in Lancaster County. Amazing, that it's in such fine shape."

"It is, isn't it?" Barbie ran her hand over the smooth grain of the top, blue eyes sparkling. "You know what? This is a genuine antique. I'll bet we could get a lot of money for it from one of those dealers in town."

"Money?" Rebecca let her outrage show in her face. "Barbie, that's a terrible thing to say. This is a piece of your family's history."

Rebellion flared in those blue eyes. "Family history. Is that all you can think of—stuff that's old and dead? I'd rather concentrate on the here and now. And on the future."

Rebecca sat back on her heels, looking at her cousin. Barbie's pert face, with its fresh color and rosy lips, was filled with a mix of impatience and eagerness, and Rebecca had a sense that there was more going on in her cousin's busy mind than sorting her grandmother's attic.

"Your future?" she asked, not sure she really wanted to encourage Barbie's confidences. It seemed an eternity since she'd been so young and eager.

"Maybe."

For a moment Rebecca thought Barbie wouldn't say any more, and then the words seemed to burst out of her as if she couldn't hold them back.

"Don't you know what it is to be bored to death with the same old thing?" Barbie's hands fluttered, as if trying to express something she wasn't sure how to say. "Sometimes I feel so restless I think I'm going to burst right out of my skin. I want to go places, do things. I want to see what's on the other side of the ridge. Didn't you ever feel that way?"

Rebecca wanted to empathize, but she couldn't lie to her cousin. "No, I never did. I always knew that what I wanted was right here—marrying Paul, having his children, being together always."

"I can't imagine feeling like that about anyone." Barbie's gaze rested on her face, questioning. "But your dream didn't work out the way you thought it would."

Rebecca winced. "No."

"I'm sorry." Barbie's expression changed, quick as a

hummingbird darting from one flower to another. "I didn't mean to be unkind. I just feel so trapped sometimes."

Feeling inadequate was becoming a habit with her, Rebecca decided. But what on earth was she to say to Barbie? Presumably she'd confided in Rebecca because she wanted understanding or advice. Rebecca felt ill-equipped to offer either.

"Maybe you need to get away for a bit," she suggested. "Take a trip to Ohio, for instance, to visit the relatives out there."

Barbie's snub nose wrinkled at that idea. "Are you kidding? The church is even stricter out there than it is here."

"There are good reasons for all the church's decisions, Barbie. They're meant to keep us separate and humble, the way the Bible teaches, ain't so?"

Barbie didn't look in any mood to appreciate the reasons behind the church's rulings. "I know, I know. Be humble, be patient, accept what happens as God's will. Honestly, sometimes I just want to smash something when people say that. Don't you?"

How could Rebecca deny it, with the realization of her anger against God for Paul's death still fresh in her mind? But she could hardly tell her young cousin so. What if Barbara cut loose and did something drastic, and it was her fault?

"Barbie, don't." She touched her cousin's hand. "You don't really mean that."

Barbie gave her a pitying look. "I suppose you're past feeling the way I do." She made it sound as if Rebecca were a hundred and two, with all her passion burned to ashes.

Well, maybe that was true. Certainly she felt that way sometimes. But what was she going to say to Barbie?

Fortunately for her, since she couldn't think of a thing, Grossmammi called up the stairs.

"It's time you girls had a break. I have lemonade and cookies on the table for you."

Barbie stood with her characteristic quick grace. Rebecca got up as well, shaking out her skirt, wrinkled from kneeling. Relief was her predominant emotion, but she couldn't let Barbie's comments go so easily.

"Why don't you talk to Grossmammi about how you feel? She wouldn't tell anyone."

But Barbie dismissed that with a quick shrug of her shoulders. "It's nothing. Forget it." She darted down the steep, narrow stairs before Rebecca could urge her.

Rebecca followed more slowly, her own concerns temporarily eclipsed by her apprehension over her cousin. Barbie was so impulsive—quick to act and quick to anger—but she had a warm heart. Rebecca felt sure of it. Still, that might not keep her from making a mistake she couldn't easily mend.

By the time Rebecca reached the kitchen, Grossmammi and Barbie were already sitting at the table, a pitcher of lemonade and a plate of oatmeal cookies between them.

"You must have dropped this when you came in." Her grandmother pushed an envelope across the table to Rebecca.

Rebecca looked at it blankly for an instant before remembering. "Ach, I took yesterday's mail from the box when I came past and then forgot all about it."

"Go ahead and open it." Grossmammi poured a glass of lemonade for her, and Barbie pushed the cookie plate closer.

Barbie bit into a cookie. "Yum." She seemed to have recovered her equilibrium already. There was no hint in her face of the girl who'd spoken so passionately of being trapped. Clearly she had no intention of speaking to their grandmother about her feelings.

Trying to dismiss the sense that she ought to have been of more help, Rebecca turned the envelope over in her hand. Usually she walked out to get the mail before going to meet Katie when she came home from school, but she'd completely forgotten it yesterday.

She stared at the return address sticker. Mr. and Mrs. Roy Strickland. Memory struggled back to the days before her life had crashed into rubble. Mr. and Mrs. Strickland had been among their first guests when they'd opened the house to visitors. A retired couple from Baltimore, they'd been enchanted with their taste of farm life, following Paul around like lambs. But why were they writing to her now?

She tore open the envelope and spread out the single sheet of paper, vaguely aware of Grossmammi telling Barbie something about her herb garden.

The letter was written in Mrs. Strickland's flowing hand. Rebecca stared at the words, her forehead furrowed.

"Rebecca?" Grossmammi reached across the table to pat her arm the way she'd done when Rebecca was a child. "Is something wrong?"

She roused herself, managing a smile. "No, not wrong. It just took me by surprise, that's all." She glanced up to find both her grandmother and her cousin looking at her expectantly. There were no secrets when you were part of a big, caring family, not that this was exactly a secret.

"It's from a lady who stayed with us the summer we opened

the house to visitors. She and her husband want to come back again."

"Well, that's great, ain't so?" Barbie said. "When you open for the summer, you'll already have guests lined up."

When? Her thoughts echoed the word. "If," she said. "I'm not sure I can do it."

"But why not?" Barbie's face was bright with enthusiasm. "I'd do it in a minute. It's a great way to earn money."

"It's . . . It's not that easy. Without Paul . . ." She let the words die away. Even with Paul there to carry the load, she had found it difficult to open their home to strangers, and Englischers at that. How could she possibly do it alone?

"It is up to you," Grossmammi said quietly. "You'll make the right decision."

Rebecca shook her head slowly, but she wasn't at all sure whether she was denying the possibility of opening or her ability to make the choice.

Lancaster County, November 1941

Anna closed the lid of her dower chest on the dish towels she'd finished hemming last night. She ran her fingers over the fading paint on the front of the chest. It had come down to her from her great-grandmother Martha Esch, and it gave her a little spurt of happiness each time she put something away in it for the day when she and Jacob would move into a home of their own. She and Mammi would start work on a log cabin quilt soon. She'd already decided on the colors. No Amish girl would think of marrying without having five or six quilts tucked away for her future home.

"Anna?" Her mother's voice echoed up the stairs. "Where are you?"

Giving the chest a little pat, Anna hurried to the steps and down to the warm kitchen. "Here I am. What is it, Mammi?"

"This will be a gut day for you to take those bushels of extra apples around to the neighbors, ain't so? It's getting colder, and they won't keep in the shed much longer without freezing." Mamm drew a black wool sweater more snugly against her body, as if she was cold even when standing next to the wood stove. "Tell Seth he must go with you."

Each year she took the last of the apples around to the neighbors. Since none of them had the big apple crop that Daad did, they were usually happy to buy a last bushel for applesauce or drying.

"I don't need Seth along just to drive down the lane." Sometimes Mammi treated her as if she were eight instead of eighteen.

"Do as I say, Anna." Mammi's voice was sharp, and she rubbed her arms as if she couldn't get warm. "You're not to go without your brother along."

Knowing an argument wouldn't get her anywhere, Anna nodded and took her black jacket from the hook by the door. Even though Mammi hadn't seen the book burning, she seemed far more affected by it than Anna, who had.

For sure it was upsetting, but that was no reason to go around acting scared to death. Anna hurried toward the barn, eager to find Seth and get going before Mamm found an excuse to call her back. After all, nothing else had happened. School went on as usual for the young ones, while the rest of the community prepared for winter.

It would soon be time for long evenings in the warm house, reading or sewing or playing board games with her younger siblings. Jacob would come over as often as he could, and they'd find some moments to talk and make plans for their future. Everything would be fine.

When she reached the barn and found her brother, Seth made a face at the idea of doing anything so tame as selling apples with his sister. But at a look from Daad, he helped her hitch the mare to the wagon, and together they loaded the baskets. In a few minutes they were rolling down the dirt lane to the gravel road that connected a string of houses and farms.

"It's gut to get out of the house." Anna lifted her face to the thin November sunshine. "Ain't so?"

Seth just grunted, snapping the lines against the mare's back.

Anna poked him with her elbow. "What are you in such a bad mood about? Did someone else take Susie King home from the singing?"

Seth glared at her. "It's nothing to me what Susie does. Anyway, there's no point in sweethearting when the world's turning upside down."

"Whatever are you talking about?"

Seth hunched a shoulder. "You should know. You were there, weren't you?"

"Are you still fussing about the book burning? You're getting as bad as Mammi. So what if some people we don't even know decided to do a mean act? It's nothing to do with us."

Seth's young face hardened. "Yesterday it was the German books. Next time maybe it'll be the people who speak German, like us. And maybe it will be coming from people we think are our friends."

"That's nonsense." She had to make her voice sharp, because her heart was thudding in a very unpleasant manner. "Everybody around here knows we don't have anything to do with what's going on clear across the ocean in Germany. Our family has lived here in Lancaster County for almost two hundred years already."

Seth just shook his head. He turned the mare into the next driveway, the one that led to the Cochrans' house. Mary Cochran could usually be counted on to buy a bushel of apples or two. Anna glanced back at the eight bushels they'd loaded into the wagon. Maybe they'd be able to move all of them today. That would please Daad and Mammi.

Seth pulled the mare up when they reached the back door, and Anna slid down. As grumpy as Seth was today, she'd better be the one to do the talking.

No sooner had she knocked than Mrs. Cochran was coming to the door, wiping her hands on her flowered housedress, clearly visible through the glass panel. She paused for a moment when she saw who it was, and then she opened the door a few inches.

"What is it?"

Anna's confident smile slipped at the curt tone. "It's nice to see you, Mrs. Cochran. We have some late cooking apples from the orchard, and we thought—"

"No." Mrs. Cochran cast a quick look behind her and then leaned toward Anna. "I'm sorry, Anna," she whispered. She started to close the door, but Mr. Cochran appeared behind her, grabbing the door with a beefy hand.

"You heard what she said. We don't want anything the likes of you are peddling. Go home and don't come back." The door closed with a resounding slam.

Anna stood where she was, too startled to move.

"Get in the wagon, Anna." Seth's voice was urgent. "Hurry up."

She scurried back to the wagon and climbed up to the seat, suddenly awkward and clumsy, and realized her hands were shaking. Seth slapped the lines. The mare moved off quickly, as if infected by their emotion.

They'd reached the end of the lane before Anna found her voice. "I don't understand. We've always been gut neighbors, ain't so? Why did they act that way?"

"We talk German. We dress funny. We think fighting is wrong." Seth's voice was tight.

"I know some people think that way. But not the Cochrans. How could they? When Mr. Cochran was laid up with a broken leg, Daad cut his hay for him. Mrs. Cochran always asked us in and gave us gingerbread cookies. Remember how she always gave us gingerbread cookies?" She felt as if she were holding up a tiny match in a windstorm.

"Forget it. They have." Seth's face twisted. "You'd better get used to it. How are we going to get along if nobody will buy what we grow? And don't talk to me about living separate. Nobody's going to be able to live separate, not anymore."

Anna wanted to deny the words. More than that, she wanted to take the pain out of her brother's heart. But she couldn't. She couldn't find a thing to say.

Chapter Five

Rebecca had returned home from her grandmother's with her head a jumble of thoughts—the letter, Barbie's confidences, her own uncertainties about the future. Emptying a jar of beef stew into a casserole dish, she tried to empty her mind at the same time.

The kinder would be hungry for their supper before long. Concentrate on that, nothing else, she told herself. Seizing an onion from the bin, she cut it into thin slices to put atop the stew. With homemade drop biscuits over the onions, twenty minutes in the oven would turn it into a dish Katie and Joshua loved.

As she mixed the biscuits, she glanced out the window over the sink. Daffodils fluttered in the breeze along the hedge, and the tulips wouldn't be far behind. She could see the first hint of purple from the old lilac bushes along the creek. Soon their fragrance would perfume the air.

She reached for comfort from the familiar, peaceful scene, but still her worries jostled one another in her thoughts.

Consider the lilies of the field . . . The scripture, with its reminder that worry was a useless exercise, touched her heart. If only she had the strength to cling to that promise—she hadn't realized, when she was young, that following the Lord's teachings with all her heart could be so difficult.

A car pulled in next to the house, startling Rebecca from her train of thought. She wasn't expecting anyone, that was certain-sure.

The car door opened, and Rebecca immediately recognized the man who stepped out. Mr. Philmont, thin, graying, neatly dressed in his businesslike banker's suit, wasn't just an officer of the local bank. He and his wife lived no more than two miles down the road, and Molly Philmont was a familiar sight, always working in her flower beds when Rebecca went past on her way to Grossmammi's house. Wiping her hands on the dish towel, Rebecca hurried to the back door as he mounted the porch.

"Mr. Philmont. It's nice to see you." At least, she hoped it was going to be nice. He'd worn a solemn expression when she'd first glimpsed him, but now his face creased in a smile.

"You're looking well, Rebecca. How are the little ones?"

"Thriving," she said, standing back to gesture him into the kitchen. "Please, sit down. You'll have some coffee?"

"None for me, thank you. I can't stay long, but there's something I need to discuss with you." He pulled out a chair and seated himself at the kitchen table, hands folded on its surface, much as he'd sat at his desk when she and Paul met with him about buying the farm. A slight chill touched her.

"Is something wrong?" She slid into the chair across from him, trying to keep the apprehension from her voice.

He hesitated, and she suspected he was trying to find a good way of saying something he didn't want to. "It's just a little matter of business to discuss. I didn't see any need to ask you to come to the bank when I go right past your house on my way home."

The chill intensified. "That's sehr kind of you." She took a breath. "If it's something about our loan, my father has been taking care of business for me since . . ."

Since Paul got sick. Paul had dealt with finances, and when he couldn't handle them any longer, Daad had taken over, saying she had enough to deal with.

"Yes, I realize that, but since you're the owner of the property, I felt it was appropriate to speak to you, and then you can discuss it with your father if you wish." He paused, as if considering how to go on. "Your father and I had a long conversation about your situation when Paul was ill. Clearly it was impossible then for you to keep up with your regular mortgage payments, and your father agreed to make such payments as he could."

She nodded, trying to look calm despite the fact that her heart was thudding against her ribs. "He told me everything was taken care of."

Mr. Philmont's smile seemed strained, but his narrow face was kind. "We've never had cause to worry about any of our loans to our Amish neighbors, and I knew I didn't have to be concerned that you were falling behind a bit on your loan. You would always honor your commitments. However—" His words died out.

Rebecca gripped her hands together in her lap, reading what he didn't say. "Something has changed."

He nodded, and she could sense his reluctance. "Small local banks like ours have been facing some difficult times lately. We've had to tighten up on our policies in order to survive. I don't like it, but there it is."

The meaning of his words sliced through the fog that seemed to be clouding her thoughts. "You mean I have to pay what's owed or lose the farm."

"Not all of what's owed," he said quickly. "Not all at once. But I need to assure my board that you'll begin making regular payments or . . . or I'm afraid they'll insist on taking action."

Humiliation mixed with her despair. Why hadn't she realized what was happening? Poor Daadi. He wanted to take care of everyone, but he had the younger ones to provide for, to say nothing of Grossmammi moving in. She should have realized.

And poor Paul. He'd never have insisted on taking out a mortgage to buy the farm and a loan for the new stable if he'd had any idea she'd be left facing the repayment without him.

"Denke." She managed to keep a quaver from her voice. "I appreciate all you've done for us." Thank goodness she had something positive to offer him. "I just recently rented the stable, so that's bringing in money now. I'll be able to pay that over to the bank each month."

She spared a moment's regret for the plans she'd had for the extra money—new shoes for the kinder, a little put back for a rainy day. It looked as if the rainy day had come already.

"That is good news," he said, relief relaxing the taut muscles in his face. Poor Mr. Philmont—she hadn't realized until now just how difficult he was finding telling her. "And it's a sensible solution to the difficulty, since you no longer have a use for the building. I'd suggest you discuss the whole situation with your father. I'm sure he has a record of what's been paid and what's still owed. Then you'll have a better idea of where the repayment schedule is at the moment."

"I will." And she'd find some way to make it clear to Daadi that she had to stand on her own feet.

And can you? The voice of doubt whispered in her ear.

She had to. Her thoughts flickered to that letter about the farm-stay. Paul had seen taking in summer guests as a means to earn the added income they'd needed even when he was alive. Much as she shrank from the idea, there was a way at hand to earn the money she needed, if only she had the courage to seize it.

Matt held the two rocker pieces up to the light, comparing them to be sure the curve was exactly the same on each. Onkel Silas had said they might as well knock off early today with the kitchen job finished, so Matt should have plenty of time to work.

Matt smiled, running a work-roughened hand over the smooth wood. If Joshua came in today, he'd recognize the piece as a rocking chair this time.

Joshua had continued to visit the shop despite Simon's opposition, so that probably meant Simon hadn't spoken to Rebecca about it. Matt's smile faded at the memory of that encounter with Simon. He'd done nothing that he knew of to get Simon's back up, so he had to assume Simon was reacting to Matt's reputation.

Well, he couldn't fault Simon for wanting to take care of his sister and her little family, even if in this case he'd gone after the wrong person. Matt certainly didn't intend any harm to them.

Rebecca surely knew that Joshua had been hanging around the workshop, as careful a mother as she was. So apparently she didn't object, and it was her call, wasn't it?

As if thinking about her had summoned her, Matt heard Rebecca's light step behind him.

"Matt? I'm sorry if I'm interrupting you."

He swung away from the workbench to give her a quick smile. "No problem."

Now, what had put that added strain in her eyes? Something was worrying her. Maybe he'd been too quick to assume she didn't mind Joshua hanging around him.

"I just wanted a word." She crossed to him and then seemed distracted at the sight of the rocker. "How lovely. It's near finished. Josh was telling me about it." Her gaze shifted. "What's this?"

Belatedly he realized that the birdhouse he'd been helping Josh make lay on the workbench in plain view. He reached out to toss a piece of canvas over it.

"That's something you'd best pretend you didn't see. Josh wants to surprise you with it."

Those expressive green eyes of hers softened. "Ach, Matt, you mustn't let my son take up too much of your time. It's wonderful kind of you to be bothered with him at all."

"It's no bother to be kind to such a sweet kid." Joshua must get his lovable nature from his mother. It would be way too easy to be kind to Rebecca as well.

"He is sweet-natured, isn't he?" Rebecca's eyes lit at his words. "I can usually tell just what he's thinking. Now, Katie is another story." Her face clouded.

"I haven't seen much of Katie," he said, wishing he could wipe the cloud away. "She always seems to be busy with her grossdaadi and onkel when I'm here."

"Katie loves nothing better than to help them with the chores. Far more than she enjoys helping me in the house, I'm afraid. I'm sure she's not trying to avoid you."

Her tone said the opposite was true. Fixing his gaze on the chair, he proceeded cautiously. "Maybe she doesn't like to see someone else using the stable built for her daadi's business. That's not surprising."

"It's not, isn't it?" Rebecca seemed to be seeking reassurance. "She remembers much more about Paul than Josh does, since she's older. So it's natural she'd be more troubled by . . . well, changes." She said the word as if it held a world of meaning.

Matt studied her face, wondering how far he dared probe into things that were rightly none of his business. "It wasn't Katie who had you looking so upset when you came in here, was it?"

Color bloomed in Rebecca's cheeks. "I don't know what you mean."

He shrugged. "When I see Mr. Philmont from the bank driving away and you looking as if the weight of the world has been dropped on your shoulders, I sort of put two and two together."

"It's nothing," she said quickly. She pressed her lips tightly, as if afraid the truth would slip out.

"Not my business, I know. But if you want to talk, I can listen." He continued fitting the chair leg into the rocker, trying to look intent upon the task, much as he had when encouraging Joshua to come closer.

He could feel Rebecca standing there, could sense her indecision as she struggled between the longing to air her troubles and her caution about him. Finally she sighed with a soft exhale of breath.

"As you said, you can put two and two together. The problem is nothing very surprising, I suppose. We fell behind with the mortgage payments when Paul was sick. Now I must find a way to catch up."

He could have afforded more than the five hundred a month rent he was paying for the use of the building. Why hadn't he offered more? If he tried to do so now, she'd interpret it as charity.

"Your daad . . ." he began.

"Daad has been wonderful kind," she said quickly. "He's been taking care of all the business and farming my land along with his. But it's time I took care of things myself."

Her hands were in his range of sight as he worked. They moved restlessly among the objects that lay on the workbench, picking up a finishing nail and putting it down again. They were small hands, but strong and capable.

"Before Paul got sick, we opened the farm to visitors one summer—what they call a farm-stay vacation." Rebecca sounded as if she were talking to herself.

He made a sound of understanding, afraid of interrupting the flow of words.

"I've had a letter from one of those visitors, wanting to come back. It made me think. If I took in guests this summer, it could make all the difference, you see."

He nodded. He could see, yes, but it was obvious from the reluctance in Rebecca's manner that her answer wasn't that simple.

"I take it you're not so eager." He glanced at her, surprising her into a smile.

"You know, back when we were in school together I once overheard one of the older girls say that you knew what to say to girls because you always understood what they were thinking. Maybe that's still true."

Now it was his turn to smile. "I was never that smart." Full of misplaced confidence was more like it, but for some reason that cockiness had seemed to charm the girls.

"You're right this time," she said. "That's certain-sure. Paul was always so natural with the visitors. They'd follow him around like a row of little ducklings, and he had a way of making every single chore sound so interesting they wanted to try it."

Paul had always been filled with enthusiasm, even when he was a kid, as far as Matt could remember. "Maybe that was his gift."

"For sure. He could talk to anyone. As for me . . . well, I was better at hiding in the kitchen and cooking the food."

Matt leaned against the workbench to concentrate on her face, trying to understand. "Food is important when you have guests in the house. I suspect you did your share."

"Maybe so." She shrugged. "Folks said they liked the meals, anyway."

"You and Paul made a good team." It seemed to him she was too ready to put down her contributions.

"We did." Sorrow shadowed her face for a moment, but she seemed to shake it off. "But doing it alone—I just don't see how I could. I couldn't do all the cooking and cleaning and have time to involve folks in doing all the things around the farm the way Paul did."

True enough. He supposed that sort of thing really was more of a two-person operation. "Maybe your daad could do that part of entertaining the guests."

She shook her head. "Daad has so much to do already, running my farm along with his own. And I don't think he'd like it much anyway."

From what he remembered of Rebecca's father, he was a typical taciturn Amish farmer of the older generation. No, he probably wouldn't enjoy trying to teach an Englischer how to milk a cow.

"What about Simon, then? It seems he's over here working most of the time, and I imagine he's comfortable around the Englisch." He had an inward smile at the thought of Simon hearing Matt recommend him for the job.

"Simon?" Rebecca's eyebrows lifted. "I never thought— Well, maybe he could, at that. I'm so used to thinking of him as my little brother that I didn't even consider him."

"Simon seems pretty well grown to me." Matt trusted it wouldn't occur to her to ask how he knew.

"Even if Simon could handle it . . ." She paused, the struggle obvious in her expression. "It wouldn't be easy to do this without Paul."

"No." He discovered that he hurt for her. "No, it wouldn't."

He bit back the urge to offer advice. Hadn't she said she needed to handle things on her own? She wasn't finding it easy. He reached for the right words and hoped he'd found them.

"You've grown into a strong woman, Rebecca. Whatever you decide, I think you can find a way to make it work."

She blinked, as if surprised. "Denke, Matthew." She smiled, and it seemed to Matt that her smile traveled right to his heart.

Rebecca walked toward the barn after supper, snuggling her jacket around her. The weather might feel like summer in the middle of the day, but once the sun slipped over the ridge, the air was still chilly. Still, the threat of frost was past, according to Daadi. He had his own method of predicting the weather, and mostly he was right.

Katie had said that Onkel Simon was still in the barn, working on something, though Daad had gone home. This would be a fine opportunity for Rebecca to speak with him about helping her with guests without anyone else around. She wouldn't want him to say yes just because Daadi thought it was his duty.

Asking Simon had been a sensible suggestion of Matt's. She had a tendency to see Simon as the little brother she had to look out for instead of the young man he was. Maybe that was only natural, but she should give him credit for the man's work he did.

Simon could certainly do what had to be done with the guests, and he would probably enjoy it. After all, he had many Englisch friends and seemed much more comfortable around the Englisch than she was. It was odd that Matt, coming on the scene after so many years away, should be the one to see Simon as an adult.

Rebecca's thoughts flickered to the passages she'd read in Anna's diary last night. She'd been trying to stay awake an extra fifteen minutes each night to do some reading, especially since she suspected Grossmammi would be asking what she thought of Anna's story.

Anna and her family had lived in a time so frightening it was difficult to imagine, but even so, her relationship with her younger brother was familiar enough to make Rebecca smile. Maybe the fact was that families didn't change, no matter how much the world around them did.

Matt hadn't offered an opinion on the wisdom of her plan. Most people were quite free with their advice on other people's business.

Maybe he'd been embarrassed, not expecting her to confide in him. But that didn't make sense, since he was the one who'd seen that she was worrying about something.

Funny, how that forgotten memory of the older girls talking about Matt had popped back into her head. She could see them now, clustered in a corner of the schoolroom, giggling and glancing at the boys as they came in.

Rebecca's reminiscent smile faded as she neared the barn. She'd told Matt that she wanted to stand on her own feet. It was true, but it was also a rather lonely business.

The barn door stood open, and Rebecca stepped inside, pausing for a moment. Simon was trying to hold a flashlight under his arm while he repaired a loose ring on one of the stanchions.

"Looks like you need another pair of hands." She reached him in a few steps and took the flashlight, focusing its beam on the screw he was tightening.

"That will do it," he said, not taking his gaze from his work. "I should have lit the lantern, but I thought there was enough daylight left to do it." Another quick turn of the screwdriver, and he pulled on the ring to test it. "Finished." He glanced at her. "What are you doing out here?"

"I came to talk to my baby brother," she said, teasing. To her surprise, Simon didn't answer her smile.

"Was ist letz?" he asked. "What's wrong?"

"Nothing. Well, nothing unusual. I just . . ." She took a breath. Just tell him what she wanted.

"The fact is, I've had a letter from a guest we had that summer Paul and I opened the farm to visitors. She says they want to come back, so I'm thinking maybe I should open the farm-stay again." She hurried on to the meat of the matter. "But I'll need someone to do the kind of thing Paul did—show them how the farm operates, teach them and let them help with the work. I wondered if you'd like to do it."

Simon didn't answer right away, and her heart sank. She couldn't read his expression in the dim light, but his lack of response probably meant he was trying to find a way to say no.

"Have you asked Daad about it?"

"Not yet. But you know Daadi doesn't really like to talk to strangers. He wouldn't be happy showing a bunch of Englischers around the farm, but I thought you might like it." She didn't need to point out that Simon was much more outgoing than Daad. They both knew it.

Simon frowned, and the expression made him look older.

"I meant did you talk to Daad about opening the farm to visitors at all?"

"Not yet. I will." Her hands moved with a gesture meant to express what seemed so obvious to her. "Daadi's been doing so much for us since Paul got sick. I should be taking care of things for myself. I couldn't have done it last summer, but now I think I can."

Simon's expression softened. "You know Daadi wants to take care of you and the kinder. And it's not as hard as it could be, running the two farms, since the land is adjoining. If you and Paul hadn't wanted to buy the place when you did, he probably would have bought it himself."

"I know. He's been so much help. And you have, too. I don't know what we'd do without you. But Daadi has you younger ones to take care of and help, and now Grossmammi is moving in, as well. It's time I stood on my own feet."

"Is that what Matthew Byler told you?" Simon's voice was suddenly so sharp it was as if a stranger had asked the question.

For a moment she could only stare at him. "I don't know what you're talking about."

"I'm talking about you spending too much time with a man like Matt Byler."

"Simon, what are you thinking? He's renting the stable for his workshop, so of course I see him from time to time." What had got Simon riled up about Matt, of all things?

"You see him. Joshua sees him, practically every evening. Is he the kind of man you want your son looking up to?"

She stiffened. Simon was going too far. "Matt has been very kind to Josh. Why shouldn't Josh look up to him?"

"You ought to know his reputation." The edginess in Simon's voice was so unlike him. "He drove his poor parents to leave the community with all his carrying on. Pushing the boundaries at every turn, keeping girls out late, hanging out with Englischers and coming home drunk—"

"That's enough." Rebecca's temper nearly got away from her. Simon didn't sound like himself. In fact, she'd guess they weren't even his words, and that they'd come straight from the mouth of Simon's sweetheart.

"No, it's not enough, Rebecca. Don't you know people are talking about you?"

"Who is talking?" she demanded. "Mary Ann King and her mother?"

Simon met her gaze for a moment, and then his slid away from hers, answering her question. "People," he said stubbornly. "Mrs. King remembers all the stories about what Matt did when he was in his teens. She wouldn't make those things up."

Wouldn't she? Rebecca tried to remind herself to be charitable toward the woman who might well become Simon's mother-in-law, but she was too angry. Rebecca wouldn't put any exaggeration past Ada, if it made a good story.

"Ada King is the worst blabbermaul in the county, and everyone does know that, at least. I'm surprised at you, holding whatever Matt might have done during his rumspringa against him. He's long since outgrown such foolishness, just like most people do."

Including you, she wanted to add, but didn't. Simon's follies had been pretty innocent, as far as she'd ever found out.

"What if he hasn't?" For a moment her worried little brother peeked through the stern facade he was trying to maintain. "You don't want people saying there's something going on between you and him."

"Nobody should be saying that, because it's not true." Rebecca's supply of patience was running out, but she managed not to point out that a little thing like the truth didn't seem to deter Ada King. Or, even worse, that Mary Ann would be turning into her mother if she didn't watch out.

"Ada says—"

"I don't want to hear what Ada says," she snapped. "Who I rent my stable to is my own business. And whether or not I open for visitors is my decision, and I've made it." With a start, she realized that was true. She had decided. "I would like to have you help me, Simon." She held her voice calm. "But if you don't want to, I'll find someone else. You can let me know what you decide."

Before she could change her mind, she turned and walked quickly back toward the house.

CHAPTER SIX

Lancaster County, December 1941

*A*nna slid from her bed, shivering when her toes touched
the bare floor. Moonlight slanted through the window,
and in the other half of the double bed, eight-year-old Sarah
slept, curled on her side. She'd had a bad dream a few hours
ago, so Anna had let her go back to sleep in her room, instead
of insisting Sarah stay in the room she shared with Becky.

But a different sibling was the reason Anna was awake in
what felt like the middle of the night. Seth. Had Seth come
in yet?

She felt at the bottom of the bed until her hand brushed the
socks and heavy sweater she'd left there. With a cautious
glance at her little sister, she pulled on the pair of socks. Easing
herself off the bed, she drew on her sweater as she padded
softly to the back window and peered out.

This window, like the one in the boys' room next to it,
looked out over the back porch roof toward the barn. Hours
earlier she'd heard the betraying creak of the porch roof and

reached the window in time to see Seth slipping over the edge to the porch post. A few minutes later, after shimmying down the porch post, he'd darted across the yard to disappear into the shadows under the trees.

Anna hadn't given him away to Mamm and Daad, naturally. That was an unwritten law between brother and sister.

Anyway, there was no cause to worry her parents about it, was there? All teenage boys slipped out at night sometimes. He was probably off with his friends, doing something he'd rather Mamm and Daad didn't hear tell of.

Still, it was a cold night for gallivanting around, and she'd been concerned enough to try to lie awake for what seemed like hours, listening for the creak of the porch roof that would tell her Seth was back.

It hadn't come. Or at least, she hadn't heard it. She'd intended to stay awake, but she'd had a busy day, and her pillow was soft. She'd drifted off into a dream of herself and Jacob standing before the church as man and wife.

She shook off the remnants of the dream, denying herself the luxury of living in it a bit longer. Seth must have come home while she had dozed off. He was probably sound asleep by now.

Shivering a little, she crept out into the hallway. The long braid into which she put her hair at night hung heavy against her breast. The cold in the floorboards seemed to seep right through her socks. Anna eased open the door to the boys' room and peeked inside. The younger ones were sound asleep, but Seth's bed was empty.

Anna rubbed her arms, trying to chase away the chill. How late was it? Was it late enough to be really worried? Late enough that she should discard her loyalty to Seth and wake Daad?

Even as Anna had the thought, she heard a sound. Relief swept over her. Seth. She'd give him such a scold for worrying her this way—

But when she peered out the window, she saw nothing but the moonlight touching the shingles.

The sound came again. Downstairs. It was coming from downstairs. Hurrying into the hall, she stood at the top of the stairs, listening. The creak came again, followed by the unmistakable *click* of the back door closing.

She stood, hand on the stair railing. Surely it was Seth, but what was he doing coming in the back door instead of climbing the elm tree and stepping onto the porch roof as he usually did?

Well, she couldn't stand here wondering. She tiptoed down the steps, staying close to the inside edge so they wouldn't creak, avoiding the noisy third step automatically.

Someone brushed against a bench in the kitchen, and Seth's voice muttered something she couldn't make out. Anna scurried into the kitchen.

"Shh. Do you want to wake Mamm and Daad?"

Seth jerked around at the sound of her whisper. "Anna. Don't scare me like that."

"You deserve to be scared," she scolded. "It's one thing to sneak out, but to stay out this late . . ."

She let the words trail off when she saw that he was shivering. "Ach, you're chilled through. No wonder, as cold as it is. What possessed you to stay out so late on a night like this one?" Her fingers closed on his damp jacket, and she pulled it off him as if he were a child. "Sit by the stove."

Anna hung the jacket on a hook in the back hall, praying Mamm wouldn't notice in the morning how wet it was. When she turned back, Seth was hunched in a chair by the wood stove, hugging himself, still shivering.

"Of all the foolish things to get up to, this takes the cake." She jerked open the stove door and shoved the poker into the coals, stirring them up, knowing full well she was angry because he'd worried her so.

A flicker of flame appeared, but she'd need more to get Seth warmed up. The wood box next to the stove was well filled, and she seized a couple of pieces of river birch, knowing they'd flare up quickly. Anna shoved them into the coals and had the satisfaction of an instant blaze.

"We'll have to hope Daad doesn't notice the fire's been monkeyed with," she murmured.

"He won't." Seth's voice was a low mutter. "Just go to bed and leave me alone. You shouldn't have waited up for me. I'm not a kid."

"You're my bruder, ain't so? Mammi always wants us to look out for each other." The fire's light flickered on Seth's face, and Anna gasped. Bruised, dirty, a streak of blood on one cheek—

"Seth! You've been fighting."

"Hush." He nearly snarled the word. "You want to wake Mamm and Daad? Go to bed. I'm fine."

Ignoring his words, Anna tipped his face up to have a closer look at the damage. It wasn't pretty, and her heart twisted to see him that way.

Tight-lipped, she seized the teakettle from the back of the stove, thankful to find it still warm to the touch. Grabbing a clean dishcloth, she soaked it with the warm water and began cleaning his face.

Neither of them spoke. She was probably hurting him, trying to get the dried blood off, but he didn't move.

Anna rinsed the cloth and began again, more gently this time. "You might as well tell me," she said softly. "You know I'll keep asking until you do."

He shook his head, looking very young and very stubborn. "Leave me alone."

"If I leave you alone, Daad will know you've been fighting in a minute. Now tell me."

His blue eyes blazed for another second and then his gaze dropped. He looked tired, young, and maybe a little bit ashamed of himself.

"I was supposed to meet Johnny Wexler down by the mill, but he didn't show up. So I ran into some Englisch guys, and they had some beer."

"Stupid," she said, without heat. Seth was seventeen. For sure he'd do some dumb things before he was grown.

"Ja, well, I didn't have more than a couple swallows. The guys were all talking about how probably a war was coming. And Jack Jacobson, he said as how he'd enlist right away. And the others said the same."

"You should have come away." She could imagine the scene only too well. All the kids boasting about how brave they were, and Seth the odd man out. "We are Amish. We don't fight. We turn the other cheek, like Jesus said."

"Well, nobody else sees it that way. And Tommy Millard said I was a coward. That everybody knew all the Amish were cowards or worse."

"So you thought it would make things better to hit somebody." She pressed a cool, wet cloth against his eye. "And they hit back."

"I don't want to talk." He snatched the cloth from her hand. "If you're gonna tell Daad, go ahead and do it."

Anna could only look at him . . . at the sweet face she'd washed so often, now halfway between the baby he'd been and the man he would become. Her heart hurt so much she could hardly breathe. What was happening to them?

"You'd best have a story ready for Daad about how you hurt your face," she said, and fled before she could burst into tears.

Rebecca put her arm around Katie, drawing her closer as they sat next to each other at worship on Sunday. The benches grew a bit hard for lively kinder toward the end of the three-hour service. Katie leaned against her, and Rebecca savored the moment. Her daughter was growing so fast that soon she'd reject such a display of affection in public.

She tried to concentrate on Bishop Jonah's closing words, but found her thoughts straying to her brother. It was all very well to tell Simon she'd manage without his help with the guests, but if he didn't come around, what was she to do? Would one of the younger boys be capable? Or perhaps one of her male cousins?

Rebecca glanced across the aisle to the men's side. Joshua was so pleased to be sitting with his grossdaadi and onkels for worship, instead of being stuck on the women's side with her as if he were a baby. At the moment, despite his claims of being so grown-up, he had clearly dozed off on Simon's lap.

Her heart clenched. Simon was so good with the boy, and such a help to her in so many ways. She didn't want to be at odds with him, but she certainly wasn't going to let his sweetheart's mother govern what she did.

Ashamed of the surge of annoyance she felt at the thought of the woman, she looked down, shielding her eyes for a silent prayer for forgiveness for her uncharitable attitude. Criticizing Mary Ann and her mother was certainly not the way to reconcile with Simon.

The service moved on to its conclusion. As she slid down to her knees for prayer, guiding a half-asleep Katie, she made up her mind. She wouldn't wait for Simon to speak—she'd go to him with an apology for her angry words. After all, if Simon ended up wedding Mary Ann, she'd have to . . . Somehow she couldn't finish the thought.

There was a rustle of movement as worship came to a close. It would take a few minutes for the men to convert the backless benches into tables, and they'd probably set them outside on such a warm spring day.

"Komm, Katie. I'll see if I can help in the kitchen. You may go and find your friends, but mind you stay out of the way while people are setting up for lunch."

"I will, Mammi." Katie's lively smile flashed, and she darted off in an instant.

Rebecca joined her grandmother, who was looking after Katie with an affectionate smile.

"The little ones need to stretch their legs a bit after sitting so long, ain't so?" She took Rebecca's arm for a step or two, moving slowly. "And so do the old ones." She chuckled, never one to take herself too seriously.

They walked together out of the long concrete-floored shed that was attached to Eli Esh's machine shop, and as she looked at her grandmother, Rebecca's thoughts turned to the diary she'd been reading.

"Grossmammi, do you remember anything about the Second World War?"

Her grandmother's eyes lit. "You are reading Anna's book, ain't so? I remember a bit, I suppose, but I was just a child then. And if times were hard . . ." She shrugged. "Well, a child thinks however he or she lives is normal. I didn't have anything to compare it to."

Rebecca nodded, realizing how true that was. Probably that was why Josh seemed less affected by the loss of his father than Katie. He didn't remember a time before his daad was sick.

"It makes you think, reading someone else's thoughts," she said. "Some things about Anna's time seem so different, but other things—things like family troubles—well, they're just the same."

Grossmammi gave a brisk nod. "Families don't change much, that's certain-sure. There are always marryings and buryings, quarrels and making up, love and jealousy and worry all mixed together most of the time." She shook her head, as if shaking off any melancholy in her own words. "I'd like to hear all about it later, but I know you don't have time now. You run on and help with the food, there's a gut girl. I'll chust have a seat under the tree in the shade."

Rebecca delayed long enough to see her grandmother settled with a few old friends before she hurried off to the kitchen. Ella Esh would have all the work done by the time she got there, if she didn't hustle.

Sure enough, when Rebecca entered the kitchen, Ella already had women cutting sandwiches and mixing up the peanut butter and marshmallow cream mixture that the children loved. And some who were no longer children loved it, too. The laughter and chatter of a dozen women at work echoed from the kitchen walls.

Rebecca squeezed past one group filling dessert trays, wanting to wash her hands before touching the food. Sadie Byler, Matt's cousin, was among them, and her voice seemed to ring out suddenly.

"Matt's supposed to have come back to Brook Hill to help Daad, but as far as I can see, he's spending more time over at Rebecca Fisher's place than he is ours."

Rebecca froze, praying she wasn't flushing, feeling mortified and angry all at once. Maybe Simon's claim that people were gossiping wasn't as far-fetched as she'd thought.

The other women around Sadie fell silent when they saw Rebecca standing there. Sadie, maybe warned by their stillness, swung around and saw her.

Rebecca had to speak, had to do something to refute the implication that Matt came over to see her. Sadie was staring at her, lips pressed together, eyes snapping.

Say something, Rebecca commanded herself, but she couldn't.

Mary Stoltzfus, the bishop's wife, set a cake pan on the table with a clatter that sounded loud in the silence. "Since your cousin is renting a building for his business from Rebecca, it isn't surprising that he should spend time at the Fisher place, ain't so?" Her tone was mild, but she spoke with the assurance of one who knew that what she said made a difference to those who heard.

Sadie flushed, an angry red that stained her cheeks. For an instant it seemed she didn't intend to respond.

"Ja," she said at last. "That's true." With a flash of temper she added, "But he's supposed to be helping my daad." She dropped the slice of cake she was holding and turned to shove her way out of the kitchen.

Rebecca had an intense longing to sink right through the floor. But that was impossible, and she wouldn't run off as Sadie had done.

"Rebecca, would you give me a hand with the salads? And some of you can start carrying the sandwich trays and the lemonade out." Ella Esh spoke as if nothing had happened, and Rebecca was profoundly grateful. She hurried to Ella's side and began dishing out macaroni salad as if it were the most important job in the world.

The crowd in the kitchen began to thin out as they started serving the lunch. "Denke," Rebecca murmured to Ella.

"Ach, it's nothing." Ella was brisk and angular, with cheeks as rosy as apples whatever the season. "You don't want to listen to anything Sadie Byler says. She's got a bee in her bonnet about her cousin Matt coming back and taking Isaiah's place. Everybody knows that."

Ella made a shooing motion. "Go on now and get your lunch. I'll be out as soon as I start another pot of coffee."

There was nothing to do but obey. Rebecca paused at the bottom of the porch steps, reluctant to join the rest of the church around the tables. What if they were talking about her?

She made a detour around the side of the house to admire Ella's flower bed, where tulips, daffodils, and hyacinth bloomed profusely against the side of the house.

A flicker of movement caught her eye from the line of buggies parked along the lane. She frowned. Why was a woman wandering between the buggies? It was natural enough to see someone going back to her buggy to fetch something or perhaps to load something, but this woman was doing neither of those things. Instead she seemed to be drifting aimlessly from one buggy to the next.

A vague uneasiness took shape, sharpening when she realized who the woman was. Lovina Byler. Everyone knew Lovina wasn't well. They knew, too, that her husband or daughter generally kept a close eye on her when they were away from home.

Maybe she should get Sadie—but her heart rebelled at the thought of a conversation with Sadie at the moment. Instead she walked quickly toward Lovina. Maybe she could encourage Lovina to come back to the others.

The woman didn't seem to notice when she approached, not until Rebecca touched her arm lightly.

"Lovina? Are you looking for something?"

Lovina's eyes were misted, as if she might cry at any moment. She wore a puzzled, almost lost expression. "No. I don't think so."

Poor soul. How terrible it must be to feel your mind slipping away.

"You haven't had your lunch yet, have you? Komm. I'll walk back to the table with you." She tucked her hand securely in Lovina's arm and tried to steer her back toward the others.

Lovina took a few obedient steps and then stopped. "I have to find him."

"Your husband? I'm sure he's back here with the others."

"No." Lovina pulled her arm free and turned back toward the buggies. "I have to find Isaiah. I don't know where he is."

Isaiah, of course. Lovina didn't remember that her son had run off to the Englisch world. Tears stung Rebecca's eyes at the pain of the situation.

"I don't think he's by the buggies," she said, as calmly as she could manage. "Maybe he's having lunch. Shall we go and see?" She couldn't lie very convincingly, but she tried.

Lovina shook her head. "I need the buggy, so I can go and find him."

A shiver ran down Rebecca's spine at the thought of Lovina out on the highway alone in a buggy. "I don't think that's a good idea."

Where was Lovina's family? Rebecca couldn't leave her alone while she went and found them, but she couldn't drag Lovina along in the face of her obsession with finding her lost son.

She looked toward the tables, and relief flooded through her. Matt and his uncle were headed toward them.

"Look, Lovina, here's Matt and Silas. I'm sure they'll help you."

Matt, a little ahead of his uncle, reached them in time to hear her words. She sent him a look that combined pleading and sympathy, hoping he understood what was happening.

"What do you need, Aunt Lovina?" He put his arm around his aunt, his voice very gentle.

She shook her head, the lost look intensifying. "I have to find Isaiah. Where is he? I have to find him."

Silas had reached them, and Rebecca saw the pain in his eyes as he spoke. "It's all right. I'm sure he'll be back soon. Komm." He took Lovina's arm and urged her gently away toward the tables.

She held back for an instant, but then she nodded and walked docilely along with her husband.

"Denke, Rebecca." Matt's voice was rough.

"I did nothing." She looked into his face, expecting the pain she saw.

But there was more than pain written there. There was guilt, strong and unmistakable, so powerful it seemed to radiate from him. But why should Matt feel guilty about his cousin Isaiah's defection?

Almost finished." Matt guided Josh's fingers to screw the hook onto the top of his birdhouse. "We'll put a wire on this, and then you can hang it up."

"And then the birds will come and live in it. They'll really like it." Josh's small face was alive with the joy of making something almost by himself.

"That's certain-sure. How could they help but like it, when you made it for them?"

"You helped," Josh said quickly. "I couldn't do it by myself."

"That's the best way of learning something, working along-side someone who already knows how to do it. One day you'll be able to teach someone else how to do it."

Josh pondered that, blue eyes serious. "Maybe. If I had a little bruder, I could teach him, but I don't."

"Maybe someday you'll have a cousin you can teach." Matt

said the word lightly enough. Unfortunately he discovered that he was picturing Isaiah standing where Joshua was, looking up at his big cousin with admiration.

How had Isaiah run so far off track as to jump the fence? Worse, never even getting in touch with his parents to let them know he was all right? He wasn't a sixteen-year-old, running off to enjoy his rumspringa. He was twenty-two, old enough to be taking on a man's responsibilities.

Trying unsuccessfully to push his errant cousin out of his thoughts, Matt showed Joshua how to attach the wire from which the birdhouse would swing. Too bad the process didn't take up more of his attention. He couldn't help thinking of Aunt Lovina, trying so hard to find Isaiah after worship yesterday. Isaiah should have been there to put his arm around her and reassure her when her mind slipped. How could he treat her so?

It was Rebecca whose loving heart had seen something was amiss, Rebecca who'd gone quickly to the rescue. He suspected that would always be her response to someone in trouble.

"What's wrong?" Joshua took a step back, looking at Matt with wide eyes.

Matt glanced down, realizing that he'd gripped the wire so tightly it had cut his finger. A drop of blood welled up and dripped down.

He shook it off impatiently. "It's fine. The wire is a bit sharp, and I should be paying more attention to what I'm doing, ain't so?"

Joshua nodded, but his eyes were wary. Did he realize that it had been anger, not inattention, that rode Matt?

"Now we'll just twist the wire together, and your birdhouse

is ready to hang. Why don't you run and show your mammi? Just be careful with holding the wire."

Obviously he wasn't fit company for a child when his temper could get out of control that easily. It would be best for Joshua to be off.

But Joshua grabbed his hand, tugging it. "You come, too. You helped."

The boy was so eager that Matt didn't have the heart to disappoint him. He let himself be led out of the workshop and tugged toward the farmhouse.

What was wrong with him? Every time he thought he had his temper vanquished, it jutted its ugly head up again. If all he'd been through hadn't beaten it down, maybe the task was hopeless. He knew only too well how short the step was between losing his temper and striking out. If he couldn't obey the most basic Amish commitment to nonviolence, how could he be Amish?

Rebecca was bending over the flower bed at the side of the house, Katie beside her, when Joshua went running to her, the birdhouse bouncing from the wire he held.

From a few steps behind, Matt heard his excited voice. "Look, Mammi. Look, Katie. See what I made? It's for the birds, and they'll come and live in it, and I'll watch them."

Rebecca knelt and held out her arms to her son, stopping his headlong rush with a laughing gesture. "Slow down a minute, Josh." Her hand stilled the birdhouse's swinging. "Look at that. It's a beautiful birdhouse. You really made it?"

"I did." He glanced at Matt. "Not all by myself. Matt showed me what to do."

"That was very nice of him." Her smiling gaze swept up to Matt's face, and for just an instant he felt as if he were losing his balance. "Denke, Matt."

"Joshua learned very fast. He did most of it." He intercepted a doubting look from Katie and grinned at her. After a startled moment, she managed a slight smile in return.

"Katie, look at this little perch by the door for the birds to sit on. Didn't Josh do a good job?"

"I guess." She moved a little closer, seeming reluctant to show any interest. "Maybe the birds would rather build their nests in trees."

Josh's face clouded up, and Rebecca intervened quickly. "Probably some birds would rather be out in the woods in the trees, but there are others who would love a little house like this. Remember the wrens who kept trying to build a nest over the front door last spring?"

Katie nodded. "Grossmammi said wrens like being around people. Maybe they'd want to live in Joshua's little house."

Rebecca smiled at her daughter as if she'd said the right thing. "Why don't you help Josh decide on a place to hang it? Maybe somewhere near the back porch would be good, and then you can watch the birds from the kitchen window without scaring them."

"Komm schnell, Josh," Katie said, and the two children raced off, the birdhouse bouncing between them.

Rebecca smiled after them and then switched the smile to Matt. "It was wonderful kind of you to go to all that trouble with Josh."

"It wasn't trouble. I liked doing it." He hesitated. He ought to be getting back to his own work instead of standing here talking to Rebecca. Unfortunately he seemed to have problems following his own good intentions where she was concerned.

"I wanted to ask you about Lovina. How is she?" Sympathy filled Rebecca's face. "I felt so useless yesterday—wanting to help her and not knowing how."

"You were there," he said gruffly. "That's about all any of us can do."

"Especially when the person she really wants is Isaiah, ain't so? I didn't have a chance to tell you what she said to me."

He shrugged. "She was looking for him, I suppose. Sometimes she sees me and thinks I'm Isaiah, and then she's hurt all over again when she realizes I'm not."

"And you're hurt, as well." Rebecca's voice was soft. "But yesterday—yesterday she said she was going to take the buggy and go look for him." She hesitated, and a shiver seemed to go through her. "It frightened me, and I couldn't dissuade her. I was wonderful glad to see you and your onkel coming."

That shook him. "I'll tell Onkel Silas. He tries to keep a close eye on her when they're out anywhere, but it's hard to do without making her feel that he thinks she's a child." He longed to touch Rebecca's hand, but he restrained himself. "We were fortunate you were paying attention yesterday."

She shrugged. "Ach, if it hadn't been me, it would have been someone else, I'm sure." She hesitated, as if not sure whether to say more or not. "I wish . . . All of us wish . . . that Isaiah would come home. I'd never have thought he'd be so heedless of his family as to go away."

"Nobody could believe it. Maybe that's what makes it so difficult."

And how much of Isaiah's foolishness in running off to the Englisch world had come out of his wanting to copy the big cousin he'd always admired? Matt couldn't shake off the guilt, no matter what he told himself.

It was Rebecca who reached out, touching his hand lightly. "You're a gut man, Matthew, giving up your own life to come and help your aunt and onkel at such a time."

A good man? Rebecca had a generous heart. But probably even she wouldn't think that if she knew everything there was to know about him. After all, she'd never seen him in the orange jumpsuit they made you wear in the county jail.

CHAPTER SEVEN

*R*ebecca pinned the double wedding quilt on the line to dry, smoothing it with her hand. The afternoon sunlight made the deep, saturated colors glow like jewels. Her grandmother had made the quilt, using scraps collected from dresses and shirts and pants she'd sewn for her family over the years.

Grossmammi had given it to Rebecca when she was married for her new life with Paul. Now it would cover the bed used by visitors in their house.

That was what Paul would have wanted, after all. He'd taken as much pleasure as she had in deciding what to put in the guest rooms.

She was going to entertain their guests without Paul. Her stomach twisted at the thought.

Determination stiffened her spine. The answer had come from her first guests quickly. Mr. and Mrs. Strickland had responded almost by return mail. They wanted to come next weekend. One way or another, she had to be ready. Everything should be at its best.

Movement caught her eye, and she spotted Simon coming out of the barn. She still hadn't set things right with him, and the longer she waited, the more difficult it would be. Dropping a handful of clothespins in her basket, she walked toward Simon, hurrying a little so he couldn't dodge her the way he'd been doing for the past week.

"Simon, wait a minute."

He swung toward her, a bucket filled with chicken feed in his hand. "Rebecca." He glanced at the bucket, as if wondering what he was doing with it, and set it down. "I guess I . . . I'm glad you're here. I want to talk to you."

"That's good. I want to talk to you, too." She kept her voice gentle, reminding herself that no matter how much Simon had annoyed her with his criticism, he was her little brother and she shouldn't have spoken so harshly to him.

"I'm sorry." Simon rushed the words. "I didn't mean to make you mad."

"No, I'm sorry." She touched his shoulder, thinking how often she had comforted him this way when something went wrong. The only difference was that she had to reach up to touch him now. "I should never have spoken the way I did about Mary Ann and her mother. It was unkind, and it hurt you."

To her surprise, he gave her a shamefaced smile. "Don't feel bad. Truth is, Mary Ann's mamm is hard to take sometimes, ain't so?"

Her tension relaxed. "I still shouldn't have said so. I do regret it."

He grimaced. "You said nothing I haven't thought myself, that's certain-sure. Of course, Mary Ann's not like that at all."

He sounded just slightly uncertain, and Rebecca bit her lip to keep from saying how often girls, especially oldest daughters, turned out just like their mothers. Simon wouldn't want to hear it from her, not now. He might have to find out for himself, but maybe he was starting to have second thoughts.

"Anyway, I'm sorry I butted in about opening the farm to visitors again. I know you're trying to do what Paul would have wanted." Simon had rushed the words, and now he stopped for breath. "So if you still want me to help with showing them the farm chores, I will. Maybe it'll even be fun."

Fun. That was one word she hadn't used to describe her intention to open the farm-stay, but if Simon found it so, that was all to the good.

"Denke, Simon." Her eyes filled with tears, and she blinked them back quickly. "I'm wonderful glad you're willing to do it. It will make all the difference, having you working with me on the project."

He nodded, looking embarrassed at her display of emotion. Manlike, he didn't know what to do about tears. "Come on. I'll help you hang the rest of those heavy quilts."

Rebecca could do it herself easily enough, but she wasn't going to turn down a peace offering. She nodded, and together they shook out the next wet quilt and hung it on the clothesline.

"You're getting the bedrooms ready for guests, ain't so? We should talk about what you want me to do." Simon put a final clothespin in place.

Rebecca nodded. "I've been thinking about it. Why don't

we make a list of possible activities people can do around the farm? That way we can give folks some choices."

"Sounds good." He grinned. "I'd guess there might be some things we have to be careful about, too. I wouldn't want any Englischer getting too close to Daad's bad-tempered sow."

"That's so." It was yet another thing to worry about, it seemed to her. If someone got hurt, would she be responsible?

Simon bent to pick up the laundry basket, the movement hiding his face as he spoke. "Josh was telling me about building a birdhouse. He's sure a family of wrens is going to move in any day now."

She shot a look at him, stiffening. "He's crazy about that birdhouse. He checks it a dozen times every day to see if birds are nesting in it yet."

"He said Matt Byler helped him build it." It sounded like a simple statement of fact, but she feared it was leading up to yet another lecture.

"Matt has been very kind." She hoped the firmness of her tone would warn him not to repeat any more rumors about Matt.

"I know you think it's none of my business, Beck. But you can't blame me for worrying, can you?"

"I don't blame you for caring about me. But you have no reason to worry." She kept her voice firm but even. She would not let him upset her again.

Simon gave her a pleading look. "Nobody knows what Matt was doing all those years he was gone. I just want you to be careful, so you don't get hurt."

Exasperation flooded through her. What did Simon imagine? That she was going to lose her common sense over a charming smile?

"Simon, listen to me." She touched his cheek to make him look at her. Her heart softened at his expression. Poor Simon. He just wanted to keep her safe. "No one can replace Paul in my heart. Do you understand?"

He nodded. "But—"

"There's no but about it. All I want to do is carry out Paul's dreams. Renting the stable to Matt will help me do it. The fact that he's been kind to the kinder is a plus, but it doesn't change anything. That's all Matt means to me." She patted Simon's cheek. "That's all he can ever mean."

Matt felt the lift to his spirits that he always experienced when he turned into the gravel drive that led to his new workshop. He had to smile at his own feelings. The building wasn't a stable to him any longer, no matter how it looked. It was a workshop—his workshop—the place where he fulfilled his dreams.

The fact that he was already glancing beyond the building to the farmhouse where he often saw Rebecca had nothing to do with his feelings. This lightness of heart was caused by the opportunity to spend time working at what he loved, that was all.

Once the mare was settled comfortably, he swung open the double doors that had been meant to allow room for farming equipment to pass in and out. The more natural light he had to work by, the better.

Matt moved inside and stopped, frowning. The shaft of daylight from the doors illuminated the inside, all right. It also showed him that something was wrong. Someone had been in his work space.

He hadn't left his tools out of their box. Everything had been properly put away the last time he'd used them, a habit that was second nature to him. Now the tools were scattered across the workbench, with some even on the floor.

Stepping around them as carefully as a cat in a strange room, Matt let the indisputable reality sink in. Someone had been in the workshop while he was out. Moreover, it was someone who hadn't minded leaving the evidence of his trespassing scattered about.

The rocking chair Matt had nearly finished lay on its side. He knelt beside it, holding his breath. But the chair was all right—tipped over, but otherwise unharmed.

Well. This could turn into a problem bigger than an overturned jar of screws. If Rebecca's kinder had been in here while he was gone—

He pictured Josh's face in his mind. The boy had been so excited about his birdhouse, and he'd seemed genuinely grateful to Matt for helping him. Surely he wouldn't come in and make a mess in Matt's workshop.

Still, a child might not consider this a mess. It was possible that Joshua had slipped out here while his mother was occupied with something else. Maybe he'd hoped to make another birdhouse, or had intended to show Katie how to do it. Matt's blood chilled at the thought of Joshua using his tools without supervision. Maybe he hadn't been doing such a good deed after all in working with the boy.

Whatever the answer, Matt had no choice but to talk with

Rebecca about it. He couldn't run the risk of a child being hurt because his tools were here.

Quickly, before he could find an excuse not to do what had to be done, he walked out of the workshop and headed for the house.

Rebecca was often out in the yard at this time of day, but not this afternoon. As he neared the kitchen windows he had a brief glimpse of her moving about inside. It would be best if he could talk with her privately, without the children listening in.

But when he reached the kitchen door, he saw that was unlikely. Both Katie and Josh were in the kitchen, busy setting the table for supper.

Matt tapped on the screen door. Rebecca turned from the stove, smiling when she saw him.

"Matt. I didn't hear you. Come in."

He stepped inside, trying to form the words to tell her what had happened without putting too much emphasis on it. He didn't want to add to her burdens, but he certain-sure couldn't risk one of her kinder getting hurt.

"Can I help you with something?" she asked when he didn't speak. She seemed to realize she had a potholder in her hand and tossed it onto the counter.

"When I went into the workshop just now, I found . . ." He hesitated, feeling Joshua's gaze fixed on him—innocently, he thought. But it had to be done.

"Someone had been in there while I was gone. Someone who left a bit of a mess. I thought I'd better come and talk to you about it."

Rebecca's eyes widened, and he had the sense that she was bracing herself to take on yet another challenge. She turned to look at her son.

Joshua stared back, just as surprised. "But that's mean. Who would mess up Matt's workshop?"

"It is mean, that's certain-sure." Rebecca took a step toward the boy, her serious gaze intent on his face. "Did you go into Matt's workshop when he wasn't there, Josh?"

The boy's small face paled. "Me? I wouldn't do that, Mammi. Honest."

"Maybe you wanted to try and make something yourself," Matt suggested.

"No. I wouldn't." Tears filled Josh's eyes. "I would never touch your tools unless you said it was all right."

"Joshua—" Rebecca began.

"It wasn't him." Katie almost shouted the words, and she slammed the spoons she held down onto the table. "It was me. I did it."

Rebecca swiveled to stare at her daughter. "Katie? But why? Why would you do something like that?" She pressed her hands together as if in a prayer.

For a moment it seemed Katie wouldn't answer. Then the words spilled out of her. "The stable is Daadi's. He made it for his horses. Nobody else should be in there." She swung toward her brother. "You shouldn't make things with *him*." She shot an angry glance toward Matt. "That's not the way it's supposed to be."

The naked pain on Rebecca's face as she went to her daughter pierced Matt's heart. He felt an instant revulsion at his part in this trauma. He never should have gotten involved with Rebecca. He always ended up hurting people, no matter what he did.

Rebecca sank down on a chair. She grasped Katie's hands and drew the child close. Katie was rigid, resisting, her clenched fists pressing against her white apron.

"Listen to me, Katie." Rebecca's voice was soft, and he thought she struggled to hold back her tears. "I feel just like you do sometimes. I think that it isn't right that Daadi's gone. That we should keep everything the way it was when he was alive. But it's no use. We can't. We have to be strong and brave, like Daadi was. We have to get along without him, and that means we have to change."

"No. I won't. I don't want to." Katie's lips trembled.

"I'm so sorry, my sweet girl, but you have to. We all have to."

"No," Katie said again, but this time the anger was swept away by grief. Her voice broke, and tears spilled onto her cheeks.

"My sweet girl . . ." Rebecca said again, and she pulled her daughter close.

For just an instant, Katie leaned against Rebecca. Then she jerked away, still crying, and ran out of the kitchen. They could hear her feet pounding on the stairs.

Rebecca looked after her daughter, her expression bereft.

"I'm sorry." He muttered the words. "I shouldn't have—" He stopped at a gesture from Rebecca.

"It's all right. Really. You did what you had to do. I wouldn't have it any other way." She stood, resting her hand on Joshua's shoulder as if in wordless reassurance. "Katie doesn't cry. She hasn't, not since . . ." She stopped, shook her head. "Maybe it's for the best for her to let her feelings out."

"Maybe." Her words didn't assuage his guilt. "But I wish I hadn't been the one to bring it on."

"It's not your fault, Matt. You must let me pay for the damages."

"Nothing is broken. It's nothing I can't clean up. Anyway, it's as much my responsibility. I should have put a lock on the door when I moved my things in."

"You shouldn't have to clean it up," she began.

"I'll do it." Joshua stood very straight. "Let me help." He looked at Matt. "Can I?"

Matt glanced at Rebecca and caught a slight nod. "Okay. Denke."

Joshua hurried to the door. Rebecca managed a small smile. "He wants to make up for what Katie did. Thank you for letting him."

Matt nodded. There was nothing else to say, and nothing else he could do about the situation, either. He'd wanted to make things easier for Rebecca. Somehow it seemed he'd managed to make them worse.

Lancaster County, December 7, 1941

Anna took the coffeepot and began to refill cups. Only the adults remained at the table at the end of their Sunday night supper, and experience told her that Daad and Onkel Tobias would linger talking long after they'd finished their coffee and apple crumb pie.

She exchanged a quick, secret smile with Jacob as she poured coffee into his cup. Mamm had invited Jacob to supper tonight, since Onkel Tobias and Aunt Hilda were visiting and the young people weren't having a singing. Even though Rebecca wasn't alone with Jacob, it still made her happy to see him sitting there at the long table where she'd had countless meals. He seemed very much part of the family, seated next to Seth and listening respectfully to what Daad was saying.

Anna darted a glance at her brother. Seth's black eye had faded to a dull purple. He'd told Daad part of the truth, admitting he'd climbed out of his window but saying he'd fallen on the way to the ground.

Did Daad believe his tale? She wasn't sure. He'd seemed to accept it, but he might still guess there was more going on than Seth had admitted. She could only be thankful that Daad hadn't asked her any questions. She'd never been any good at fooling him.

Finishing her round with the coffeepot, Anna slid into her seat across the table from Jacob and Seth. Seeming subdued, as he had been for the past few days, Seth concentrated on his pie, not raising his eyes.

Anna hoped that meant he was ashamed. He ought to be, to say nothing of being wary. Daad might not be so accepting a second time. It would be far better, in her opinion, if Seth stayed away from his Englisch friends for a time, at least.

Not forever. She knew better than to expect that from him. But he ought to steer clear until all this war talk died down and things got back to normal.

The loud, abrupt knocking at the back door must have startled everyone. Anna rose, but Daadi waved her back to her seat and went to answer the door himself.

Ezekiel Wagner, their closest Amish neighbor, nearly stumbled in his rush to get inside. He grabbed Daad's arm, his face pale and his eyes wide with what seemed to be shock. Anna's breath caught. His family—someone hurt?

"Zeke, was ist letz? Is it Mary, or one of the kinder?" Daad put a hand on his shoulder.

"Nothing like that." Zeke took a gasping breath. "I just heard . . . one of the O'Brien boys came over to tell us. They heard the news on their radio."

The O'Brien family lived in a small house just beyond the crossroads—all ten of them. Folks used to laugh and say the O'Briens had near as many kids as the Amish.

"What news?" Daad looked as if he were infected by Zeke's panic. "What has happened?"

Zeke shook his head. "It's terrible. The Japanese—they attacked the American navy base out in Hawaii. The O'Brien boy said they thought at least hundreds of people must have been killed. The navy ships were sunk. The radio said the president is talking to Congress tomorrow. They say he's going to declare war."

War. Anna's numbed thoughts turned the word over, trying to make sense of it. She looked at Jacob, seeking reassurance, but saw only a shock equal to her own.

"Komm." Daad seemed to rally himself. "Sit. Have some coffee."

Zeke shook his head. "Denke, but no. I'm on my way to Susie's place. Her husband is working away, and I don't want her to be alone with the babies."

Susie was Zeke's married daughter. Anna could understand his need to be with her. She reached out toward Jacob, and he took her hand in his firm grasp, not caring whether her parents saw or not.

"It has come," Seth said as Daad closed the door behind Zeke. His voice was harsh. "Everyone said war was coming, but we Amish weren't listening."

"It's not a question of not listening." Daad spoke evenly as he returned to his seat, but Anna had the frightening feeling that he'd aged ten years in the past few minutes. "But we can do nothing about it. We do not resort to violence, no matter what happens."

Onkel Tobias thudded his fist against the table, his normally jovial round face bleak above his chestnut beard. "It will be chust as bad as it was during the last war. We have to face the truth."

Mammi clasped her hands as if in prayer. "Surely things won't be that harsh again. Folks understand our ways now better than they did back before the first war. They know our boys can't fight."

"The government knew that then, but that didn't stop the officials from forcing our boys into uniform." Onkel Tobias frowned at Daadi. "Don't go gesturing for me to keep silent, either. These two boys are right at the age. They'll be the ones who have to face it." He stopped short, shaking his head.

"What happened in the last war? Nobody ever talks about it." Seth sounded as if he had to make an effort to keep his voice from breaking. "Like you said, me and Jacob are at the age to be affected. We have a right to know what to expect. What happened?"

Daadi exchanged glances with Onkel Tobias. He nodded slowly. Reluctantly.

"Ja. You have a right to know." Daadi ran a hand over his forehead, maybe trying to clear his thoughts. "There was conscription—that means all the young men were called up to serve in the military. Our bishops told the authorities that it was against our faith to fight, but they didn't listen. Boys were forced to go to army camps, to put on uniforms. If they tried to refuse, the others called them cowards. They beat them."

Anna had thought Daad couldn't get any paler, but he did. She longed to make him stop. She didn't want to hear anything worse.

"Some went to prison. Others were sent off to war, where most of them died in the fighting or from illness they picked up on the battlefields." Daad's face twisted. "We thought we were finished with the military when our people left Europe centuries ago, but we weren't."

"Daadi . . ." Anna reached toward him, longing to offer comfort but not sure how.

"That's what happened to your onkel John. My older brother." Daadi's face was bleak with pain. "They gave him a rifle and told him to shoot at the enemy. The others who were with him told my mamm and daad he didn't fire the weapon. He just stood there, and the enemy soldiers shot him." He shook his head. "I prayed no one else of the Leit would ever have to make that choice. But now—"

"People understand us better now," Jacob said, as if repeating something he desperately wanted to believe. "They understand that our faith is founded on nonviolence."

"Nobody understands." Seth's face twisted. "Don't be so foolish. The Englisch are already turning against us. This will make it worse."

"I don't believe it," Jacob said. His fingers tightened on hers. "We Amish are committed to turning the other cheek. What good would it do to force us into uniform? Besides, if there's a war, people will need food more than ever. It doesn't make sense to take us away from our farms."

"Nobody's thinking about good sense right now," Seth retorted. "They're just thinking about how their own sons will have to go and fight, so we should, as well."

"Enough," Daad said, his tone firm. "If God is sending this trial to test us, we must stay strong and obedient. Think of those who were martyred for the faith before we ever came to this country." His gaze flickered from Anna to Jacob. "Jacob, you should go to your family now. They will need to have you with them when they hear what has happened."

Jacob nodded. He rose, letting go of Anna's hand, and she felt cold without his touch.

She stood, too, and went quickly around the table. She'd see him out, and they could have a moment or two of privacy on the porch before he left. She needed it.

Jacob took his black coat from the hook near the door, and Anna grabbed the wool shawl that hung there. She glanced back at the table. The family was still seated around the table, the yellow glow from the gas lamp gilding their faces, just as she'd seen them when she was pouring out the coffee. But the peace she'd sensed then was gone, shattered into bits by something that had happened a half a world away.

She and Jacob slipped out into the cold darkness of the back porch. He put his hand on her shoulder.

"You shouldn't have come out. That shawl isn't warm enough on a night like this one."

She looked up at him, his face nothing more than a pale oval in the dim light from the kitchen windows. "I had to have a minute alone with you. Oh, Jacob, this is like a nightmare."

He nodded. "Only we're not going to wake up from it, I'm afraid."

She shivered, and he wrapped his arms around her, holding her close.

"I thought you'd say everything was going to be all right." She nuzzled against his sleeve, longing to be even closer.

"I can't." His voice was solemn. He put his hand up to stroke her cheek. "I don't have any hope to give. Like your daad said, we'll have to pray we're strong enough to stand the tests ahead of us."

Tears stung her eyes. "It's not fair. Everyone else was able to get married, have babies, have a happy life."

"Not everyone," he corrected, and she was ashamed, thinking of the uncle she'd never known.

Jacob pressed his cheek against hers, just holding her silently for a moment. Then he moved, and his lips closed on hers. Tender, warm, loving.

The moment should have been full of promise, but it couldn't be. As quickly as he'd kissed her, Jacob turned and was gone, vanishing into the dark.

Anna wrapped her arms around herself, rocking back and forth, trying to find comfort, and fearing she wasn't strong enough or brave enough to stand up to the test.

CHAPTER EIGHT

*R*ebecca felt as if she'd been put through the wringer and hung out to dry by the time she got the children into bed that night. Too much emotion piled on an already shaky foundation would do that to a person.

Anger spurted up, startling her. But she couldn't be angry with Matt. It wasn't fair to blame him for bringing her yet another problem. If one of her kinder did wrong, she had to know about it so that she could deal with it. Being angry with Matt in this situation was as foolish as being angry with Paul for dying.

Something seemed to quiver in her at the thought. She didn't blame Paul, she told herself quickly. That would be both stupid and wrong. But she couldn't seem to dismiss the thought, even as she tucked the quilt around Joshua, snuggling him close in its warmth.

"There you are," she said. "Snug as a bug in a rug, just the way you like it."

He cuddled his favorite toy against his cheek—the black-and-white stuffed cow her mother had made for him. He gave her a drowsy smile.

"When I helped clear up his tools, Matt said—" Josh stopped, shooting a glance toward his sister.

What a tender heart her little boy had. Rebecca tousled his hair. "He probably said you did a fine job of helping him, isn't that right?"

Joshua nodded. Rebecca sent a quick look at Katie, but her daughter was turned on her side, presenting nothing to them but her back.

Or at least, that was most likely what Katie thought. She wouldn't know, not until she was a mammi herself, just how much a parent could be affected by the vulnerable curve of the back of a child's neck.

Uttering a silent prayer for wisdom, Rebecca smiled at Joshua. "Denke, Josh. I'm glad you helped Matt clean up the mess."

Katie didn't move, but Rebecca thought her shoulders stiffened. She knew full well that she was the one who should have done the cleaning up.

Rebecca kissed Josh with a soft good night. Then she rose and walked around to the other side of Katie's twin bed.

Probably she should have separated the two of them into different bedrooms sometime in the past year. In the normal course of events, by now there'd have been another boppli or two, and there would be a boys' bedroom and a girls' bedroom, just as there had been when she was growing up. But with Paul gone, she hadn't been able to bring herself to leave either of the kinder alone in the dark.

She sat down on the edge of Katie's bed, putting a hand on her shoulder. "We have to talk, my Katie."

Katie sniffled a little, her face woebegone, and Rebecca's heart melted. Why did life have to be so difficult?

"Don't want to," Katie muttered. She tried to frown and only succeeded in looking a little more lost.

"Ach, Katie, sometimes we have to do what we don't want to." She smoothed her hand over the log cabin quilt that Grossmammi had made, finding comfort in the love it represented. "I know you miss Daadi. I miss him, too, so much."

Katie's lips trembled. "You don't. You don't even cry about him."

That struck her in the heart, taking her breath away for an instant. Had her stoic little Katie been emulating her?

"Of course I cry," she said. "I cried every day at first, but maybe a little less often now. I just always tried to do my crying when you wouldn't see me."

Josh had turned toward them, listening intently. Maybe he needed to hear this, too. Had she been wrong, making every effort to protect them?

"I thought it might make you afraid if you saw me crying, so I tried to be strong for you. It hasn't been easy to do."

Katie's eyes were suspiciously bright. "I'm sorry, Mammi. I thought it meant you didn't care."

Rebecca's throat was tight, but she forced herself to go on. "Of course I care. What happened to Daadi was so sad, and we feel so lonely without him, but he would want us to go on, ain't so?"

Katie nodded, sniffling a little, and Joshua copied her, rubbing his fist against his nose.

"I know you hate the idea of somebody else using the stable we built for Daadi's horses, but Daadi can't use it anymore."

"I thought we could raise the horses for Daadi, just like he wanted," Katie said.

"Ach, Katie, can you see us doing that?" Rebecca managed a smile. "You, and me, and Joshie trying to take care of those great big Percherons? One swish of the tail would knock Joshie over, wouldn't it?"

Katie couldn't seem to stop a small giggle from escaping. "Well, but maybe Onkel Simon could take care of them until we're older."

Rebecca stroked her daughter's cheek. "That wouldn't be fair to him, would it? The Percherons were Daadi's dream, but not Onkel Simon's. He has his own dreams, ain't so?"

Katie nodded, the movement reluctant.

"I had to decide which things were most important to Daadi." She picked each word with care. "I think keeping our home was at the top of his list. He loved our place so much." Her smile trembled on the edge of tears. "When he hung the bell on the back porch, he said that every time it rang, it meant home to him."

"Then why don't we ring it anymore?" Josh raised himself on one elbow to put the question to her.

Her heart was being squeezed again. "I guess it reminded me too much that Daadi is gone." She blinked back tears. "Maybe we'll start ringing it again soon."

"I think Daadi would like it if we did that for him." Josh lay down again.

Rebecca studied Katie's face, encouraged by the thoughtful look she saw there.

"I intend to keep our home by taking in guests this summer, like Daadi planned. And renting the stable to Matt helps, too." She ran her hand over Katie's soft, silky hair, smoothed back in loose braids for the night. "I know doing so means changes, but if it helps us keep our home, isn't it worth it?"

Katie nodded, the movement slow. "I guess," she whispered.

Rebecca was reminded of her conversation with Grossmammi about accepting changes. Maybe she had been selfish, thinking only of how she was affected. All of them were facing changes, it seemed, and somehow they had to accept them.

"Gut." She bent to kiss Katie's cheek. "I will always take care of you and Josh. You know that, don't you?"

Katie murmured something that sounded affirmative. Then she flung her arms around Rebecca's neck in a throttling hug. "I love you, Mammi."

"I love you, Katie. And I love you, Joshua. Always and always. And now I think it's time for sleep." She smoothed the quilt over Katie and kissed her forehead. Rounding the bed, she did the same to Joshua. Then she went out of the room quickly, before she could start to cry.

Wiping tears away with her palms, Rebecca went slowly down the stairs. She breathed deeply, trying to ease the tightness in her chest. This talk with the children had been hard, but obviously it had been needed. It seemed not even a mother could guess everything that was in a child's mind.

The sound of a buggy drew her attention to the kitchen window in time to see Matt drive up to the back porch. Her stomach gave a lurch. Surely nothing else was wrong. This day had held enough troubles.

By the time she reached the back door Matt was climbing down, and they met at the bottom of the porch steps.

"Is something wrong?" She couldn't help the apprehension in her voice.

"Not exactly." His strong features were unusually solemn. There was no charming smile to distract her now. Even the cleft in his chin looked carved from wood. "I've been thinking about what happened. I just wanted to say— Well, if it would make things easier for you, I'm willing to move my shop some-where else."

"No." She pressed her fist against her ribs. "No, please don't do that." She sucked in a calming breath, realizing that she'd startled Matt with her emphatic response. "I know this incident wasn't very pleasant for you, but I promise, it won't happen again."

"That's not worrying me, Rebecca." His expression eased a little, his voice becoming gentle. "I don't want to make things more difficult for you and the kinder."

"You didn't." She shook her head, unsure how much she wanted to say. "Katie will be better now. What happened forced us to talk about her feelings, and it seems that was just what she needed. I guess I should have spoken to them more about how things had to change since their daadi died, but I was afraid to let them see how I felt." She rubbed her arms, suddenly aware of the cool evening air.

"How did you feel?" Matt's voice was low, his gaze intent on her face. He really wanted to know.

For a moment Rebecca didn't seem to see anything but the gathering shadows. But she knew the answer to the question. "Like a child left alone in the dark."

He clasped her hand. "You're not really alone."

"No, I'm not." She shrugged off the chill that wanted to settle into her heart. "I'm sorry. I shouldn't have said that to you."

Matt shrugged, letting his hand drop to his side. "It's all right. I'm glad you did."

"It's easier to say some things to you than to my family." Voicing the words seemed to clarify her thoughts. "They all care too much, you see."

Matt's smile seemed to contain a certain wry edge. "I guess that would be a problem, wouldn't it? We'll say no more about it, then. Good night, Rebecca." He swung himself up into the buggy without looking back.

Matt walked back toward his uncle's farmhouse from the barn after tending to the animals first thing the next morning, liking the silent moments at the opening of the day. Even in late May, the air was cool this early, and the sun was just making its way over the eastern ridge, its rays lighting up the parallel ridge to the west long before they reached the valley floor. A pale silver crescent moon clung to the darker sky. It had been different out in Indiana where it was so flat, but a morning like this reminded him of his childhood.

Onkel Silas walked beside him, sunk in the silence that seemed to have become habitual with him. He'd never been as talkative as Matt's daad, but now his isolation was a cold, frozen thing that seemed to chill even those who cared for him most.

Was this what his parents had been like after Matt had

jumped the fence? He didn't want to think about that time or its after-effects. He'd been a kid—young, heedless, not thinking of anyone but himself, unaware of causing pain.

Onkel Silas had set up a sink in the back hall years ago at Aunt Lovina's insistence, and they stopped there to wash up and take off their boots. He could remember Aunt Lovina standing in the doorway, lecturing him and Isaiah when they'd tried to skip this step.

There will be no muddy boots in my clean kitchen, so don't you even think about it. Would she know or care now? His smile faded.

He followed his uncle to the table, hearing the thump of feet as the younger kids rushed down the stairs, dressed for school. Sadie and Aunt Lovina were already setting bowls of oatmeal and a platter of scrambled eggs on the table.

Once they were all seated, silence fell at a glance from Onkel Silas. Heads bowed. Matt found his prayer leaping from one concern to another.

Silent prayers ended simultaneously, even though no signal had been given. If you were raised Amish, you must have an internal timer for the proper length of prayer. Dishes clattered, and the younger ones resumed an argument about whose turn it was to wash the boards after school today. He caught fourteen-year-old Thomas's gaze and grinned at the boy. It all sounded so familiar, and they both knew the boy was only persisting to tease his next younger sister.

"Sadie, we've forgotten." Aunt Lovina's voice rose over the chatter. "We haven't laid a place for Isaiah. How could we forget?"

Silence. No one even seemed to breathe. Matt glanced,

exasperated, from his uncle to his cousin Sadie. Surely they should have found a way to deal with Lovina's memory lapses by now, but they sat there like stones. When he couldn't stand it any longer, he seized control.

"Isaiah's away this morning, remember, Aunt Lovina?"

"He is?" She looked puzzled, raising a hand to her forehead. "But he has to have breakfast."

"I'm sure he'll find a place to eat. He can stop at a restaurant if need be." Matt spared a frustrated thought for Isaiah, who probably wasn't even out of bed yet, wherever he was.

"He'll be fine," Sadie echoed finally. "Daad, some more coffee?"

Talk began again, more muted this time, but at least sounding fairly normal. Matt found he was thinking of something Rebecca had said last night—something about how she hadn't talked openly about Paul's death with the kinder, and how she felt now it had been wrong not to bring it out in the open.

But if his uncle or Sadie did talk to Aunt Lovina about Isaiah, would she understand or remember? Maybe if they'd all behave more normally, she could accept the idea that Isaiah was working away someplace.

As for Isaiah, the least he could do was write to his family, or even call and leave a message on the machine in the phone shanty. It wasn't as if he'd already been baptized into the church, so that his defection would result in the bann being imposed. Whatever Isaiah's quarrel was with being Amish, it wasn't right to leave his mamm in such a state.

Matt eyed Sadie. If anyone knew what had been going on with Isaiah before he left, it was Sadie. She wouldn't want to talk to Matt about it. Well, too bad, because she was going to.

He waited until everyone had scattered after breakfast, leaving Sadie alone cleaning up. He approached the sink where she was working. Was there any way of bringing up the subject without making her angry with him? Probably not, so he might as well come right out with it.

He leaned against the counter next to her.

"Do you know where Isaiah is?"

Sadie stiffened, not turning to look at him. "How would I know? And why would you care?"

"You might know. You and Isaiah were always close. And I care because Aunt Lovina is being hurt by this whole situation."

Sadie turned on him, her hand gripping a cup so hard it was a wonder it didn't break. "You think I don't know it? I'd do anything to make it better for her. Of course, you've been here for a few weeks, so you know all about what should be done." Her tone was sharp with sarcasm, and she made a business of scrubbing the cup, splashing sudsy water so that it hit his shirtsleeve.

He took a firm hold on his exasperation. "You don't want me interfering. I understand why you feel that way. But wouldn't it be better if Isaiah at least wrote to her? Don't you think then she could accept that he was working away someplace? She wouldn't have to know that he was living Englisch."

Sadie's restless movements slowed. "She might feel that way, but he hasn't written to us. Or called. Or anything." She shot him a look of dislike. "You should know about that, ain't so?"

"I was a kid when I left, with a kid's heedless attitude. Isaiah's a grown man." He planted his hands against the counter. "Look, Sadie, I know you don't want me around, but I'm here.

Isn't it better for everyone if we try to get along instead of fighting?"

Sadie stiffened. Then she swung to face him. "I suppose that's Rebecca's idea. She told you what I said after worship, didn't she?"

The introduction of Rebecca's name jolted him. "Rebecca hasn't told me anything about you. But it sounds like maybe you'd better."

Sadie blinked. "She must have . . ." She let that die, then shrugged and turned back to the sink. "I didn't say any more than the truth—that you're spending more time over at Rebecca's than you are here."

Matt's hands clenched, and he fought to control his words. "You know full well that I'm over there to work in my shop, nothing else."

"So you say," she snapped. "Everyone knows men will be flocking around Rebecca again now that Paul has been gone for over a year."

He stopped himself from saying something unforgiveable about the source of Sadie's resentment. "As far as I can see, Rebecca doesn't have time for anyone but her family and her kinder." He kept his tone mild with an effort. "Right now all I'm interested in is getting my business off the ground and helping Onkel Silas and Aunt Lovina. It seems to me somebody ought to make an effort to get Isaiah to write to his mamm, if nothing else."

Sadie was silent for a moment, and he had an idea she was struggling with herself. Finally she picked up a dish towel and dried her hands, still not looking at him.

"I don't know where he is," she said at last. "I was so angry when he said he was thinking of leaving. . . ." She pressed her lips together, as if wishing something unsaid. "Anyway, he didn't tell me. He might have talked to Simon Lapp. You could try him."

Matt nodded, judging it as well not to say anything more with Sadie's mood as precarious as it was.

But Simon Lapp—why, of all people, did it have to be Simon? Given the way he'd acted the one time he'd talked to Matt, it seemed very unlikely that Simon would want to confide in him.

"I think we're almost finished with the sorting. We have the lists for Grossmammi of everything that's up here. All that remains is moving it out before the sale of the farm is finalized."

Rebecca said the words with a sense of relief as she glanced around her grandmother's attic. With everything she'd had to do getting ready for her first guests this weekend, she couldn't really afford many more afternoons spent in this attic.

She ran a dust cloth over the rungs of a rocking chair. All that remained was the final cleaning up.

"Lots of the relatives are stopping in over the weekend to pick out what Grossmammi wants them to have. She told me you're going to store some things for her in your attic." Judith gave Rebecca a questioning look. "Are you sure you have room?"

Rebecca nodded. "The attic was empty when we bought the farm, and we haven't really added much to it. It's fine. I don't want Grossmammi to feel that it all has to be given away. You know how she likes to tell the family stories about the things."

Judith moved a dresser a few inches and closed the top drawer. "That's certain-sure. Well, we know how busy you are with your first guests coming in so soon. Barbie and I can finish without your help. Ain't so, Barbie?"

Barbie, thus prompted, nodded. "I guess."

Rebecca closed her lips on the comment that Barbie had been late today yet again. "Denke, but I'm about ready. I just have some last-minute things to do tomorrow."

And the next day her guests would arrive. She couldn't give in to the panic she felt at the thought.

Judith nodded. "Well, don't forget we offered if you get busy. I'm sure your mamm and daad will be wonderful glad to see this place cleared out and finally get Grossmammi moved in with them."

"Mamm's been ready for weeks, I think." Rebecca straightened, setting the rocker moving with a touch of her finger. "Grossmammi reminded me that she wants each of us to have something special to keep."

"She told me that, too." Barbie's lively face grew serious. "I don't want to hurt her feelings, but really—" Her gesture took in the contents of the attic. "There's nothing here I want."

"You will hurt her if you say so." Rebecca frowned at her young cousin. At least she was thinking instead of blurting it out, but didn't she have *any* feeling for her family history?

"She'll want to choose something for you," Judith suggested, her tone that of a peacemaker. "She likes to match the gift to the person, I think."

"What if—" Barbie began, and then seemed to think better of whatever she'd been going to say. "What does she want you to take?"

"The study table, but I told her that if anyone else wanted it, I'd have something else." Judith, as usual, seemed ready to give up her choice if challenged.

"You should have it," Rebecca said quickly, darting a warning glance toward Barbara but then realizing it wasn't necessary. Barbie didn't care.

Judith ran her hand along the sturdy oak table, built with drawers along one side. "The boys can do their schoolwork at this nice piece. And that will move them off the kitchen table right when I'm busy fixing a meal or cleaning up. But are you sure this isn't what you had your eye on, Rebecca?"

She shook her head. "My heart already belongs to the dower chest with Anna's things in it, and I know Grossmammi wants me to have it. I've been reading Anna's journal when I have time, and she's starting to feel like a friend."

"Does Grossmammi remember anything about the things Anna wrote about?" Judith set to work dusting a small bookcase.

"I asked, but she said not much. She was just a little girl during World War Two, and she said you take things for granted when you're a child."

Judith seemed to consider the words. "I guess that's true. Children aren't troubled as long as life goes along steadily from day to day. And I sometimes think they can accept changes more easily than adults can."

True. Rebecca couldn't help but consider how her own two had coped with the changes that had been forced upon them. Katie had actually seemed more like her old self since the night they'd talked, and Rebecca could only thank the good Lord that difficulty had turned out for the best.

"I'll be doing my baking tomorrow," Judith said, concentrating on the bookcase. "I'll bring over a couple of loaves of bread and a coffee cake. With your guests coming in, you can use some extras."

"You don't need—" Rebecca began, but Judith didn't let her finish before she was shaking her head.

"I want to," she said. "You'll make me happy by accepting."

Rebecca nodded, her throat tightening. "Denke, Judith. I have to admit I'm nervous about the whole thing. I'll be glad to have some extra food, just in case."

Judith sat back on her heels, studying Rebecca's face. "You know, maybe that's why you're so drawn to Anna. She was facing a scary future, too."

"Maybe." Rebecca wasn't sure she wanted to think about it that way.

"You know all your family wants to help," Judith said, her expression intent.

"I know."

Judith meant well. They all did. The problem was that no matter how much anyone wanted to help, in the end it all came down to her. And she just wasn't sure she could do it.

CHAPTER NINE

Lancaster County, March 1942

*A*nna couldn't deny the truth, even to herself. She was afraid. Even as she measured oats into the feed pails for the buggy horses, safe in their own barn, doing her familiar chores, the fear and uncertainty crept in.

The past few months had been full of news about the war. It was going badly, it seemed. On a rare trip to town for Daadi, she'd seen posters everywhere urging people to participate in the war effort, saying, "Use it up, wear it out, make it do, or do without."

All the Englisch could talk about was the need for more men, more food, more guns and tanks for the war. And if they happened to see her listening, they turned away.

And now the threat of conscription hung over their young men. If they were called up—Jacob, Seth, all the Amish boys she'd known since they were toddlers—what would they do?

Anna reached across the stall bars to pat Bell, and the mare turned away from her oats for a moment to nuzzle Anna's hand.

"That mare loves you more than she loves her grain, ain't so?" Daadi, coming down the loft ladder after tossing hay down to the stalls, actually smiled at her. Smiles had been in short supply lately, it seemed to her.

"She'll turn back to her supper fast enough." Anna pulled her black wool sweater closed over her apron. The sun was setting, the air still cold in late March once it was down. "Daadi . . ." She hesitated, not sure she wanted to put her fear into words.

"What is it, child?" He leaned against the stall bar next to her, his lean face carrying new lines above his beard. "You're fretting. Did something happen when you went to the mill this afternoon? Your mamm was scolding me for letting you go alone."

"It was all right." Mammi would keep all of them under her eyes constantly if she could, these days. "Folks were talking about the war. When they saw me, they stopped talking. They looked at me funny, like I was a stranger instead of somebody they've known for years."

"People are afraid, not knowing what's going to happen. That fear makes them seek someone to blame." He shook his head. "Your mamm was right. I shouldn't have sent you there alone."

"I was fine," she insisted quickly. "I guess I should be getting used to it by now." But she wasn't, and she suspected she never would. "I heard Mr. Andrews say that this war is a just war. That we have to fight for freedom for those people who are enslaved." Somehow, when the elderly Englischer had said it, it seemed to make sense to her.

" 'Thou shalt not kill. If someone strikes thee on the right cheek, turn to him the left one also.' " Daad's voice rolled the scriptural words out solemnly. "Those are the words we live by. What others do is up to them, but we must obey Christ's teachings, even when we don't understand."

Her fingers tightened on the rough wood of the stall door. She didn't really want to talk about whether war was justified or not. Her concerns were more personal. "What will happen if our boys get conscription letters? Seth . . . Jacob . . . What will happen to them?"

"You're worrying that it will be as bad as it was in the last war because of what your onkel said, ain't so?"

She nodded. "It sounded so terrible."

"It was, but at least we're not alone this time. All of the peace churches are joining to face this trial with us. And the bishop says there are friends of the churches among the Englisch, even in the government, who are working to make sure our boys will not be forced to kill."

"But if they are sent away . . ."

Daad took her hands in his work-roughened ones. "Anna, we must have faith. We must continue to be humble and forgiving and to live at peace. No matter what happens to us, it must be God's will."

He said the words firmly, but she could see the pain in his face. Did it wonder him, too, how he could hold on to his faith and courage in the days ahead?

"I know, Daadi. I'll try my best to be faithful." But when

even her father and the bishop walked around with grave faces, it was hardly any wonder that she fretted and struggled.

Daadi held her hands for a moment longer. "You're a gut child, Anna. I wish . . ." He stopped and shook his head. Then he turned and walked toward the house, his head and shoulders bowed as if he carried a heavy burden.

Bell, finished with her oats, poked her head over the stall bars and blew gently on Anna's neck. Anna tilted her head against the mare's face.

"What is happening to us?" she murmured. She stood for a moment, feeling the warmth of the animal's body, until the scrape of a shoe on the barn ramp told her someone else was coming.

"Anna?" Jacob stood in the doorway, his gaze seeking her in the dim barn.

"Here." She stepped into the yellow glow of the lantern. "I didn't expect to see you this early in the evening."

Jacob came toward her quickly, his face lighting with a smile as it always did when he saw her. "I can't stay long, but I hoped I could catch you to talk for a moment before you went inside."

"I'm glad." She held out her hand, seeking his, and he grasped it, threading his fingers with hers.

"You were talking with your daad. I didn't want to interrupt."

"You could have." She drew him closer. "He was trying to help me make sense of things. I was just worried about . . . everything."

"We all are." His fingers moved on her hand, caressing her skin. "That's really what I wanted to see you about."

Her heart clenched. "What is it? What's wrong?"

"I just wanted to tell you that I spoke with the bishop today. It seemed to me we need more information. He agreed. He is already planning to have a gathering after worship on Sunday to talk with the young men and their parents about what to do if . . . when they get conscription notices."

"Maybe it won't happen." She tried to cling to what she feared was a forlorn hope. "So many men are volunteering, I heard. So maybe they won't need any more."

Jacob shook his head. "They will always need more, I think. The war is all over the world—in Europe, in Asia—no place seems to be spared. We'll be called to serve, just like all the Englisch boys." His face was solemn in the dim light, all strong bones and shadows.

"But you can't fight. You can't kill someone," she protested, knowing they'd been through it all before but unable to stop.

"The bishop says we will have to apply to be conscientious objectors." He said the words carefully, as if they were as strange as they sounded. "That means we are saying that we can't kill, no matter what."

She squeezed his hand. "That didn't help the last time. You know it didn't. Amish men were forced into uniform, and if they wouldn't fight, they were put in prison."

"Don't, Anna. Don't think that way." Jacob slipped his arm around her and drew her close.

She could feel the warmth and strength of him, and he was inexpressibly dear to her. What if they took him away?

"It could happen." Her voice caught on a sob.

"Our friends are working for us in Washington. That's what

the bishop says. All of us . . . Mennonites, Quakers, Amish . . . we're all in this situation together."

"If the worst happened, and they made you go into the army, could you do it?" She looked up into his face. "Could you raise a gun against another person to kill?"

He hesitated. Then he put his palms on either side of her face, cradling it in his hands. "No. I couldn't. I have searched my heart again and again. I could not take a life, no matter what the cost."

It was what she expected him to say. What she wanted him to say. And yet, some small part of her cried out that he might have to do so to protect himself.

"Keep on hoping, my Anna." He put his forehead against hers and whispered the words. "Have faith."

Something in his voice alerted her. There was more to this than he was saying.

She drew back a little, looking into his face, her eyes widening. "Jacob, why did you go to the bishop today? Did you . . ." She couldn't finish.

He nodded, his face bleak. "I received my call-up notice from the draft board today."

She should speak. She should say something encouraging, something hopeful. But she couldn't. She could only step into his arms and hold him close while it seemed her heart broke into pieces.

When Rebecca saw the shiny blue convertible pulling into the lane on Friday afternoon, her heart plummeted. Mr. and Mrs. Strickland had arrived.

It wasn't that she wasn't prepared. The house had been cleaned as thoroughly as if she were hosting worship, baked goods lined one kitchen counter, and the refrigerator was stocked with everything she might possibly need for the meals she'd be preparing.

But all of that external preparation didn't seem to help in the least when her insides didn't match her outside. She, the house, and the kinder might all look prepared for guests, but her heart was thudding, her breath coming too fast, and her hands as cold as a windowpane on a winter morning.

Rebecca took one last glance out the window, sucked in a deep breath, and headed for the porch to greet her guests.

Roy and Melissa Strickland had been among the first to visit two summers ago. In their late fifties, they both seemed to look and act younger. They'd been filled with enthusiasm about helping Paul with every farm chore imaginable, and she prayed they'd be willing to transfer that allegiance to Simon. The only hope she had of getting through the weekend was to have them out of the house as much as possible.

When they began taking bags out of their car, she hurried to meet them, arranging a smile on her face. "It's so nice to see you, Mrs. Strickland. Mr. Strickland."

"Melissa and Roy, remember?" Mrs. Strickland surrendered her suitcase to Rebecca with a smile and pulled off the silk scarf that must have been intended to protect her hair from the wind in the topless car. It must have worked, because every auburn curl was in place. "You don't know how much we've been looking forward to a nice, relaxing weekend in the country."

"Not so much of the relaxing for me, thanks." Roy, brisk

and ruddy, shook hands and smiled a greeting to Katie and Joshua.

Katie stood up very straight. "Wilkom. We are wonderful glad to see you." She'd memorized the greeting, and she brought it out quickly in English.

Joshua, still uncomfortable when he was expected to speak English, gave a quick nod and then sidled behind Rebecca, his hand clutching her skirt.

"Komm." She detached Joshua and turned toward the door. "I've put you in the same room you had the last time you were here. I hope that suits you."

"Fine, fine." Roy reached out as if to tousle Joshua's hair, but he stopped when Josh pulled back. Obviously the talk she'd had with him about how to behave around guests hadn't been enough to help him overcome his shyness.

She couldn't scold him, since she felt much the same herself. Rebecca led the Stricklands inside. *Talk*, she commanded herself, but she couldn't seem to think of anything to say.

Melissa glanced around the downstairs as they paused inside the door. "Where's Paul?" she said, her voice loud in the quiet house. "We thought he'd be here to meet us."

Rebecca could feel the color drain from her face. Josh pressed against her, and she patted him automatically.

"I'm sorry. I thought you understood. Paul passed away over a year and a half ago."

Melissa gasped, taking a step back. "No, we didn't realize. I mean, we saw the letter was only signed by you, but . . ."

She let that trail off, and Rebecca found she was wondering how much difference it might have made to their coming if they'd known. But she might say the same about Melissa's original note, asking whether they were open this year. It had just been addressed to Rebecca.

"That's such a tragic thing," Roy said quickly. "You and the children have our deepest sympathies." He hesitated. "I suppose that's going to make a difference to our stay. I mean, we were expecting to be able to join Paul in doing the farmwork, and since he's not here, well—"

"My brother Simon is taking over for Paul. He's looking forward to working with you." Was Roy implying that they wouldn't have come if they'd known? Rebecca wasn't sure, and the uncertainty made her, if possible, even more nervous. "Let's take your bags upstairs, and then I'll show you around. There are a few changes since you were last here."

Besides the fact that Paul is gone, she added silently. She led the way upstairs to the room she'd prepared for them and put Melissa's suitcase on the luggage rack they'd bought for each bedroom. Katie set the tote bag she'd carried on the floor next to it and then came to stand by Rebecca, slipping her hand into hers.

Somehow the feel of that cool little hand gave Rebecca a spurt of courage. "Please take all the time you need to settle in. I'll be waiting downstairs to take you around and introduce you to my brother Simon." Clutching Katie's hand, she left them alone.

Unfortunately she wasn't quite out of earshot when Melissa began to speak. "Well, she might have told us that her husband was gone. I don't think this—" The words were cut off by the door closing.

Keeping the smile pinned firmly to her face, Rebecca continued down the steps. It would be a relief to express the doubt and dismay that filled her, but she couldn't do that in front of the kinder. They had to feel assured that their mammi had everything under control, even if she didn't.

At least she did have the cooking organized. They had set up the farm-stay so that they provided breakfast each day to their guests as part of their room rent. The other meals were available at an extra cost.

That first summer, some people had wanted to use the farm as a sort of base for exploring the surrounding area, and that was fine. As Paul had said, the whole idea of a farm-stay vacation was that folks could enjoy living on a real working farm in a rural setting. They could join in and help if they wanted to, but that was entirely up to them. Guests could do exactly as they wished when they were here.

Roy and Melissa had chosen to book supper for tonight, maybe because Friday was a short day since they'd arrived in midafternoon. The meal, at least, didn't have Rebecca worried. It was every other part of entertaining their guests that made her want to shrivel up inside her shell.

Hearing footsteps overhead, she turned to the kinder. "I want you to stay with me and the guests at least until we've introduced them to Onkel Simon. After that, if you want to slip away you can. But remember, they are our guests, and you should try and make them feel at home, ain't so?"

They both nodded, Katie with a little more emphasis than Joshua. Katie would do her best, Rebecca felt sure, because she'd remember how much her daadi had enjoyed having people here. Joshua was a little too much like his mother to enjoy having them in the house, but he was obviously trying to be brave about it.

Roy and Melissa came downstairs, Roy having changed to a pair of jeans, a flannel shirt, and shiny boots that looked as if they'd just come from the store. He rubbed his palms together in what Rebecca supposed was enthusiasm.

"Well, let's get going. What do you have for us to do this afternoon?"

"All I want is to sit in the shade with my book," Melissa announced, showing the fat volume she held under her arm. Its glossy cover was bright red with a bold black illustration. Rebecca couldn't quite make out what it was, but she suspected it wouldn't be a book she'd care for, even if she had time to read much of anything these days.

"If you wouldn't mind coming along on a short walk first, I'd appreciate it."

Rebecca feared she was being too tentative. Paul had insisted that each party of guests had to be taken around when they first arrived, just so they'd know where everything was and what was off-limits. The last thing they wanted was someone having an accident.

"I suppose so." Melissa hugged her book against her chest. "Lead on."

"You'll remember the downstairs." Rebecca tried to copy Paul's words. "Please make yourself comfortable down here. If you need help turning on the gas-powered lights, just let me know."

She led the way through into the kitchen where she paused, glancing at the baked goods lined up on the counter.

"You can have a snack and something to drink anytime you like. There will always be something out on the counter for you."

She led them on out the back door and then stopped at the bottom of the porch steps. "The porch swing is a nice spot for relaxing."

"That's new, isn't it?" Roy was staring toward the stable, and Rebecca had to swallow before she could answer.

"Yes. We built the stable shortly after you were here, I believe. It's now rented out to an Amish friend who makes handcrafted furniture."

"Ooh, I'd like to see it." Melissa's face lit up, apparently at the thought of buying something. "Can we go there now?"

"I'm afraid Matthew isn't in the workshop at the moment, but anytime you see a buggy parked outside, please feel free to go over." Matt might not be overjoyed by visitors, but they were potential customers, after all.

"Later, Melissa." Roy put his hand on his wife's arm. "You can spend some money later, okay?"

Melissa pouted a little, but nodded. Rebecca suspected the woman was a dedicated shopper to judge by her expression. That was a thing Rebecca would never understand. She bought something because she needed it, or because she was giving it for a gift, not just for the sake of buying something. They had a roof over their heads and plenty of good food to eat—what else did anyone need?

Shepherding the pair along, she showed them the vegetable and flower gardens, pointing out that weeding was always appreciated, and that the fresh lettuce, spinach, and spring onions would be on the supper table tonight.

If there had been children along, she'd have had to show them the creek, pointing out where it was safe for a child to splash around and where the deeper parts were. She judged that was not necessary for Roy and Melissa.

The carriage horses were in the field next to the barn, and they moved to the fence at the sight of people coming, probably anticipating a handout.

"Oh, look, isn't he sweet?" Melissa reached over the fence to pat Star's glossy face, and Ben leaned over to get his share of the caress.

"Katie, why don't you show Mrs. Strickland how to feed an apple to the horses?"

Nodding, Katie darted to the barrel near the barn door and rushed back with a double handful of small, withered apples.

"See," she said importantly. "Put the apple on your hand and hold it out flat, like this, so the horse doesn't get a finger by mistake." It was, word for word, how Rebecca had taught her.

Ben reached over the fence to snaffle the apple while Brownie, the pony, trotted over, obviously afraid he was missing something. Roy fed the animals without hesitation, but Melissa squealed and dropped the apple the minute Star's lips touched her hand. Star picked it up daintily with her lips, and Melissa was persuaded to try again with Brownie, Katie helping by holding her hand.

Rebecca relaxed enough to smile more naturally. Katie was her father's daughter, it seemed.

Simon came toward them from the barn. His fresh young face was clouded with a little uncertainty, but he grinned when he saw what was going on.

"Katie is being the teacher, ain't so?" He flicked her cheek with his finger, making her grin. "I'm Simon Lapp, Rebecca's brother."

Rebecca hurried to make the introductions, relieved to see that Simon conquered his reluctance very quickly once he started talking. He took over, answering Melissa's questions about the horses and the pony without any hesitation.

Rebecca breathed a little more easily. She should have known she could count on Simon. While he wasn't as outgoing as Paul had been, he did seem relaxed around Englisch people.

And he was good-looking, if she did say so herself. She could see that Melissa thought so, tilting her head to the side and hanging on his words.

Ach, she wasn't going to start worrying about women flirting with her little brother. Simon was old enough to deal with that himself, and she had plenty of more sensible concerns.

"I'll leave you with Simon now, so that I can get supper started. Please remember that you can do just what you want." She glanced at the book, still tucked in Melissa's arm, but the woman seemed to have forgotten her desire to sit and read.

Rebecca glanced at the children to remind them that they didn't have to stay with the guests any longer right now. Joshua, predictably, darted off in the direction of the apple tree, but Katie hung on Simon's hand.

The relief Rebecca felt as she hurried back to the house gave her a flicker of guilt. She was the one who'd insisted on opening the farm-stay. She probably shouldn't be so eager to leave her guests behind.

Paul had been skilled at coping with their guests. He'd answered endless questions about what it meant to be Amish, even though they were repeated time after time by each new set of guests. He'd kept the conversation going at the supper table, making sure that everyone was drawn in, telling stories, making jokes.

She couldn't possibly copy him in that respect. It just wasn't in her nature. She loved feeding people, and it would make her happy to prepare their supper and watch them eating it with enjoyment. But she didn't have the social gift Paul had, and now that the time had actually come, she was afraid that what she had to offer wasn't going to be enough.

Matt was spending his Saturday morning working on a small chest of drawers. His teacher, Asa, used to say that a craftsman could sometimes earn more making several small pieces instead of one large one, because people were quicker to make up their minds over something small. This one had a curve to the top that added a touch of something different, it seemed to Matt, and the fine grain of the maple had been a pleasure to work with.

When he heard a step in the doorway, he knew he'd been waiting for it all morning. But when he glanced up, it wasn't Rebecca. An Englisch couple stood there, lingering in the doorway as if not sure whether to come or go. Rebecca's guests, no doubt.

"Komm in. Were you wanting to see what's happening in here?" He rose, smiling as they approached.

"Rebecca said you wouldn't mind if we had a look around. My wife wants to see what you're making."

"I'm happy to have you look around all you want. If you have any questions, just ask. I'm Matthew Byler."

"Are you another of Rebecca's relatives?" The woman paused in her inspection of the rocking chair he'd recently finished.

"Just a friend." At least, he hoped he was. "She rents the building to me for my workshop."

The man had already turned away, casting a cursory glance at the few pieces Matt had set up on display. Until the furniture he'd had in storage in Indiana arrived, he didn't have much that he could sell, so he hadn't bothered to try to drum up any business yet. Time enough for that later.

It was the woman who was the buyer, he'd guess. She went from piece to piece, keeping up a running commentary to her husband on what she liked, what would fit into her decorating scheme, and whether she had space for another chair in her bedroom.

The man made indeterminate sounds indicating that he was listening. Matt hid a grin. They were much like his daad and mamm when they went to an auction.

"Roy, look at this one." She stopped at a small wooden piece that could be either a stepstool or a child's chair, depending on what a buyer wanted. "It's the perfect stool for the kitchen."

"Do you really need . . ." he began in the tone of one who'd said the words many times before.

"Of course I do. You know how I'm always calling you to reach things on the top shelves for me. This is just perfect."

She patted it, and then stepped up on the stool by way of demonstration. "See?"

"Very nice." He reached toward his pocket and pulled out a wallet, turning to Matt. "I guess it'll be a nice souvenir of our weekend. More useful than most of the things we bring home. How much?"

Matt made what he thought was a fairly accurate guess at what the couple would expect to pay for such a thing in the city, naming a price that would let him come down a little if the man proved to be a bargainer.

But he handed the money over without argument and gave Matt a man-to-man grin. "Let's get it in the car before she sees something else she can't live without."

Rightly judging that he was expected to carry the stool, Matt picked it up. "Is your car over in Rebecca's driveway?"

The man nodded. "Come on, Melissa. We'd better get this loaded up if you want to go looking for that quilt shop you were talking about before lunch."

Matt shoved the door farther open with his elbow and walked out into the sunshine. The woman fell into step with him.

"I suppose you must have known Paul, if you're a friend of the family."

Matt nodded.

"We were so surprised when we arrived and found he was gone. I'm not sure we'd have come if we'd known."

"Now, Melissa." The husband frowned at her. "I'm sure Rebecca's made us very comfortable, and her brother is a nice young man."

"I suppose. But Paul was so outgoing and friendly, he just

made you feel like one of the family. It doesn't seem quite the same without him."

Matt had to suppress the desire to give the woman a shake before he could speak. "Rebecca is doing her best to carry on without Paul." What did they expect from her?

"I'm sure she is," the man said quickly, probably thinking his wife had been tactless. "They haven't offered the same activities we did the last time, though. I really enjoyed helping to cut the hay, messy as it was." He laughed. "I felt like I was getting the dust out of my hair for a week."

Matt had to increase his effort to control his annoyance. It wouldn't help Rebecca if he alienated her first guests.

"That's how it is on a working farm. There are different jobs to be done at different seasons. It's not time for the first cutting of hay yet. Come back in several weeks, and I'd guess Simon would be glad to have your help."

"I suppose." Roy still sounded a bit disgruntled, as if they ought to be able to manipulate the growing seasons for his enjoyment.

They were approaching the car by this time, and Matt was only too ready to stow away the stool and return to his work. He stood back, waiting while the man opened the trunk and did some rearranging of its contents.

Just then Rebecca came around the back of the house, carrying a basket and heading for the garden. She stopped when she saw him, and his eyes met hers.

Matt was conscious of a quick disorientation, as if the ground had shifted under him. Rebecca. He'd been telling himself that he wanted to help her for old times' sake, and because she so obviously needed help.

But another motive had just become abundantly clear to him. He was attracted. Very attracted. Attracted enough to rock him off his balance for an instant.

But only for an instant. Some things were possible, and some weren't. And the idea of any relationship between him and Rebecca clearly fell into the category marked impossible.

CHAPTER TEN

*I*f only she could stop obsessing about everything she feared she'd done wrong with her guests over the weekend, Rebecca told herself on Monday, she might be able to figure out what to do next.

"I think we should put the dill along the back of the bed." Grossmammi reached out as if to plant the herb on her own, and Rebecca pulled herself together and caught her hand.

"No, you don't." She managed a smile. "Remember what we decided? You're going to plan your herb bed, but I'm the worker, ain't so?"

Grossmammi would be moving in soon, and she'd insisted she couldn't leave her herb garden behind. So Mammi had offered her flower bed, and Rebecca had agreed to do the transplanting. If it made Grossmammi more content with moving, it was certainly worth the time.

"Ach, it's a fine thing when I can't even transplant a few herbs without all this fuss." Grossmammi settled back onto the porch steps at Mamm and Daad's place, but Rebecca could see she still wasn't convinced she couldn't do the job herself.

"You know what the doctor said. No lifting, no bending. Don't you trust me to do it right?" Rebecca, kneeling on the mat she used when she gardened, plunged her trowel into the earth and picked up the next plant.

"Not if you're going to put that peppermint there," her grossmammi pointed out. "You should know how it spreads."

Chagrined, Rebecca tried to focus. "I remember. After all, I had a gut teacher." Memory gave her a quick image of the day Grossmammi had arrived with a basket full of seedlings to help Rebecca establish her own herb garden soon after she and Paul had moved into the farmhouse. "I'm just . . . distracted, I guess." She clamped her lips closed.

"You are feeling bad about your first guests," Grossmammi said. "Everyone can see it, even though you haven't said a thing about it. Now, it's time you talked."

"No, I . . ."

"Rebecca Lapp Fisher." Grossmammi grasped her shoulder, forcing Rebecca to look at her. "You are fooling no one. Now, tell me what you are brooding about. Was it Simon? Did he do something wrong?"

"No, no, Simon was fine."

"Then what?" Her grandmother was gently persistent, her soft, wrinkled face filled with loving concern. "What is the problem? No one can help you to fix it if we don't know what it is."

"I was the problem." The words came out even though Rebecca tried to hold them back. "It was *my* fault the weekend didn't go as it should. I just can't do what Paul did so well. I couldn't relax and talk and tell stories the way he did." She wiped away a tear with the back of her gardening glove. "I keep thinking it should get easier to go on alone, but it doesn't."

Grossmammi patted her cheek. "Ach, Rebecca, I know. Do you think I didn't feel the same after your grossdaadi passed?"

"At least you didn't let anyone else down. It's been well over a year. I should be doing better."

"Nobody can put a time on how long it takes to grieve." Grossmammi gestured to the plants Rebecca had already set out. "Those will wilt at first from the shock of being transplanted, ain't so? But in a day or two they will come back and start to grow again. People take much longer to put down new roots, and you can't rush it."

Rebecca nodded, absently pressing the warm soil down around the basil plant she'd just put in. As Grossmammi said, its bright green leaves were drooping, but they would come back quickly with a little water and a little time.

"I have Katie and Joshua to raise. I can't wait until the season of grieving is past. I have to do better for them."

"You will. You know you always let Paul take the lead." Grossmammi patted Rebecca again, the way she did when Rebecca was a small child who'd taken a tumble. "That's not wrong, but . . ." She paused, as if trying to find the right words. "You would not put that tiny basil plant right next to the dill, because if you did, it wouldn't grow strong. The dill would shade it out, ain't so?"

Rebecca wanted to protest at the comparison, but she understood what her grandmother was saying. "I always followed Paul and relied on his strength. I know."

"That's true, but it's not all I mean." She hesitated, as if she was going to say something Rebecca might not want to hear. "Dill and basil are both gut, useful plants, but they grow better if they're not too close together. Leaning on Paul might have kept you from growing as strong as you could have."

"If so, it wasn't Paul's fault. He loved me and wanted to protect me." Surely Grossmammi wasn't saying that Paul had been wrong to love and care for her.

"Of course he did." Her grandmother frowned slightly. "But sometimes when we love someone, we protect them too much. Sometimes each of us has to try things and succeed or fail on our own."

She wanted to argue, but unfortunately she could see the sense of what Grossmammi was saying. If she'd protected her children from falling, they'd never have learned to walk.

"If you want your Katie to grow into a strong woman, you must give her an example of it." Grossmammi seemed to be reading her thoughts.

Rebecca sat back on her heels, looking up at her grand-mother. "I know. I'm just afraid that I'm going to fail with the farm-stay, and then what will I do?"

"This was Paul's dream, ain't so? It doesn't have to be yours. But if you want to do it, then maybe you should find someone to help. Even with Simon doing the outside work, you're still taking on everything else Paul did, besides all the cooking and cleaning for the guests."

"I suppose you're right." She hadn't realized until she'd tried it just how big the job was. "But that would mean someone who could be there whenever the guests are, who can talk easily to the Englisch and make them feel at ease, even make them laugh the way Paul did. I don't know—"

"Your cousin Barbara," Grossmammi exclaimed. "She would be perfect at it."

"Barbara?" Rebecca couldn't conceal her dismay. "Barbie wouldn't be right. She's too young, for one thing. And she's too frivolous, not responsible enough . . ." She ran out of steam, but surely Grossmammi couldn't be serious.

Her grandmother just smiled. "You think about it. Those are all things Barbie will outgrow, ain't so?"

"I guess." She hoped so, certainly.

"You'd be surprised at how long people can keep growing in ways you don't imagine. And Barbie is outgoing enough to do what you need done, that's certain-sure."

At Rebecca's expression, Grossmammi chuckled softly and patted Rebecca's cheek. "People keep on growing even when you're as old as I am. Chust think about it. All right?"

All Rebecca could do was nod.

Matt ran his hand along the edge of a drawer. If it didn't slide smoothly, it would be a reflection on his work. He'd come straight into the workshop when he'd arrived, not so much as letting himself glance toward the farmhouse. But his restraint didn't seem to be doing him any good. The feelings he'd discovered he had for Rebecca were growing stronger without any encouragement at all.

Any relationship with Rebecca was out of the question. She was still mourning Paul, who'd quite clearly been the only man in the world for her.

As for him . . . well, he knew how tenuous a grasp he had on being truly Amish in his heart. His reckless temper was still likely to flare up just when he thought he'd beaten it down. The last man Rebecca needed was someone like him.

He tossed aside the cloth he'd picked up to rub down the finish on the chest, wincing at the word his mind had chosen to describe his battles with his temper. *Beaten.* Even in his thoughts, he used images that were not Amish. If a man did not embrace nonviolence in his heart, how could he live in peace? And if he did not live in peace, how could he call himself Amish?

Feeling the dark memories rise, he stalked to the doorway and stood looking out at the late-afternoon sun. The time he'd spent in jail had given him a need to feel the breeze on his skin frequently. If that experience hadn't taught him the need to conquer his impulses, what would?

He'd fled back to the Amish community afterward, seeking refuge where violence had no place. He'd found a commitment he hadn't known when he was a restless teenager, eager to taste all the world had to offer. But until he could be sure, beyond a doubt, he couldn't—

A sound cut off his fruitless train of thought, and he frowned. Maybe the kinder shouting while they were playing? He took a step or two clear of the stable so that he could look back toward the house and the fields beyond.

No one was in view but Rebecca's daad, James Lapp, heading toward the house. Even as Matt began to turn away, he registered something odd about the man's pace. He looked almost as if he were stumbling. Then, slowly, the lean figure crumpled to the ground.

Matt ran toward him, heart thumping, shouting for Rebecca. Where was Simon? He usually worked with his daad . . . either Simon or the next younger boy, Johnny. Matt shouted again and then saved his breath for running.

Matt skidded to a stop and dropped to his knees beside the figure. James's fingers dug into the grass, and he seemed to be trying to raise himself.

"Easy. Just lie still. Let me help you." Matt put his arms around James's shoulders, raising him just enough to see the man's face.

Concern tightened its grasp. James's lean face was ashen above his beard, the skin seeming drawn against the bones. His eyes flickered open and then closed again.

The door of the house slammed, and Matt heard Rebecca's running footsteps.

"Daadi!" She fell to her knees next to Matt, reaching for her father. "What's happened?"

"He's fainted, I think." Matt put his hand against James's skin, finding it clammy. Cold perspiration was soaking his hair. Apprehension growing, Matt felt for a pulse. It was weak, fluttering under his fingertips. "We'd better call for an ambulance."

He'd barely gotten the words out when Simon joined them, his face white. "What did you do?"

Matt's muscles tightened. Even in a crisis, Simon was determined to blame him.

"He might be having a heart attack," Matt said bluntly, and heard Rebecca's quick, indrawn breath. "Simon, go to the phone shanty. Call nine-one-one. Ask for the emergency squad to come immediately. Understand?"

The instant antagonism faded from Simon's face, and he looked very young and frightened. He nodded, then turned and sprinted away.

"What can we do?" Rebecca took her father's lax hand in both of hers. "There must be something."

"Maybe a blanket." Matt frowned, trying to remember what he'd heard about heart attacks. He didn't want to do the wrong thing, but it couldn't be a mistake to keep him warm.

"Right away." Rebecca scrambled to her feet and ran to the house. No sooner had she gone than the kinder appeared from the barn. They came running and stopped a few feet from their grandfather, faces white, looking very alike in their fear.

"Grossdaadi." Katie's eyes filled with tears, and she looked to Matt as if begging for assurance.

"He's sick," Matt said quickly, not knowing what else to say. "Katie, do you think you could run to his house and get your grandmother?"

She seemed able to fight back tears at the prospect of helping. "I'll get her." She took off running, the strings of her kapp flying behind her.

"Can't I help?" Josh stepped cautiously around his grandfather and squatted next to Matt. "Please?"

"Mammi went to get a blanket. Can you run and tell her to bring a pillow, too?" It was better for the boy to be doing anything other than staying here and staring at his grossdaadi's ashen face.

Josh nodded. He touched his grandfather's hand with a quick, light movement and then raced off.

"Hang on, James." Matt felt again for a pulse. Weak, but there.

"They are on their way." Simon, breathing heavily, slumped down next to his father. "It's not far—only about five miles. They'll get here soon. They'll be in time."

Simon was trying to convince himself, Matt knew.

"That's certain-sure." He looked up as Rebecca reappeared, arms filled with a blanket. Behind her Joshua scurried along, carrying a pillow snatched from someone's bed.

"Help me lift him a little to get the blanket under him. No use his lying on the damp ground."

Simon nodded, sliding strong young arms under his father. Together they raised James enough that Rebecca could slip the blanket underneath. They eased him back down, and she wrapped it snugly around his body, tucking it in as if she were tucking one of her kinder in for the night.

"Here's the pillow." Joshua, his eyes wide in a pale face, passed it over, and his uncle pushed it into place.

Rebecca tore her attention away from her father long enough to glance around. "Where's Katie?"

"I sent her for your mother." He hesitated. Rebecca probably thought he was taking too much on himself, telling everyone what to do. "She wanted to help."

"That's gut." Rebecca's gaze clouded. "Poor Mammi. She'll be so worried. If only Daadi could say something . . ." Her voice broke.

"He's going to be all right." Matt tried to put some confidence in his voice. They were the words people always said at moments like this, expressing the thought that was surely the last thing they could guarantee.

Rebecca nodded. She took her father's hand again, her head bowing, and Matt thought she was praying.

It seemed like hours, but it was only minutes before they heard the wail of the siren. Rebecca's mother arrived at the same time as the paramedics. She was shaken, but in control of herself.

"Your grossmammi is at the house, so I asked Katie to stay with her," she said in answer to a questioning glance from Rebecca. "I thought it best for both of them."

Rebecca nodded. Grossmammi probably wanted to be with her son, but the stress wouldn't be good for her. And Mammi had no doubt persuaded both Grossmammi and Katie that they needed to take care of the other one.

The paramedics took over, moving everyone else away, conversing in low voices and using phrases that made little sense to anyone else. Matt took a step or two away from the family, feeling he was out of place and yet not wanting to leave in case he could be of some help.

The EMTs talked with the hospital. An Englisch neighbor pulled in, drawn by the siren, eager to drive anyone wherever needed. Finally James seemed to be communicating, answering something the paramedic asked. Matt, looking on, discovered that Joshua was clutching his leg.

He put his hand on the boy's shoulder. "They're taking good care of him." It was impossible to say "Don't worry," since this was a child who'd lost his father already.

Josh nodded, pressing closer, as if he was comforted by Matt's touch.

Finally the paramedics prepared to load James into their van. Rebecca hurried over to Matt. "Mamm is going with Daad in the ambulance. Mrs. Johnson has said she'll drive me and Simon." Her gaze touched Joshua, and she tried to smile. "Maybe Josh can go—"

"Let Josh stay with me." The offer came quickly, without thought. "We can work on a project together until you get back."

"I don't know when it will be." She seemed torn between acceptance and doubt.

"It doesn't matter. We'll be fine."

Josh nodded. "I want to stay with Matt. We'll be fine," he echoed. "Take care of Grossdaadi, Mammi."

"I will." She touched her son's cheek, smiling. Then she looked at Matt, and the smile trembled a bit. "Denke, Matt. I . . . I don't know what we would have done without you."

All he could do was nod, and smile, and pretend her pain didn't wrench his heart.

Rebecca felt as if they'd been sitting in the hospital's emergency room waiting area for hours. She glanced at the large round clock on the wall above the uncomfortable plastic chairs, sure it must be later than the time it showed.

Mamm sat next to her, her hands clasped together in her lap, her head lowered, while Simon paced to the window and back again. At a look from Rebecca he sat down, but almost immediately he stood up again. Rebecca recognized the symptoms. When a situation was out of his control, Simon could never be still.

"Why don't you go and get some coffee for us?" she suggested. "The snack bar is just down the hall." She remembered it only too well from all the times she'd been at the hospital with Paul.

Amy Johnson, who'd been waiting patiently all this time,

grasped her handbag. "I'll go along with Simon and help carry the coffees."

Simon nodded, obviously relieved to have an excuse to move. He set off so quickly Amy had to hurry to keep up.

Rebecca put her hand over her mother's clasped ones and found them icy. "Daad is strong, ain't so?" She wanted to say he'd be all right, but she was almost afraid to use those words. How many times had she told herself that about Paul?

Mamm nodded. "If only they'd let us stay with him. I could keep him from fretting if they had."

"I know." They'd been allowed to stay with Daad for only a few minutes in the curtained cubicle before he'd been whisked off for tests. "But the ER doctor said he had to have the test results right away. And they sent for Dr. Cartwright. You'll feel better when he's here."

Their family doctor had seen them through so much. Many of his patients were Amish, and he understood them. Mamm needed that understanding now.

They both looked up at the sound of a door opening. Bishop Jonah Stoltzfus came in, his white beard ruffled from the breeze, his kind, wise eyes searching for them. Behind him was Onkel William, her father's brother, without the smile that always seemed to crinkle his eyes.

Mamm rose to greet them, pressing her lips together as if she feared she'd cry if she spoke. Rebecca stood as well, clasping her mother's arm.

"I'm sehr glad you're here." Rebecca couldn't manage a smile. "We don't know anything yet," she added quickly, knowing they'd ask. "Daad is having tests."

"Sit, sit." Onkel William urged her mother back into her

seat and sank down himself in the chair Simon had vacated, planting his hands on his knees. "Someone said it might be a heart attack."

Rebecca, pulling another chair over for Bishop Jonah, gave him a warning look. "We don't know yet."

"How did it happen? Was he by himself?" Her uncle always wanted to know all the facts.

"He'd been in the barn with the kinder, and for some reason he'd started toward the house without them. Maybe he was feeling ill and didn't want them to know." That would be like him. He'd understand how frightening it would be for them.

"He didn't say anything to you?"

She shook her head. "Matt . . . Matthew Byler . . . had come out of the workshop just then and saw him fall." She relived those awful moments when she'd heard Matt shouting for her. "If he hadn't been there—" She stopped, not wanting to go on.

"God puts all of us where He wants us," Bishop Jonah said, his deep voice confident.

"We sent for the paramedics at once, and they were there in minutes. That's gut, ja?" She looked from Onkel William to the bishop, longing for reassurance.

"That's certain-sure." Onkel William's voice was an echo of its usual hearty tone. "The sooner the better, ain't so?"

"The good Lord put Matthew in the right place," Bishop Jonah said again. He patted her hand, seeming to know how much she needed to be comforted. "All we can do now is pray and wait."

Onkel William nodded, even though he looked as if waiting

wasn't suited to him. Like her brother, he preferred action. "Your aunt Miriam and cousin Judith have gone over to the house to fix supper and look out for the kinder. And the boys will make sure the animals are taken care of."

Rebecca knew it was all happening just as he said. Even without seeing it, she could be sure that neighbors had rushed to help as soon as they'd heard the news. The chores would be done, the children would be cared for, and no one would expect to be thanked. Grossmammi was probably already surrounded by women ready to do whatever was needed, and Katie no doubt was being kept busy.

As for Joshua . . .

Maybe she shouldn't have accepted Matt's help. He had other things to do than look after a small boy. But Josh had clearly been leaning on him, and she hadn't doubted for a minute that Matt meant the offer. He'd been so kind to all of them, even Katie, who'd made no secret of her resentment.

Simon returned, causing a little stir in the room as he nearly dropped the container that held three cups. Amy, behind him, moved quickly to rescue it. Before anyone could speak, Simon nodded toward the man who'd just come through the treatment room door.

Dr. Cartwright wore his usual flannel shirt and jeans with a white jacket slipped over them. With his longish, graying hair, his casual clothes, and his relaxed manner, he might have been a local farmer instead of a doctor.

He reached Rebecca's mother as she rose from her chair, a painful question clear on her face. He took both her hands in his.

"Now, Sarah, take it easy. You know James won't like it if you're upset." His swift glance swept the rest of them, lingering for a moment on Rebecca as if assessing her condition. "He's resting comfortably now, and you can see him in a few minutes."

"His heart . . ." Mamm began, her voice fading.

"Yes, it was a heart attack, but a fairly mild one. And you did everything right, getting the paramedics there so quickly. Too often people wait, thinking it's not serious enough to call. That's when things can go bad in a hurry."

"But he'll be all right?" Mamm clung to the only important part of what he'd said, at least for her.

"As far as I can tell, he will. We're going to keep him for a few days, and then I'll be giving him some strict instructions about what to do and what not to do." He smiled. "He won't like me telling him he can't work like a twenty-year-old any longer, will he?"

Onkel William blew out a relieved breath. "No, that he won't. Sarah will have to make him behave himself, that's certain-sure."

"We'll do just as you say." Mamm still clutched Dr. Cartwright's hands, but Rebecca thought some of the strain had left her face. "Can I see him now?"

"We'll go up together." Again the doctor glanced at them. "You can all come along and have a peek, but I don't want him excited by having too many people at once."

They made a little parade, it seemed to Rebecca, following Dr. Cartwright down the hall to the elevator. Just before they reached it, Aunt Anna, her mother's sister, came scurrying in from outside. Mamm went into her sister's arms with a little cry, and Rebecca met her aunt's gaze over Mamm's head.

"We're just going up to see him now," she explained quickly.

Aunt Anna nodded. "Komm now, Sarah, don't you be crying. You don't want to show James red eyes, do you?"

Rebecca couldn't help a smile. It always amused her to hear the two sisters squabbling and bossing each other as if they were ten-year-olds, but she could count on Aunt Anna's sound common sense in a situation like this one.

By the time they approached the hospital room, Aunt Anna had everyone straightened out. Almost without Rebecca realizing how it had happened, it had been decided that she'd go into the room just long enough to see Daad, and then she'd head off home to take care of her children.

". . . and Simon can stay here, in case we need to send him to make any phone calls or take messages. Otherwise, Sarah is all the company James needs, and I'm all the company my sister needs." Aunt Anna, always the dominant one of the sisters, laid down the law and no one, up to and including the bishop, was inclined to argue.

Mamm and Aunt Anna went into the room with the doctor. Rebecca had a quick glimpse of shiny tile floor and the metal base of a hospital bed before the door swung shut again.

Not much, but it was enough to send her mind spiraling backward—back to Paul, back to hours spent in rooms like that one, back to praying and hoping and trying to sound encouraging no matter what.

She must have swayed a little, because Bishop Jonah took a firm grasp on her arm.

"Your aunt is right." His tone was kind but firm. "Your place is at home with your kinder. Promise me you'll let Mrs. Johnson take you home as soon as you've said good night to your daad."

Her throat was too tight to speak, but she nodded.

"Gut. I know you will be sensible."

But whether he felt sure of it or not, he continued to keep a firm grip on her arm until it was time for Rebecca to go into the hospital room.

She should have been prepared. She'd seen this sort of scene plenty of times, but it was still a shock when it was Daadi, always so big and strong, lying flat on his back, attached to machines on either side of the high bed.

His face was turned away. Was he asleep? She touched his hand. "Daadi?"

At once he turned toward her. Despite the hospital gown, the apparatus, the sounds and smells of the place, it was just Daad. His fingers moved against hers.

"Don't worry." His voice was a hoarse whisper. "I'm not done yet."

"Don't try to talk." She smoothed the blanket over him. "Just rest. Everything is going to be fine."

"Rest," he murmured, and his eyes drifted closed.

She should leave, so Simon could come in. She should go home to the children. But all she could do was stand there, holding her father's hand, and fight back tears.

Daad had been carrying such a heavy burden ever since Paul got sick. He had been her rock, and she'd turned to him for everything. Was it any wonder that even his generous heart couldn't keep up with the strain?

No more. She made a silent promise. She would not be a little girl relying on Daadi. She no longer had a choice. She'd been telling herself for months that she had to take control of her own life and her children's future. She had to make good on those words before anyone else had to pay the penalty.

CHAPTER ELEVEN

Lancaster County, April 1942

*A*nna moved along the plowed row of fresh-turned earth, pushing the wheel that dropped the corn seed in and pressing the soil over it. The wheel slipped on the loose earth, and she straightened it. Seth was always saying Daad should get one of the horse-drawn planters, but Daad clung to the older method of planting the corn.

The spring day was chilly, with a bite in the breeze, but her father had been impatient to get the seed in the ground. Impatience seemed to be affecting everyone these days. She glanced at the next row, where Seth was doing the same thing she was, but with scant attention. His every movement was jerky, as if he struggled with something more than just the planter.

Not that she was much better herself. All the worry about Jacob and the conscription letter had her feeling constantly on the verge of tears.

"Was ist letz?" Seth murmured the words, low enough that

Daadi, occupied with the plow and team of mules at the far end of the field, wouldn't notice.

"I was just going to ask you the same thing." She pressed dirt over the seeds with her foot. "What's wrong?"

"I asked you first." Her brother gave her the quick, mischievous grin that made him look about six again.

Anna was so glad to see it that she hated to answer, knowing that to refer to the war was to banish any amusement from Seth's heart. "I was thinking about Jacob." Her throat seemed to close on the words.

Seth stared down at the row, his face hidden. "What has he done about the draft?"

Draft. It seemed a funny word to use for calling a man into military service, but there was nothing funny about the situation.

"The bishop talked with him and his mamm and daad. There was a letter he had to write and a form declaring that he could not serve in the military because of his religious beliefs. And the bishop had to write something as well."

Seth moved his shoulders restlessly and stamped down so hard on a seed that it would probably never come up. "What gut is that going to do? It didn't help in the last war. People went to the army or to prison."

A chill gripped her heart, and Anna fought against it. "The bishop says everything is different now. Jacob might be allowed to stay and work on the farm. After all, growing food is important."

"Not likely," Seth grunted.

She wouldn't let Seth's attitude destroy her faint hope. "If not, he says the peace churches are setting up special camps for those who can't serve in the military to do other things for the good of the country. He might be sent to one of those."

"Or he might be sent to an army camp." Seth's gaze met hers, and he flushed. "Sorry, Anna. I just—"

"You are upset, like everyone else. Jacob says we must hope and pray for the best."

"The army needs men. The war is going badly." Seth sent a cautious glance toward Daad, probably to make sure he was well out of earshot.

"You don't know that for sure." The best thing for everyone would be if this war were over quickly. "You know what Daad feels about listening to talk about the war."

"I hear anyway from my friends, whether Daad likes it or not. They say a whole group of nurses from Australia was shot in the Pacific. And hundreds, maybe thousands of soldiers and just ordinary people were captured. Bombs are killing children while they sleep."

His words were like weapons, wounding her. "It is dreadful," she said. "Wicked. But at least it's not here."

"It could be." Seth's face hardened into that of someone she didn't know. "I heard German subs were going to attack American ships right off the coast."

"There's nothing we can do," she protested. "We live separate from the world, ain't so?"

"I don't think we can stay separate, not with everything that's going on." Seth frowned down at the plowed row, but he didn't seem to be seeing it. "Some of my friends are joining up."

Her heart gave a little thud. "Englisch friends," she said quickly.

"Amish, too. Thinking about it, anyway."

She stared at him, her shocked mind taking it in. "You mean you are thinking about it. Seth, you must not."

"Why not?" His eyes flashed defiance. "Everybody my age is going, one way or another. I might as well join before they drag me off."

"But you can't." She'd thought they'd already experienced the worst that could happen, but bad things just kept coming. "You can't become a soldier. You can't lift your hand in violence against another person. We are to forgive. To turn the other cheek. Not to take up a gun and shoot someone."

"This is different," he said, his voice passionate. "Think of all the innocent people who are being killed, Anna. It can't be wrong to try and stop the enemy from doing it."

"But not by violence. That's what our history teaches us. We have always believed in nonviolence, no matter the cost. Think of the martyrs who sacrificed themselves instead of fighting back."

Seth had been raised on those stories, just as she had. Surely he couldn't forget them so easily.

"It's one thing to sacrifice yourself. What if it means letting somebody else be killed?" Seth had given up even the pretense of planting. He stood, frowning and intent, and stared at her. "If someone tried to harm you, don't you think I'd stop them?"

His passionate conviction confused her, and she couldn't find an answer, even though she felt sure he was wrong. "But . . . even so, we're doing something positive. We're raising food. People have to eat, whether there's a war or not. Already folks are saying there will be shortages."

Seth waved that argument away with a choppy gesture. "I'm

telling you we won't have a choice about serving. They'll take us, one way or another. I might as well join up like the other guys. At least maybe I'd be with people I know."

"You can't." She grasped for something that would deter him. "Daad won't let you."

"I'm old enough. I don't need Daad's permission."

"Seth—" She was failing. Her brother was slipping away from her, and she couldn't stop him.

"Hush," he said in a sharp whisper. "Daad's coming." His gaze pinned hers. "Don't tell, Anna. I trusted you. Promise."

She didn't want to promise. She wanted to put the whole problem on Daad's shoulders. But if she told now, Seth would never talk to her about it again, and she might still be able to convince him to take a different path.

Finally she nodded. What else could she do? At any cost, she must talk Seth out of doing something so irrevocable. If he joined the military . . . Well, even if he survived the fighting, it wouldn't change the outcome. He would never be able to come home again.

Matt hadn't seen Rebecca for several days, with all of his news about how her father was mending coming from the always-active Amish grapevine. But now, as he drew up at the workshop, he spotted her in the backyard, taking laundry from the line.

For a moment he hesitated, frowning. Still, it was natural enough to ask about her father, wasn't it? Not letting himself probe too deeply about why he wanted to see her, he strode briskly toward her.

Rebecca dropped a folded sheet into her basket and straightened, smiling at him. "Matt. Have you heard the news? Daad is coming home tomorrow."

"That is wonderful gut." And it was even better that the stress had vanished, at least for the moment, from her face. "Your mamm will be glad to have him home, ain't so?"

Rebecca's eyes sparkled with laughter. "You should hear her. She has memorized all the restrictions the doctor has put on him, and he won't dare put a foot out of line."

"I hear your grossmammi moved in, too. Is that right?"

Rebecca nodded. "She kept delaying and delaying until this happened. I think now she feels that she's needed, so she didn't make any more fuss about it. My cousins moved her in yesterday, and to talk to her you'd think she's been living there for years."

"I guess she is needed. Between your mamm and your grossmammi, your daad will have to behave." He could imagine just how much James Lapp was going to enjoy having them hover over him.

Rebecca nodded, the amusement fading from her green eyes. "I'm just so thankful you were here that day and—"

"You thanked me already," he said, cutting her off. "There's no need to say it again."

"I was so upset I don't know what I said." She shivered, even though she couldn't be cold standing in the warm sunshine. "The doctor mentioned how fortunate it was that you spotted him right away and knew what to do."

"You'd have managed fine if I hadn't been here." Her gratitude made him vaguely uneasy. So what if he'd done a good deed? It didn't cancel out all the wrongs he'd done in his life.

Rebecca seemed to consider his words, her face tightening. "I would have to. I will have to."

Matt frowned, wondering what was going on behind that somber expression. "No need to worry about it now. It was scary, that's for sure, but your daad is going to be all right. That's the important thing."

Rebecca shook her head slightly, as if shaking off the comfort he offered. "He's been doing too much. Ever since Paul got sick, he's been carrying the load of both farms, and I've leaned on him so."

She turned away, snatching a pillowcase off the line with a jerk that sent the clothespins flying. She was hiding her face from him, he suspected, not wanting him to see how upset she was.

What could he say? She might be right that all the work and worry had precipitated James's health problems, but what else could he have done in the circumstances?

"Komm, Rebecca. Think about it. How could you have stopped your daad from helping when Paul was sick? You could no more do that than you could stop the sun from setting."

For a moment all he could see was the curve of her cheek and the downward sweep of her eyelashes. Then she turned back to face him.

"I know." She gave a little sigh. "He kept saying it was no harder to grow twice the number of fields in corn and cabbage and pumpkins, and the boys helped with our two milk cows and the buggy horses and chickens. We all did what we had to then. But now—now I should be standing on my own, not still leaning on him."

Matt studied her face, trying to understand. "I don't think he'd agree with you."

"Probably not." She managed a slight smile. "But this time we have to take care of him. And I must find a way to make a success of the farm-stay."

She didn't sound optimistic about it, and based on what little he'd heard from her first guests, maybe she had a right to be concerned.

"Are you sure that's what you want to do?"

She looked surprised. "Of course. It was always our dream."

He was getting onto dangerous ground, but he couldn't seem to help himself. "Don't you mean it was Paul's dream?"

She blinked. "Well, ja, but—"

"That doesn't mean it has to be yours," he pointed out.

She didn't speak for a long moment. Then she shrugged. "My grandmother says that, as well. But it has to be. I have the children to support, a mortgage to pay off, and I can't keep relying on my daad."

Matt thought again of what her first guests had revealed. "Maybe you could find some other way."

Rebecca shook her head. "You're thinking I'm not very gut at running the farm-stay, ain't so?"

"I didn't say that."

"You were thinking it." Her voice was tart. "Maybe I'm not—some parts of it, at least. But I either have to learn how to be or find someone else to help me with it."

She had a determination that had been completely lacking in the little girl he remembered, but he'd long since stopped thinking of Rebecca as a little girl. She was a woman, and a stronger one than perhaps even she realized.

"Whatever you decide," he said carefully, "it's not wrong to accept help when it's offered. If you need anything from me—"

"No, denke," she said quickly. "You have your own business to run. And I have mine."

That sounded final. And it was probably just as well. Hadn't he just been telling himself that Rebecca didn't need someone like him?

Rebecca still wasn't sure she was doing the right thing in inviting her cousin Barbara to help with running the farm-stay. Even as she drew up at the hitching rail alongside the Schultz sisters' bakery in town, Rebecca was scouring her thoughts for another solution.

She couldn't come up with one. As her grandmother had said, if she wasn't good at one aspect of running the business, it made sense to enlist someone who was. And given that was the case, who else was there but her cousin Barbie? Rebecca couldn't think of another soul who would be good at it, who would be free to do it, and most important, who would not expect a fancy salary.

The mare waited patiently at the railing, no doubt wondering why Rebecca was still sitting in the buggy. With a quick shake of her head, Rebecca slid down. She had to make a move. She had a whole family booked for the weekend—parents, grandparents, and two children. Her palms grew damp at the thought of coping with all six on her own. Barbie, whatever her faults, was her best hope.

Walking quickly around to the front of the building, Rebecca paused for a moment on the sidewalk leading to the shop. You couldn't really call Brook Hill a town, since it was hardly more than a village. When the Amish had begun moving from Lancaster County into the hills and valleys of central Pennsylvania fifty years ago, the town had been a collection of houses with a name that referred to the whole area, including the outlying farms.

Nestled in the creek valley between two wooded ridges, it hadn't grown all that much since then; a few businesses mingled with the houses along the street, and there was a school and a post office down a ways. If people wanted to do any serious shopping, they went elsewhere. Still, folks knew one another here and felt at home.

Rebecca pulled open the glass-paneled door and stepped into Two Sisters Bakery, inhaling the scents of baking bread and brewing coffee. Even though the two Amish sisters considered that they operated a bakery, not a restaurant, this was still a popular gathering place, especially in the morning when the small round tables would be filled with folks sharing the latest gossip over their coffee and crullers. Barbie worked a few early hours on weekdays whenever the sisters needed her.

By now, the busy time had ended. Only a pair of elderly Englisch men sat at the table in the front corner, and they were a familiar fixture. Widowers, both of them, and according to Ruth, the older of the Schultz sisters, if those two didn't get out and see folks once a day, they'd probably shrivel up and blow away.

Rebecca nodded when the men turned and waved to her but she went on to the counter, knowing that if she stopped, Ed and Ben would be capable of bending her ear for the next hour, at least.

"Rebecca." Barbie straightened from sliding a tray of streusel muffins into the glass case. Her rosy cheeks were flushed still more by the warmth of the shop, and the all-enveloping white apron was tied snugly enough to show off her slim figure. "I'm surprised to see you in town this early. Doing your grocery shopping?"

"Not exactly." Rebecca took a breath. Just do it. "Actually, I wanted to have a chat with you. Do you think Ruth and Susie would mind if we had a cup of coffee and talked?"

"No problem," she said, using the Englisch slang that Rebecca knew annoyed her father. "I'll just pop my head in the kitchen and let them know."

Barbie was back in an instant, looking pleased—probably at the idea of a break in the day's routine. "Coffee for two." She poured as she spoke. "And Ruth says to try her apple cinnamon coffee cake."

"I shouldn't . . ." Rebecca began, but let the words fade as Barbie pulled two wedges of coffee cake from the case. The cake did look delicious, and it had been a long time since she'd had breakfast.

"There we are." Barbie plopped everything on a tray and led Rebecca to a table in the rear. She grinned as she set the tray down. "If we keep to Deutsch, those two won't be able to listen in."

That was the sort of pertness that made Rebecca wonder whether Barbie was really suitable to the task she had in mind. There isn't anyone else, she reminded herself.

She took the coffee mug and added sugar, stirring unnecessarily long.

Barbie didn't wait. "How is your daad? I hear he's doing better."

"He's happier now that he's home, that's certain-sure. Mamm and Grossmammi are fussing over him, and he likes sleeping in his own bed. But it'll be a job to keep him from doing things he shouldn't."

"They'll gang up on him," Barbie said. "I'm glad we finished up at Grossmammi's house before this happened." She shrugged, wrinkling her nose a little. "But things are back to being boring now."

It seemed to Rebecca that Barbie too easily lost interest. She could only hope that if Barbie agreed to her proposition, she wouldn't become dissatisfied with the farm-stay after a few weeks.

"You know I started having guests at the farm last weekend?"

Of course Barbie would know. Everyone knew. If she sneezed now, six people would offer her cold remedies before the day was over.

"Ja, I heard. How did it go?" Barbie's gaze evaded hers, which might mean she already knew the answer to her question.

"Not too bad. Simon took over showing them the outside work, and I think he enjoyed it once he got started." Her younger brother had been surprisingly competent, in fact. "But I found . . ." She hesitated, still not sure how to put it. "The truth of it is, I'm just not very gut at talking to the Englisch. You know, making them feel at home and telling them about our ways."

A spark of interest lit Barbie's eyes. "It doesn't sound hard to me. I talk to Englisch folks every morning here. They're just like us."

"For you, maybe," Rebecca said. "Not for me. Anyway, that's what I wanted to talk to you about. Do you think you'd like to work with me on the weekends I have guests?"

"Me?" Barbie's eyes widened. "You want me?"

"Why not?"

Barbie grinned. "I didn't think you approved of me."

Rebecca suspected she flushed, despite her best efforts. She hadn't realized that Barbie had picked up on her feelings.

"I think you have just the personality to greet the guests and keep them happy. I can manage getting the rooms ready and doing the meals, and Simon will do as much as he can outside. Of course, with Daad not well . . ."

How much time would Simon have to spare for her? He wouldn't want to let her down, but Daad's illness placed an extra burden on the boys.

"That's not a problem." Barbie's face lit up. "I'd guess there's nothing Simon does that I can't do. And I'd love to be sort of a hostess. That's what you want, isn't it? I can do it. How soon can I start?"

Barbie's enthusiasm bubbled. Energy radiated from her so strongly that Rebecca wouldn't have been surprised if she'd shot out of her chair. She made Rebecca feel as old as the ridge above the town.

"I have a family of six coming on Friday for the weekend," she said. "If you can start then—"

"Of course I can."

"Maybe you should talk to your parents about it first,"

Rebecca cautioned, wondering what her aunt and uncle would think about the idea.

"They won't mind. After all, it's helping family, ain't so? And they'll be wonderful glad to have me busy. What do you have planned for the guests? Grown-ups or children? What things do they like to do?"

Rebecca held up her hand to stop the flow, feeling as if she were being swept away by the wind. "Wait, wait. We haven't even talked about what hours you'll have to work, or what you'll be paid, or anything. So long as I know you're interested, we can set up a time to make plans together."

"We can do it now. Please, Rebecca."

Barbie reminded Rebecca of Katie, trying to wheedle her into playing a game instead of getting on with the mending. "Not now. I've taken up enough of your time. You're supposed to be working for Ruth and Susie now, remember?"

"They won't care." Barbie wiped them away with a quick gesture.

"Well, I do. It would be wrong for me to take the time they're paying you for." She could only hope Barbie wouldn't have a similar attitude toward the work she was supposed to do with Rebecca's guests.

Barbie had the grace to look abashed. "Ach, you're right. I'll make sure I do everything here before I go. I promise. It's just that running a farm-stay is much more exciting than serving behind the counter. Don't you think so?" Without giving her time to answer, she swept on. "I have lots of ideas. I'll bet we can come up with all sorts of things for people to do at the farm. When can we meet?"

Barbie's enthusiasm reminded Rebecca irresistibly of Paul's

when they'd planned that first summer. What was it about the farm-stay that so appealed to them? And what was missing in her, that it seemed such a scary ordeal to her?

Matt's words seemed to echo in her thoughts. *Don't you mean it was Paul's dream? That doesn't mean it has to be yours.*

Was it her dream? She hauled her thoughts back to Barbie.

"Can you come out tomorrow after you get off work here? We can figure it out then."

"I'll be there." Barbie leaned forward, her whole body seeming to express her excitement at the idea. "I'll start making a list of all the things we can do with the guests. By tomorrow, I'll have dozens of ideas."

"I'm sure you will." There wasn't any doubt of that in Rebecca's mind.

What doubt there was went in exactly the opposite direction. Barbie's enthusiasm threatened to sweep the farm-stay program right out of Rebecca's hands.

Nonsense. The farm belonged to her. The business, such as it was, did as well. Barbie was only coming in to help.

But she couldn't keep from feeling that by inviting her cousin in, she was unleashing something she wouldn't be able to control.

Chapter Twelve

*M*att was earlier than usual in getting over to his work-shop, but the fact didn't especially please him. He was only arriving in midafternoon because Onkel Silas had given up. Matt couldn't think of another expression that fit, no matter how he tried.

The mare trotted toward the lane at Rebecca's place, so used to it now that he hardly needed to touch the lines. He frowned at the road ahead between her ears, seeing instead the day's fiasco.

He and Onkel Silas had gone over to the new development on Bentley Road to talk to a homeowner about a job. The houses all seemed alike to him, sitting back from the streets with manicured lawns in front of them, surrounded by tidily mulched shrubs instead of the overflowing flower beds of an Amish home.

The house they'd visited had seemed plenty big enough for the two people living there, but Mrs. Hansen wanted a sunroom added on the back. It would be a well-paying job, Matt thought, especially since the couple seemed to have more money than they knew what to do with.

Their visit was intended to view the site, take measurements, find out what the homeowner wanted, and then go home and work up a bid on the job. It was the sort of thing Onkel Silas had done more times than Matt could imagine, and he was a pro at it.

Until today. Today Silas had been so distracted that he'd commented almost at random about the project, barely making a note. Finally Matt had taken the notebook from his hands and started asking the necessary questions.

He'd half expected Onkel Silas to snatch the notebook back, but not even that served to rouse him. He'd followed Matt and the Hansen couple around the house, sunk so deep in his distraction that Matt suspected he barely heard a word.

It wasn't hard to figure out the reason. After all, Matt's bedroom was right across the hall from the one belonging to his aunt and uncle. He'd heard his aunt crying in the night, heard his uncle trying vainly to comfort her. The sounds had broken his heart.

How could Isaiah disappear this way? Anger rose, and Matt's hands tightened on the lines so that the mare turned her head in reproach. If Isaiah didn't want to come back, that was one thing. Matt could hardly quarrel, since he'd done the same himself. But to cut off contact with his family so completely—that wasn't acceptable, no matter how much Isaiah thought he was going to find happiness by jumping the fence.

Happiness. Matt's jaw tightened, but he kept his hands light on the lines with an effort as the buggy turned into the lane to the workshop. Amish parents didn't consider that happiness was a suitable goal for their children, and he'd begun to understand that for himself. A person didn't find happiness by looking for it. If it came, it was a by-product of something else entirely—a good marriage, maybe, or a job well-done, or the knowledge that you were living the way God intended.

Well, wherever Isaiah had gone and why, he had no right cutting off his family. Maybe it was time somebody found him and told him so.

Sliding down from the buggy, Matt let his gaze travel across the fields behind the farmhouse. Simon was the person he needed to question, and he couldn't put it off any longer. If anyone could give him a clue to where Isaiah had gone, it might be Simon, assuming his cousin Sadie had been speaking the truth. It was time he and Simon had a little talk.

And sure enough, there was Simon at the edge of the cornfield. It looked as if he was mending a fence. Matt set off toward him, not giving himself time to change his mind.

The path led along the pasture, already green and lush from the spring rains and the warm sunshine. A wave of nostalgia swept over Matt as the scent of it rose to meet him. Funny, how a smell could take a person back. He might have been walking through the fields on his daad's farm, either the one here in the valley where Matt and his siblings had grown up or the one in Indiana.

The Amish settlement in Indiana had seemed very different from the Pennsylvania valleys. Acreage there was flatter and easier to cultivate, cheaper besides. Still, he'd missed the narrow valleys and wooded ridges he'd grown up with, even if he hadn't realized it at the time. The reckless teenager he'd been hadn't slowed down long enough to know what he was feeling.

Simon must have been aware of Matt approaching him, but he didn't look up from the strand of barbed wire he was mending as Matt drew near.

"Deer getting into the corn, are they?" he asked as he came to a stop a few feet from Simon.

"Worse." Simon grunted out the word. "A bear ripped through here last night. Took the fence right out, and trampled his way through the corn."

Now that he looked, Matt could see the tracks. Fortunately the corn was only about a foot high, so it would probably recover from the mauling it had taken under the bear's broad feet.

Matt followed the trail with his gaze. It led right through the cornfield and on toward the trees beyond, where the land lifted toward the ridge.

"Probably going from the stream back up to the woods," he commented.

"Ja." Simon rose, giving Matt a frowning glance. "You didn't come here to talk about bears. What do you want?" The words were little short of rude.

Matt couldn't help tensing at the animosity coming off Rebecca's brother. *Rebecca's brother,* he reminded himself. He couldn't get into a quarrel with him.

"I hear you were close friends with my cousin Isaiah." He kept his tone easy. "I hoped I could talk to you about him."

Simon shrugged, avoiding his gaze. "We used to hang out. So what?"

"So I thought you might have some idea of where he went."

Simon's face seemed to close. "I don't know anything about it."

Matt wasn't about to be put off so easily. "You were friends. He must have talked about going away. About his plans for the future."

"No." The word came too quickly to be true, and it was accompanied by a glare. "Anyway, why should I tell you anything?"

"Because I'm his cousin. Because I want to find him, and you can help."

"Seems to me if I'm his friend, that's the last thing I'd do. If he wanted you to know, he'd have told you."

Matt tried to count to ten. He didn't make it. "You might want to think about his parents. They haven't heard a word from him."

"What do you care?" Simon's face darkened, and he clenched his fists. "You've already got what you wanted, ain't so? You took over Isaiah's place so fast, if he did want to come back, he couldn't."

"That's ridiculous." Matt's fragile control on his temper was fraying. "I'm just helping out until Isaiah returns. His daad can't carry on alone."

"Yeah, right." The words were contemptuous, and Simon swung away from him.

"I'm not finished." Matt grabbed his arm. "Wait—"

Simon twisted with an abrupt movement, trying to jerk his arm free. He swung his arm back, knocking Matt off balance.

Matt stumbled, tripped, and fell backward. His left hand, flying out, hit the barbed wire, and the wire tore his flesh.

Matt scrambled to get his feet under him, cradling his left hand in his right. Blood flowed from the jagged cut on his palm. Pain stung him.

If his hand was injured, he couldn't work. Fury ricocheted through him. He charged at Simon, his pulse pounding like a drum in his head.

"Matthew!" Rebecca's voice stopped him. Maybe it was the only thing that could. "What are you—" She stopped as she came even with them and saw the blood dripping from his hand.

"You're hurt." She grasped his wrist in a surprisingly strong grip and transferred her glare to her brother. "What is the matter with you? With both of you? Out here squabbling and fighting like a couple of kinder. I'm ashamed of you. What do you have to say for yourself, Simon Lapp?"

Simon managed to combine looking abashed and defensive. "It's not my fault—" he began.

"You were raising your hand in anger against a brother. I won't have it."

"But he—" Simon made a vain effort to stem the tide.

"Enough. I am ashamed of you. Think what Daad would say if he knew. But he's not going to, because I won't tell him. It would upset him to know, and that should make you feel even worse."

She interrupted her scolding to look down at Matt's hand even as a drop of his blood splashed on her dark blue apron. "What a mess." She tugged him. "Komm. We'll go into the kitchen and get you cleaned up."

"I don't need—" he began.

"Don't you start," she said tartly. "I've heard enough fool-ishness from my brother to last me all day. You'll get that cleaned and bandaged right now."

Matt had never heard Rebecca so assertive. Or so angry. She marched him toward the house as if he were Joshua's age, gripping his wrist the entire time.

Matt glanced back at Simon, who was studying his shoes, clearly not risking a look at his irate sister. *We're not finished,* he promised silently.

Once inside the house, Rebecca led him to the sink and turned the water on, letting it run cold over his palm. He was almost afraid to look at the cut. The pain wasn't important, but his livelihood was his hands. Without them, he couldn't help his uncle or himself, and his business would be over before it had begun.

Rebecca pressed a folded-up dish towel against his palm. One hand held the pad in place while the other still grasped his wrist, as if she feared he'd yank it away from her. They were as close as if they were about to embrace. The curve of her neck was inches away from him, and the scent of her diz-zied him for an instant.

No. He couldn't let himself feel anything, not when he'd just come so close to breaking all his promises and using vio-lence against another person. No use saying Simon had started it. If there was one thing he'd learned the hard way, it was that that excuse never helped when all was said and done. If you couldn't turn the other cheek to aggression, what kind of an Amish person were you?

Rebecca eased the pad away from the cut and inspected it. Blood still oozed sluggishly, but it wasn't as bad as he'd feared.

"That looks better than I thought," she said, echoing his thoughts. "Cuts to the hand do bleed badly. I don't think it will need stitches, but if you want to see a doctor—"

"Not unless I have to." His head swam as she looked up into his face, the movement bringing her lips perilously close to his.

Rebecca seemed to freeze for a moment, her gaze widening, her eyes growing darker. Awareness trembled in the air between them.

And then she was moving, pulling him away from the sink and pushing him into a chair at the kitchen table. She turned to the stove, speaking without looking at him. "Just hold the pad firmly against it. I'll get you some coffee, and we'll check the cut again once you've rested a few minutes."

"Ja, Doktor Rebecca." *Keep it light,* he cautioned himself.

"You mean I'm being bossy, ain't so?" She set a mug of coffee in front of him and pushed the sugar bowl within reach. "Women have to be bossy when grown men act like small boys. What were the two of you fussing about, anyway?"

He couldn't see any reason not to tell her. "I hoped that Simon might have some idea where Isaiah went when he left home. According to my cousin Sadie, they were always close friends growing up."

Frowning a little, Rebecca sat down in the chair across from him. "They were, I'd have said, but it seems to me that we hadn't seen as much of Isaiah in the weeks before he went away. I suppose he might have been hanging out more with Englisch friends, since he was thinking of leaving."

"You're probably right, but I have no idea who any of them were. Simon is my only hope of finding a lead to where Isaiah has gone."

She was silent for a long moment, still frowning just a little. "Maybe I can get something out of Simon after he calms down." Her green eyes flashed. "Your method certainly didn't do any good. Scrapping like a couple of kids on the playground. I thought better of you, Matthew."

I thought better of you. The words reverberated in his thoughts. Rebecca wasn't the first person to say that to him.

"You shouldn't." He ground the words out through the pain that had nothing to do with his hand. "You'll be better off if you expect the worst."

Rebecca stared at Matt's bent head for a long moment, turning his words over in her mind, unable to make sense of them.

"Why?" she said simply.

"Sorry," he muttered, looking down at his hand. "I shouldn't have said it. Forget it."

"I can't."

Realizing he hadn't touched his coffee, she dumped a spoonful of sugar into the cup and stirred. Sugar and caffeine seemed to help when someone had had a shock.

She urged the coffee mug into his left hand and scooted her chair closer so that she could hold the pad against the cut. Judging by the stubborn line of Matt's firm lips, she wasn't going to get an answer to her question, so she changed it to a different one.

"What made your talk with Simon turn into a fight?"

He shook his head, not looking at her. "Don't get involved, Rebecca."

"I am involved already." Her voice was resolute. "Something must have led up to this business." She gestured toward his hand. "I want to know what it is."

And she wanted to know why he thought so little of himself, but she'd have to work her way around to that question again.

"Tell me."

Rebecca considered grasping his wrist again, but the memory of those moments when she'd looked into his eyes and felt something she'd never expected to feel again—no, better not. They were close enough to each other as it was.

"Simon seemed to take offense at my trying to find out where Isaiah has gone." Matt's shoulders moved in the smallest of shrugs. "He seems to think I'm taking advantage of the situation, moving into Isaiah's place."

"That's ridiculous," she said sharply. From everything she'd seen, Matt would be just as happy to give Isaiah back his job, so that he could get on with his furniture-making. "And I'll tell him so. As for Isaiah . . . You mean his mamm and daad haven't heard from him?"

People left, jumped the fence, usually boys younger than Isaiah, but generally they were predictable about it. Their family had some notion, at least, where they were.

Matt was shaking his head. "Nothing at all, and they've no idea where he's gone. Apparently he left a note saying he wanted more than this life. They haven't received any word since. Aunt Lovina . . . well, you saw how she is."

Rebecca's heart hurt at the thought of poor, confused Lovina. "I know. She can't understand."

"She keeps searching for him." Matt stared bleakly into his

coffee. "I've tried telling her he's working away, but then she wants to know why he hasn't written. In the night I hear her weeping."

Her heart twisted in sympathy. "He should at least write. He should let them know he's safe, even if he doesn't want to come back."

"He should, but he hasn't."

Rebecca couldn't understand it. "Isaiah always seemed so . . . well, typical. At his age, everyone expected him to be getting baptized, joining the church, finding someone to marry. It's not as if he was a sixteen-year-old."

Matt looked at her then, and Rebecca could see the pain in his eyes. "Sadie says it's my fault. That he was copying me, just like he always did."

"That makes no sense at all," Rebecca said quickly. Not that it surprised her to hear Sadie was taking out her pain and worry on the nearest available person.

"She ought to know. They were always close."

Rebecca's lips tightened when she thought of her own recent experiences with Matt's cousin. "Sadie is too quick to blame everyone else when things go wrong. Think about it. You have been away from Isaiah for years. Any decision he made was formed recently, we both know it. You surely have more sense than to believe her."

Matt grimaced. "Sadie can be pretty convincing. And she knows I already have plenty of guilt where Isaiah is concerned."

"Why? How could you possibly . . ." She stopped, recalling nearly forgotten fragments of grown-up conversations.

"You remember." Matt studied her face.

She shook her head. "Only that there was something people talked about. I don't think I ever knew the rights of it."

"Your parents probably thought it wasn't suitable for you to hear."

Was it guilt or bitterness he felt? She wasn't sure. Maybe, if she treated it lightly, he'd go on.

"Kids do foolish things every day." She took the pad from his palm and studied the cut, not looking at him. "I don't suppose you were any more foolish than most."

"Foolish, maybe. But they don't all nearly cost someone's life."

"Isaiah's life?" she guessed. That was the only thing that seemed to account for his attitude.

When he didn't respond she rose, retrieved the first-aid box from the kitchen cabinet, and resumed her seat, trying not to betray too much curiosity.

He watched as she dealt with his hand, not wincing when she applied the antibiotic cream to the cut. She could sense the struggle in him. He wanted to talk; she was sure of it. But she shouldn't force his confidence.

Folding gauze into a thick pad allowed her to focus on the task. If he spoke, it would be his decision.

"Isaiah," Matt said heavily. "He was just a kid then. I was thirteen—old enough to be responsible, so my daad said. I took him fishing over at Miller's pond."

She nodded, fitting the pad over the cut. His hand, callused and strong, lay relaxed on the table. She forced herself to concentrate on the job, not on the warmth that radiated from him.

"Isaiah must have liked going someplace with his big cousin."

Matt's fingers twitched. "I guess he did. We were fishing down by the old dock. I don't know if it's still there."

"It fell down a couple of years ago," she said. "All for the best, since it was so rickety it was a danger."

"It was dangerous then, too. I let Isaiah sit on the end closest to the bank, where it was fairly stable. Told him we couldn't go farther out—it wasn't safe."

Rebecca risked a glance at his face. He seemed to be staring into the past, probably at two barefoot kids sitting on a dock with fishing poles on a summer day.

"Anyway, a couple of Englisch teenagers came by, looking to go fishing, too. Older than I was, with a cooler of beer and plans that didn't include sharing the spot with us."

Rebecca found she was visualizing the scene as he spoke, and she didn't have much trouble seeing what was coming next.

"So they told us to get out. Said this was their spot, we shouldn't be there, acting big. Isaiah . . . I don't know if he was afraid or not, but he wanted to go. I said no. I said we had just as much right to be there as they did." His fingers twitched again. "There was some pushing and shoving. I saw red. Lost my temper. Waded into the biggest guy with fists flying." His right hand curled into a fist as he spoke, his fingers closing over the bandage.

"Something happened to Isaiah," she said softly.

"Right in the middle of it I heard a cry, a splash—it was Isaiah. He'd gone clear out to the end of the dock, maybe trying to get away from the fighting. Backed into the railing, and it broke and went right into the pond with him." Matt's jaw was so tight it wondered her that he could manage the words.

"We had an awful time fishing him out. He was tangled up in the broken boards and the reeds. Muddy bottom, so you couldn't get a grip—" He was reliving those moments too strongly, and beads of sweat appeared at his hairline. "I thought he was dead when we pulled him to the bank."

"But he wasn't," she said gently, longing to comfort him but sure that words weren't enough. "Isaiah is fine."

"No thanks to me. It was my hot temper that nearly killed him." His gaze met hers. "You should know. You saw it in action just now. Every time I think I have my anger conquered, it crops up again."

"Everyone has some failing, Matthew. You're only human."

"Human, ja. But Amish?" He pulled away from her, smoothing down the tape she'd put over the bandage. "I left the faith because I thought I could never live up to our beliefs. And I came back because . . . well, because I thought it was safer. But even here—" He gestured with his injured hand. "You see what happens."

"Matt . . ." She felt so inadequate to deal with what he'd said. "You're not solely to blame for what happened. My brother bears an equal share of responsibility."

He only looked more stubborn. "He's still hardly more than a kid, for all he's doing a man's work. I'm older. I should be able to control myself."

"We're not meant to be perfect, Matt," she reminded him. "Not in this world. That will happen only in the next."

"Maybe." He stood, pushing his chair back, and his gaze focused on her face. "You're a kind person, Rebecca. But you'll be better off if you don't trust me. The Lord knows I don't trust myself."

Before she could find the words to reassure him, he'd swung away and strode out the door. Rebecca sat where he'd left her, turning the whole conversation over in her mind.

Safer. What had Matt meant when he said he thought it would be safer for him to return to the Amish? She didn't know, and she suspected he wasn't likely to tell her.

Lancaster County, May 1942

Anna stepped over the strawberry plants, eyes searching the thick green mat for a sparkle of red. Nothing ripe yet, it seemed, but it wouldn't be long. She stooped at the row of rhubarb and began to pull stalks, snipping off the fanlike leaves and dropping the ruby-red stalks into her basket. Maybe by concentrating really hard on what she was doing, she could keep her thoughts from running round and round after her worries.

All the rhubarb in the world couldn't do that, she feared. She waited daily for Jacob to learn his fate, praying and hoping and too afraid to talk about it. If only they'd let him stay here, where he belonged, and work the farm . . .

Her gaze caught on her daad and brother, hoeing weeds away from the rows of corn seedlings. Was Daad talking to Seth again about applying, as Jacob had, to be exempted from service because of his religion? He'd been pushing Seth to start the process. So far, Seth had managed to evade the prompting. He'd evaded her, too, each time she'd tried to renew their conversation about fighting.

She spun around at the sound of buggy wheels, spilling rhubarb from her basket. Jacob pulled to a stop, lifting a hand in greeting, and jumped down. By the time she'd gathered up the rhubarb, he was coming to meet her.

"Jacob. I'm wonderful glad to see you."

His answering smile didn't seem to reach his grave eyes, and a little chill settled on her.

"Will you take a walk with me, Anna?"

She nodded, her heart thudding. Had he heard something? She wanted to know, but she was afraid, as well. "Toward the woods or down to the creek?"

"The creek," he said, and fell into step with her. "Your mamm won't mind waiting for the rhubarb?"

She shook her head. "It's just a small batch for supper. Will you stay?"

"I can't." He was frowning, his gaze shadowed by the brim of his straw hat.

The fear bubbled up. He couldn't stay to eat. And he wanted to walk down by the creek, where the willow trees would hide them from view.

"Has Seth gotten his notice yet?" he asked.

"Not yet." She hesitated. "I suppose it will come soon. Daad has been trying to get him to start applying for exemption, but he won't."

What about you, Jacob? She shouldn't ask. She should let him tell her in his own way.

"Why not?" They were under the willows now, with the stream running smooth and high from the recent rain.

"Oh, Jacob, I'm afraid of what he might do. He hasn't talked to Daadi about it, but he spoke to me a little. He's thinking that maybe it's not wrong to go and fight if you're doing it to help other people. I'm so afraid that if he's drafted, he'll go in the army."

Jacob turned to face her, taking both her hands in his. "I'm sorry. I know how much it must worry you." He shook his head. "I guess every one of us has been tempted."

"Not you." Her voice wobbled a little. "You couldn't take up a gun against another person."

"I don't think I could." His clear blue eyes were troubled. "But sometimes I wonder if maybe I'm just a coward, not a pacifist."

"Ach, Jacob, how silly." The foolishness of it would make her laugh if the subject weren't so deadly serious. "I remember when that gelding my daad got at the auction started rearing and bucking and trying to kick the cart to pieces. Everyone else stood clear, but you jumped right in and grabbed its head. I was so scared, and you were as cool as can be."

"That's not the same." But there was the ghost of a smile on his face, and some of the tension had gone out of it.

"It is. If you're brave in one situation, you will be in another."

"My Anna, just being with you always makes me feel better. I will miss your sweet smile."

"Miss?" Her voice choked, and she knew the moment she'd been dreading had come.

"I got my orders." He was surprisingly calm about it. "I'm being sent to a Civilian Public Service camp to work for the duration of the war. So I won't have to find out if I could shoot at a person."

Anna told herself she should be relieved. She was relieved,

of course she was. At least he wouldn't be given a choice between the army and jail. But why couldn't they have let him stay here and work the farm?

She couldn't say that to him. She had to be brave, no matter what she felt inside. He was still clasping her hands, and she moved her fingers against his in a silent caress.

"Where?" She managed the word without letting a sob escape.

"I don't know yet. I'm to report in at Harrisburg, and then I'll be sent to the camp from there. They won't tell us anything about where it is except . . ."

"What?" Her heart twisted at his serious tone.

"It won't be anywhere nearby. Not even in the state. All the conscientious objectors are being sent to camps in a different state, the bishop says. Maybe the authorities are afraid we'd try to come home again if we're too close. Or maybe they think that if the Englisch boys have to go far away, we should, too."

"But that's not fair." Tears stung her eyes. "If you were closer, maybe we could come to see you, at least."

He blotted a tear from her cheek with the touch of his finger. "I'm sorry, Anna. I know it's hard on you."

The idea came, so quickly it might have been hiding there all along. She could hardly get the words out fast enough. "Jacob, we should get married before you leave. You talk to the bishop. I'll speak to Mamm and Daad—"

"No, Anna." She'd never heard him sound so stern. "We will not rush into a wedding that way. It's not fitting."

"But we could be together." Her cheeks flamed with what she was saying, but she meant it. If they could be together as husband and wife, even for a little while, it would be worth anything. Somehow, if they were married, she could find a way to bear this separation.

"No." He grasped her shoulders and gave her a little shake. "I love you, Anna Esch, but that is not the way to approach being united by God. Promise me you'll let it go."

The brief flare of hope died away. She wanted to argue, but she couldn't.

"I promise." She blinked rapidly to hold back the tears. "We'll wait. We'll wait until you come home to stay."

"Right." His voice was husky, and he cleared his throat. "I leave for Harrisburg on Friday morning."

"But . . . so soon?" It was Wednesday already, and Jacob would be gone in less than two days.

"I know." His face was bleak. "I must be on the bus in town at eight in the morning. If you come to see me off—"

"Of course I will be there." How could he think she wouldn't?

"Will you promise me something?"

He was looking at her with so much love shining in his eyes that she would promise anything. She nodded. "What?"

He lifted her hands to his lips and spoke against them. "Promise me you won't cry. Because if you cry, I will, too. So you must promise."

She struggled to produce a smile. "I promise." She wouldn't cry when she saw him off. But when he was gone . . . well, there would be plenty of time then to cry.

CHAPTER THIRTEEN

*R*ebecca snapped the gas off under the kettle, feeling as if she were beginning to boil herself. Hadn't they agreed that Barbie would come straight here after work? That should have been two hours ago. Rebecca had anticipated having plenty of time to talk before Katie got home from school.

But Katie was here, sitting at the table with Joshua having a snack, and talking a mile a minute about what they'd done in class today. Josh hung on her every word, fascinated.

"Mammi, when will I go to school?" he asked for probably the hundredth time, interrupting Katie, who was reciting a list of the spelling words she had to learn for Friday's quiz. "Soon?"

"You don't start school until September, Joshua. Remember when we looked at the calendar? Summer comes first, and then it will be time."

"I wish it was September now already," he said, his lower lip coming out.

"Soon enough." She tousled his hair, but she couldn't help joining in his longing.

By September, her first summer of running the farm-stay alone would be over. She'd know whether she could do it or not. Still, she couldn't help thinking of her mamm's comment each time she'd wished for something to happen more quickly.

Don't wish your life away, Mamm would say. Rebecca hadn't understood the words then, but she'd begun to. This moment, now, with the kinder sitting at the kitchen table, deserved her appreciation and her focus. She shouldn't waste it on worry about why Barbie hadn't arrived.

She heard the creak of a buggy and the sound of hooves on the dirt lane, and a second later the buggy, with Barbie on the high seat, passed her kitchen window and came to a halt at the back door.

"Somebody's here!" Katie jumped from her chair, her oatmeal cookies barely touched, and raced toward the porch with Josh close behind.

Rebecca wiped her hands on the dish towel and followed them. It would be impossible to make her disappointment known to Barbie with the two children looking on.

Jumping lightly down from the buggy seat, Barbie seemed impervious to the notion that she'd done anything wrong. She greeted Katie and Josh with a hug.

"You two are growing like weeds, ain't so?" She measured Katie against herself with the flat of her hand. "Soon you'll be as tall as me."

"I will, too," Joshua said instantly. "I will, Cousin Barbie."

"You'll be even taller before you're done," Barbie said.

She looked over their heads, still smiling, and saw Rebecca's stare.

Innocent blue eyes met Rebecca's gaze, the innocence replaced after a moment with a puzzled look.

"Go back in and finish your snack." Rebecca shooed the kinder toward the kitchen door. "Cousin Barbie and I need to talk."

She watched them until the door closed behind them and then turned back to Barbie. They'd have to have this issue out right now. How could Barbie possibly help her if she was this unreliable?

"What's going on?" Barbie's eyebrows lifted in a question. "You look as if you're ready to bite someone's head off. Mine, for instance."

"I thought we agreed you were coming here directly from the bakery." Rebecca kept her voice low. "If I can't count on you for that—"

"Didn't you get my message?" Barbie interrupted, eyes flashing. "I called and told you on your answering machine as soon as I knew I couldn't be here."

Rebecca's righteous indignation fizzled, leaving her guilty and embarrassed.

"Oh, Barbie, I'm sorry. I haven't been out to the phone shanty all day. I should have checked it when you didn't show up. I just thought . . ." She let that trickle off, because what she'd thought made her feel ashamed.

"You thought I'd wandered off with some friends and forgotten all about you, ain't so?" Anger flickered briefly in Barbie's eyes and then was gone. "You just chalked it up to Barbie being irresponsible."

"I'm so sorry. Please forgive me." She had been irresponsible herself, jumping to conclusions that way. "I should have known better."

For an instant Barbie stared at her. Then her face crinkled in its usual dimpled smile. "It's okay. Sometimes I deserve a scolding, but not this time. Ruth had a dentist's appointment today, and at the last minute she got panicky and wanted Susie to go with her." She shrugged, her face clearly expressing what she thought of such silliness. "Imagine a grown woman, afraid of the dentist! So I said I'd keep the bakery open until they came back. What else could I do?"

"Nothing," Rebecca said quickly, reaching out to clasp Barbie's hand. "You have a gut heart, and I should have known better than to make such an assumption."

Barbie shrugged. "Forget it. Can we still work on plans for the weekend?"

"Of course." Thank goodness Barbie still wanted to. Rebecca had half expected her to go off in a huff. "Why don't we sit at the picnic table since it's so nice today? I'll get my notebook and check on the kinder."

She hurried inside without waiting for a response, scolding herself. If she didn't think of such a simple thing as checking the message machine, how did she imagine she was going to run a business?

Checking for messages would have to become part of her daily routine. Her Englisch guests might not be as forgiving as Barbie was.

When she came back out with the loose-leaf binder that held all her notes, Barbie was sitting at the picnic table. She'd shed the black bonnet she'd worn for the drive and sat with her head tilted back, her face to the sun.

"Here we are." Rebecca plopped the binder on the table and pulled out a manila folder. "I made copies of what I thought you'd need to know."

Barbie nodded, flipping the folder open. "Very business-like," she commented.

Was there any sarcasm in the words? Rebecca wasn't sure. She certainly didn't feel businesslike.

"You see there are going to be six people. I've marked down what meals they'll take here, the children's ages, and their arrival and departure times."

"What do you have planned for them already?" Barbie looked at her, pen in hand, apparently ready to take notes.

"Not much, I guess. Simon is willing to do outside work with them, show them anything they want to learn about, but this time of year . . . well, it doesn't seem like it would be that interesting. I mean, there's plenty of work to be done, but why would they want to be out hoeing or planting?"

"They're from the city," Barbie said, putting her pen on their address. "Anything that's done on the farm will be new to them. They'd probably get a kick out of shoveling manure if they've never done it before."

"I don't think—" she began, and then she saw Barbie's grin.

"If you can get some Englischer to muck out the stalls, I'll give you a bonus," Rebecca said, returning the grin.

"Deal," Barbie said. "You'd be surprised what I can get people to do. Let's make a list of all the possibilities. Then they can choose what they want to do."

"What about the children?" Rebecca said, getting out a fresh sheet of paper. "Simon was always concerned about making sure they didn't get hurt, what with the farm machinery and the animals."

Barbie nodded. "We can make a second list for the kinder. You can trust Katie and Josh to do their chores and amuse themselves, but I don't know that you can think that about Englisch children. You wouldn't believe how some of them behave when they come in the bakery."

"Don't tell me," Rebecca said quickly. "I'm nervous enough already."

"Scaredy-cat," Barbie teased. "Okay, now, let's just think of as many things as we can, no matter if they sound silly. We can weed them out later."

It was a sound plan, Rebecca realized, and her mind was already sparking with ideas. This was what she'd needed—someone to talk to and plan with. She hadn't realized how much that lack had been troubling her.

They began jotting down ideas. Every one of Barbie's, no matter how silly, sent another one popping into Rebecca's head.

"No one in their right mind is going to want to clean out the chicken coop," she protested when Barbie added that suggestion. "I don't want to, and they're my chickens."

Barbie grinned. "Can't you just picture a woman in high heels and a tight skirt chasing chickens around the coop? It would be worth the price of admission. Maybe we could give a prize for the most chickens caught."

Rebecca met Barbie's eyes, sharing the image, and began to giggle helplessly. "Ach, don't. We're supposed to be working." She mopped at her eyes, wondering how long it had been since she'd laughed that way.

"Well, I still say city folks will think just about anything is a treat if we tell them it is." Barbie glanced over Rebecca's head at something. "I see your handsome friend is here."

"What?" She swiveled on the bench and realized that Matt had pulled up to the workshop.

"Handsome," Barbie repeated. "Matthew Byler. You have noticed that, haven't you?"

Barbie couldn't know just how much she'd noticed about Matt. "I suppose he is nice-looking." Rebecca made an effort to sound as if the idea had never occurred to her.

"Nice? He's better than nice." Barbie raised her arm and waved at Matt.

"Don't do that," Rebecca exclaimed, pulling her arm down.

"Why not?" Barbie's blue eyes sparkled. "He saw. He's coming over."

That was why not, but it was useless trying to explain to Barbie. The truth was that Rebecca wasn't sure she was ready to face Matt so soon after the personal things he'd shared with her. After the moment when she'd been so close to him that she could smell his skin and see the tiny lines around his eyes and felt—well, she didn't know what she'd felt. But she knew she didn't want to talk to him with her cousin Barbie looking on.

"Rebecca Fisher," Barbie said softly. "You have feelings for that man, don't you?"

"No, of course not. Don't be silly." But warmth rose in her cheeks at the question, and surely Barbie could see her blush.

He was too close to say anything more, but Rebecca was very aware of her cousin's gaze on her as she greeted Matt.

"You two look like you're having a fine time over here. What's all the laughing about?"

"Wouldn't you like to know?" Barbie smiled up at him, her dimples flashing.

Flirting, Rebecca thought. It was almost second nature to Barbie, it seemed to Rebecca.

"We're making up lists of activities for the guests I have coming this weekend. Barbie has some funny ideas of what our Englisch visitors might enjoy."

"Here, see for yourself." Barbie waved her list, and Matt moved closer to look over her shoulder, scanning what she'd jotted down.

Or was he looking at Barbie? Rebecca couldn't be sure.

Well, that wouldn't be surprising, would it? Barbie was probably nice for a man to look at, with her rosy cheeks, her dimples, and her flashing eyes. Next to her, Rebecca felt as old and worn-out as a used dishcloth.

Matt transferred his gaze to Rebecca, eyeing her a little quizzically. "What about offering your guests a tour of a real handmade-furniture workshop? I could give a demonstration."

She wanted to leap at the prospect, but . . .

"That would be asking too much," she said. "You're wonderful kind, but you have your own work to do. I can't expect you to spend your time on my guests."

"I offered. You didn't ask." His gaze was so warm she seemed to feel her skin heating under it. "It's simple enough, and anyway, maybe they'll buy something."

Before she realized what he was doing, he bent over, took the pen from her hand, and printed the words on her list. *Tour an Amish handcrafted furniture workshop.* He put the pen back in her hand, his fingers brushing hers.

"There. I'll be disappointed if you don't send anyone over." He was leaning with one hand braced on the table close to hers. He smiled down into her face, and she couldn't seem to stop looking at him.

With a rustle of her skirt, Barbie stood. "Since I can tell you two want to be alone, I think I'll go in and check on the kinder."

Rebecca could hear the teasing laughter in her voice, and she didn't know where to look. Her gaze dropped from Matt's face, but it was nearly as bad staring at his strong, tanned hand so close to hers.

Once she heard Barbie go in the house, she managed to clear her throat. "Barbie likes to tease. Don't pay any attention to her."

"I'd guess that your little cousin is used to getting a lot of attention." Now the teasing came from him. "She doesn't bother me."

"I wouldn't want you to think . . ." The words trailed off, because she didn't know where to go with them.

"What, Rebecca? What shouldn't I think?" His voice was low, and it seemed to force her to meet his eyes. Whatever he saw in her face seemed to deter him, because he smiled suddenly.

"Forget it. I just couldn't resist the temptation to tease you."

"You and Barbie have the same idea." She tried to say it lightly, as if none of their interactions had any meaning. "Was there something you wanted? When you came over, I mean."

"Just to thank you." He gestured with his hand, still bandaged. "I don't think I told you that yesterday."

"It was nothing." She found she could relax, at least a little. They were on safer ground. "My foolish little brother caused it, after all. I just hope the cut didn't keep you from doing your work today."

"We're between jobs right now." He frowned slightly, as if he was troubled. "There's something else on my mind, and I'd best get it out. It's about what I told you yesterday." His face tightened, and he seemed to be looking past her. "I'm not sure why I spilled all that to you. Just upset, I guess, that my temper got the better of me again."

She said what she should have said yesterday. "It seems to me it is Simon whose temper needs some improvement. And I don't suppose he's been blaming himself the way you are."

Matt's face was like a mask, not giving any hint to his feelings. "He's young. I'm not, and I've been dealing with this failing for too long. There's never an excuse for an Amish person to turn to violence. We both know it."

He was trying so hard to hide his feelings, but Rebecca began to think she knew what lay behind the mask. Pain. A great deal of pain. She longed to help him, but she didn't know how.

"I think you're being too hard on yourself, Matt." She kept her voice soft.

His only response was to shake his head. Then he turned and walked quickly toward the workshop, his shoulders stiff.

Confused thoughts tumbled through Rebecca's mind. The words she'd read in Anna's diary the night before came back to her, adding to the jumble. Jacob, fearing his refusal to fight might be rooted in fear. Seth, looking for reasons why violence might be all right. And now Matthew, fighting his own battle about much the same thing.

Where were the answers? She knew what the scripture said. But she didn't know how that worked out in the real world, with real people who were struggling.

Matt laid out the slats for another rocking chair on the worktable. If Rebecca did send any of her guests over for a demonstration, this was one thing he could show them—how to fit the back of a rocking chair together.

He frowned down at the grain of the maple. Had that suggestion really been a good idea? It would benefit him, too, as he'd told Rebecca. People who came to watch might very well buy. The couple she'd hosted last weekend had bought something from him.

But the benefit to his business hadn't been in his mind when he'd mentioned giving a workshop tour to her guests. He hadn't been able to resist the temptation to involve himself even more in Rebecca's life.

Rebecca had looked younger when laughter softened her face, erasing the lines of remembered grief and current worry. Maybe Barbie's company was good for her.

And when he'd teased her, Rebecca's green eyes had sparkled, a wash of color spreading from the delicate column of her neck to the creamy skin of her face.

Stop. He shouldn't be thinking of Rebecca that way. But he was a normal, healthy male, wasn't he? He couldn't help—

The train of thought broke off abruptly at the sound of someone entering. Rebecca? His smile died before it reached his lips when he turned and saw who it was.

Simon. Now what did Simon want with him? Hadn't he done enough already?

Giving the boy a curt nod, Matt turned back to his worktable.

"Do you need any help?" Simon approached as he spoke. "If you need a hand . . ."

Matt looked at him. Simon flushed, appearing very young. "I'm sorry. Guess I should apologize first of all. I never meant for you to get hurt. I just didn't want to talk about Isaiah."

Matt leaned back against the workbench, studying the boy's face. "You mean you didn't want to talk to me."

"No." Simon looked momentarily startled. "It wasn't just you. I didn't want . . . I mean, I haven't talked to anybody about Isaiah's leaving. He's my friend. I have to be loyal to him, ain't so?"

The kid looked so conscientious and worried that Matt's annoyance faded away. "I'd say that you should do what's best for your friend."

"Ja." Simon stared at the floor, as if he'd find some answer written there. "But sometimes it's hard to know what is best."

Everything stilled in Matt as he focused on Simon's face. There was an opening here, if only he could keep from rousing Simon's antagonism toward him.

"Isaiah's mamm has been pretty bad since he left." He made his voice low, deliberately keeping the urgency out of it. "Her memory is going. She doesn't understand why he's not there. Well, you must have seen that for yourself."

Looking miserable, Simon nodded.

"My onkel Silas has just lost heart. He doesn't even seem interested in the business without Isaiah. I'll stay as long as he needs me, but . . ." He gestured to the half-finished pieces around them. "I really want to get on with my own work."

Did Simon believe him? Or did he really think that Matt's goal was to steal Isaiah's place?

"I can't make Isaiah come back," he said, when Simon didn't speak. "But if I could find him, I could at least tell him how hard his folks are taking his absence. Maybe it wouldn't make a difference, but I feel I have to try."

Simon's hands twitched. "I guess I owe you something after what I did." He shot a glance at Matt's bandaged hand. "I don't know where he is, honest. But he talked once about some website he found where they'd help people who wanted to leave the Amish."

Matt wasn't as surprised as he would have been ten years ago. It wasn't that unusual these days to find Amish youth owning cell phones and using computers at the homes of their Englisch friends. Isaiah should be getting past that stage, but he hadn't been baptized into the church yet, so Onkel Silas would have been unlikely to interfere, even if he'd known about it.

"Do you know what the name of the website was?" He could always use a computer at the library to try to trace it.

Simon shook his head. "No, but Isaiah had an Englisch friend he was pretty close to. He might know." He paused, as if considering whether or not he was crossing some line that he'd drawn in his mind. Finally he shrugged. "His name is Richards. Carl Richards. He lives in town."

It shouldn't be hard to find a Carl Richards in a town as small as Brook Hill. Matt was filled with a probably unreasonable optimism.

"Denke, Simon. I appreciate it. You're not making a mistake in telling me."

Simon turned away, shrugging, as if to divorce himself from the whole subject. He took a step or two and then stopped. "Rebecca has been through a lot." His voice was gruff, and he didn't look at Matt. "If I've been acting foolish—well, I just don't want her to get hurt worse."

Was he being that obvious? Matt felt a pang of remorse. "I don't, either," he muttered.

He didn't. And if that was true, he'd better stop giving in to temptation each time he was near her.

The path along the pasture between her house and her parents' was so familiar to Rebecca that she didn't have to pay attention to where she put her feet. She hadn't been over to see Daadi yet today, and she wanted to check on him.

She'd seen Simon, though, when she'd helped her brothers with milking her two dairy cows this morning. They'd insisted she didn't need to, and they actually seemed to be carrying on fairly well with Daadi laid up. Johnny was taking on more responsibility than she'd expected of him, and he and Simon hadn't engaged in their usual brotherly rivalry.

When he was leaving, Simon had caught her arm. Face averted, he'd muttered that he'd told Matt what he wanted to know.

Before she could say anything, Simon had scooted off,

obviously not wanting to talk about it. Rebecca could see he was ashamed of himself.

She didn't understand Matt as well, even though she was trying. Matt carried a heavy burden for his cousin Isaiah. After hearing his story, she knew why a little better, although she still felt he might be overreacting.

But how could she know? The secrets of another person's soul were hidden, even from the individual himself sometimes. Matt may not truly understand why he felt as he did about Isaiah.

He certainly seemed intent on finding his cousin. Did Matt picture himself persuading Isaiah to come home? That certain-sure would make Isaiah's parents happy. And it would free Matt from his duty.

For what? Her mind ran up against a blank wall. What did Matt really want? Would he leave Brook Hill then?

Maybe so. There'd be no obligations to keep him here, and he could start his furniture business anywhere. The thought seemed to make the sunny day a little darker, and she tried to push it from her mind. It wasn't any of her business what Matt did.

Rebecca crunched across the gravel driveway and started up the back porch steps. She'd best keep her mind on her own goals, and not go wandering off into other people's. Today, in addition to checking on Daad, she intended to pick up the file with the mortgage information.

She could remember Daad taking it when Paul was so ill, saying she shouldn't worry and he'd deal with it. She had to take it back—should have done it long before this. Somehow just having the folder in her hands would be a sign that she was ready to assume that responsibility for herself.

"Anyone here?" Rebecca opened the screen door.

Three faces turned toward her in welcome. Daad and Grossmammi sat at the table, while Mammi held the coffeepot poised above their cups.

"Rebecca." Mammi put the pot back on the stove and came to hug her. "I didn't know if you'd find time to stop and see us today. You're busy getting ready for your guests coming, ain't so?"

Rebecca returned the hug and then moved to her father, smiling. "I'm not as rushed as all that, Mamm. You're looking better today, Daadi."

She pressed her cheek against his. *Better* was a relative term. Certainly he'd improved from the sheet-white complexion he'd had when he went to the hospital, but his face was thinner and more lined than it had been before his attack. Worse, his spirit seemed to be dampened.

"I'm fine. I wish everyone would stop fussing over me." He drew away from her hug.

Rebecca studied his face. The irritability was unusual for her father.

"I'm only trying to get you to do what the doctor said." Mamm looked even more frustrated than he did, and it seemed as if Rebecca had interrupted an argument of some sort. "You tell him, Rebecca. Your daad has to rest in the afternoon. The doctor said so."

"All I do is rest," Daad snapped.

Rebecca exchanged a look with her grossmammi and patted

his shoulder. "Daadi doesn't need me to tell him something so plain. He knows he must do as the doctor says in order to get well as quickly as possible."

Daadi tried to glare, but he couldn't keep it up. His smile was a shadow of its usual self, but it was there. "Ach, you're all picking on me. There's not a man alive who can hold out against three determined women."

"That's right." Rebecca kissed his cheek. "I should have been here earlier, so it didn't run into your rest time. But I can't stay long anyway."

Daad patted her hand where it lay on his shoulder. "You're busy, like your mamm said. Are you ready for your guests tomorrow? Maybe we should—"

"Now, there's nothing you should do," she said quickly. "Barbie is helping me, and everything is working out fine. So you're not to worry."

Clearly this wasn't a time to ask him for the mortgage folder. It would just make him start worrying about that subject or feeling less needed. She'd have to put off reclaiming it for the moment, even though she'd already made a payment for the month, turning over the rent Matt had paid her.

"So Barbie is working out better than you thought?" Grossmammi's eyes twinkled at her.

"You were right. I admit it. She's so enthusiastic she's almost wearing me out."

Mammi was fidgeting behind them, picking up the coffeepot and then putting it down, wiping the counter unnecessarily. Rebecca glanced at her, lifting her eyebrows in a question.

Mammi communicated silently, giving Daad a look that combined worry and frustration.

Rebecca gave a slight nod and reached across the table to pat Daadi's shoulder again. "You know it is past time for you to go and rest, Daadi. Will you do it, or do I have to leave?"

Her father grunted. He rose to his feet, bracing his hands on the table like an old man.

Her heart twisted. Daadi wasn't old. He was in the prime of life, tough and strong. Or at least, he had been.

"I'll go, stop nagging. But you send over if you think of anything you need this weekend, ja? Simon will do whatever you want, and Johnny can always help, too."

"I know," she said. "Denke, Daadi. Rest well. I'll see you later."

She watched as he went out of the room, walking far more slowly than she'd ever seen him move. Mamm kept pace with him, and as they went up the steps, Rebecca could hear him insisting that he didn't need Mamm's help.

Rebecca turned a troubled face on her grandmother. "She keeps fussing over him, and the more she does, the more irritable he becomes."

"I know." Grossmammi's voice was gentle. "They're worried about each other, ain't so? They'll find their way. It's not easy. You know as well as anyone."

Rebecca nodded. She certainly did know.

"You're right. As always." She managed a smile. "How does it feel to be moved in? Are you settled?"

"Pretty nearly. There are still the pieces that are going to be moved to your attic to take care of, but your uncle promised to get his boys to do it." Her grandmother frowned. "I'm still working on getting all the family to choose something to treasure, but it's going to take some time, I think."

"It's not a problem. I have plenty of room in the attic, and I'm happy to store everything. It will give you time to tell me all the stories connected with them, ain't so?"

Grossmammi smiled at the reminder of her storytelling. "Ach, you young ones should be glad there's still someone who remembers the family stories."

"We are. Or at least, I am."

Rebecca moved to the chest that stood against the back wall and pulled open the top drawer. Daad always kept business papers there, and sure enough, the manila folder with the words *mortgage information* marked in Paul's printing lay to one side. She took it out and slid the drawer closed.

As she turned back to the table, she realized that Grossmammi was watching her with curiosity.

"This is mine," she said, holding up the folder. "The information about the mortgage Paul took out to buy the land and build the new stable. Daad has been taking care of it, but it's time I dealt with it myself."

"Your daad wanted to help you, like always," Grossmammi said.

"I know." Rebecca sat down opposite her, opening the file. "But I don't want him worrying about it, especially now. I've started making the payments—"

She stopped, staring at the figures on the sheet in front of her.

"Rebecca? Was ist letz?"

Rebecca swallowed hard, tried to release the tension that had her throat in a cold grasp. "I didn't realize. That's stupid, isn't it? But I never knew how much Paul had borrowed. He handled everything that had to do with business, and I let him."

She was appalled to think how passive she had been. This was her future, too, and the children's. Why hadn't she involved herself in the decision?

"Paul thought he could take care of everything," Grossmammi said. "He never imagined getting sick."

"No, but . . ." The amount shook her. "It's so much."

Grossmammi put her hand over Rebecca's. "If you're worried about the payments, I can help when my house is sold."

"No, no." That much was sure. "I'm not going to switch from being a burden to Daad to being a burden to you. Anyway, with renting the stable to Matt and the money coming in from the guests, I can manage to meet the payments every month." She tried to sound confident and wasn't sure how well she did.

Well enough, apparently, because Grossmammi didn't press her. She studied Rebecca's face, and her own expression was troubled.

"What are you thinking, Rebecca? Tell me."

She shook her head. "I'm just . . . I'm angry."

She stopped, aghast at her own word. *Angry.* But it was true. She was angry with Paul. Angry that he'd pursued his dream at the cost of security for her and the children. Angry that he'd done it without consulting her.

But she couldn't be. How could she be mad at Paul, who was gone?

She'd been thinking that it was hard to know the secrets of Matt's soul. But it was her own soul that should have concerned her.

Chapter Fourteen

Lancaster County, June 1942

*A*nna rose while it was still dark. Lighting the lamp on the dresser, she tried to force herself awake. It had been another long night of sleeping very little and having bad dreams when she did. Thank goodness her position as eldest had afforded her a bedroom of her own. She needed a place to escape to when her worries about Jacob threatened to overcome her.

Shivering a little in the predawn chill, she pulled her night-gown off and began to dress. The dream she'd had just before waking still seemed to hold her in its grasp.

She'd seen Jacob so clearly, and even in the dream her heart had leaped with joy. She'd reached out her hands, running toward him, knowing his strong arms would close around her and hold her tight. There would be nothing to keep them apart.

But she couldn't run. She was slogging through thick mud.

It pulled at her shoes, dragging her back like a living thing. She cried out to Jacob for help.

But Jacob's expression didn't change. He didn't look at her. Instead he turned slowly, staring ahead as if drawn that way. He moved, but not toward her. Away from her, never turning back, never hearing her cries. He vanished into a gray unknown, and she was left behind.

Anna's throat was tight with unshed tears. She attacked her hair with the brush, drawing it to the back of her head with the ease of long practice.

It had been a dream, nothing more. Jacob was gone, true, but he would come home. Someday this terrible war would be over, and they'd surely let the boys come home.

The hairpins secured her kapp in place. Anna took her sweater from its peg on the wall and stood at the window to put it on. The eastern sky was beginning to brighten. Daad would want the boys up and dressed to help with the milking while she and Mamm prepared breakfast.

Maybe today she'd finally get another letter from Jacob. May had mellowed into June, the days growing warmer and the corn sprouting in the fields. Jacob had been gone a month, and she'd had only one letter from him.

She'd read it so many times that she had it memorized.

. . . keeping us very busy here at the camp in Maryland. The barracks are in bad shape, but the boys are all handy enough with tools to make improvements.

Had they made the place livable? She had visions sometimes of Jacob sleeping where a respectable Amish farmer wouldn't keep his pigs, with the roof leaking and rain dripping down his neck.

Ach, that idea was foolishness. Jacob would fix any leaking roof—that was certain-sure.

At least Jacob had been able to send her his address, so she could write to him. Each day she added a little more to the letter, recounting all the little things that made up her life, so he would remember and think about his true life here.

On Friday she had mailed the letter. *Today,* she prayed silently. *Let me get another letter from him today.*

She went quickly to the boys' room, not bothering to tiptoe. It was time everyone was up. Seth was usually an early riser, so he was probably almost ready.

But she opened the door to darkness. Frowning, she fumbled her way to the gas lamp and lit it. "Do you boys think it's a holiday? Komm, schnell. Get up."

She turned as she spoke, smiling at the row of three single beds. Eli pushed himself up on one elbow, but Peter, the youngest, pulled the pillow over his head. Her gaze went to the bed by the window, and she felt as if someone had hit her in the stomach.

The bed was empty, still made, with the nine-patch quilt drawn up over the pillow. On it rested a single sheet of paper, folded in half.

Anna forced herself to walk toward the bed. The reluctance that dragged at her was like her dream, except that this was real. And she knew what she would find before she picked up the paper.

"What is it, Anna?" Eli slid from his bed and padded barefoot to her side. "Where's Seth?"

"Hush a minute." The paper had her name scribbled across

the outside. Anna sank down on the quilt. With stiff fingers she unfolded the paper.

I have gone to join up. I know what you will say—what everyone will say—but I have to. It can't be right to stand back when innocent people are being killed.

Try to break it gently to Mamm and Daad. I know you will look after everyone.

I love you all. I hope you can forgive me.

"Anna, what happened to Seth?" Peter, drawn by the hint of trouble, joined them, pressing close to her side. "What does it say?"

She brushed the fringe of blond hair back from his eyes. "I don't—"

The door opened to reveal Daad, with Mammi right behind him.

"What is going on?" Daadi's voice seemed loud in the quiet room.

Mammi's step caused a board to creak. Her startled gaze took in Anna and the two boys. And the empty bed. She gasped, reaching out to grab Daadi's arm.

"Anna?" Daadi looked at her, and she saw the knowledge dawn in his eyes even before she could speak.

"I'm sorry." Her throat was so tight she had to force the words out. She gestured with the note. "Seth is gone. He says he's sorry, but he must. He's joined the army."

"No. No." Mammi shook her head. "He can't, not Seth. Not my baby." She clutched at Daadi's arm. "You must stop him. Go after him. Make him come home."

Anna had never seen her father look as he did now. The skin seemed drawn tight against the bones, his eyes dark with pain.

"It's no use." He sounded defeated, the words dragging. "We can't keep him if he's determined to go."

Mammi broke into sobs that shook her whole body. Peter, frightened even if he didn't understand, began to cry as well. Anna cradled him close and put her arm around Eli, who stood as stiff as a board, his face working with the effort to hold back tears.

Beyond Daad and Mammi, Becky and Sarah appeared, drawn by the commotion, their faces white and frightened.

Daadi's gaze met Anna's over her mother's head. He seemed to try to focus, but he looked as dazed as if he'd been struck by a falling timber.

"The cows must be milked, and . . ." He let that trail off and stared helplessly at Anna.

He was relying on her. Anna struggled to swallow over the lump in her throat. Somehow, she had to be strong.

"Becky, take Sarah and start fixing breakfast. I'll help you when I can. Peter, stop that crying. You boys komm. We'll tend to the milking."

The kinder seemed paralyzed, not moving.

"Now," she said sharply. "Schnell."

Becky nodded. Taking her little sister's hand, she vanished toward the stairs. Eli and Peter began to scramble into their clothes.

Daad patted Mammi's back, his touch gentle. "I should help . . ."

Anna shook her head. "You should stay with Mammi. Don't worry. We'll take care of everything."

Everything. But they couldn't do the important thing. They couldn't change what had happened and undo what Seth had done.

Daadi nodded. He reached out to grasp Anna's shoulder in a rare embrace. "You are a gut girl, Anna."

Chasing her brothers ahead of her, Anna headed for the door. Daadi was wrong about one thing. Her time of being a girl was over. It had been ended abruptly by forces none of them could control or understand. Now she must be a woman, and she must somehow find the strength that would be needed in the dark days to come.

You really don't have to help make supper," Rebecca protested as Barbie dropped potatoes into the pot. "You've done so much already."

By Saturday afternoon it seemed to Rebecca that Barbie had actually accomplished more than she had in making their guests feel welcome and comfortable.

"I want to," Barbie said. "You've been doing all the work, ain't so?"

"Me?" Rebecca paused, rolling pin in hand, to stare at her cousin. "It's you who've been doing everything. You've been keeping them all busy and happy all day long. You must be exhausted."

Barbie's dimples appeared. "But that's just playing for me. You've been making beds and cooking meals for all these people and ensuring they're comfortable. That's the work part."

Rebecca felt a giggle bubbling up inside her. "You have a

funny idea of what's hard to do. I could never do what you've been doing, but I love cooking and dishing up and seeing folks enjoy the food I prepare."

Barbie shook her head, grinning. "Now, that would be work to me. I'm wonderful glad we want to do different things."

Had Grossmammi seen from the beginning how their talents would mesh? Probably so. She seemed to see most things better than anyone else Rebecca knew.

"So you're happy with helping me?" She asked the question on impulse, but realized she really wanted to hear Barbie's answer.

"For sure." Barbie studied a potato thoughtfully before dropping it into the water. "I guess it's because I feel as if what I do is important to the success of the business." She made a face. "I certain-sure can't say that about the bakery. Anybody could help out there. You could probably train a cat to do it if you had enough time."

"Now, I'd like to see that for myself." Rebecca was amused, but at the same time she felt a little qualm. Did she want Barbie to claim so much of a share in their success? But that was a selfish attitude.

"What each of us does is important," she said firmly.

Barbie nodded. "Even the kinder are feeling that way, I think, especially Katie. She's been so helpful in keeping the Englisch children occupied."

"She has, hasn't she?" A glow of maternal pride filled Rebecca.

Life with Katie had been easier lately, and not just because she was occupied with their guests. The bond that had formed when they'd cried together over Paul seemed stronger each day, and it humbled Rebecca to think she might have missed that if she'd gone on trying to protect the kinder from her own pain.

"Simon was having a fine time with the grandfather today," Barbie observed. "It seems the old man lived on a farm when he was young, and he asked for nothing more than to get his hands dirty again."

"Not so his son-in-law." Rebecca peeked through the kitchen window. Sure enough, the man was leaning against his car in what he'd declared was the best spot for cell phone reception. He tapped away at the tiny keyboard.

"I thought he was going to walk out when you told him there was no electricity to recharge his little phone." Barbie giggled. "I could have suggested he use the generator in your daad's barn, but I figured it was more fun to let him figure it out on his own."

"His wife said she wanted to get him away from business for the weekend, and that's one reason they came here." Rebecca rolled out the potpie dough and tested the thickness with her fingers. It should be just a little thinner. "I don't think her plan is working."

Barbie shook her head. "You're not going to make everyone happy," she said. She was silent for a moment, and then she shot a mischievous glance at Rebecca. "Matt certainly was great, especially with the little boy, Parker. He managed to keep him interested until he'd finished his birdhouse, and I'd say that's pretty good for that kid. He's as lively as a grasshopper."

"Schnicklefritz," Rebecca said, using the word for a mischievous child.

"Don't you think Matthew was great with him?" Barbie prompted.

"Ja." Rebecca concentrated on the dough. "He's very gut at what he does."

"Gut at other things, too, I'd guess." When that didn't get a reaction, Barbie poked Rebecca in the back with a wooden spoon. "Come on, admit it. You like him."

"He's a gut friend," Rebecca said. It was probably impossible to repress Barbie, but she could try.

"He doesn't look at you the way you look at a friend," Barbie declared.

Rebecca met her gaze involuntarily. "He doesn't?"

"No, Miss Innocent, he doesn't. And that's not how you look at him, either."

"I . . . I don't know what you mean."

Barbie made a sound of exasperation. "Why shouldn't you be interested in each other? You're both free."

Maybe so, but it wasn't that simple. And if she was growing to care for Matt, she would have to be cautious.

"All right." Barbie sounded resigned. "I won't tease you anymore. Let's talk about something else." She paused for a moment, as if trying to think of something. "Are you still reading that diary you were telling me about?"

Rebecca nodded. "I can't resist it, even though the part I'm reading now is so sad. The boy she loves has been drafted and sent away to a camp for conscientious objectors in another state, and she hardly hears from him."

"She should have married him before he left," Barbie said quickly. "That's what I would do."

"She tried to get him to agree, but he insisted it wasn't right to marry all in a rush."

"I'd have convinced him." Barbie didn't seem to doubt her ability to get anyone to do what she wanted. "Or if he wouldn't, I'd go to where the camp was and settle in the nearest town. At least then I'd get to see him."

Rebecca had to smile at her cousin's resolute tone. "I don't think it was as easy as all that then. And I doubt Anna was like you." In fact, Anna was more like herself, she realized. Maybe that's why she was so attracted by Anna's story. "I think—"

Her words were cut off by a clatter on the back porch. In an instant the bell began to toll, loud and fast, shocking in its strident demand.

Rebecca's heart jumped, and she pressed her hand against her chest. Then she tore across the kitchen and out onto the back porch.

Ten-year-old Parker had climbed onto the porch railing where he could reach the bell. He clanged it so hard it seemed it must fly off its bracket, ignoring Katie's pleas that he stop and his mother's ineffectual suggestions that he find something else to do.

Rebecca grasped his arm. "Stop. Now."

Her tone was the one she used when she expected instant obedience from her kinder. Apparently it also worked on Englisch children. His hand dropped from the bellpull. He slid down off the railing.

"I'm so sorry, Mrs. Fisher," the mother declared. "I just can't do a thing with Parker some days."

Since the woman hadn't so much as stirred from her chair or dropped her magazine, it was difficult to think she had tried very hard.

"I want to ring the bell," Parker said, reaching for the rope again.

"No." Rebecca gave him the look that most children, at least most Amish children, knew meant business.

"Why not?" He pouted. "It's there. Why can't I ring it?"

"Because that's not what it's for." *Because it's a precious memory of my husband and I don't want you to touch it.*

"What's it for, then?" Parker didn't seem to understand what the word *no* meant.

"It is a dinner bell. When it's rung the way you were ringing it, people will think there's something wrong." She grasped his shoulders and turned him. "See? There is Matt coming out of his workshop because he thinks there's an emergency." She waved to him, to let him know it was all right. "And there's my brother and your grandfather coming out of the barn." Again she turned him. "I think you should go and tell them there's nothing wrong, don't you?"

He got a faintly mulish expression that wilted when she stared at him. "I guess. Will you let me ring it when it's time for supper?"

We don't ring it. That was what she wanted to say. But why not? Wasn't that what Paul had intended, that it should call his kinder in for supper? How foolish she was, to deny them the pleasure of building memories around it, the way their father had.

"Katie will be in charge of the dinner bell tonight," she said firmly. "She may let you help her, ain't so, Katie?"

Gratified, Katie nodded. "I might." She tugged at Parker's sleeve. "Let's go tell your grandfather and my onkel Simon everything is okay." Together they ran toward the barn.

Rebecca leaned against the porch post, feeling as if she had been running as well. Or maybe as if she'd finished a race.

Matt's trip to the library to use the computer had netted some surprising results, and he was still considering them as he released the mare from the hitching rail and climbed into the buggy. The library was new since his time—a sprawling modern edifice of brick and glass with a large parking lot and a hitching rail for the convenience of the Amish. The librarian had shown no surprise at seeing him using the computer. Many Amish were great readers and frequent visitors to the library, and if they had need of the computer—well, using one in the public library wasn't like having one in your home.

He clucked to the mare. He'd been taken aback to find several websites whose purpose was to encourage Amish youth to leave the church. And a couple of the sites seemed to represent groups that offered help to those who'd decided to jump the fence.

Such a thing hadn't existed back when he'd jumped the fence. It bothered him a bit, to tell the truth, but most likely a young person wouldn't find the sites unless they went looking, and they'd only be looking if they were already thinking of leaving. Probably the people who ran the sites thought they were doing work that needed to be done.

It was true that the average young Amish male who jumped the fence had few of the skills he'd need to succeed in the modern world. The Amish philosophy had always been to train their young through eighth grade in the information and skills they'd need to live Amish, not Englisch.

Matt had jotted down the particulars of one group that seemed most likely to appeal to Isaiah if he'd been looking for help to run. It was in Holmes County, Ohio, not all that far from central Pennsylvania, and it offered help in terms of advice, housing, and finding jobs.

The information given was a bit vague about exactly where it was located, probably deliberately. The person running it would want to know that the one asking was genuine before giving out specifics.

Matt understood, but it presented him with difficulties. If he had to go out to Holmes County in search of Isaiah it would mean hiring a car and driver, possibly for several days, and he'd rather be sure he had a more accurate location first.

He'd had a driver's license when he'd been living Englisch, of course. But there was something inherently wrong in attempting to persuade his cousin to come back to the faith while breaking one of that faith's traditions himself.

Well, he was on his way to find Carl Richards, the Englisch friend Simon had thought might know something about where Isaiah had gone. Asking around had netted the information that Richards worked at a local garage owned by his girl-friend's father, and it wasn't far from the library.

By the time Matt had reached the garage, he'd hammered out an approach to Richards. The best possibility seemed the simple truth. Isaiah's mother was ill, and she'd been made worse by not hearing anything from him. Matt wanted to find Isaiah to tell him about his mother, so that he'd write to her.

If he could get Isaiah to come home, he would, but there was no point in telling Richards so.

The garage was like most small, independent ones in the area—a low cement-block building with an office at one end and four bays for working on cars. If it had ever had gas pumps, they'd been removed, and the concrete yard held several junked cars that looked in immediate danger of collapsing into a pile of rust.

A buggy was out of place in a haven for motorized vehicles, and there was no convenient hitching rail. Matt guided the mare to a spot on the edge of the lot where a tree provided shade for her and a branch to tie her to. In a moment he was approaching the office.

Somewhat to his surprise there was a girl behind the wooden counter, talking on the telephone. Her dramatic makeup and snug, low-cut top would be more appropriate for a cosmetic counter, he'd think, but she was reeling off parts numbers into the phone and still had time to eye him with a certain appreciation.

She hung up and gave him a teasing smile. "Now, don't tell me you brought a car in for service, because I'm not going to believe it."

If playing up to her would get him what he wanted, he didn't mind. He leaned against the counter, smiling down at her. "I don't suppose there's anything you can do with my buggy. I'm Matthew Byler. I'd like to see Carl Richards if he's here."

"He's working, but I'm sure he can take a little break to talk to you, Matthew." She rose and wafted toward the door into the garage. "Follow me."

He followed, well aware that he was supposed to be

admiring the back view. And since this was presumably the girlfriend, he was also meant to think what a lucky fellow Richards was.

The garage wasn't as busy as he'd have expected. Only two bays were occupied. The woman approached the man who was bent over the engine of the compact in the nearest bay and ran her hand down what was visible of his back.

"Somebody to talk to you, sweetie."

He straightened abruptly, a wrench in one hand. He had a wink for the girl, but he sent a frowning look at Matt. Richards was stocky, with the heavy shoulders and muscled torso of someone who worked out. His square face had straight black brows and a level mouth, giving it the look of a face cut into a wood block.

"I'm busy. I promised this heap for this afternoon."

"Come on," she said. "Talk to the nice gentleman. I told him you would." A red-tipped finger touched his cheek. "Don't be rude."

"All right, all right." Richards gave her a gentle shove. "Get back to the office if you don't want grease on you."

Giving Matt another smile, the girl brushed past him and headed to the office. He noticed that she lingered just inside the door, obviously intending to hear whatever was said.

"So, what's up?" Richards advanced to within a couple of feet of him. "We don't usually get Amish in here."

"I guess not. I'm Matthew Byler," he said, and added, "Isaiah Byler's cousin."

The frown darkened. "So?"

Matt reminded himself not to respond to the obvious antagonism. "I understand you're a friend of my cousin."

Heavy shoulders moved in a shrug. "We hung out sometimes. What's it to you?"

It seemed he was determined to be antagonized no matter what Matt said, so maybe it was best just to get on with it.

"I'd like to find him. I hoped you might know where he is."

"Sorry." The word was short. "Haven't heard from him."

"Maybe not, but you still might have an idea where he went. Isaiah's family hasn't heard from him since he left. I really need to get in touch with him."

"Not my business." Richards turned, as if to go back to his work.

Matt was losing him, not that he'd had much chance from the beginning of getting anywhere. "Look, his mother is sick, and she's fretting because she doesn't know where he is or even if he's safe. If you could tell me anything about his whereabouts, it might make the situation a little easier for her to accept."

"How would I know?" He cast a quick sideways glance as he said the words, and Matt felt reasonably certain he knew.

"You're his friend. He probably told you where he was headed, even if you haven't heard from him since. You could save his mother a lot of grief if you'd tell me what you know."

Richards's face reddened. "How do I know if any of this story is true?" He took a step closer to Matt, shoving his face forward. "I'm not saying I know, but if I did, Isaiah would have made me promise not to tell. I don't rat on a buddy." He seemed to be picking up steam and gaining courage as he talked. "So I got nothing to say to you. Just get out."

He planted the hand without the wrench on Matt's chest and gave him a shove that sent him back a step or two. Matt saw red, and his hands had doubled into fists before he realized it.

He forced them to relax. First Simon, now this guy. He was beginning to think he wasn't popular here.

"I don't want to start a fight." He spread his hands open. "I'm just trying to help my aunt. Think of how Isaiah would feel if she got worse and he didn't know."

"Not my business," Richards repeated stubbornly. He was a man with a single thought. He'd said he wouldn't tell, and he wasn't telling.

Matt hated to admit defeat, but he could see that nothing he'd say would do any good. "If you change your mind, you can get in touch with me at the Byler place."

He hesitated for a moment, but Richards didn't move. Finally Matt turned and walked out. There was no use waiting for a response he knew wouldn't come.

He was halfway to the buggy when he realized someone was coming after him. Richards's girlfriend hurried up to him.

"You don't need to be in such a rush." She put her hand, red nails and all, on his sleeve, and he had to resist the temptation to shake her off. There was no point in alienating her. Maybe she'd be willing to intercede with Richards.

"I don't have any reason to stick around," he said. "Your boyfriend's not going to help me."

She gazed into his face. "Look, is that really true? Is his mother really sick?"

"Yes. She really is." He hesitated, but he thought he detected caring in the heavily made-up face. "She cries for Isaiah all the time. It's enough to break your heart."

"Poor thing." She paused, then sent a quick backward glance

toward the garage. "Look, I don't know exactly where Isaiah is, but I can tell you the town, if that helps. It's Millville, Ohio."

He studied her face, and the expression in her eyes convinced him she was telling the truth. Behind the makeup and provocative clothing there was a soft heart, it seemed.

"It helps a lot. Thank you."

She squeezed his hand. "Just don't let on who told you, okay?"

"I won't," he promised, wondering whether she feared retribution from Richards. "You've done a good thing."

And she'd opened the door for *him* to do a good thing. He just had to figure out the right way of using the information he had.

CHAPTER FIFTEEN

Matt was still trying to figure out the best way of getting in touch with Isaiah the next afternoon. He stood at the workbench, rubbing down the rocking chair with linseed oil. The repetitive movement was soothing, and it gave him time to think. Unfortunately, he wasn't coming up with any great answers.

He could try sending something to the post office in the small Ohio town, but there was no guarantee it would reach his cousin. And the Internet had probably been all the help it was going to be in tracking Isaiah.

Englisch people might be fairly easy to find that way, but not the Amish. Some teenagers and business owners might be active on it, but if Isaiah was determined to cut ties with his past, he wouldn't make himself easy to locate.

Going out to Ohio was probably the only answer, but what excuse could Matt give his uncle for going all that way? If he told Onkel Silas the truth, he could be raising hopes and then causing additional grief if they came to nothing.

Matt looked up from the rocker, glancing toward the back wall of the workshop. He'd been hearing noises off and on from outside for the past half hour. Maybe it was time he went to see what was going on.

He walked around the outside of the building. The sounds were coming from the old apple tree that was a favorite haunt of Joshua's. He stepped under the tree and glanced up just in time to dodge away from a plummeting board, which came so close it brushed his shoulder.

Matt dusted off his shirt and looked up. Two scared faces peered down at him through a circle of leaves.

"We're sorry. We didn't mean it." The words tumbled out of Joshua.

"Are you hurt?" Katie looked as if she'd come down and render first aid in an instant.

"It's all right. I'm not hurt." Matt bent and picked up the board. Not one of his, he saw, but an old piece of one-by-four pine that had probably been knocking around in one of the sheds. "Are you allowed to have this?" He gestured with it.

Joshua nodded. "Onkel Simon said it was okay."

Katie's forehead crinkled. "But I think he was busy. He didn't even ask why we wanted it."

It sounded as if that lack of interest might have hurt their feelings. They were used to having quite a bit of attention from their grandfather and uncles.

"What are the two of you trying to make?" Matt asked.

They exchanged glances, and then Katie seemed to appoint herself spokesperson. "We thought if we could put the board across between the branches, we could make a bench to sit on." She wrinkled her nose, looking suddenly like a young Rebecca.

"We keep losing hold of it. It's harder to do it than I thought it would be."

Matt smiled at the rueful tone. "Things often are."

Joshua nodded. "Katie says that Daadi was going to build us a tree house, but then he got sick."

The kid's words lodged in Matt's heart. Paul had probably left undone a lot of things that he'd thought he'd be able to do with his children.

"Why don't I get a couple of boards and my tools? Then I can come up and help you. But only if you want," he added, mindful that Katie might still harbor some resentment toward him.

"Would you really?" Katie's eager smile dismissed that concern.

"But Mammi said we aren't supposed to bother you when you're working," Joshua said.

"It's no bother. I can take a little break." He put out of his mind the work he'd planned to accomplish yet this afternoon. If it didn't get done today, it would tomorrow. That was one of the reasons he liked being in business for himself. "Do you want to help me carry things?"

"For sure." Joshua shinnied down the tree in seconds, all smiles, and Katie followed him.

"We'll carry everything," she said. "You can just show us what to do. Maybe, if there are Englisch kids the next time we have visitors, they'd like to sit on our bench, too."

Joshua, trotting beside Matt as they headed into the workshop, didn't look thrilled with that idea. "I thought maybe it would be our own secret place."

"But we're supposed to help Mammi with the Englischers,

remember?" Katie seemed to take the responsibility seriously. "It's our job."

"I guess," Joshua said reluctantly.

Matt decided not to venture an opinion. Rebecca could deal with this one. Certainly Amish children learned from an early age that everyone in the family contributed to its work, but he could understand Joshua's wish for a secret hideout. What kid didn't want one?

In a few minutes they were back at the tree, laden down with supplies. "I'll use a rope to hoist the boards up into the tree," he said. "That's how we do it whenever we're working on something high."

Joshua nodded, face serious. "I saw Grandpa and Onkel Simon do that when they mended the barn roof. You can climb up the ladder I made, okay?"

The ladder was a few crosspieces nailed to the trunk. Matt buckled on his tool belt before starting up. He didn't want to hurt Joshua's feelings by nailing the steps more solidly, but he went up cautiously.

The spot the kinder had picked for their building operation was actually suitable—a natural crotch in the tree where two branches formed a rough triangle with the trunk.

He lowered the rope down to them. "Just tie that around the boards, and I'll haul them up."

They scurried to obey, and in a moment stood back. "It's ready," Katie said. "We made it really tight."

The boards rose, swaying a little, and he lashed them to a handy branch while the kinder were climbing up.

"Did you ever build a real tree house?" Joshua asked, with thinly disguised hope in his voice.

"I did make a few," he admitted. "But I was older than you are by then."

He hadn't actually been much older than Katie when he and his brother had built their first tree house. He had a sudden, vivid memory of sunshine hot on his back and the smell of manure coming from the barn. He could almost feel himself sitting with his skinny knees wrapped around a rough branch, pounding a nail in and grazing Caleb's fingers. He could see the small hand snatching back and hear Caleb's shriek.

He hadn't been very sympathetic, as he recalled. He'd called Caleb a baby, which hadn't helped matters, and then said if he didn't shut up, Daadi would make them stop. That threat had produced instant silence, and they'd finished their project in harmony.

Matt fitted a board across the branches and let Joshua and Katie push it firmly against the trunk.

"That's it," he said. "Let's put a few nails in to hold it fast." Remembering Caleb's bruised fingers, he made sure small hands were well back from the hammer. "My brother and I used to build tree houses. Then as soon as one was finished, we'd want to build something else, so we'd tear it apart and make a fort or a nest or even a different style of tree house. That was all part of the fun, I guess."

"I wish I had a brother." Joshua gave his sister a quick glance. "I mean someone younger than me. If I had a little brother, I could teach him things, like Katie does me."

"Maybe you will someday." If their mother married again. The thought was vaguely disturbing. "Or you might have a boy cousin when Onkel Simon gets married."

"Maybe." Joshua didn't sound too hopeful. *Someday* sounded like never when a boy was five, Matt supposed.

"I hope he doesn't marry Mary Ann," Katie blurted out, and then looked guilty. "I shouldn't say so. Don't tell Mammi."

"I won't say anything." Matt had the impression that no one was exactly thrilled with Simon's friend except, presumably, Simon.

They fitted another board into place beside the first. Matt figured about four planks would give a wide enough platform for the two of them.

"Was this why you were so interested in my tools?" He focused on Josh's face. "Because you wanted to make a tree house?"

Joshua shrugged. "Not just a tree house. I like to build things. But Mammi doesn't know how, and Onkel Simon used to help me but now he's too busy."

Joshua sniffed, as if Simon's defection was a sore point.

Katie nudged him. "Onkel Simon has more work to do now, remember? Mammi said."

"I guess everyone has to pitch in and help more since your grossdaadi is sick," Matt pointed out. "Your onkel Simon is busy with his planting and your mammi's as well."

Joshua nodded. "I heard Mary Ann say that he had time for everybody but her. What do you think she meant?"

Katie looked as if she had her own ideas on the subject, but she didn't speak.

Matt suspected he shouldn't touch that, either, but he had to say something. "I don't know. Maybe she was just missing spending more time with him, and it made her sad."

"She didn't sound sad." Joshua helped him put the last board in place. "She sounded mad."

He definitely wasn't going to touch that one. Time for a change of subject. "We're almost done. You two can show Mammi what you made. You'll let her come up, right?"

Josh grinned. "Mothers don't climb trees."

"Your mother did when she was about Katie's age. I'll bet she still can."

"I'll go get Mammi," Joshua said, scrambling across the platform for the ladder.

"Mammi is here," a voice said.

Matt peered over the edge to see Rebecca smiling up at him, the sunlight that filtered through the leaves gilding her face.

It was the strangest thing. Matt had a sudden longing to pretend that the past few years, with their burden of guilt and grief and pain, hadn't happened, that the two of them could be young again, just for a few minutes.

He smiled down at her. "Komm up. See what Joshua and Katie have built."

"Not just us," Katie said quickly. "Matt did most of the work."

Rebecca eyed the climb warily. "Maybe I'll admire it from down here."

"Coward," Matt teased. "Where is the little girl who climbed to the top of the oak tree in the schoolyard if someone gave her a boost?"

"She got stuck there, as I remember."

"Komm." He held out his hand. "We won't let you fall."

She met his gaze for another moment, and then she nodded,

laughter seeming to tremble on her lips. "All right. But there will be trouble if I do."

Rebecca grasped the crosspieces, checking their sturdiness, and then stepped off the ground. One step, two, and then Matt's fingers reached hers. He held her hand, liking the sense that she relied on him, and she scrambled up to perch on the platform next to him, her legs dangling.

"Isn't it great, Mammi?" Josh threw his arms around her neck in his excitement, and Matt had to steady them both.

"Matt says he had a tree house when he was a little older than us," Katie added.

Matt saw the swift shadow that passed across Rebecca's eyes, probably because she was remembering Paul's plans. Then she was smiling again.

"This is a fine job. You can sit up here and see everything that's going on. You could even have lunch up here sometime, if you wanted."

"Could we do it now, Mammi?" Katie said quickly. "Not lunch, I mean, but a snack? We're hungry from working."

"I guess you are due for a snack. There are some snicker-doodles in the cookie jar. I'll get them—"

"No, no, me!" Joshua exclaimed. "Let me." He climbed over his mother like a little monkey.

"Me, too," Katie said. She swung down to the first rung of the ladder. "We'll be careful. We'll put the lid back on and wrap the cookies up in a paper towel." She jumped the last rung, Joshua right behind her, and set off running across the yard.

"There's no use hoping they'll remember to wash their

hands before they get the cookies," Rebecca said. "I hope you don't mind a little dirt."

"Keeps you healthy, so my mamm used to say."

They were sitting very close of necessity on the small platform, and Matt was intensely aware of Rebecca—the gentle curve of her mouth, the soft flush in her cheeks, the way her gaze followed her children's sturdy little figures until they disappeared into the house.

Her eyes swept up to his, and his throat went dry.

"You are wonderful kind to build this with Joshua and Katie," she said.

"It's nothing." He tried for a light touch but didn't think he succeeded. "I found them trying to manhandle a board into the tree on their own. I figured helping them would be the safest course."

Her face clouded as if he'd scolded her. "Ach, I should have been watching them closer. They could have gotten hurt doing something like that and—"

"Rebecca, don't start blaming yourself," he interrupted. "That wasn't what I meant. They're normal kids. Trying things, failing, falling, getting hurt, getting up again . . . That's all part of being young." His fingers closed on her wrist, and he could feel her pulse beating against his skin.

"I know. I try not to fuss. It's just . . ." She smiled suddenly. "I'm a mother. That's what we do."

That smile seemed to go right to his heart. They were so close, and her smiling lips were only inches from his. He couldn't help it. He closed the distance and found her lips with his.

For an instant Rebecca was still. Then she leaned into the kiss, and her breath came out with a little sigh. He touched her face, longing welling inside him. He wanted . . .

The back door slammed, announcing that the children were coming. Rebecca drew away, the movement slow. A blush colored her cheeks but she was smiling, her eyes bemused.

"The kinder," she said, as if in explanation. "I . . . I think I'll get down and let you have your snack with them."

He nodded. Rebecca wasn't running away, or being offended, or reacting in any of the ways he might have expected to his kiss. She was just putting a little distance between them.

He didn't speak, because he didn't know what to say. But as he helped her climb down from the tree, he knew that soon he would have to speak. He'd have to tell her the whole truth about himself, no matter how much it hurt.

Rebecca slid the beef noodle casserole into the oven and straightened, only to catch a reflection of her face in the tray on the counter. Her lips were curved in a smile she hadn't seen in a long time.

She moved the tray, but it didn't help. She could still feel the smile. And she knew what had put it there. Matt had kissed her.

She should be embarrassed, shouldn't she? Or upset? But was it wrong for a man—a good man—to show an interest in her? It had been so long.

Rebecca lifted an earthenware mixing bowl down from the shelf. She'd make a loaf of corn bread to go with the casserole. Josh and Katie loved corn bread.

The thought of her children reminded her that she must be careful. She wasn't an eighteen-year-old girl any longer, and she had to put her children first in any relationship.

Not that she had a reason to suppose Matt meant anything serious by his attentions. He had probably kissed dozens of girls in his time.

Kissing her had been an impulse, nothing more. She should treat it lightly.

And if it hadn't been just an impulse? She discovered, to her surprise, that she'd like to believe it. Even so, it was far too soon to think of anything serious.

Rebecca couldn't seem to keep from feeling optimistic, though. The farm-stay was up and running, she had money coming in to provide for her children, Daad was improving every day, and Matt had kissed her.

A buggy passed the kitchen window. Rebecca put the lid back on the cornmeal box and wiped her hands before she hurried outside.

To her surprise, it was Mary Ann King, who stopped at the sight of her.

"Mary Ann. How nice to see you. Have you been over at Mamm and Daad's?"

Mary Ann nodded, not smiling. "My mamm sent supper over for them."

"That was wonderful kind of her. And of you, to bring it." Maybe Mary Ann was beginning to gain that maturity Mamm had mentioned. "Do you have time to come in and visit?"

"I can't stay." Mary Ann looked like someone on a mission she couldn't figure out how to complete. "I just wanted to talk to you."

"Of course." Rebecca looked up at her. What could Mary Ann possibly want with her?

"Simon wouldn't dream of complaining, but I thought you'd want to know how he's feeling. I'm sure I would in your position." Mary Ann's gaze avoided hers, fixed firmly on her horse's ears.

"I see." But she didn't. If there was a problem with her brother, she wasn't aware of it. "Why wouldn't Simon come to me about whatever it is?"

"He wouldn't want to hurt your feelings," Mary Ann said quickly. "And he wants to do his duty."

There was a righteous tone to Mary Ann's voice that Rebecca didn't care for. She tried to be fair, but did Mary Ann actually imagine she was telling Rebecca anything she didn't already know about her own brother?

"You must see you're asking too much, Rebecca." Mary Ann leaned toward her suddenly, flushing a little. "Simon is taking care of his daad's farm and yours, and now you've got him involved in the farm-stay business of yours. And you're not even paying him! How can you treat your own brother that way?"

Rebecca felt as if she'd been struck. She took a step back, shaking her head. She didn't want to believe what she was hearing.

Guilt rushed in. True, Simon was doing all those things. No doubt it didn't give him time for anything else.

It wasn't right. Simon was only twenty. He ought to be free to be courting, to be enjoying himself, not be tied to responsibilities that weren't rightfully his.

"I just thought you'd want to know," Mary Ann repeated.

She picked up the lines and clucked to the mare, leaving Rebecca shaken and torn.

It was only when the children were tucked up in bed that Rebecca allowed herself time to think again about the distressing visit from Mary Ann. By then, she'd calmed down and could look at it more objectively.

The girl was young and she was interested primarily in herself, but Rebecca couldn't blame her. Naturally Mary Ann wanted her come-calling friend to have time for her.

More important, what had Simon said to set Mary Ann off? Rebecca stood for a moment in the kitchen, staring absently at the back window and the view beyond. Was it really only a few hours ago that she'd been celebrating the fact that her business was going well?

That happiness now seemed to be even more selfish than Mary Ann's attitude. She had taken her brother's help for granted when, without him, how could she proceed? Even if Simon felt he could cope with helping her now, what would happen if and when they got busier? Mary Ann was right about one thing—Simon couldn't run two farms and deal with her visitors as well.

She had to talk this over with Simon. Of course he wanted to help her. He was her brother. As the two oldest, they'd always been close. But she couldn't go on taking advantage of him.

Maybe, if they could discuss it openly, they could figure out some solution. But what? It seemed each time she'd solved one problem, another cropped up.

Simon might be still at the barn. She stepped out into the mild evening, pausing on the porch. The sun had slipped behind the ridge, painting the western sky in shades of pink and purple, and twilight had begun to draw in. The barn doors were closed, and if Simon were there working, he'd have left them open for the light. Their conversation would have to wait for tomorrow.

"Rebecca."

She spun, startled, to see Matt approaching from the workshop.

"Matt." A little flutter in her chest made it hard to sound normal. "I thought you left already."

"I had some work I wanted to finish first."

His face was solemn, and her heart thudded. He looked so serious—she hoped he wasn't going to say he was sorry he'd kissed her, especially since she feared she'd made it very plain that she'd enjoyed being kissed.

"Are the kinder in bed?" He paused, one foot on the bottom step.

"They're in, although it gets harder to settle them now that it's light longer."

"We need to talk." The words were heavy, as if they were weighted with something. Regret, maybe?

She could hardly say she didn't want to listen. "Komm." She gestured to the porch. "We can sit out here, where I'll hear the kinder if they call."

She sat down on the porch swing, the motion producing its familiar creak. It was a pleasant place to relax in the summer when the day's work was done. "Please." She gestured to the space beside her.

Matt didn't seem to notice. He leaned against the porch railing, hands gripping it, as if he was bracing himself. He frowned, maybe trying to figure out where to start.

She might as well save him the trouble. "If you are worried about kissing me—"

"No, Rebecca." His expression didn't lighten. "I'm worried about caring for you."

The serious tone touched her heart. He meant it. She seemed to tremble on the edge of a precipice. Matt meant it, and she cared for him, as well.

It was one thing to admit it to herself, but quite another to say it out loud. She was afraid—afraid of what that might mean.

Matt didn't seem to expect a response. His frown deepened, and his knuckles must be white considering how hard he was gripping the railing.

"I don't go around telling people about my past. But you have a right to know the truth about me."

"I know that you're kind, and caring, and responsible," she said quickly. "I don't need to know anything else."

Matt's gaze rested on her face, and she couldn't quite interpret what it said. "No." He shook his head. "I've made so many mistakes in my life. They were all caused by the same thing—a temper I can't control. A temper that can lead to violence."

Everything in her denied it. "You're beating yourself up, but there's no need."

"Listen to me, Rebecca." He leaned toward her, his face a mask to hide his feelings. "That's why Isaiah nearly drowned, because I couldn't control my urge to hit back."

"Matt, you were a kid. You've grown out of it. You can't go

on blaming yourself for something that happened when you were just a teenager."

"You're quick to defend me." His grim expression lightened for an instant. "But I'm not a kid now, and look what happened with Simon."

"It seems to me Simon is the one who should feel guilty about it."

Matt couldn't seem to accept any excuse. "You don't understand. I was so furious that I nearly struck him with my fist."

"But you didn't." She longed to touch him, to comfort him, but she was afraid to move lest he stop talking.

"I didn't because you were there." A ghost of a smile appeared and was gone. "I've tried again and again to live in peace. I've failed."

"You've done nothing wrong. Just because you get angry sometimes—well, none of us is perfect. Don't you think all of us fail to live up to the church's teaching?"

"Not like me." He sucked in a breath. "I thought I'd be happy when I jumped the fence. I thought I'd fit in to the outside world. But I didn't. I ended up in jail."

She stared at him for a long moment, unable to accept the words, thinking he must be joking. But he was serious.

"What happened? Why?" An Amish person might go to jail for failing to obey a law that he felt went counter to God's will. She could understand—

"I got into a fight in a bar. A man was injured, so badly he had to go to the hospital." He raised his hands in front of him, looking at them as if they belonged to someone else. "I struck someone. I injured him. I was arrested and sentenced to six months in jail."

Rebecca's throat was dry, and her stomach twisted. "Matt, I . . . I'm sorry." For him, for the other man, for the whole situation.

His jaw clenched. "When I got out, I made up my mind to come back to the church. To start over. I thought I could live in peace."

"You can," she said, forcing the words out through a tight throat.

He shook his head. "It's not something I could leave behind in the Englisch world. It's something inside me." He looked down at his hands again, as if he saw something she didn't. "I wish I could be the man you think I am, but I'm afraid I can't. So the safest thing is not to let anyone rely on me." His face twisted. "Especially not you and the children."

"Matt, that doesn't make sense. It doesn't have to be that way." She reached out to him, but he didn't seem to see her.

He shoved himself away from the railing, took the porch steps in a long stride, and headed toward his buggy at something just short of a run.

Her heart clenched painfully. She couldn't think of anything else to say, any way to reach him. Matt had locked himself behind the barrier of his guilt, and he wouldn't come out, even for her.

Chapter Sixteen

Lancaster County, September 1942

*A*nna shoved a basket of tomatoes into the wagon and stood leaning against it for a moment, hand on her aching back. The wagon wasn't quite full, but this was the last picking of the summer. It was the first week of September already.

She nodded to her youngest brother. Peter looked smaller than ever perched on the wagon seat. He slapped the heavy lines on the back of the workhorse, and the wagon moved slowly down the field.

Eli, who seemed to have grown a foot since Seth had left, came to her, automatically measuring himself against her. He seemed to be living for the day when he'd be taller than she was.

Because he felt he had to take Seth's place? It might well be. He wasn't the only boy who had to do a man's work before his time, now that so many of the county's young men had gone off to the war.

Anna tapped her brother's frayed straw hat. "Komm. Let's get back to the barn. Daadi will be needing us."

He nodded, his young face tightening. "He works too hard. I wish . . ."

"Ja. I know." She wished it, too. If there had never been a war, if Seth hadn't thought he had to fight . . .

A wave of anger swept through her, startling in its power. Had Seth thought about them when he left? Had he known Mammi would be crying every night, Daadi aging ten years in a day, Anna and the kinder taking on a man's work to keep the farm going without him?

The government kept announcing that farmers should produce more food because of the war. But how could they when their young men were gone, either into the military, like Seth, or to the Civilian Public Service camps, like Jacob?

Jacob's family was struggling, too. They were missing him and challenged to bring in a decent crop with only kinder and old people to help. Jacob would be missing it. He'd always said he was never so happy as when he had his hands in the earth.

She remembered teasing him. *Not even when you're taking me home from singing?* she'd asked. *Not even when you kiss me good night?*

He'd responded with a grin and a light kiss on her lips, and she'd thought she'd always be as happy as she was right in that moment.

"Everyone is in the same situation," she told her brother, not sure how that was supposed to make Eli feel better.

"Not everyone," he said, his mouth twisting a little. "Not the Yoders. Zeke Yoder got exempted from going to the camps. How did he do it?"

Everyone, even the Amish, had a new vocabulary these days, it seemed. She and Eli left the field for the easier walking of the yard and headed toward the barn. *Exempted*—she wouldn't have expected her little brother to know the word in an ordinary world.

"You mustn't blame the Yoders for Zeke not having to go," she said. "That would be as bad as our Englisch neighbors blaming us for speaking German."

"Well, I still say it's funny. Why should Zeke get a farming exemption and not Jacob?"

She couldn't deny the fact that she'd asked that question herself sometimes, especially when she woke in the night and thought of Jacob so far away.

"I don't know." That was the only honest answer she could give. "It seems like the folks on the draft board don't know exactly what to do with us. We just have to be thankful that none of our boys have been forced to bear arms."

"I don't want to hear any more war talk."

They'd gotten close enough for Daadi to hear, and his voice was sharp.

"Sorry, Daadi." Anna knew how he felt about it. She should have been more careful.

Daadi's gaze rested on her face, softening. "We've done enough for now. We'll finish up after supper. Go, all of you, and have a break."

The two boys didn't need an excuse. They darted off across the yard as if they'd been fired from a slingshot, making Anna smile.

"If you're sure you don't need me now, Daadi, I'll go and see if there is any mail."

His worn face creased in an answering smile. "You mean you will see if there's a letter from Jacob, ain't so? Go ahead and check. I hope you'll find one." He waved his hand toward the road.

Anna's tiredness slipped away as she hurried down the lane toward the mailbox out by the road. Now that Jacob was settled at the camp in Maryland, he wrote more regularly, although Jacob never had been much of a letter writer.

At first he and the other men, mostly Amish and Mennonites with a few Quakers and Englisch, had been kept busy renovating the dilapidated buildings that were their barracks. The only thing that had held them back initially was the lack of supplies, but the sponsoring churches had quickly brought in what they needed.

Now, according to Jacob's last letter, they had been put to work planting trees. He'd said he heard that some men would be picked to help with the harvest on area farms, and he hoped to be chosen.

Planting trees is okay, but harvesting crops would be better. It seems like farm work would be a better use of a bunch of farm boys!

Anna smiled, thinking of his words. At least he was well and safe. The peace churches had to provide everything that was needed for the camps, and folks were generous, knowing it was their own boys and their neighbors' sons who were far from home and needing them.

She'd nearly reached the gravel road, and she quickened her steps, reaching the metal mailbox at what was almost a run.

Yanking open the door, she thrust her hand in and pulled out the contents: a newspaper for Daad, a round robin letter from Mammi's cousins, and finally a letter from Jacob. She held the envelope in both hands, gloating over it.

Waiting to read it was impossible. She ripped the envelope open and pulled out two sheets of paper covered with Jacob's sprawling hand. If he—

The sound of an engine startled her. She'd been so preoccupied with her letter that she hadn't heard the pickup coming, and her breath caught in alarm. The truck bucketed down the narrow road, too fast, surely, weaving from one side to the other and then heading straight for her.

Anna stumbled backward, feet slipping on the gravel, fear sending her heart thudding. Tripping into the ditch, water in her shoes, the truck screaming down on her . . .

Brakes shrieked. Laughter—someone was laughing. Two boys hung out of the bed of the pickup. Before she could speak something struck her once, then again and again.

Tomatoes. They were pelting her with tomatoes. She winced away, trying to shield her face and hair with her hands. Almost before she knew what had happened, the truck lurched off down the road, weaving from side to side.

Anna looked down. Her skirt and apron were splattered with red that looked like blood, her shoes and socks soaked and muddy. Her stomach lurched, but she couldn't be sick, not out here in the road for anyone passing by to see.

"Are you all right?" A teenage Englisch girl scrambled off a bicycle and came running toward Anna. Anna hadn't even noticed her in the wake of the truck. "Did they hurt you?"

"No, no. I'm fine." But she was shaking uncontrollably.

The girl leaned over, grasping Anna's hand. "Come on. I'll help you. Just lean on me."

She pulled, and Anna managed to control her shaking legs enough to climb up out of the ditch. Once there, she couldn't seem to move. Shivering, she looked at the girl.

"Denke. Thank you." She shook her head. "I can't seem to think straight. It's kind of you to help me."

"I saw what they did. You should tell the police." The girl brushed ineffectively at the mess on Anna's skirt.

"It's all right." She caught the girl's hand, her voice rising. The Amish didn't go to the police, not even if they were attacked. "Really. I don't want to cause any trouble."

The girl straightened, smiling at her, and Anna realized she was older than she had thought at first. The pants she was wearing made her look like a kid, but her face was mature. She had brown hair pulled back in a ponytail and curly bangs, and her lips were slicked with pink.

"You're Anna, Seth's sister, aren't you? I'm Patty Felder." The young woman was looking at Anna as if that should mean something to her.

"I'm sorry . . ." Anna began.

"I guess Seth didn't tell you about me." She smiled, showing a dimple in each cheek. "I'm a friend of his."

Why she should be so surprised that one of Seth's Englisch friends was a girl, Anna couldn't say. "I'm wonderful glad to meet you, Patty."

Patty's smile widened. "You'll be even happier when you see what I have for you." She pulled a folded paper from her pocket. "It's a note from Seth."

"From Seth?" Anna's heart swelled until it seemed about to burst through her chest. "For me?"

"I guess for the family, but Seth said in his letter that I should only give it to you." She shrugged. "He didn't know how his dad would feel about his writing to the family. He says you'll know what to do about it."

"Thank you." The words didn't seem big enough for what she was feeling. Anna grasped Patty's hand. "I can't tell you how much it means to hear from him."

Patty nodded. "I figured as much. He did tell me that his family wouldn't understand his joining up, and he said they'd take it hard."

"It goes against our beliefs." Anna longed to have this unexpected friend understand, strange as it was to stand beside the road and talk this way. "We don't stop loving Seth and worrying about him, but it grieves my parents that he went against our faith by joining the fight, and Daadi doesn't want us to write, even if we knew where he is."

"I guess that would make it worse," Patty said. "Most folks act like they're proud when their boys join up, but I bet they do a lot of worrying and crying, too."

"It's hard on everyone," Anna said. And how much harder was it going to get? She couldn't even guess.

"Sure is." Patty's lips twisted. "You know, at first all this business about the war was exciting. Scary, but exciting, too, with all the boys going into uniform and everything. But now . . . now it's just sad."

"Yes." Anna met her gaze and saw understanding there. "It is."

Patty drew away. "I'd better go. I don't want your dad to spot me. Or my dad, either, for that matter, not that he's likely to. So if I hear again, I'll come see you. If I happen to come past the mailbox at this time of day, will you be the one picking up the mail?"

Anna nodded. "If I possibly can, I'll come to the mailbox every day. Although after this, my mother will probably make a fuss." She gestured toward her stained apron.

"I still say you ought to tell the police. I recognized that truck, and I'd back you up."

"No, I can't." She could see that Patty didn't understand, and it seemed useless to try to explain the Amish aversion to dealing with the authorities. "People are already upset with us. I don't want to make it any worse."

"It's up to you." Patty appeared doubtful. "Tell you what—if you want to write a letter to Seth, I'll send it on to him."

"I would love to write to him," she said quickly. "Would you really do that for me?"

"I sure will. I'm supposed to work at the Red Cross all day tomorrow, but I'll come by the next day, same time. I'll wait out here for you. Okay?"

"Thank you." For an instant Anna held back, but her feelings were too strong. She gave Patty a quick hug and felt the girl's arms close warmly around her. When Anna drew back, there were tears in Patty's eyes as well as hers.

Rebecca found parts of Anna's diary slipping back into her thoughts at odd moments of the day. Anna had begun to seem so real to her—as if she were a dear friend Rebecca talked to daily.

Rebecca unpinned sheets from the clothesline in the backyard, enjoying the fresh scent of air-dried linens as she folded them. One challenge about having guests was keeping up with the constant laundry. And she'd thought she had plenty of sheets.

Rebecca's thoughts turned to the segment of the diary she'd read last night before bed. Anna's experience with Englischers had aroused emotions from disappointment to downright fear, and yet she'd managed to stay open to possibilities when she'd met her brother's Englisch girlfriend. She clearly hadn't suffered from being tongue-tied around strangers.

Tomorrow's guests would give Rebecca another opportunity to become the friendly, open hostess she longed to be, she reminded herself. This time she would try to be more like Barbie. Surely the whole experience would become easier with practice, wouldn't it? She was counting on it.

Glancing toward the stable was becoming a habit for her. It was too early for Matt to be there, of course. Still, she couldn't help praying he would come. He might well want to avoid the whole place after what he'd said to her yesterday.

Matt had told her things he apparently hadn't spoken of to anyone else. In the aftermath, he might well be regretting it. What if he felt he couldn't face her, now that she knew?

A jagged edge of pain sliced through her. She should have handled the conversation better. She should have thought of something to say that would show him he was the good man she knew him to be, despite his past.

But she hadn't. She'd stood there silently, hardly able to say a thing. She hadn't been smart enough or brave enough or strong enough to make a difference for him.

When he came . . . If he came . . . she must try harder.

A flicker of movement caught her eye and sent her heart jumping before she realized it was Simon. She had to talk to him, as well, and that task loomed nearly as difficult as finding the words for Matt.

Well, it had to be done. She must make it clear to Simon that he didn't have to dedicate his life to helping her. And she'd have to try to keep Mary Ann's name out of it, if she didn't want to figure as an interfering possible sister-in-law. She put the folded sheets in the basket and waved to her brother.

Simon came toward her with his lanky stride, still moving as if he was getting used to having a man's body instead of a boy's. The reflection produced a twinge in her heart. Simon was trying so hard, but he was too young to have so much responsibility thrust on him, wasn't he?

And he certainly was too young to be thinking of marriage to Mary Ann or anyone else, in her opinion, although she didn't suppose he'd agree.

"I have some ideas for things I can do with the guests when they come tomorrow." Simon spoke as soon as he was within earshot. "I've been thinking about it since last weekend, and Daad had some suggestions, too."

Rebecca was momentarily sidetracked by the mention of their father. "He's not fretting about it, is he? Mammi doesn't want him worrying."

Simon grinned, pushing his straw hat back farther on his head. "I don't think she can stop him from being involved, ain't so? He always thinks none of us kids can do anything without him standing right there watching."

"Ach, Simon, you know that's not true. Daad has to trust you with so much just now, and you're not letting him down."

He shrugged. "It's just the same things I always do, and the young ones are more help than you'd expect. Johnny keeps telling me he doesn't want to be a farmer, but he's so gut with the animals I think he'd be a dummy to do anything else."

"Maybe he'll see that for himself as he gets older." Johnny had a bright, inquiring mind, and she'd often wondered what he'd settle to in the end. "But I wanted to talk to you about . . ." She gestured, palms up. ". . . well, everything. You've been doing so much between running the farms and taking over for Daad, and now you're putting in so much time helping me, as well." She thought of Mary Ann's complaint. "And I'm not even paying you. It's not fair."

Simon just stared at her for a moment, his blue eyes very wide. "What are you talking about?"

He honestly didn't seem to understand.

"You, putting in so many hours helping me run the farm-stay. It was one thing for Paul to do it, because it was his business, but I shouldn't be depending on you—"

"Who else would you be depending on?" Anger edged his voice and made his face suddenly older, surprising her. "You're my sister. Of course I am helping you. What would make you think I would have it any other way?"

"I just don't think I should take up so much of your time." She went on doggedly. "You're young. You should be enjoying your running-around time, not stuck here working every minute."

"Who put that idea in your head?" He stared at her as if waiting for an answer.

She didn't speak. She couldn't.

Simon's cheeks flushed slightly. "Anyway, it's crazy. We're family. We help each other. Who would we be if we didn't?" He slung an arm around her shoulder in a rare, awkward caress. "Ach, Becky, you've got a bee in your bonnet for nothing. Anyway, I like working with your visitors."

"You're sure?" She searched his face and was comforted by what she saw there.

"Positive. The Englischers are all different, and that makes it interesting. Like the old man last weekend—he said it made him feel like a boy on his father's farm to help me. But his son-in-law couldn't figure out one end of a pitchfork from the other and didn't want to try."

"You really do enjoy it, don't you?" She sighed, perplexed and relieved. "You and Barbie both. And I'm always worried to death I'm going to say the wrong thing, or they're going to ask me something I can't answer, or—"

"Borrowing trouble." He gave her shoulder a final squeeze and let go. "You just keep them well fed, and let Barbie and me do our parts."

"All right."

"And don't worry," he said.

She smiled. "I promise." It seemed to her that Mary Ann had come up with the wrong idea. If she didn't know Simon better than that, it probably didn't bode well for their future happiness.

Don't interfere, she reminded herself. Besides, it seemed to her that Simon might have guessed who'd put the idea in her head. He wouldn't want to admit it, of course.

She started to turn back toward the house, but Simon touched her arm. He was frowning a little, not meeting her eyes.

"One thing I wanted you to know." He said the words reluctantly.

"Ja?" She stiffened, trying to be ready for anything.

"I talked to Matt. I told him I was sorry for how I acted with him."

"I'm glad," she said, relieved. It wasn't easy for Simon to admit his fault, but he'd done the right thing. "Matt has been very kind to me and the kinder." She would not let herself blush. "I'd hate to think you were on the outs with him."

"No. I mean, we're not." It was Simon's turn to flush, the tips of his ears reddening as he seemed to force himself to go on. "But I still . . . Well, I can't help worrying that you're getting too close to him."

What could she say? *I'm not*? But that wouldn't be true. "You don't need to worry about me."

He gave her a look. "I'm your bruder, ain't so? I'm supposed to worry."

"I think I'm a little old to need your advice on this subject." She tried to put a hint of warning in her voice.

"I know." The stubborn set to his jaw said he wasn't finished. "I'm wonderful glad to see you getting interested in living. I want you to be happy. But Matt— I'm just afraid Matt will end up hurting you." He looked as if he expected to have his head bitten off, but she was too touched by his obvious concern to be angry.

She patted his hand. "I'll be careful," she said.

But even as she said it, she knew it was too late for caution. Her feelings were already too strong to back away and pretend there was nothing between them. And given Matt's determination that he couldn't be involved with anyone, she had already been hurt.

What had possessed him to tell Rebecca the one thing he never talked about? Matt didn't understand himself, and he hated the feeling. Even at his worst, when he'd been living Englisch, drinking too much, hanging out with the wrong people, he'd at least known what he was doing. Now . . . well, now he didn't.

He leaned against the workbench, frowning at what was meant to become a bookcase. This was still his chosen work— the kind of creation that brought a sense of satisfaction. And he could hardly back out of the agreement he'd made to rent the building from Rebecca. That would be a dirty trick when she was obviously counting on the money.

But the safest course for both of them was probably to stay as far apart as possible under the circumstances. He shouldn't have to worry about that where Rebecca was concerned. After what he'd told her yesterday, she wouldn't want to have anything to do with him.

He told himself that was the best solution. Unfortunately, his heart seemed to require a little more convincing.

He heard voices outside, and a moment later two small tornadoes swept through the door.

"You're finally here." Joshua rushed over to the workbench to see what he was doing. "You were late today."

"We were afraid you weren't coming." Katie skipped to his side. "Tomorrow our guests are going to be here, so we'll be busy."

"We wanted to ask if we could have a couple of pieces of wood to make a little shelf in our tree house." Josh looked up at him, blue eyes very serious. "But only pieces you don't need."

Matt couldn't help smiling. "I think I can find something. But does your mammi know you're here?" Hard to imagine that Rebecca would want her kinder anywhere near him.

"Mammi said it was okay, but we were supposed to say that if you're busy, just tell us to leave and we will." Katie's forehead crinkled. "Oops. I think we were supposed to say that first."

"You're not too busy, are you?" Josh tugged on Matt's sleeve.

"I could sweep up for you," Katie offered. "I always help Mammi."

Matt didn't quite know what to make of Rebecca's attitude. Maybe she didn't want to make an issue out of forbidding them to come here. If so, she was being kinder than he had any reason to expect. If she had kept the children away from him, word would inevitably get around the community that he must have done something to cause such a thing.

"I'll have some pieces left over that should be just the right size once I finish cutting the shelves for the bookcase I'm making. Okay?"

They nodded vigorously, and Katie ran to grab the broom that leaned against the wall. "You help me, Josh. You can hold the dustpan."

Josh didn't argue with her bossing him, and Matt continued to measure and cut to the accompaniment of their light voices chattering happily.

By the time the children were getting restless, he had the pieces of pine cut for them to make a small box. Joshua looked ready to object to the suggestion until Matt explained.

"See, if you put it together this way, you can set it on its side for a shelf or use it as a box or turn it over and make it a table, ain't so?"

"I see." Katie's face lit up.

Josh nodded vigorously. "Can I hammer?"

"You can take turns," he said.

Their enthusiastic hammering must have drowned out the sound of her approach. Matt didn't realize Rebecca was there until she touched his shoulder. He swung around to find her smiling at him.

"It looks as if you've let these two talk you into helping them instead of getting on with your work."

He shrugged, taking a careful step away from her. "It was no problem." *Keep it brief,* he reminded himself.

Rebecca's eyes clouded at his curtness. "It was kind," she said, and glanced at the children. "Supper's ready now. You can finish up tomorrow." Then she turned back to Matt. "We'd be pleased if you'd have supper with us." The words seemed a bit hesitant.

Because she was unsure of herself? Or because she was hoping he'd refuse?

"I have plenty to do here. Denke."

The children were already scrambling for the door, but she paused for a moment longer. "You really are wilkom, Matt."

Whatever he could have answered was interrupted by a call from Katie, just outside the door.

"Mammi, there's a car pulling up at the house. I thought the guests weren't coming until tomorrow."

"They aren't." Rebecca shook her head slightly. "It must be someone else."

"They're getting out suitcases," Joshua said.

Something that might have been panic seemed to freeze Rebecca, eyes wide and frightened.

Matt could hardly ignore what seemed a plea for help. "Maybe we'd better go and find out." He touched her arm lightly, but even that brush of his fingertips on her sleeve sent his awareness of her shimmering.

Rebecca spun and hurried to the door. "It can't be," she protested. "They aren't due until tomorrow."

But when they got outside, it was only too clear that Rebecca's guests had arrived. Two men were taking suitcases from the car's trunk while their wives looked around, clearly expecting to be welcomed.

"They can't be here." Rebecca's words were edged with fear. "We're not ready."

Matt tried to think of something comforting to say and couldn't think of anything. "I guess you'd better go and speak to them."

She jerked a nod and walked toward the group by the car, her movements stiff. Matt hesitated a moment and then followed her. There was no point in telling himself that he shouldn't get involved when Rebecca so obviously needed help.

"Here we are." One of the middle-aged women was thin and nervous-looking; the other was chubby and placid. It was, predictably, the nervous one who spoke. "We're the Thompsons and the Bidlemans."

Rebecca seemed to struggle to produce a smile. "We did not expect you until tomorrow."

"No, no, today." The woman reached into her oversized bag and rummaged. "Today. The fifth, see?" She waved a piece of paper triumphantly.

Her three companions stared at her for a moment. One of the men shook his head, a rueful expression touching his face. "Doris, honey, today is the fourth."

"It is?" She looked inclined to argue, but in the face of a unanimous agreement that it was the fourth, she shrugged, laughing a little. "Well, if that isn't the silliest thing. I had it set in my mind that it was Friday, of course, and I never even went back and looked at the date." She turned back to Rebecca. "Well, it doesn't matter, does it? If you don't have any other guests, surely we can stay."

Everyone looked at Rebecca, including Matt. He wasn't sure what the others saw, but he knew what he saw. Rebecca was paralyzed.

He nudged her. "Can you show them to their rooms? They'll understand if the beds aren't made up yet."

Rebecca's gaze fastened on his. "But . . . the meals, Barbie, Simon—"

"We don't expect you to fix supper for us this late." The man who was apparently Doris's husband stepped in. "I'm sorry about the mix-up. If you can direct us to a restaurant, we'll go get some supper and give you a chance to get ready for us."

"I can do that, of course." Matt spoke, since it seemed Rebecca couldn't. "Why don't you set your bags on the porch, and we'll take them up later."

The man nodded. "Come on, let's get unloaded and we'll go eat."

As the unexpected guests began carting their things onto the porch, Matt took Rebecca's arm. "Rebecca, snap out of it. This is going to be all right. I'll call Barbie and tell her to get over here. The kinder can run and let Simon know what's happening."

Rebecca gulped in a breath, the color returning to her face. "Ja, of course. I'm sorry. I just—I couldn't think what to do." Seeming to collect herself, she turned to the children. "Katie and Josh, run over to Grossmammi's house and tell her and Onkel Simon what happened."

Matt started for the phone shanty and then hesitated. "You're all right?"

Rebecca nodded, her face set. "I'm fine."

She didn't look fine. He felt a familiar exasperation. If she dreaded this whole business so much, why should she do it? Surely enough time had passed that she could stop trying to fulfill her late husband's dreams.

Or maybe that was the point. Maybe she couldn't.

Chapter Seventeen

*I*t wasn't until evening when Rebecca was finally alone. The children were in bed and she hoped asleep. The two couples, apparently unable to face a night without television, had gone off to a movie theater, some fifteen miles away in the nearest larger town.

Barbie, after appearing promptly in response to Matthew's call and jumping into action, had gone home after they'd left, promising to return first thing in the morning, and Simon had activities lined up for the next day.

Rebecca could finally stop smiling . . . a good thing, as her face had begun to feel frozen. She stood at the sink, washing the bowl she'd used to mix up a breakfast casserole for the morning. She was alone. She could relax.

Unfortunately, being alone also gave her time to consider her performance when the guests had arrived unexpectedly. She put wet hands to her cheeks and found them burning with humiliation. She'd been faced with a challenge, and she'd frozen.

We must be ready for the unexpected. That was what Paul had said repeatedly the first summer they'd opened. People cancelled at the last minute, people arrived on the wrong day, people had allergies they hadn't mentioned or couldn't live without electricity or expected to have high-speed wireless in an Amish home. In all those situations, Paul had smiled and dealt with the problem.

And what had she done when faced with the smallest hiccup? She'd failed. A tear slid down her cheek and dropped into the dishwater.

"Rebecca?" Matthew stood at the screen door in the dusk, looking in at her. "Was ist letz? What's wrong?"

"Nothing." She turned her face away to wipe her eyes.

The screen door creaked, and she heard Matt's footsteps cross the kitchen floor.

"It can't be nothing when you're standing here crying." He was close behind her, and his voice was gentle. "What happened to the guests? They didn't leave, did they?"

She shook her head, forcing herself to turn and face him. "Only to go to a movie. I think they weren't prepared for how quiet it is."

Matt's chuckle was a low sound in his throat. "There's something to be said for knowing how to amuse yourself. But if the guests are all right, why are you crying?"

A flicker of anger went through her that he'd force her to say it aloud. "You know why. You saw me. At the first little problem, I panicked. If you hadn't been there . . ." She let that trail off, not willing to say how much she'd relied on him in that moment.

"It wasn't as bad as that, was it?" Matt almost sounded

amused. "You were shocked, and you couldn't think what to say for a minute. If I hadn't been there, you'd have done fine on your own."

"No. I wouldn't." The anger turned from a flicker to a flame. "Don't you see? I'm just not capable."

"That's ridiculous." He didn't look amused any longer.

She shook her head stubbornly. "You mentioned one time when I climbed that big oak tree in the schoolyard, but you conveniently forgot what really happened. I climbed up all right, because someone teased me about it. But then I saw how high I was and I froze, just like I did today. Paul had to come up and rescue me. I couldn't do it alone."

"Komm, Rebecca." Matt leaned against the counter next to her, and she couldn't help being aware of his warmth and strength. "There's a big difference between a child afraid of heights and a woman who has a momentary hesitation in the face of the unexpected. You're not a failure because this particular job is a little hard for you."

She pressed her fingers to her forehead, because her head seemed to be thudding in time with Matt's words. Why couldn't he just go away and leave her alone?

"I know you mean well. I appreciate your help. But I don't want to talk about this anymore."

"You want me to go away, ain't so?" There was an edge of anger in Matt's voice, and his straight brows drew down over his eyes. "Then you can sit here and feel sorry for yourself because you think you can't do what Paul wanted."

Her head came up at his words. "I'm not sitting. I'm working. And I'm not going to cry anymore, but even so, it's true. I can't do what Paul would have wanted, and that hurts."

"What Paul wanted." Matt's hands shot out and grasped her wrists. "It was Paul's dream, not yours. You can do it, but why should you?"

"You don't understand." She tugged at her hands, and he let them go at once, but his cleft chin looked as if it were carved from stone.

"No, I don't understand." His gaze searched her face as if looking for answers. "Don't forget, I knew Paul, too. He was a good kid, and I'm sure he grew into a good man. But he wasn't a saint, and he didn't have all the answers."

"I never said he was a saint. But—"

"But you think you can keep him alive by doing what he would have done."

She gasped at that, feeling as if he'd hit her. She wasn't trying to keep Paul alive. She wouldn't. Matt was wrong, and he had no business talking to her that way.

"You're a fine one to be telling me how to live." She flung the words at him, wanting to hurt. "If I'm a coward, I'm not the only one. You're busy using your past mistakes as an excuse for not living your life now."

Silence. No one had ever made her as angry as Matt had. She had gone too far, and she wanted the words back, but she didn't know how to retrieve them.

"You know, you might just be right about me." Matt's lips twisted in what could have been meant for a smile. Then he turned and walked away.

Matt tossed clothes at random into the duffel bag he'd put on his bed, impelled by a fierce need to get moving. There was only one thing he could do after the mess he'd made of things with Rebecca.

He'd known all along it would be a mistake to get involved with her, hadn't he? So he had only himself to blame for caring so much that leaving her felt like wrenching his heart right out of his chest.

"Are you running away again?"

The tart female voice had him spinning to the door. His cousin Sadie stood there, one hand on the frame almost as if she'd bar his way.

Matt gritted his teeth together. That was unlikely to happen. Sadie would be far more willing to give him a swift boot out of her family's life.

"Is that what you want me to do?" He ground the words out. The last thing he needed right now was a hassle with Sadie.

She wrapped her arms around herself, her face clouding. "No. But isn't it what you always do?"

Her words echoed too closely what Rebecca had said to him, jabbing him in whatever was left of his heart. But for once there had been no malice in Sadie's tone or her face. She'd asked as if she really wanted an answer.

Matt glanced down at the shirt he held and tossed it in the direction of the duffel bag. "I'm going after Isaiah."

Sadie took a hasty step toward him, her face lighting. "Do you know where he is? Tell me."

"Not exactly." He didn't want to watch her face, but he couldn't help seeing the hope battling doubt in her eyes. "I talked to Simon, and he gave me the name of an Englisch friend of Isaiah's. The upshot is he might be at a place out in Holmes County."

"How long have you known?" she demanded. "Why didn't you tell me before now?"

"I didn't want to tell you because it's so vague. I guess I hoped I'd find out a little more before I raised anybody's hopes."

Or maybe he'd just been too preoccupied with his own affairs. With Rebecca. But that was over now, and the only really useful thing he could do for anyone here was to find Isaiah.

"Anyway, I've decided to go out there and have a look around for him. If he's not there, maybe someone has been in touch with him and knows something. It's better than doing nothing."

A glimmer of hope remained in Sadie's face as she nodded. "I wish I could go. If only I could see him . . ."

"I know." For the first time Matt felt completely in sympathy with Sadie. It was the hardest thing in the world to see someone you loved making a mistake and being powerless to help. "But your mamm needs you here. Onkel Silas doesn't have much work planned for the next week, so I can be spared more easily." He managed a smile. "Besides, this might be a situation where my having lived Englisch comes in handy."

"I guess you're right." Sadie pressed her lips together, and he thought she was trying hard not to let her emotions out. "But how will you manage the trip if you don't know exactly where he is?"

"Rebecca's father put me in touch with a retired Englisch teacher who likes to drive the Amish, a guy named Joe Davis."

Sadie was nodding. "Everyone knows Joe. He's always driving the Leit when they need to make a trip."

"Anyway, he doesn't mind driving me out and doing some wandering around to look for Isaiah. I explained that I couldn't be sure exactly where we'd have to go. I booked Joe for three days. We'll find a motel if we have to stay over. If I haven't learned anything in that time—" He stopped, not willing to face the idea of failing.

"Even if you find him . . ." Sadie paused, the muscles of her face working. "If you do, what do you think will happen?"

Her pain seemed to communicate itself to him, and he reached out to touch her hand. For an instant she clung to him, reminding him of the small cousin she'd been when he left Brook Hill.

"I don't know. It's probably too much to hope that he'd come home with me, but even if I can get him to stay in touch with the family, that would be better than what you have now. Maybe I can knock that much sense into Isaiah's thick head." He tried to smile, but knew it for a failure. "At worst, at least I can tell Aunt Lovina I saw him. I'll give her a happy report of him even if it's a fairy tale."

Sadie nodded. "Anything would be better than not knowing." She took a deep breath, dropping his hand and straightening. "But what are you going to tell Mamm and Daad about going away?"

He shrugged. "As little as possible, I guess. I don't want to raise their hopes."

"Ja, that's so." Sadie picked up the shirt he'd crumpled, flipping it out and folding it properly. "We can't have you going around strangers looking like a rag bag, can we?"

"Denke, Sadie." He leaned against the footboard, knowing she was finding relief in the simple physical action.

She tucked the shirt neatly into the bag. "What does Rebecca think about what you're doing?"

The name hit him like a blow. He'd actually managed not to think about Rebecca for a few minutes.

"Nothing. I mean, I didn't talk to her about it."

Sadie eyed him. "That's funny. I thought you two were getting kind of close."

His throat was tight, and he had to force himself to speak. "Rebecca . . . Well, maybe Rebecca is still too wrapped up in Paul to get close to anyone else."

Sadie didn't speak for a moment. Then she startled him by patting his arm.

"Don't give up," she said. "There's always a chance, ain't so?"

He'd like to believe it, but he couldn't. "Not this time."

Lancaster County, October 1943

Sometimes it seemed the war had been going on forever. Anna trudged down the road toward the neighbor's house, the basket she carried heavy on her arm. Not even the bright golden colors of the hedgerows could lift the weight on her heart today.

So many boys had been lost from the county—it seemed every week there was another. The early optimism, the thought that the fighting would be over by Christmas, by spring, by summer, had faded into a dull endurance for Englisch and Amish alike. Nobody talked any more about when it would be over.

People—all people, no matter their beliefs—struggled with grief that was not made any more bearable because others suffered, too.

This time the pain had struck close to home. Neil Cochran, son of their closest Englisch neighbors, had been reported killed, dying in the fighting in a place so far-off that no one had ever heard of it. Not even his body had come home for his family to grieve over.

Anna's basket held a heavy casserole dish filled with chicken potpie and two loaves of bread. She and Mamm had started cooking at dawn. They wouldn't attend the memorial service for Neil, held in the small white church down the road, but at least they would send food.

She followed the power lines that led along the lane to the house. When the electric had come out this way a few years ago, the Cochrans had been among the first to hook up. The Amish didn't, and a number of the older Englisch farmers had eyed it with suspicion.

A year ago Anna might have been worried about her welcome as she neared the house. But shared hardships had seemed to dissolve some of the early antagonism against the Amish, at least among neighbors. She prayed that this fresh loss wouldn't renew it for the Cochran family.

She went, as always, to the back door, threading her way past a few parked automobiles. The Englisch didn't drive as much as they used to, what with the shortages of everything, including fuel.

Balancing the basket against her hip, she knocked on the door, hearing the muted sound of voices from beyond it. In a moment it swung open. Mr. Cochran stood staring at her, his eyes red-rimmed with tears, his face haggard and suddenly old. She held her breath, waiting for him to speak. If he turned her away . . . She remembered that long-ago day before the war when she and Seth had come by with the apples.

"Anna." His voice rasped with pain, and he pressed his lips together as if he couldn't say anything else. He gestured her in, touching her sleeve lightly in mute welcome.

"We are so sorry." Her own eyes filled with tears on the words. That Neil would be gone—his laughing eyes and freckled face stilled forever—seemed impossible.

Mr. Cochran nodded, his face working, and turned away.

Anna carried the basket to the kitchen counter, nodding and exchanging soft greetings with the women who'd gathered there. They wore their Sunday print dresses and flowered hats, and their faces were uniformly solemn.

The radio around the corner in the dining room was turned on, and someone was singing a mournful song. *I'll be seeing you in all the old familiar places* . . . She shivered at the words. No one would be seeing Neil.

A woman she recognized as Neil's aunt took the basket, peeking inside. "So kind of you to bring this. Please tell your mother how much it's appreciated." She took Anna's arm. "Come into the living room. Mary will want to speak to you."

They passed through the doorway, leaving behind the kitchen with its muted bustle. Mary Cochran sat on the sofa, the coffee table in front of her covered with photograph albums. A framed picture of Neil, proud and smiling in his uniform, stood on the mantel.

"Mary, here is Anna Esch come to see you. She brought a nice hot casserole. Maybe you can eat a bite after a while."

Mrs. Cochran, her plump cheeks sunken and her eyes

swollen with crying, ignored the well-meant comment about eating. She caught Anna's hand and drew her down on the couch next to her.

"I'm glad you came. Neil would have liked it. You children were all such good friends when you were little, weren't you?"

Anna nodded, remembering those times that seemed so long ago now. "He and Seth used to go fishing together. They always complained I scared the fish if I went along."

Mrs. Cochran's pain seemed to ease a little with the happy memory. "Such good times those were. But tell me, what do you hear from Seth? Is he safe?"

"He's fine. Somewhere in the Pacific is all we know."

Luckily by the time Seth's friend Patty had left the area to work in a defense plant somewhere in Virginia, Daad had come around to letting Anna write to Seth openly. He pretended not to listen when she read his letters aloud, but when she carefully left them open on the table, she knew he devoured every word.

"We'll pray he stays safe." Mary patted her hand.

Were they more acceptable to their Englisch neighbors because Seth had abandoned their ways and gone to fight? Anna suspected she'd never know the truth of it.

"Thank you. Your prayers are appreciated." She sought for something else to say and glanced at the picture albums.

Mrs. Cochran saw the movement and pulled one onto her lap. "Poor Frank can't stand to look at these pictures of our boy, but it comforts me. I like to see the happy faces and remember. Look at this one."

Anna obeyed, and her heart seemed to stop. Neil, barefoot

and grinning, stood holding a string of fish. Next to him was Seth.

Anna touched the faded black-and-white picture lightly. "I've never seen a picture of Seth before." Her heart seemed to cramp. He'd probably been about twelve in the picture, his hair as fine as corn silk under his summer straw hat, his face caught between childhood and maturity, his grin an echo of Neil's.

"I'd forgotten you don't believe in taking pictures." Mary's face clouded. "I don't know what I'd do if I didn't have these."

"I'm glad you do." If Seth never came home, they would have to rely on their memories of him. How long would it be before his image blurred and faded? Or would it always stay young and strong in their minds, like Neil in these photographs?

A movement in the doorway caught her eye, and she realized Neil's aunt stood there with another visitor, probably waiting for her to relinquish her place. Anna rose, bending to press her cheek against Mary's for an instant. "May God be with you." Blinking back tears, she headed for the door.

Neil's aunt linked arms with her. "It was good for her to see you, Anna. Will you stay and have something to eat?"

She shook her head, just as relieved that she had a reason to go and didn't have to linger in the house of sorrow. "Denke, but I must get home to help my daad and the boys with the chores."

"Let me get your basket, then." She disappeared into the group of women arranging food on the counter and reappeared with the empty basket in her hand.

"I'll walk out with Anna." Mr. Cochran took the basket. "I could use a breath of air."

Together they slipped out the back door. He stopped on the porch, holding on to the basket for a moment when she took it. "Your family . . . are they well?"

She nodded. "Ja, fine." Or as fine as they could be, working harder than ever and worrying over Seth.

"Good, good. And your young man? He's in one of the camps, isn't he?"

She hadn't realized he would know about Jacob, hadn't expected the question, and had to compose her face before she could answer.

"He's in a camp in Maryland right now. He's been working on a nearby farm over the summer, and they have classes in the evenings."

Jacob was busy. That was why he didn't write so often anymore, she told herself. That only made sense.

"I'm glad he's safe. I know you miss him."

She nodded. "There's talk some of them might be sent out west to fight forest fires. He has volunteered to go." Jacob hadn't asked what she thought about it. He'd just volunteered to go even farther away. "They might be jumping out of airplanes to fight the fires—smoke jumpers, they call it."

"That would be a big change for an Amish boy, wouldn't it? Still, I guess it's natural a young man wants to see a little bit of the world. Even when the war ends . . ." He stopped, seeming to fight for control when he thought of that eventuality. "Well, things won't ever be the same as they were before."

"No. I suppose they won't."

She turned away quickly, before he could read too much in

her face. Their world wouldn't be the same. How many of those who'd left would come back from the army or the defense plants or wherever this war had taken them?

Now it would take Jacob out west, to a place she couldn't imagine and a job that seemed terrifying and impossible. And he wanted to go.

That was the hardest thing. Jacob wanted to go. His latest letter was tucked inside her dress, and when she put her hand over her heart she could feel the thin paper.

Jacob had written it—his handwriting was perfectly familiar. But nothing else about the letter was familiar. He didn't sound like the Jacob she had fallen in love with at all. It seemed he'd turned into another person . . . a man who no longer mentioned the future they'd dreamed of.

She had been fighting against the conviction that grew steadily in her heart, but she was losing. It must have been another world in which she'd sat at her desk, writing in her diary while she waited to hear the bobwhite call that told her Jacob was there. Wherever Jacob was now and wherever he went, she feared he would never come back to her.

CHAPTER EIGHTEEN

Rebecca knelt at the edge of the strawberry bed. A few berries had ripened already, enough, anyway, for a little treat after supper. If the warm, sunny days continued, the patch would be overflowing in a week.

She held a ripe berry in her fingers, lifting it to inhale its aroma for an instant before dropping it in the small berry basket. It would be nice if the only thing that clouded her thoughts was wondering what to do with this year's crop of strawberries.

The sound of voices interrupted her before her worries could climb back onto the same familiar track. She glanced over her shoulder.

Barbie and Simon stood talking in the backyard—teasing each other, by the look of it. Cousins so close in age were really more like brother and sister, and Barbie was always one to tease.

Simon walked off toward the barn, grinning, and Barbie came to join her.

"The beds are made up, and the rooms are clean and ready for the next batch of guests." Barbie bent, picked a ripe berry, and popped it in her mouth.

It was on the tip of Rebecca's tongue to say there wouldn't be any more guests. Cancelling the season would be easy enough—she didn't have that many reservations. Maybe it was time to give up and admit that she couldn't run this business.

"What's going on with Simon?" Barbie asked, dropping a few berries in Rebecca's basket.

"Going on?" Rebecca blinked, a flock of new worries presenting themselves. "What did he say? Did he have trouble with the guests?"

"No, nothing like that at all." Barbie's smooth forehead wrinkled in thought. "We were just joking around, the way we always do. And all of a sudden he comes out with asking me how sure a person should be before deciding to get married."

"Goodness." Rebecca would have been dumbfounded if he'd said it to her.

Barbie's eyes sparkled. "Maybe he's having second thoughts about Mary Ann. Wouldn't that be a shocker for her and her mother!"

"Barbie, you shouldn't. Maybe . . . maybe they are having problems, but that doesn't mean they're going to break up."

"You know something." Barbie seized her arm. "Tell me, schnell."

"You're going to spill the berries." Rebecca removed Barbie's hand from her arm. "I don't know anything. I just thought . . . Well, Simon has been spending so much time helping Daadi and working on the farm-stay that he hasn't had much left for Mary Ann."

"Has she been complaining? No, don't bother to deny it—I'm sure she has. Don't forget we're about the same age. What you don't know about somebody after going through eight grades of school with them isn't worth knowing. Mary Ann always complains."

"It's natural that she'd be jealous . . . I mean, that she'd want more of Simon's time. I shouldn't expect so much of him." And there she was, right back at another reason why she should give up the farm-stay.

"Rubbish," Barbie declared. "Only a girl who was totally self-centered would give a man a hard time for helping his family when they need him. She ought to realize that if he'd let them down, he'd let her down, too, sooner or later."

Rebecca sat back on her heels in the warm grass, staring at Barbie. The girl was constantly surprising her. Who would expect such wisdom from her?

"Mary Ann's not so bad." She felt obliged to defend Simon's choice. After all, Mary Ann might well become her sister-in-law.

Barbie shrugged. "She'd be all right if her mother would stay out of things, but she never will. Ada is such a busybody. And haven't you ever noticed how often girls turn out just like their mothers?"

"That's what I've always thought, but I certain-sure wouldn't say so to Simon."

"Maybe somebody should," Barbie said. "Imagine waking up and finding you've married somebody like Ada King."

"You can't tell Simon so. And anyway, that's not necessarily true."

"It's especially so with oldest daughters," Barbie said, sounding sure of herself. "Look at you. You're just like your mamm— always putting other people first, devoted to your family. And if Mary Ann turns out just like her mother . . ." She grinned. "Well, all I can say is that Simon better get out while he can."

Rebecca couldn't stop her mouth from twitching in response. "You're full of wisdom today, ain't so?"

"You didn't expect it of me." Barbie's eyes twinkled. "Nobody gives me credit for having any brains."

"That's not true. Look how well you've managed with the guests." Rebecca frowned down at the berries. "Better than I do. Those people this weekend . . ." She hesitated. They'd made her feel like a failure. Worse, they'd convinced her.

"A farm-stay vacation isn't for everyone." Barbie ruffled her fingers along the row of bright green leaves, looking for more ripe berries. "Those four didn't know what to do with themselves when they didn't have all their electronics. And they didn't want to join in on any of the chores." She made a face. "Did you hear that one woman complaining about ruining her manicure if she so much as patted a horse? It's just too bad they didn't realize a farm-stay wasn't going to suit them *before* they came instead of afterward."

"There should have been something I could do." Although the truth was that Rebecca couldn't think of anything, which maybe just proved that she was in the wrong business.

"Nothing would have helped with them," Barbie said darkly. "By the way, is Matt going to be back before the next guests arrive? Because if he isn't, we'll have to think of something to take the place of visiting the workshop."

Rebecca's heart jolted so at the sound of his name that it was a moment before the meaning of Barbie's words sank in. "What do you mean, back?"

Barbie blinked, her lips forming a silent O. "I assumed you knew. He's gone away. You mean he didn't mention it to you?"

"No, he didn't say anything." Her heart hurt at the thought of the words they'd hurled at each other the last time she'd seen him. "Where did you hear he'd left?"

"I ran into his cousin Sadie at the grocery store. She mentioned it."

"Did she say where he's gone?" Rebecca hoped she didn't sound too eager.

"No." Barbie frowned slightly. "Now that I think of it, she was rather vague about it. She didn't say where, or why, or when he'd be coming back."

Or if, Rebecca thought.

She shouldn't jump to conclusions. After all, he'd been talking about trying to find Isaiah. Maybe he'd gone in search of his cousin. Maybe his leaving had nothing to do with her at all.

Even so, she couldn't see that it made much difference. Matt had left without a word to her about it. She shouldn't be so surprised, after what had happened between them.

She hadn't thought it could hurt any more than it already did, but she'd been wrong.

Matthew had put a wall between them. She'd seen it going up, brick by brick, with every hurtful word.

Now he wasn't only safely behind his protective walls. He was gone entirely, and with his leaving, she realized something. She loved him. She'd never intended to. Never even thought of it until it was too late.

A chill went through her. Too late. Matthew was gone, and even if he returned, he wouldn't be coming back to her.

Matt slid out of the car and stood for a moment, stretching. He'd rather put in a hard day's work than sit in a car for hours. In contrast, Joe Davis seemed perfectly satisfied to stay behind the wheel. Even now, he unfolded a newspaper and leaned back in his seat instead of getting out and moving now that they were stopped.

Matt bent down to speak through the open window. "You sure you're okay to wait?"

"Fine. Take your time." He waved Matt away. "I'm in no hurry."

With a nod of thanks, Matt turned and started up the driveway of the small ranch-style house. He thought he knew why Joe enjoyed driving the Amish so much. Joe liked to talk.

Maybe he didn't have anyone else in his life who wanted to listen to his stories. Joe had enlivened the long drive from central Pennsylvania with a steady stream of tales that stretched back over the past fifty or sixty years, none of which required much comment. It had given Matt plenty of time to think his own thoughts, not that he'd enjoyed them very much.

Their first few stops hadn't yielded much information. Either no one knew or admitted that they knew Isaiah. After a few negative reactions from the people he'd spoken to, Matt had changed his approach. When he'd entered a country store mentioned in a post on the website Isaiah had visited, he'd started by merely mentioning where he'd seen the name of the store.

The elderly proprietor had given him the once-over, assessed his clothes, and told him he must want to see Fred Zimmer. At Matt's nod, he'd provided directions. It had been as simple as that. Clearly the man had assumed Matt was a fence-jumper looking for help.

Well, Matt would do whatever it took. He considered the house as he approached. Small, modern, unpretentious. The front door opened directly onto a small stoop, and the drapes of the windows on either side of the door were closed. He hoped Fred Zimmer, whoever he might be, was at home.

Repeated knocking failed to bring a response. Matt dropped his fist, frowning at the door in frustration. If he'd come to a dead end already—

From somewhere around the rear of the house came the sound of a hammer. Matt stepped down from the stoop and strode toward the noise. He rounded the house, moving quickly.

A man stood at the back door, apparently trying to simultaneously hold it in place and repair a hinge. As Matt approached, the door slipped, earning a muttered oath.

"Looks like you need an extra pair of hands." Matt helped the man lift the door back into position.

His action got him a startled look followed by a grin.

"You got that right." Zimmer, if this was he, hastily set the screw with a few taps of the hammer and then screwed it into place. "One more, and she'll hold, I think." He suited the action to the words, and in another minute or two the door was secure.

"That'll do it." He dusted off his hands and turned to Matt with a friendly smile. Fortyish, maybe, with a broad, ruddy face under the baseball cap he wore. "I'm Fred Zimmer. Might you be looking for me?"

Like the proprietor of the store, he'd made a quick assessment of Matt's clothes and come up with his own answer.

"I guess I might be, if you're the Fred Zimmer who runs a certain website."

Zimmer tossed his tools into the bright red toolbox at his feet and straightened, taking another long look at Matt. Something Zimmer saw brought a frown to his face. Matt hoped his attitude wasn't too obvious.

"You're not the usual fence-jumper looking for a hand into the outside world," Zimmer observed, his sharp eyes narrowing a bit. "You're too old, for one thing."

Matt shrugged. At least the assumption had gotten him this far. "Most of the people who come to you are in their late teens or early twenties, I'd guess."

"You'd be right." Zimmer moved a few steps away from the door. He leaned back against a redwood picnic table and crossed his arms over a beefy chest. "So what's your story? You're not the average Amishman, either."

"What makes you think so?"

Matt didn't mind sparring with the guy, not if it gave him some notion of how his mind worked. If Zimmer knew where Isaiah was, Matt suspected he wasn't the kind to blab it easily to the first person who asked him.

"It's unusual to see an Amish male your age unmarried." Zimmer gestured to his chin. "No beard. And you talk like someone who's spent a good bit of time among the Englisch."

Matt wasn't sure he liked being read so easily. "Several years among the Englisch, in fact. It convinced me I was born to be Amish."

That was true, wasn't it? He couldn't let doubts assail him, not at this particular moment.

Zimmer nodded. "It happens. Not everybody who jumps the fence stays out."

"Does that disappoint you?" Matt couldn't help a certain amount of tartness in his voice.

"Disappoint? No. If somebody comes to me for help adjusting, I help them. I point out that doubts are natural. But if a person really wants to go back—" He shrugged. "I can't stop them."

Matt looked at him, his drive to get answers about Isaiah momentarily diverted by curiosity. "What led you to do this kind of work? Is that what it is—a job?"

Zimmer grinned. "Not one I get paid for, that's for sure. Mostly it takes money out of my pocket." He paused, studying Matt's face, and then shrugged. "I grew up Amish. When it came to me that I just didn't want to live that way anymore, I took off. And then I found out just how hard it is to make it in the outside world with no friends, no family, and an eighth-grade education that doesn't prepare a person for much of anything."

"It prepares you to live Amish." That was really the only possible response. "If you want to learn something more, you can do it on your own."

"That's not so easy for a lot of young guys."

"Maybe not, but it works." Matt took a deep breath, trying to focus. "I'm not here to argue with you."

"You're not here to argue, and you're not here for help in adjusting to the Englisch world. So why are you here?"

It was time to come out with it. "I'm looking for my cousin, Isaiah Byler. Do you know him?"

Zimmer paused, considering. "I might. What do you want with him?"

Matt's jaw tightened, and he had to unclench his fists deliberately. "That's family business."

"If you want my help, it better be my business, too," Zimmer said promptly.

Matt fought back his temper. He wouldn't gain anything by letting it rip, no matter how he felt.

"Isaiah's mother isn't doing very well. He needs to know what's going on with her, so he can decide what to do about it. I'm here to tell him."

"You mean you're here to put a guilt trip on him about going home."

"Sometimes it's right to feel guilty." That was a subject he'd had plenty of experience with. "Isaiah's family hasn't heard a word from him since he went away. Not even a line or two to say he's safe."

Zimmer's face hardened. "He might think it was safer not to let them know where he is. Maybe he didn't want any visitors like you. That's his right."

"It's not your right to keep him from knowing about his mother." Matt took another deep breath and counted to ten. "Look, I can't force him to go home. I know that. I just want to see him. If he won't write to his folks, he won't, but at least I can tell my aunt I've seen him and he's all right."

Zimmer studied him for a long moment, and Matt couldn't

tell what was going on behind that guarded expression. Finally Zimmer shrugged. "I'll talk to Isaiah. Come back in the morning, and I'll let you know."

If Zimmer thought he'd be content with a secondhand message from Isaiah, he'd better think again. Still, there was no harm in trying it his way first.

Matt gave a curt nod. "I'll be back in the morning."

He'd turned away when Zimmer spoke again.

"Are you sure you're not looking for help yourself? Seems to me the fact that you're not married means you have some doubts."

Matt shook his head and kept walking. The man was just trying to needle him, he supposed. He couldn't give him the satisfaction of seeing that his words had an impact.

Maybe he did have a few doubts, but he didn't need Zimmer to tell him so. Anyway, his issues had little to do with being Amish.

He'd lost Rebecca before he'd even admitted how important she was to him.

So, was his determination to bring Isaiah home for his aunt and uncle's sake? Or because it would free him to leave behind the wreckage of what he might have had with Rebecca?

The truth was, he didn't know.

Lancaster County, Spring 1944

Another spring planting season had come—another time of struggling to do more with less. Anna knelt in the vegetable garden, setting out the small pepper plants she'd been nurturing on the windowsill. The family would be all right for food as long as the earth continued to bring forth its fruit in its season, no matter what else happened.

Did Jacob miss the spring planting, now that he was out west fighting fires? His last letter hadn't sounded as if he missed anything. He'd sounded so caught up in what he was doing, seeming to delight in the challenge of something new. It was hard to reconcile the writer of that letter with someone who would come back to Lancaster County, slip into his old place, and be content with his old life.

Eli finished helping Daad unload the wagon after their trip to the feed mill. They exchanged a word or two, and then Eli came striding across the yard toward her. He walked with a sureness that he hadn't had even six months ago, as if he'd finally adjusted to the way his body was sprouting up.

She sat back on her heels and watched him, smiling. He was going to be taller than Daad if he kept on growing so fast.

"Need some help?" He squatted next to her.

Anna raised her eyebrows in mock surprise. "You're volunteering? You sure you didn't get too much sun on the ride back from town?"

He grinned. "I can help my favorite sister sometimes, ain't so?"

"Ach, I'm only your favorite when you want something. What is it this time? An extra dessert?"

Still smiling, he firmed the soil around a pepper plant and reached for the next one. "I'm still growing, remember?"

"You'll start growing a belly if you don't watch out."

This was the way she used to be with Seth, Anna realized, a pang touching her heart. She and Seth were so close in age they had been almost like twins.

Funny how the family had paired off—her and Seth, the two younger girls, the two younger boys. But now Eli was old enough to be more of a friend to her. It moved her to gratitude even as it made her miss Seth all the more.

"What was new in town?" she asked, suspecting he was only too eager to tell her everything he'd heard at the feed mill, that center for male gossip.

He paused, his face kindling with excitement. "If only you could have heard them, Anna. Everyone was talking about all the American victories in the war, especially in the Pacific. Folks are sure the war will be over soon."

"They've been saying that since 1941, ain't so?" She concentrated on setting out another plant. "They haven't been right yet."

"It's different this time. Honest it is. Why, even old Mr. Drumheller says so, and you know he never has anything hopeful to say."

Her heart softened when she glanced at him. "Maybe this time they're right. I'll pray it's true."

Eli crumbled a clump of earth in his hand. "I wish I were a man already. Then I could do something to help make the war end."

"Don't be foolish." Anna couldn't prevent the edge in her voice. "What would you do? Run off like Seth and break Mamm's heart again?"

He flushed. "I didn't mean that, honest."

She couldn't look at his earnest young face and be angry with him. "I know. It's all right."

"You're missing Jacob. But think of it, Anna. If the war ends, they'll let Jacob come home, too, ain't so?"

"I don't know." It was like a splinter in her heart. "There's been nothing said about when they'll let the CO people go. And when they do . . . well, who's to say Jacob will want to come back to Lancaster County after everywhere he's been?" Her throat tightened with the pain.

"Anna!" His face expressed shock. "You don't mean it. Jacob will come back. You'll be married, just like you always planned. Won't you?"

It wasn't right to share her worries with Eli, so she nodded. "Of course, you're right. I was just thinking Jacob might find it dull around here after being out west fighting fires. That keeps him busy."

Too busy to write to her, it seemed.

"It will be all right. You'll see." Eli patted her shoulder awkwardly. "Jacob loves you. And Seth will come home, too. He can go before the church and ask forgiveness, and then he'll be baptized and find somebody to marry and it will all be the way it should have been all along."

Eli wanted the rosy picture he'd painted so much. She only wished she could believe in it, too.

"Look, here comes Mammi to ring the bell for supper," she said, trying to distract him. "I have to hurry and get these last two plants in. I'll water them after supper."

"I can do it."

Moving quickly, they set out the rest of the pepper plants just as Mammi rang the bell on the back porch. In a moment Daadi was heading in from the barn, Peter running ahead of him.

There was the usual scramble of washing up at the pump, and finally they were all around the table, with Mammi and the two girls setting out the food. Meatless tonight, Anna saw. That was happening more often these days, but nobody would complain. Everyone had to make do with less, especially with so many things rationed.

Daadi had no sooner bowed his head than they heard the rattle of a car coming down the lane to the house. His head jerked up again, and he looked toward the window.

Anna followed the direction of his gaze. The Mitchell's Grocery truck moved past the window and stopped at the porch, with old Mr. Mitchell himself driving.

They hadn't ordered anything from the store, had they? And besides, if it were a delivery, usually the youngest Armstrong boy would be driving.

But the grocery store was also the telegraph office, and everyone knew that if it was a telegram, Mr. Mitchell would come himself.

A cold hand gripped Anna's heart. She saw everyone around the table frozen in place, and she had a wild desire to stop this moment so that time couldn't move forward, so that Mr. Mitchell wouldn't climb the steps and walk to the door.

But she couldn't. The knock sounded. Anna glanced at Daad, and he nodded. Numb, she managed to force her feet to carry her there, and then force her hands to open the door.

Mr. Mitchell stood on the porch, facing her. Tears stood in his faded blue eyes. He held the envelope out to her with a hand that trembled, and she knew that he'd had to do this too many times to be borne.

"I'm sorry, Anna," he murmured. "So sorry." Moving as if he'd aged thirty years in the last three, he headed toward his car.

Anna turned, holding the thin envelope with her fingertips. She held it out to Daad.

He gave a quick, negative movement of his head. "Read it." He rasped out the words.

Mamm's hand was over her mouth. The younger ones' faces were white, their eyes wide.

Anna ripped open the envelope and fought to find her voice. *Don't think. Just read.*

"The Department of the Army deeply regrets to inform you that your son Seth Daniel Esch Private First Class U.S. Army was killed in action in the performance of his duty and in the service of his country." Her voice wavered, but Anna pushed the words out, knowing she had to keep going before she couldn't speak at all. "The department extends to you its sincerest sympathy in your great loss. On account of existing conditions the body if recovered cannot be returned at present."

Her voice choked entirely. She clamped her lips together, and the tears spilled over onto her cheeks.

Mamm let out a wordless wail, and Daadi gathered her in his arms, holding her tightly. The younger ones burst into frightened tears. Anna gathered the girls against her, trying to find some words of comfort to murmur. On the other side of the table, Eli had put his arm around Peter and was patting him. Their eyes met over the heads of their younger siblings.

Eli's longing to be a man flitted incongruously through her mind. She must remember to tell him. He was one already.

As for her . . . she must stop being a girl, longing for a safe and simple future that was never going to be. Seth was gone permanently now. There would be no homecoming for him, and her heart felt as if it had turned to stone.

A wordless cry formed on her lips. How could the trees outside the window still put forth their blossoms? How could the sun still shine? All creation should join in the endless wave of sorrow that enveloped so much of the earth. All over the world there must surely be families like hers, torn to pieces by the endless tragedy of this war.

CHAPTER NINETEEN

Rebecca stood at the counter, the steaming kettle forgotten in her hand, and stared out the window toward Matt's workshop. Strange, how quickly she'd gone from thinking of it as Paul's dream to Matt's reality. But now . . .

Now Matt was gone. Two days had passed, and she'd heard nothing from him. She could hardly ask his family if they knew where he was. She had no excuse, no standing where Matt was concerned. What if he wasn't coming back at all?

Nonsense. He'd hardly leave all his things in the workshop if he didn't intend to return. He'd have to do something about his business.

"Rebecca, are you making tea or not?" Grossmammi's voice recalled Rebecca to what she was doing.

"Sorry." She forced herself to smile and poured the hot water into two mugs. "I was just . . . thinking." She turned back to the table. "I'm sehr glad you felt strong enough to walk clear over here today."

Grossmammi stirred sugar into her tea, the spoon clinking. A homely sound, reminding Rebecca of the hundreds of times she'd had tea with Grossmammi, starting when her feet didn't even reach the floor from her chair and her "tea" had been mostly warm milk with a drop or two of tea added.

"Barbie is having fun playing with the kinder, ain't so?" Grossmammi nodded toward the backyard, where Barbie was engaged in a vigorous game of kickball with Josh and Katie.

"Sometimes I think she's not much older than they are," Rebecca said, smiling. She reached across to touch her grandmother's hand. "You are doing better since you moved in with Mamm and Daadi, I think."

Her grandmother's hand turned to clasp Rebecca's, still warm and confident despite the apparent fragility of the blue veins standing out over fine old bones.

Grossmammi nodded, her expression rueful. "Your mamm was right all along, much as I argued. It was too much for me, keeping up the old house. Worrying about all the family things I'd saved."

"All of those things are going to people who will care for them," Rebecca said. Did her grandmother still worry about those family pieces? She'd already given many of them away, and the rest were safely stored in Rebecca's attic.

"They are going to people who need them," Grossmammi corrected. "Like you, ain't so?"

The question startled her. "I . . . I don't know. I've been touched by Anna's story, for sure."

Touched, yes. Sometimes she'd been startled, even shocked,

by how much she identified with what Anna had gone through. But need? She wasn't sure she wanted to look too closely at that idea.

"I knew you would be. Just open yourself to what you have to learn from others, Rebecca. At this end of my life, I see how important that is." Grossmammi smiled. "I am content."

Grossmammi almost sounded as if she were preparing to pass on. Rebecca was shaken by her reaction. She wasn't ready to get along without Grossmammi, not yet.

"You're doing so much better now," Rebecca said, determined to show her conviction that her grandmother would be with them for years to come.

"I'm even working in my herb garden a bit. You should see how fast the mint is growing, despite my sinking the pots to keep it from spreading too much."

Guilt flared. "I'm sorry I haven't been over to help you with the herbs this week."

"Ach, it's all right. You have plenty to do with the business." Grossmammi patted her hand. "I'm getting along fine. You must take care of your own work."

"I guess so." She couldn't hide the clouding of her expression from someone who knew her as well as Grossmammi did. "To be honest, I've been thinking it might be time to give up on the farm-stay. But don't say anything," she added quickly. "I haven't told Barbie yet."

Grossmammi's eyes widened. "Why would you close? I thought it was going well. Isn't Barbie enough help?"

"Barbie is wonderful gut at it." Rebecca looked down at her tea, not wanting to meet her grandmother's keen gaze. "I'm the one who isn't. I just can't manage the farm-stay on my own."

Grossmammi set her cup down with a decided thump. "And who says you have to?"

"No one. But even with Simon and Barbie helping, I need to be the one in charge. Paul could have done it single-handed, but I can't."

"He could not." Grossmammi's voice was tart, forcing Rebecca to look at her. "Rebecca, you are acting as if all the things you did were of no importance. Paul had the dreams, ja, but it was always your common sense that made them into reality."

"No, I—"

"Ja, you." Grossmammi looked at her sternly. "I don't like to hear you denying your own gifts, Rebecca. The gut Lord gave them to you to be used. And Barbie needs the chance to use her gifts, as well. And Simon."

Rebecca stared at her grandmother, trying to find a response, when Barbie and the kinder burst into the room, all talking at once and seeming like far more than one adult and two children.

"Mammi, you'll never guess . . ." Katie said.

"Let Cousin Barbie tell her," Josh declared. "It's not your news."

"Enough, you two." Barbie silenced them with a hand on each of them. Her eyes were dancing. "But Katie is right. You'll never guess."

"Then I won't try," Rebecca said. "What's happened to make you all so excited?"

Is Matt back? The thought slid into her mind and was

quickly dismissed. They'd have no reason to find his return so exciting.

"We heard the phone ringing in the shanty, so Katie ran and grabbed it," Barbie said.

"And it was someone asking about the farm-stay, so I said they should talk to Cousin Barbie," Katie added.

"The woman had heard about us from one of the couples who was here last week. Apparently they must have enjoyed their stay more than we thought. Anyway, this woman wants to bring her whole family for a visit—eight of them. And she didn't even hesitate when I told her the cost. Think of it—eight people for three nights."

"Barbie—" How to find the words for what she'd been thinking of telling her?

"So I said yes, and they're coming tomorrow!" Barbie finished triumphantly. "Isn't that great?"

"Tomorrow?" Rebecca's stomach gave a nervous lurch. "Barbie, you should have asked me first."

"Why?" A shade of defiance came into Barbie's face. "We're running a business, aren't we?"

The words hovered on the tip of Rebecca's tongue. The words that would end the business for good.

But they were all looking at her, all expecting something from her—Grossmammi, her wise old eyes weighing Rebecca's decision. Barbie, torn between hope and disappointment. Her children, and the future she wanted for them.

Maybe, as Matt had said, this wasn't her dream, but if she wanted it, she could do it. She had a new life to make for herself and her children, and it was time she stopped looking backward to what had been and faced the future.

She looked at them, and slowly she began to smile. "Well, what are we waiting for? If we're having a houseful of guests tomorrow, we'd best get busy."

Matt had breakfast with Joe Davis at the motel, and they were headed out toward the Zimmer place by nine the next morning. Matt still hadn't figured out just what he was going to say to Isaiah—always assuming he actually got to see his cousin. Maybe he'd be better off leaving the words to the good Lord and trusting in His guidance.

He glanced at Joe, who had been uncharacteristically silent so far. At the moment, he was frowning at the road ahead of them.

"Joe? What's wrong?"

Joe shot him a startled look that turned to a reluctant smile. "Guess it shows, huh? I was trying to decide how to tell you something."

Just as he had been trying to decide what to say to Isaiah. "Just say it, whatever it is. Do you need to go home?"

"No, it's nothing like that. Well, like you say, I'd better just spit it out. You know that tavern that's next to the motel?"

Matt nodded, mystified. "I noticed it."

"Well, I stopped over there last night before I turned in. To have a beer, but I figured maybe I could pick up something helpful about this Zimmer guy."

It hadn't occurred to Matt to involve Joe in his search, and maybe it should have. "That was good of you. Did you find out anything?"

The frown was back, and Matt had a sense that he wasn't going to like what Joe had learned.

"Well, I got to talking to one of the locals. I mentioned Zimmer, and it was like I'd put a match to straw. He flared up right away, talking about how Zimmer was bringing all these troublemakers to the area. Kids who couldn't get along at home, so he said, so they'd come out here to make trouble." Joe paused. "About that time another guy chipped in. He said the Amish kids weren't so bad. Some of the ones Zimmer helped were really trying to adjust, getting jobs, working hard, that sort of thing. So the first guy, he snorts, says he's talking about the ones who spend all their time drinking and starting fights."

Joe came to an abrupt halt, but Matt knew there was more.

"What else? You asked about Isaiah, didn't you?"

Joe nodded, looking embarrassed. "It turns out his name was familiar to them. This guy I was talking to had had a run-in with Isaiah and a couple of his buddies a day or two ago. He said a lot of folks have been complaining to the police, and there's word around that the cops are going to crack down on them."

"The police." Matt's very soul winced. This was worse than he'd thought. It was what had happened to him. Was Isaiah destined to follow every bad mistake he'd ever made?

Joe gave Matt an apologetic look. "Sorry, but I figured you should know what was going on. It seems like Isaiah's got himself mixed up with a bad crowd. And he was always such a fine young man, too." He shook his head. "I don't know what gets into kids sometimes."

No more did Matt, and he was a living example. "Thanks, Joe. It's better to know the worst going in."

"It makes it harder for you, I'm afraid." Joe seemed to relax now that he had turned the burden over to Matt.

Matt nodded. Harder, and even more important. Isaiah seemed determined to make every mistake in the book, just as he had done. The difficulty was to stop him before his young cousin did something irrevocable.

He felt a moment of despair. Would anyone have been able to stop him, when he'd vowed to live life his own way no matter how much it hurt himself and others?

They'd reached the house, and Joe pulled up into the driveway. The place looked as deserted as it had the previous day, but someone had been here then. Maybe, very soon, he'd see Isaiah and face the truth. Tension gnawing at his nerves, Matt slid out of the car.

"Are you sure you don't want me to go with you?" Joe asked, leaning across the front seat.

"Thanks, Joe. But I think I'd better handle this on my own." The offer was kind of the man, but Matt didn't want the responsibility of taking care of Joe when he was confronting a possibly angry Isaiah.

"Good luck." Joe's pleasant face crinkled with worry. "You shout if you need me."

Matt nodded, raising his hand in acknowledgment. He headed for the back of the house, where he'd found Zimmer yesterday. If anyone was here, that was likely to be where he'd find them.

No one was outside when he rounded the house, but when

he approached the door it opened. Three men came out, jostling one another as if each was trying to be first. The one in the lead was Isaiah.

But not an Isaiah Matt could have easily recognized. His light hair straggled nearly to his shoulders, and it looked as if he'd neglected to wash it lately. A stubble of beard seemed to proclaim a desire to look tough, but the hair was so light it probably failed to deliver. Isaiah wore frayed denim jeans and a black T-shirt that looked a size too big for him, and a beer can dangled from one hand.

The other two were carbon copies of Isaiah. Or maybe it would be more correct to say that he was copying them. They both looked older, tougher, and meaner than Isaiah ever could.

Matt focused on his cousin, ignoring the other two. "I'm sehr glad to see you, Isaiah. It's been a long time."

Too long, obviously. If Matt had been around, he might have headed off Isaiah's rebellion before it turned to grief.

"Fred Zimmer told me you were here." Isaiah's young face was hard, rejecting him. "You come to take me home?"

"I'd like to." But what were the odds he could get through to this older version of the youthful cousin who'd once idolized him?

Isaiah acted as if he found that hilarious, and the other two joined him, laughing and poking each other in the ribs. Matt stood, stoic, waiting for them to finish.

"Come home?" Isaiah jeered. "What would I go back there for? So I can be a dumb Dutchman all my life?"

"No. So you can be with your family. So you can have a gut, useful life." Probably the only way he could ever reach

Isaiah was to stay calm and answer his jeering comments as if they were really questions that deserved consideration.

"Hear that, Ike?" The older of his two buddies punched Isaiah's arm. "He wants you to be useful."

Matt felt the underlying menace coming from the other two, and found himself wishing Zimmer were here. He'd at least seemed mature and well-intentioned, no matter what his attitude was.

"I've got the life I want now," Isaiah said. "You can just take off again. There's nothing for you here."

"Yeah, not unless you're ready to break free, too," his buddy added.

Matt ignored him, looking into Isaiah's eyes. "What about your family?"

A trace of uneasiness passed over his cousin's face. "Tell them I'm fine."

"It's going to be hard to do that when you don't look fine to me. From what I've heard, it seems like you've been getting into trouble."

"What do you mean, trouble? Nobody's got anything on us."

The older guy flared up instantly, and Matt recognized the hair-trigger temper that had him itching for a fight. He'd seen it too often in the bad old days to mistake it.

"Isaiah, look." He reached out to put a hand on his cousin's shoulder, feeling bone and muscle. "Your mamm's getting worse all the time. All she does is cry since you left."

Isaiah pressed his lips together. "I couldn't do anything for her." It was a feeble protest, and they both knew it. "Sadie's better at—"

"Sadie tries to help, but how can she comfort her? It's you she wants. And your daad's lost heart for the business without you. I'm trying to help him keep it together, but it's you he needs, not me."

Isaiah's hard expression cracked, showing the boy underneath. "Mammi . . ."

"Don't listen to him." The older man gave Isaiah a buffet on the shoulder that made him stagger. "Can't you see he's just trying to guilt you into going home? It's probably not half as bad as he's saying."

"Yeah," the other one echoed, his hands clenching and unclenching, his eyes dark and staring.

Matt balanced on the balls of his feet, muscles tightening. If this turned into a physical confrontation . . . No. He couldn't let it.

"This is between me and my cousin." He kept his tone even with an effort. "I think he knows I'm telling him the truth." He focused on Isaiah's face, staying aware of the other two in the periphery of his vision. "Isaiah, stop and think before it's too late. From what I've been told, people around here are tired of dealing with you. The police have been called in. You keep on the way you're going, and you'll end up in jail."

Isaiah managed a sneer for that idea. "So what? You're trying to scare me, but it's not working. I'm not afraid of a little jail time."

"You should be." Memories assailed him.

"You don't know anything about it." But Isaiah's voice had lost some of its bravado.

Matt looked into his eyes, knowing what he had to say. "I know too much about it. I've been just as dumb as you in my time, and I ended up spending six months behind bars. Believe me, it's not something you walk away from easily."

Isaiah's face was shocked. Open, the way it used to be.

Matt grasped Isaiah's arm. "Listen to me. Komm home. Now, before it's too late."

Matt was intent on his cousin's face, longing to see understanding—and then the blow, coming from nowhere; he'd forgotten to keep his eye on the other man. Matt fell, sprawled on the ground, trying to clear his head, bracing himself for another punch.

The older man stood over him, fists doubled. "We don't need your kind around here. Get out before I let you have more than a taste."

Matt got slowly to his feet, eyeing the man as he would a rabid dog. A quick glance showed him Isaiah—still shocked, looking young and afraid. The third guy stood a step away, fists doubled, face eager. He'd jump in if necessary, Matt decided, but the main adversary was the older man.

"Go on. Get out." He tried to emphasize the words with a shove, but Matt ducked it.

He could take him, he thought. Or at least, give a pretty good accounting for himself.

But how would that show Isaiah that the Amish life was right for him, if Matt himself deserted their ways because of a bully?

"Get out!" The man swung at him again, the blow striking his ear when Matt dodged. It stung, infuriating him.

His hands automatically doubled into fists, the rage rose in him, he pulled his arm back—

He saw Isaiah, watching him. Ready to copy him, just as he always had. He saw Rebecca's face, expecting the best of him.

The rage died, replaced by a great weariness with the whole idea of settling anything by blows.

"I won't fight you." He wouldn't run, either. He stood, waiting.

The bigger man rushed him, the other close behind, and they were both on him, landing blows, and he absorbed them, trying to keep on his feet—

"Stop it!" Isaiah rushed into the fray, putting his body between Matt and the other two. "Leave him alone."

"You siding with him against us?" The bigger man struck, not waiting for an answer, and Isaiah stumbled into Matt.

Matt grasped him, holding on, not sure how they were going to get out of this, but sure that this time, he was going to be the man he wanted to be.

A motor roared, and Joe's vehicle shot past the house, across the lawn, and braked feet away from them. He swung open the door, holding up his cell phone like a banner.

"I've called the cops," he yelled. "You better back off, before you get in any deeper."

For a second the choice hung in the balance. Prudently, Joe got back in the car and locked the door. The older man's face twitched, the desire to mindlessly strike out obvious. Then he took a step back, fists slowly lowering. He jerked his head toward his buddy.

"Let's get out of here." The two of them fled, disappearing around the far side of the house.

Matt grasped his cousin's shoulders. "Are you okay?"

Isaiah nodded, his face young and vulnerable again. "I'm okay. You . . ." He looked at Matt, and tears filled his eyes.

"Hey, we're both okay. That's what counts, ain't so?"

Isaiah grinned at the familiar phrase. "For sure." He took a deep breath, seeming to shed something that had been holding him. "Let's go home."

Together, they walked to the waiting car.

Lancaster County, September 1945

The war was over, but the knowledge seemed to do little to bring peace to Anna's heart. She sat at her desk, staring down at the pages of her diary, for once having little to say. For the past four years the diary had been a solace to her, a place to express the thoughts she couldn't say out loud to anyone. She'd come to cherish the time she spent writing, trying to record even her daily routine in a way that would help her remember it sometime in the distant future.

Anna ruffled back through the pages, looking for the day she'd written about the end of the war. When she found it, she flattened the page to read what she'd said.

It's over at last. I can hardly believe it. We can finally begin to hope for the future. Surely Jacob will come home soon.

She felt comforted in a way, knowing the killing was finally at an end. But while the whole county celebrated the return of those who had fought, what about those who would never come home?

And what about the conscientious objectors, still in their camps even now? No news had come about when they'd be released. Some people said the government didn't want to let them go too soon after the soldiers had returned, but surely it wouldn't be long now.

Still, even when they were released . . . She suspected she wasn't the only one wondering whether their faith had survived their years in another world.

Jacob's last letter had been devoted to an account of a fire they'd fought. He'd praised the courage of his fellow smoke jumpers and spoken of their comradeship. He'd sounded so different—as if that life was all he wanted. Only at the end had he mentioned the future, and then just to say he thought very little would be the same as it had been before the war.

Was that his way of preparing her for the news that he wouldn't be coming home to stay? If so, how would she bear it?

A sound she couldn't immediately identify had her straightening. One of the younger ones? Maybe Peter had had a bad dream, like he did sometimes. She got up from her chair and hurried barefoot to the hall.

The sound wasn't coming from any of the bedrooms, but from downstairs. Her heart ached. It would be Mammi, maybe, waking in the night to grieve where Daad couldn't hear.

Anna slipped down the stairs, her hand sliding on the bannister worn smooth by generations of hands, her bare feet making no sound. She'd reached the kitchen door when she stopped, stunned.

It wasn't Mammi. It was Daadi who sat at the kitchen table, Seth's letters spread in front of him. It was Daadi who wept.

Anna's heart convulsed. She had never seen her father weep before, not even when the telegram had come.

She ran to him, putting her arms around his shoulders, bent down with grief and toil. "Ach, Daadi, I'm so sorry."

He made an effort to straighten at the realization of her presence, but then he gave it up, his hands moving on the sheets of thin paper as if he'd caress them.

Anna touched the nearest page, covered with her brother's scrawl. "We're never finished with grieving for our Seth." Her voice choked on the words.

Her father shook his head, putting up one hand to shield his eyes. "It's my fault. I should have stopped him."

She pulled a chair close and sat down next to him, longing to comfort him and not sure how. "I don't think you could have, Daadi. Seth was determined. He'd have found some way to do what he thought he should, no matter what."

"He was just a boy, swayed by what his friends were doing." There was a trace of anger in Daad's voice. "If I'd talked to him more, listened to him, I could have helped him find the courage to resist."

She'd thought this grief couldn't hurt any worse, but it did. "Seth had plenty of courage. That wasn't why . . ." She had to find the way to ease this burden. She grasped her father's hands tight in hers. "Daadi, listen. Seth talked to me about the war.

I truly believe he didn't make the decision lightly or because of what his friends were doing."

"Then why?" Daadi lifted a tear-ravaged face to her. "Why would he go against all he'd been taught?"

"You know that Jacob's conscience told him to resist conscription, and he did, no matter what the penalty was for it." She paused, feeling her way. "But Seth was different. He was so moved by the suffering of people who were being persecuted that he couldn't let it go. His conscience told him to try to protect them. He didn't join the army because he wanted to fight. He joined because he wanted to save others."

"Even if it meant killing." Pain filled Daad's voice.

"We don't know that he killed," she said. "But we do know that God gave him his conscience. You believe that, ja?"

Daad rubbed his palms against his face and nodded.

Anna hesitated. She hadn't said this, even to herself, and she had to get it right.

"I think we must accept God's will and trust that He gave Seth his conscience for a reason we don't see now. It's not in our hands to judge. That's what Jesus teaches. Our only task is to forgive."

With the words it seemed a weight was lifted from her heart. Whether her words helped Daad or not she couldn't say, but they helped her.

Daadi looked at her for a long moment. Then he nodded, the pain in his face easing. "There's much in what you say, my Anna. I've been fighting with God instead of trusting Him." He patted her hand, and she could see that the storm was passing for him. "It takes strength to forgive. Whatever else it has done, this war has made a strong woman out of you."

She clung to the words, praying they were true. Praying that if Jacob chose not to return, she would be able to understand and to forgive.

Chapter Twenty

Rebecca and Barbie stood by the driveway with the children, waving as the cars pulled out. Their biggest party of guests ever was departing, singing their praises of a delightful stay.

When the last car turned onto the road, Rebecca let her arm drop, so tired she couldn't hold it up any longer. She turned to her cousin. "They're gone. We can relax at last."

"Just what I'm going to do," Barbie said.

Suiting the action to the words, she collapsed into the nearest lawn chair, stretching her legs out in front of her, looking like an Amish cloth doll. Except that the dolls were faceless, while Barbie's features sparkled with her lively personality.

Katie and Josh, released from the need to behave better than they wanted to, vented their energy with a game that seemed to consist of chasing each other around the yard while squealing.

Rebecca shook her head. "How they can run around on

such a warm afternoon I don't know." She sank down in the matching lawn chair, only too glad to stay motionless for a bit.

"It's going to be hot," Barbie agreed, fanning herself with her hand. "I'll take them wading in the creek later if you want."

"Don't let the two of them talk you into it," Rebecca said. "I thought you wanted to rest."

Barbie grinned. "Only for five minutes or so. Did you hear what the guests said when they were checking out? I've never heard such raves. I think we're a success."

"I guess so." Rebecca could only marvel at how smoothly everything had gone. Was this whole thing actually becoming easier?

"Your meals were great," Barbie said. "And that was really a fine idea, showing those women how to make a quilt patch. They loved it."

"At least it was something we could do sitting in the shade," Rebecca said. She wouldn't have expected the Englisch women to take to sewing, but they'd seemed to like it. And it was surprising how easy it was to chat over a piece of handwork, even with people who were so different.

"The younger woman, Leslie her name was, said she'd go online and post rave reviews about our farm-stay vacations." Barbie seemed to think that was good news.

"It was wonderful kind of her, but do you think that will really make a difference to the business?"

"Are you kidding?" Barbie brightened even more, her eyes sparkling. "People do everything online anymore, especially booking vacations. We'll be overwhelmed with business."

Rebecca couldn't resist chuckling. "I thought we were already overwhelmed."

Barbie's lively smile faded as her face took on a more serious tone. "You feel better about running the farm-stay now, ain't so? For a while there I wondered if maybe you'd decide you couldn't do it."

"I had doubts," she admitted. She thought back over the events of the past few days. "It's a funny thing," she said slowly. "I was thinking I had to do everything myself to prove I can handle the farm-stay without Paul. But I didn't." She smiled at Barbie. "It's okay to share the dream with others."

Barbie nodded, her serious expression making her seem older. "It is strange, isn't it? I mean, you wouldn't have known that if Paul hadn't started so many things and left them for you to deal with."

Rebecca could only stare at her cousin, absorbing the words. Was that what people were saying about Paul?

Apparently thinking she'd said too much, Barbie flushed. "I'm sorry. I didn't mean anything by what I said."

"It's all right." Rebecca made an effort to chase the idea away. "I hadn't thought of it that way."

Or had she? The question seemed to linger in her mind.

Barbie glanced around, as if looking for a change of subject. "You know, I was thinking we might try to line up some other options for the guests. Like different Amish businesses they might visit. I could make up a flyer listing them. They'd probably buy things, and that would help everyone."

Rebecca nodded. "We'll need them if Matt doesn't come back." She'd tried to keep her voice firm, but it wavered a little on the words, and Barbie was quick to catch her doubt.

"You don't really think he's leaving for good, do you? He's

probably just away for a few days. Maybe some business for his onkel took him. He'll be back."

"Maybe."

Rebecca wished she could think so. Wished she'd done a better job of talking to him when she'd had the chance. She'd been so obsessed with her own shortcomings that she hadn't paid attention to what he was feeling.

As for accusing him of letting the past dictate his actions in the present—well, who was she to say that to anyone else? She and Matt were more alike in some ways than she'd have believed possible. Only the reasons behind their attitudes were different.

"I know one thing for sure," Barbie said, her voice lifting. "You can stop thinking Matt has gone for good."

"What do you mean?"

Barbie nodded toward the workshop. "Because he's here now."

Rebecca swung around, and her heart leaped. A wagon had just pulled up outside the workshop. Matt . . . She realized suddenly that she'd recognize his particular figure anywhere, in any group of Amish men all dressed alike, in any crowd of people.

She was getting another chance. She could talk to him, show him that she wasn't so tied to the past as he'd thought, and that he needn't be, either.

"He'll be coming over to see you," Barbie said, getting up. "I'll keep the kinder busy so you can talk."

"You don't need to," she began.

Barbie chuckled. "You wouldn't say that if you could see

your face. Talk to him. Let him know how you feel. You'll both be idiots if you let a chance to be happy slip away."

Barbie had obviously been noticing a lot . . . maybe more than Rebecca had been aware of herself.

Feeling the warmth in her cheeks, Rebecca looked again toward the workshop. And froze. Barbie had said Matt would be coming to see her after having been away. She'd been wrong. Matt wasn't coming this way. He'd disappeared into the workshop.

"It looks as if we were wrong." She tried hard to keep her tone light. "Matt has other things to do than explain where he's been to me."

"I don't believe it." Barbie glared at the workshop. "What is he doing? Where is he going with that rocking chair?"

Rebecca's throat closed. Matt was loading the rocker he'd made into the wagon. It didn't take much to figure out what he was doing. Hadn't she told herself that he wouldn't leave without coming for his things?

She had to force the words out past the lump in her throat. "It looks as if he's clearing out the shop."

Barbie seized Rebecca's hands. "You're not going to let him go without a word, are you? Stop him."

"I can't." She'd like nothing so much as to dissolve into a weeping heap on the ground, but she couldn't. She had to be the strong person her children needed. "If he's decided to leave, I've no right to stop him."

"That's just plain stupid." Barbie gave her a little shake. "If I ever saw two such stubborn people in my life, I don't know where. Go after him. Make him talk to you. You can't give up without trying."

You can't give up without trying. The words repeated themselves in her heart. She'd certainly done that often enough in
the past, convinced that she couldn't do this or that. She'd told
herself she was finished with thinking that way.

"Go on." Barbie gave her a little push. "Go after him."

Rebecca hesitated. Go after him? That seemed so shameless.
But she knew how to make him come to her, didn't she?

She went to the porch, up the steps, and stopped at the bell.
Her hand paused, almost without volition, as she reached for
the rope.

She hadn't rung it, not in all this time. She'd finally gotten
used to having the children do it, but she hadn't herself.

That was all the more reason to do it now. She clasped the
rope. Paul had said that the bell would call him home. Would
it call Matt in the same way? She pulled the rope, over and over
again.

The clamor of the bell shocked Matt, sending him spinning
around so quickly he nearly lost his balance. Something was
wrong—Rebecca? The children?

Then he was running toward the sound, his heart thudding,
hardly able to breathe. If something had happened to Rebecca . . .

He was close enough to see who was ringing the bell.
Rebecca. She didn't look hurt or upset. She looked angry.

As he neared the porch she stopped pulling the bell
rope. She stalked down from the porch, coming to meet him.
Beyond her he spotted Barbie with Josh and Katie. She was

waving off Simon, who'd started running toward them from the far field.

Barbie had a firm hold on each child. She steered them toward the barn, with Katie looking back over her shoulder and Joshua loudly protesting that he wanted to see Matt.

Matt focused on Rebecca. "What's wrong?"

"How could you?" The words burst out of her.

He could only stare at her. "How could I what?"

"You were loading up to leave." She flung out a hand, pointing at the wagon. "You didn't even tell me."

He was so unaccustomed to anger from her that he didn't know how to respond. "I wouldn't, Rebecca. You should know I wouldn't."

"How? How would I know it?" Rebecca demanded, her cheeks flushed and eyes snapping. "You've already done it. You went away for days with no word to me. And now that you're back, you're loading your things up, getting ready to leave—"

"No, Rebecca. No." He took a step closer to her, close enough to touch her if he dared. "I was just loading the rocker in the wagon because it sold. A neighbor of Aunt Lovina's bought it."

Obviously he'd caught her off guard. She stared at him, her anger visibly deflating like a child's balloon.

He couldn't let it go at that, could he? "I'd tell you if I were thinking of giving up the workshop."

Rebecca studied his face. "Are you?" she asked softly.

Now it was his turn to be caught off guard. He hadn't actually thought about what he was going to do now that Isaiah had come home.

His silence seemed to lead Rebecca to her own conclusion. Her lips trembled, and she pressed them together. "You are, aren't you?"

She started to turn away, and he reached out to grasp her wrist and stop her. "Wait. It's not like that. I brought Isaiah home."

"Really?" Her face came alive with joy. "Ach, Matt, how happy everyone must be. How did you do it? How did you even find him?"

She was in pain herself, but she could share the joy his family felt at having the prodigal home. It humbled him.

"Simon helped. Those leads he gave me eventually took me to people who knew something."

Her smile trembled. "I'm wonderful glad of it. But surely Simon didn't know where Isaiah was all this time."

"No, no. It was just a pointer, and then it was a question of going out to the area of Ohio where Isaiah might be and looking for him."

"It can't have been that easy," she said.

Matt still held her wrist, but she made no effort to pull away. She wanted to know.

And he wanted to tell her. He wanted to say that he knew now his temper couldn't get the better of him. That the image of her dear face had kept him from striking a blow against another person. That he knew what he wanted—a life of peace and forgiveness. An Amish life. With her and the children.

How could he say those things to her? She was still so set on pleasing Paul, and he wouldn't get into line for her love. But—

A reflection of sunlight caught his eye, and he realized he

was staring at the bell. She had rung the bell, probably for the first time since Paul's death. She had rung it to call him. That had to mean something.

He held her two hands between both of his and looked into her eyes. "Something's changed with you, Rebecca. Since the last time we talked—"

"Since we argued, you mean." Tears shone in her eyes. "I was so angry, but what you said made me think." She shook her head, as if to chase the tears away. "Yes, something did happen while you were gone, something that forced me to make a choice. And I realized that I wanted to go ahead with the business, but not because it was Paul's dream. Because it is mine, and the children's, and Barbie's."

He let that settle into his thoughts. He was glad for her sake that she knew now what she wanted to do and why. But did it also mean she was ready for something more?

"I finally saw something else that's even more important." She went on as if she'd read his thoughts. "I haven't been at peace with Paul's memory." She stopped abruptly, as if she didn't know whether she should confide in him.

"What, Rebecca?" He tried to keep the urgency from his voice. This wasn't about him—it was about Rebecca and her feelings.

She nodded slightly, as if making up her mind. "I've been angry—angry because all his dreams left me and the children in such a difficult place when he died. And I never even realized it." She shook her head, a smile trembling on her lips. "But I know now. I forgive him. Now I can cherish the memory of what we had together without pain or regret. I'm ready to move into the future."

A surge of confidence flooded through him. Matt lifted her hands and held them close against his heart. "With me?" he asked.

Rebecca's smile blossomed. She reached up to touch his face with her fingertips. "With you," she said.

People would see. He didn't care. He pulled her into his arms and kissed her, pouring all his love, all his wholeness, into that kiss. The past was gone, for both of them. But they would have a wonderful future, with the Lord's help.

Joshua's high voice penetrated the haze in which they stood, lips pressed together. "Look! Matt is kissing Mammi!"

"And Mammi is kissing him back." Barbie sounded as if she was laughing.

"I think they should get married," Katie said. "Don't you?"

"I'm certain-sure they will," Barbie said.

Matt felt Rebecca's lips tremble with barely suppressed laughter. He released her gently, reluctantly. And together they turned and held out their arms to the children.

Lancaster County, November 1945

Anna sat once more at the desk in her bedroom, alternately staring out the window at the dusk and trying to write. Maybe it was time she gave up keeping a diary. She didn't seem to have much time for it these days. She was too busy helping Daad and the boys run the farm and taking over Mamm's job of teaching her little sisters what they needed to know to be good wives and mothers.

Poor Mammi. She just didn't seem to have the heart for

much of anything these days. Sometimes Anna thought she felt the same way.

Other Amish boys had come home at last from the camps. Their families had welcomed them, glad to let the bad years slip into the past. They had been absorbed back into the fabric of Amish life as if they'd never been gone.

But she had heard nothing from Jacob. Was that how it would end between them, with no final words of release, just a slow fading away of all their hopes and dreams?

A chilly breeze filtered through the open window she'd left open an inch or so. She should close it, get ready for bed. But she couldn't seem to find the energy to move. Instead, she just stared out, longing for something and not even sure anymore what it was.

It came faintly at first, carried on the breeze so soft she might have imagined it—the bobwhite call. Anna froze, hands pressed against the desktop, eyes straining to see through the shadows. Her imagination, she must have been dreaming it. . . .

And then it came again, and a shadow moved under the tree outside her window. Her breath caught in her throat. It was not a dream.

She shoved the chair back so hard it fell over, and then she was running, running down the stairs, through the kitchen, past the astonished gazes of her family, out the back door, around the house. Heart pounding, unable to breathe, she hesitated. Where . . .

Jacob stepped out of the shadow, taller and broader than she remembered, but otherwise the same Jacob—black pants, white shirt crossed by suspenders, straw hat set squarely on his head.

For an instant they just stood, looking. Then he held out his arms. Anna flung herself into them and they held each other, half laughing, half crying, as Jacob pressed kisses on her face.

At last Jacob drew back a few inches, still holding her, but as if he wanted to see her face. "My Anna," he murmured. "It's been so long."

"When did you get back?" Her words came so fast they tumbled over one another. "Why didn't you tell me you were coming? Have you seen your family yet?"

He chuckled, putting a finger against her lips. "Ja, I've seen my family. I got there at suppertime. They were so shocked I thought for a minute my mamm would faint."

She pinched his arm to make sure he was real. "You should have told them. You should have told me."

"I didn't know, honest, Anna." He grinned, his eyes crinkling with laughter. "They just told us all of a sudden that we could go, and I rushed to catch a train. Never got out at all until we got to Harrisburg, and then I hitched the rest of the way."

The more he spoke, the more real he became. The same Jacob, only a little more . . . well, sure of himself, she guessed. More mature after four years of life in the camps.

"You're here." It was silly, to keep thinking the same thing. She looked at him, cherishing the line of his strong face, the crinkle in his eyes, the lips that had touched hers.

Reality kicked in. He was here. But— "Are you home to stay?"

Jacob didn't pretend to misunderstand her. He led her to the bench under the willow tree where they'd sat so often. Once they'd sat down, he clasped both her hands in his.

"You guessed. You always did know me better than anyone else did. I have to be truthful and say that I wondered. I thought maybe my life was going in a different direction. All that time away, working with the Englisch—well, I suppose it changed my way of thinking."

This was it, then. Anna tried to steel herself. He was going to tell her he wasn't back to stay. Maybe he was going to ask her to leave with him. Her heart grew bleak. She couldn't. With Seth gone, she couldn't possibly hurt her family that way.

She moved, trying to stand, but his hands held her still. "Don't, Jacob. If you're here to say you're going . . ."

"Listen, Anna. Listen." He leaned closer, so close she could feel his breath on her face. "Maybe I thought that way. But then they told us we were free to leave, and you know what happened? It swept over me like a . . . like one of those wild-fires, consuming everything in its path. I wanted to come home. I wanted to come back to you, to marry you, to buy the farm we always talked about, to start a family." He made a gesture with his hand, as if he were throwing something away. "Those other ideas were just daydreams. This is real. I love you. I don't want anything more than our life together." He hesitated. "But maybe I should ask. After all this time, do you still feel the same?"

Tears spilled over onto her cheeks, and she was laughing and crying at the same time. "Ach, Jacob, how can you even ask? It's always been you. Always."

As if he couldn't wait another instant, Jacob pulled her close. Her arms went around him, she lifted her face for his kiss, and her heart danced.

It was over. The long war was over, and Jacob had come home.

Epilogue

Rebecca made her way through the chattering after-worship crowd. She had been extra busy since worship was at Mamm and Daad's place today, but now that lunch was nearly over, she could relax a little.

Fall was in the air, with apples ripe on the trees and pumpkins getting fat in the gardens. They had already entertained their last guests of the season at the farm-stay, and now she could focus on something more important.

She and Matthew had been together for only a brief moment since their upcoming wedding had been announced in worship that morning.

Matthew had been cornered by a bunch of men, mostly those his own age, although she noticed some younger ones, including Isaiah and Simon, among them. They were determined to give Matthew a hard time about settling down to marriage at long last.

She wasn't worried. Matthew could handle it.

Grossmammi sat in a rocking chair placed on the grass behind Mamm and Daadi's house, looking very much at home there. A cluster of young ones sat on the ground around her, and Rebecca didn't need to go any closer to know what Grossmammi was doing.

"She's telling the family stories to a new generation." Judith paused next to her, smiling as she looked at their grandmother. "It makes her happy."

"It makes them happy, as well," Rebecca said, wondering at the shadow that seemed to cloud her cousin's eyes as she looked at the children. "It's gut for them to know about those who have komm before."

"I suppose. But sometimes I think . . ."

Whatever Judith thought, Rebecca wasn't destined to hear it now. Barbie burst upon them with her usual impetuousness, putting an arm around each of them.

"Here we are, together again. And now that Grossmammi's house has sold, we never have to sort family mementoes again."

"Ach, you know it wasn't that bad." Rebecca could smile at her words, knowing the warm heart that lay behind Barbie's sometimes careless words. "I liked working with the two of you, even though . . ." An unanswered question dampened her mood.

"What?" Barbie poked her in the side. "You can't leave us hanging that way. What did we do wrong?"

"Nothing, nothing," she protested, laughing. "I was just thinking about the diaries I brought back from Grossmammi's. You remember. I told you about them."

Judith nodded. Barbie looked puzzled for a moment, and then she seemed to recall. "You mean the girl who wrote about what it was like during the Second World War. What is there to worry you about it?"

"Not worry, exactly." Rebecca was far too busy with her own life for worrying about something that had happened so long ago. "But the diaries ended very suddenly. I thought there might be another one in the chest, but I couldn't find it. So I never knew how Anna's story ended, except that the boy she loved came home from the CO camp at last." She shrugged. "It's silly, maybe, but I'd like to know life worked out well for her after all she went through."

"Ask Grossmammi," Judith said with her usual practicality. "If anyone knows, it's Grossmammi. Look, the kinder are finished hearing their story for the moment. Ask her now."

Rebecca nodded. She should have done it before this, but she'd had little time for old, far-off things. She'd been too busy living for looking back, and maybe that was a good thing. Still, she'd like to know.

"Are you telling stories, Grossmammi?" She sank down on the low stool next to her grandmother's chair that one of the children had brought out of the house.

"Always." Grossmammi patted her cheek. "You'd best learn them all, so you can tell them in your turn. You are looking very pretty today, Rebecca. Happiness brings out the best in people."

"I am certain-sure happy." Her cheeks were probably glowing with it. "There was something I wanted to ask you. About the diaries and Anna Esch."

"You learned something from Anna's story, I think," Grossmammi said, with that air of always knowing more than folks told her.

"Maybe I did," she said, thinking about it. "Anna let trouble make her grow. Make her stronger. That was what I had to do, ain't so?"

"And you did," Grossmammi said, her face crinkling into a thousand lines of love and experience when she smiled.

"But I don't know the end of Anna's story. I know her love did come home after the war, but I don't know if he stayed, or if they married, or anything else."

Grossmammi studied her face for a moment. Then she nodded, as if feeling satisfied. She gestured toward the basket that sat beside her on the grass. "Here is the family Bible. I brought it out to show the kinder something. Lift it up here."

Rebecca picked up the heavy Bible that Grossmammi so cherished and placed it on her grandmother's lap, supporting it with her hands.

Grossmammi opened the cover and turned to the family charts that had tracked family members since they had first come to America in the 1700s. She ran her finger down a page and then stopped.

"There. Look at it."

Rebecca turned the Bible slightly so that she could read the faded ink of the entry. "Anna Esch," she read aloud. "Born 1923. Married Jacob Lapp, March 1946. Died December 1998."

Sorrow swept over her for the passing of a woman she'd never met yet seemed to know so well. A relative, who'd married into the Lapp family just as Grossmammi had.

"Look below their names." Her grandmother pointed.

"Eight children." Rebecca slid her finger along the list of names. Most of them showed marriages, more children, more marriages.

"You said you wanted to know the end of Anna's story." Grossmammi's voice was gentle. "But no one's story ever really ends. They are all here, a part of the family line, just as you and Paul and your children are. And as Matthew and the kinder you'll have with him will be. The family story doesn't end, Rebecca."

Grossmammi put both her palms on the pages, and her gaze seemed fixed on something Rebecca couldn't see. "Faith. Humility. Peace. Forgiveness. This is the true heritage we leave for those who come after us."

Rebecca put her hands over her grandmother's, seeming to feel all those stories flowing through her. Grossmammi was right. Her gaze sought out Matthew's tall figure. Her story with Matthew was just beginning, but it was part of a bigger story that would go on and on, God willing.

RECIPES

Creamed Celery

Creamed celery is a traditional Amish wedding dish, served as a side with roast turkey. There are a number of different ways of fixing it, but here is my favorite.

4 tablespoons butter or margarine (not a softened blend)
4 cups celery, about 2 bunches, trimmed and cut in ½-inch
  slices
4 green onions, sliced
3 tablespoons flour
1 cup chicken broth
½ cup half-and-half or whole milk
salt and pepper, to taste

Melt the butter in a pan over medium-low heat. Add the vegetables and sauté lightly for about 5 minutes until celery is tender but still slightly crisp. Sprinkle the flour over the celery and onions, stirring until smooth and well blended. Slowly add the chicken broth, stirring constantly, and cook until the mixture begins to bubble and thicken. Stir in the half-and-half or milk. Add salt and pepper to taste and pour into a serving bowl. Serves 6.

Molded Cucumber Salad

A cool taste for a summer picnic!

1 3-ounce package lime gelatin
¾ cup boiling water
1 cup cottage cheese
2 tablespoons grated onion
¾ cup peeled, grated cucumber
dash of salt
1 cup mayonnaise

In a large bowl, dissolve the gelatin in the boiling water. Stir in the remaining ingredients and blend well. Pour into an 8 x 8–inch glass pan. Refrigerate for several hours until firm. Serves 6 to 8.

Baked Lima Beans

This recipe for baby lima beans is a delicious sweet-and-sour twist on traditional baked beans.

1 pound dry baby lima beans
1½ sticks butter or margarine
¾ cup brown sugar
½ teaspoon salt
1 tablespoon molasses
1 cup sour cream

Wash the beans, cover with water, and soak overnight. Drain the soaking water, cover with fresh water, and cook at a low simmer until tender, about 1 to 2 hours. Drain the beans. Add the other ingredients, stirring gently until blended, and pour into a greased 2-quart baking dish. Bake for 1 hour in a 350°F oven. Serves 12.

Dear Reader,

The Forgiven is the first book in my new Amish series, Keepers of the Promise. Three cousins are drawn by their grandmother into helping preserve the story of their Amish family in America. Each book will combine a story from the present with one from an important point in the past of the Amish community.

I became fascinated with the impact of World War II on the Plain community in America, and the more I learned, the more I was captured. Their story presents a powerful dilemma: How can a person be both a good citizen and a pacifist during a time of war? I hope you'll find much to think about in the story of Anna and Jacob's response.

I would love to hear your thoughts on my book. If you'd care to write to me, I'd be happy to reply with a signed bookmark or bookplate and my brochure of Pennsylvania Dutch recipes. You can find me on the Web at martaperry.com and on Facebook at facebook .com/MartaPerryBooks, e-mail me at marta@martaperry.com, or write to me in care of Berkley Publicity Department, Penguin Group (USA) LLC, 375 Hudson Street, New York, NY 10014.

Blessings,
Marta Perry

Available June 2015

THE RESCUED

Book Two in the

Keepers of the Promise

series by Marta Perry

Two Amish women living in different times struggle to defend their faith—and learn what love means to them. . . .

Amish wife and mother Judith Wagler acts as a buffer between her husband and his young brother, whom she has raised as her own. As tensions rise between them, Judith longs for a closer relationship with her husband, who never speaks of the tragic night that changed his family forever. When she discovers a long-forgotten packet of old letters, Judith reads a story of courage and loyalty told by an Amish woman of a previous generation, and finds insight into her own situation. . . .

Available wherever books and eBooks are sold

martaperry.com

penguin.com

BERKLEY BOOKS, NEW YORK

Penguin
Random
House

Photo by Lorie Johnson Photography

A lifetime spent in rural Pennsylvania and her own Pennsylvania Dutch roots led **Marta Perry** to write about the Plain People who add to the rich heritage of her home state. She is the author of more than fifty inspirational romance novels and lives with her husband in a century-old farmhouse.

Visit the author online at martaperry.com and facebook.com /MartaPerryBooks.

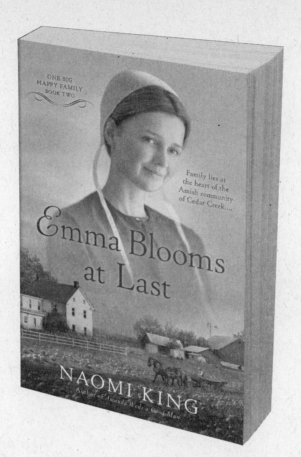

ONE BIG
HAPPY FAMILY
BOOK TWO

Family lies at
the heart of the
Amish community
of Cedar Creek....

*Emma Blooms
at Last*

NAOMI KING

Author of *Amanda Weds a Good Man*

Don't miss the second book in the
One Big Happy Family series!

Romance is in the air during the fall wedding season in the Amish
community of Cedar Creek. But as Abby Lambright and James Graber
prepare to tie the knot, Amanda and Wyman Brubaker's large, recently-
merged family faces a threat from outside their happy circle. Meanwhile,
James's sister Emma resists romantic overtures from Amanda's fun-loving
nephew Jerome. Can she overcome the regret of past disappointments, and
find the courage to make a leap of faith into a new future?

naomikingauthor.com
 NaomiC.King